RAVEN: PART ONE

PIPER SCOTT

VIRGINIA KELLY

To everyone who knows that
the villain will always be the villain
if the hero tells the story.

ACKNOWLEDGMENTS

A huge thank-you is owed to all Piper Scott & Emma Alcott Patrons for their support and encouragement throughout the publishing process, but an especially huge thank-you is owed to...

Bri
Crystal C
Kelly G
Kim H
Kayla M
Renee P
Sophie P-M
Tine P
Sue W

... for going above and beyond with their generosity. Your contributions have directly supported the publication of Raven: Part One and other great books still to come. Sorin, Bertram, and the rest of the Drake crew all send their thanks—and this author does, too.

CONTENT WARNING

Those who are sensitive to topics including violence and acts of torture, death (of secondary characters, none of which are previous main characters,) trauma due to off-page sexual assault, human trafficking, unwilling removal of children from parents, feelings of helplessness and anger with regards to social injustice, depictions of mental health struggles, suicidal ideations, and strained family relations (especially between father and son) should proceed with caution when reading Raven: Part One. While a happily ever after is guaranteed, there are scenes involving the above that some readers may find triggering.

1

SORIN

Sorin didn't make a sound when the first egg was born, not because it wasn't painful, but because he knew all too well what would happen should they discover he had laid. Drenched in sweat from his efforts, he gritted his teeth against the agony of his labor and pushed his face into his pillow. He was hot—too hot—and the bedsheets were sticking to his skin, but he couldn't risk leaving the bed. If anyone heard him, it would be over. It was best to stay as still and as quiet as he could, no matter how uncomfortable.

He needed to do it for his babies.

He needed to do it for himself, lest he truly go insane.

The only reprieve was that the first egg was here. Carefully—quietly—he lifted himself onto his elbows and inspected it from his place on the bed. It was the color of the sky the moment before the sun set and let night take over, a luxurious dark purple that edged on black. Instinct begged him to reach out and touch it—to take it into his arms and hold it to his chest, where it might feel his beating heart—but he knew better.

He had survived a great many terrible things, but not even he could survive a bleeding heart.

"I love you," he whispered to it, both a heartfelt declaration and an apology.

It deserved far better.

But for now, it was the best he could do.

He was not able to wallow in his suffering for long—a contraction rocked through him that forced him back down onto the bed, and in the solitude of his bedchamber turned prison cell, he pushed and labored through gritted teeth. The pain mounted. Sorin turned his head to the side and bit into his pillow, stifling a hiss that should have been a scream. Minutes passed. The rising sun stole through his bedroom window, creeping across the floor to crawl up and over the foot of his bed.

It was not welcome here.

It meant he was running out of time.

"Come on," he begged, barely daring to speak the words. They came out thin and breathy, little more than a desperate puff of air. "Come *on*."

He bore down, pushing, as another contraction rippled through him, but it was useless.

The next egg did not want to come.

It seemed to be stuck somewhere inside.

In a panic, Sorin glanced at the sunbeam striping his bedding and found it had crept up over his ankles. The chamberlains would be by to check on him soon—their day was already well underway. If they arrived and found him like this, it would all be over. He would lose his chance to escape—and then, he would lose his eggs.

He couldn't let that happen.

Couldn't bear to think of it—not this time.

Not again.

Hands shaking, short-winded and unsteady as his own fear stirred to life painful memories that screamed inside his head, Sorin squeezed his eyes shut and brought his hands to his rounded stomach. He pressed in with his fingertips, searching,

3

following the contours of the hard masses beneath his skin until he found a spot that was noticeably more painful than the others.

Tongue pinned between his teeth, breath held, Sorin pushed and palpated it.

Pain surged through him, but something else did, too.

The egg lurched, and tumbled, and fell into place… and during the next contraction, while Sorin lay sweating and silently screaming, it was finally born.

It was the same color as its brother—a gem in midnight purple that deserved far better than the old, bloody linens it was currently nesting in. Sorin looked down upon it, panting, exhausted, wanting to collapse, wanting to give up, and yet somehow at the same time so utterly, blissfully happy he had to blink tears out of his eyes.

His eggs.

How was it that he could love something so completely, so wholly, that even without touching it, without having known it for any length of time, he would give his life to keep it safe? That feeling—that radiant happiness—swelled inside him, making the pain worth it and shushing the racket in his head.

He would persevere.

He would lay his clutch in secret, and take them out of this wretched, evil place.

No scullery maid could stop him. No groom. No steward. No chamberlain.

With the dragon lord gone on business, not due back for another few days, he would have the time he needed to escape—to take his eggs and disappear, never to be seen again.

Another contraction struck. Sorin dropped onto the bed and screamed soundlessly into his pillow, bearing down until it felt like he'd very nearly split in two. A third egg moved through him, stretching him, and then, suddenly, emerged.

Three eggs.

Three beautiful, precious eggs.

And when his next contraction came, it revealed a fourth was on the way.

Sorin gasped, squirmed, and prepared himself to push, but right before he bore down, there came an awful commotion from outside his bedchamber door.

Footsteps.

Heavy, hurried.

A moment later, the door burst open, and through it stormed a stout figure wrapped in a dark travel cloak.

It was a waking nightmare by the name of Unwin Drake.

"I'm sorry," Sorin choked out automatically as the dragon grabbed him by the front of his tunic and lifted him up and out of bed like he weighed little more than a paper doll. "I'm so sorry, I—"

"*Traitor*," Unwin snarled, his rank breath on Sorin's skin. "Did you think I wouldn't find out? Did you think I wouldn't know?"

"No, that's not—"

"Silence." Unwin's nostrils flared and his lip pulled back, revealing dragon's teeth. Teeth meant for breaking skin, for crushing bone. Teeth that would rip through Sorin like he really was a paper doll, leaving him shredded and torn.

In a panic, Sorin kicked wildly at Unwin, but although the kick connected, Unwin did not drop him.

Rather, his grip tightened.

Eyes dark—dark and endlessly angry—he raised his free hand and snapped his fingers.

Magic popped in the air like a spark off a burning log, and just as suddenly, Sorin was set aflame.

Dragon fire ate through his tunic. It devoured the hairs on his arms, bit into his skin, and scorched the insides of his nostrils. The pain was terrible, but the heat was worse—it swelled up all at once, swallowing him, stealing the oxygen out of the air so he was left gasping and choking while his skin cracked and blistered.

While his nerve endings lit up white-hot in anguish, then went cold and numb as they died.

"*Stop!*" he screeched, using the last of his breath to speak. "Make it stop. *Make it stop!*"

Unwin scoffed.

Without a word, he tossed Sorin onto the bed, narrowly dodging the eggs.

"Your cloister has done a shoddy job with you," he muttered, taking hold of Sorin's bare thigh. A rush of scalding magic flowed between them, from Unwin into Sorin, repairing his burnt skin, but in the process, causing him incredible pain. Sorin screamed, but the sound was so high-pitched, it came out as a squeak. "Omegas are meant to be docile and pliant. Obedient. You deserved what you got for stepping out of line, but do not delude yourself—I am no monster. I will not let you die. If you had behaved, none of this would have happened, but you chose not to alert the chamberlain when you began to lay, and you chose to act in violence against me when I discovered you in your lie. Actions have consequences, and you have been dealt yours."

Sorin heard Unwin speak—heard the words leave his mouth, the rumble of his voice, every noun and verb—but his attention was fixated on the agony of the healing process. It burned him from the inside, like the only way it could undo the damage done was to reduce him down to ash and rebuild him like the phoenix.

He was dying.

He had to be.

His skin was smoothing over and his hair was growing back, but beneath the surface, he was being charred alive. It was worse than any contraction. Worse than amputation. Worse than broken bones. Pains like those were crisp and measurable, worse and then better, the kind of pain that promised there would be an end—but this…

This was constant, and it was endless.

Rationally, he knew it couldn't go on forever, but he had little rationality left to ground him.

Not only was he in immeasurable pain, but his only chance at escape was gone.

He would not get to disappear with his eggs.

They would be taken from him, just like all the others, and he would be haunted by their screams.

There were no sounds left in him, but there were tears left to cry. They streamed down the sides of his face as Unwin's magic burned through him, coming on harder as he retreated into his own mind. It was supposed to be safe there, but instead, it was made inhospitable by his own failures.

If he had laid quicker, this wouldn't have happened.

He had doomed his babies.

Because of his own actions, he would forever be a dragon's plaything.

There would be no escape.

"Are you done laying?" Unwin asked quizzically, flicking his gaze to Sorin's abdomen as Sorin spiraled. His thoughts grew darker, and the more they swirled around his head, the more they woke his old memories. Past failures. Prior clutches. Eggs taken from him. Eggs he'd never gotten to touch, but who had found him anyway and filled his head with their heartbreak. Their feelings—their shrill voices, terrified and begging for him with increased desperation—took hold of him now, gaining in volume until they had drowned out all other thought.

They had wanted him.

Needed him to comfort them, and hold them, and wrap them up with his love.

They had *begged* for it.

Pleaded with him to come find them, because they were scared and alone.

The sound of them mingled into a discordant choir, louder and louder, and beat against the inside of Sorin's skull like a hammer. His temples throbbed. He clutched at his hair, opening his mouth in a scream of his own that never quite materialized, but there was no relief from the pain.

These were only memories, yet still, they felt so real.

And soon, four more voices would join them.

Four more terrified, frantic voices who didn't understand why he wouldn't hold them.

Why he didn't love them.

But he did.

He *did.*

He wanted so badly to be with them, but they would never know that. He would only ever be the father who had never been there. The one who had abandoned them.

They would never know the truth.

"I'll take that to mean no," said Unwin before taking Sorin unceremoniously by the ankle and tugging open his legs. "Out with it, now. Do make haste. We haven't got all day."

The pain in his head—the screaming—distracted Sorin from his body. He barely felt his next contraction, barely noticed as the fourth and final egg descended. The noise was overwhelming. It was only when he was empty that he noticed he had laid.

"Four eggs," Unwin observed, unimpressed. "A mediocre amount. I can't say I'm pleased with you, but I suppose it makes no difference. These will not be the last eggs you give me. I have just returned from making arrangements with your cloister, and it has been decided—you will stay here with me, and you will give me another clutch."

The news came as such a surprise that Sorin's heart didn't just throb—it felt like his entire chest heaved.

"You're keeping me?" he asked in total disbelief. "You'll... you'll let me have my eggs?"

"Don't be daft." Unwin didn't spare Sorin a look. He bent at the waist to get a closer look at the clutch, his hands tucked behind his back and his lips pursed, expression unreadable. "You'll go mad if you touch them, and we can't be having that. I have chosen to keep you here not because I want you to raise them, but because I am curious about too many things to let you go. My questions aren't even close to being answered. You've made an excellent subject thus far, and I'd hate to have to start fresh on a new specimen. Besides, should the rumors be true, you'll be able to provide me with a near unlimited source of new test subjects. If you do lay again, I can justify riskier experiments." His tone brightened. "I really do think I am close to mastering the art of regenerative magic, and I would like to see if I can use it to keep a fetal whelp alive when taken out of its shell."

No.

No.

The mismatched chorus of juvenile voices in Sorin's head didn't just scream—they shrieked.

His babies.

How could Unwin do something like that to his babies?

They were helpless. Innocent.

They didn't deserve pain.

He would kill them, Sorin knew. In his quest for knowledge, he would snuff out their lives one by one until he either learned how to keep one alive or ran out of eggs.

And what could Sorin do?

He would be locked in his bedchamber like he had always been, incubating another clutch that would succumb to the same fate. He would lie there and hear them screaming, not just in want of him, but as they suffered. As they were experimented on by one of their own.

By a monster.

It was incomprehensible, but even in his addled state, he knew he couldn't let it happen.

He was only human, but he would give his life to protect his babies.

He would not let Unwin harm his eggs.

"No," he croaked, breathing hard enough the sweat on his upper lip was pushed away.

Unwin blinked in confusion. "What was that?"

"No," Sorin ground out, more loudly than before. "You won't do that. I won't let you."

"Do you challenge me, omega?" Unwin chuckled. "I understand it must be upsetting to hear, but you should be honored, not infuriated. Not only have you played a pivotal role in the advancement of healing magic, but your eggs will, too. If a few are lost along the way, so be it. You will lay more. Their sacrifice will be our gain."

"*No.*"

Something dark was rising up in him. Something dangerous.

How dare Unwin say that?

They were children.

His children.

He could not be allowed to do this. Even if it meant his own death, Sorin would not let him. He'd kill Unwin Drake if he had to. He'd do it for the eggs.

"What in the blazes?" Unwin muttered to himself. He sniffed, then sniffed again.

Sorin scowled at him, hatred and darkness rising up hand in hand inside of him the more he looked. He wished deeply that Unwin would suffer—that every terrible thing he'd wished to do to the eggs would happen to him instead. He wished for it so badly, he shook.

Unwin deserved to pay.

If the dragon noticed Sorin's change in mood, he didn't let on —he straightened up and took a small step away from the bed in what seemed to be a state of confusion. He blinked rapidly and, sniffling, pressed his hand beneath his nose. When he took it away, it was wet with blood. His upper lip was dripping crimson.

"A nosebleed?" Unwin blinked hard, as though there was a hair stuck in his eye, then sniffled wetly and shook his head, sending droplets of blood flying. What had once been a trickle started to gush, causing him to cup his nose like he could keep it in.

He couldn't.

Blood trickled through his fingers and flowed over the side of his hand.

Let him suffer, the darkness in Sorin's mind said. *Let him bleed.*

And bleed Unwin did.

It came on harder and faster. Unwin gasped and stumbled forward, but his legs buckled beneath him and he fell, striking the side of the bed before slumping onto the ground. He coughed and gurgled, thick and wet, and when Sorin looked over the edge of the bed, he saw why—Unwin wasn't just bleeding from his nose anymore. Blood now gushed from his mouth and trickled out of his ears. As he looked up at Sorin, terrified, fat droplets of it rolled down his cheeks, shed from his eyes.

He made one last sound—some strangled noise made weak with terror—then convulsed and curled into himself.

The gurgling stopped.

Was he dead?

Sorin glanced at the eggs to make sure they were well, then cautiously climbed out of bed. His legs wobbled and his knees were unsteady, but he knew this would be his only chance. If he wanted to save the eggs, he had to run.

He turned to face the bed and reached forward to finally —*finally*—touch the eggs, but right as he was about to make contact, something latched on to his ankle and yanked him hard.

With a yelp, he lost his balance and fell, hitting the floor.

"Wretched creature," Unwin gurgled, tugging Sorin toward him. Pain pierced Sorin's ankle—dragon's claws. They anchored into him, spelling his doom. Unwin would gut him right there on the floor, and this time, there would be no magic to bring him back.

He would die, and the eggs would suffer.

They'd suffer because of *him*.

The injustice of it all—the helplessness—filled Sorin with a fury not even his exhaustion could quell. He screamed—this time not in pain, but in anger—and kicked Unwin as hard as he could. As he did, something painful snapped in his head, and blood burst out of Unwin like a grape crushed beneath a woman's heel.

It was the last thing Sorin saw before he lost consciousness.

When he awoke, the first thing he noticed was that Unwin was dead, lying in a pool of his own blood. Sorin, gasping, scrambled away from him and clawed his way up the side of the bed, rising to his feet on unsteady legs.

The eggs.

The eggs.

He had to take the eggs and run.

But as he found his footing, he noticed something else—something far more terrible than Unwin's death could ever be.

The bed was empty.

The eggs were gone.

2

BERTRAM

A scream pierced the silence of the courtyard, so desolate and filled with pain that even Bertram took note. He looked up, studying the castle before him curiously, while the lady steward at his side stiffened in fear.

He couldn't blame her.

It wasn't every day one came face to face with a mad omega, and judging from his scream alone, this one was quite mad indeed.

"How long has he been loose?" Bertram asked conversationally, allowing himself a prolonged moment spent in observation of the castle before giving the lady steward his full attention. She looked no less fearful, and had begun wringing her hands nervously, but—bless her—found the courage to reply.

"Since the day of the incident, my lord," she said in a hushed whisper, as though she feared speaking aloud would draw the ire of the mad omega onto herself. "We locked him inside as soon as we'd discovered what had happened, but he still tears about the castle at all hours of the day and night, weeping and wailing and screaming. He'll pound his fists against the doors until he's worn himself out, and sometimes he'll throw his whole body against them, as though he fancies himself a battering ram."

"Have the doors held?"

"For the most part. A few of the weaker ones have fallen, but from what we've heard from the inside, he's yet to breach the rooms in the upper eastern wing."

Bertram quirked an eyebrow. "What do you mean, from the inside?"

"There are ten napery maids trapped upstairs, my lord," the woman admitted fearfully. "The mad omega stalks the area nearby, preventing their escape. They've barricaded the door to keep him from entering, but we fear greatly for their safety. As it is, they have no access to any sort of nourishment, and we've had to devise a way to send up breads and cheeses and wines through the windows. But all our efforts will be for naught if the omega gains entry to the eastern wing. Should he succeed, we fear he'll kill them all."

"I take it none of you have attempted to stop him?"

"No, my lord. None of us have had the courage. Not after what he did to Lord Unwin."

That gave Bertram pause. His father had not been forthright about the details behind Unwin's death—he had simply told Bertram to go, and Bertram had obeyed—but the fear in the lady steward's voice suggested this was not the straightforward scenario his father had made it out to be.

What did she know that he didn't?

Wanting to find out, he pushed the conversation onward and asked, "And what, exactly, is that?"

A dark expression befell the lady steward's face and she shivered all over, from her tightly pinched shoulders to her rather generous rump. "It was terrible, my lord. A sight so dreadful, poor Sybby collapsed on the spot and couldn't be revived for hours. He's..." She swallowed nervously. "He's still in there, my lord. Lord Unwin... or what's left of him. For the good of my eternal soul, I mustn't describe to you the things I saw. If you wish to know it, you must view him yourself. But please, be careful. The omega has gone utterly mad. The eggs have done such wicked, terrible things to his mind I fear there's more devil left in him than man."

Eggs?

Bertram's interest piqued. His father had not told him a clutch was involved, but the news did not come as a surprise. Omegas were docile creatures, and for one to act against his nature to such an extent was unusual indeed. A terrible thing, egg madness. A pity the omega hadn't been spared. If only the eggs had been taken from him sooner, Unwin might have been saved.

"Is the clutch safe?" Bertram asked the lady steward. "Or shall I need to recover it?"

"The clutch has been removed. But please, my lord... I really must insist you proceed with caution. This is no normal omega. There is truly something evil about that boy."

Another scream of anguish rang out, followed by the distant sound of racking sobs. The woman flinched, but Bertram held steady. He lifted his chin and listened to check which direction the sobs were coming from, then nodded to the woman. "You have my word."

"Lord Unwin's remains are in the omega's bedchambers on the third floor of the western wing," she revealed, inching steadily backward, as though afraid of the castle doors. "I'll be waiting out here on the grounds for your return. Heaven forbid, should you not be back by nightfall, I'll send word to the Amethyst clan."

"You needn't worry," Bertram told her. "I'll return."

"How can you be so sure?"

Bertram fixed her with one of his easy smiles and raised a playful eyebrow. "I've made a nasty habit of surviving when I shouldn't," he said, "and I've no intention of giving it up now."

The castle was an old and onerous thing, its stairways narrow and steep and its cobbled floors uneven. It was never particularly sunny in England, but the dark seemed to congregate more heavily here in its halls, where it weighed down the air and filled the place with gloom. Bertram navigated his way through it cautiously, ever wary of his surroundings. Omegas were not creatures to be feared, but this one had somehow killed a dragon, and he'd be damned if he let it happen again.

He ascended to the third floor of the western wing via one of the servant's stairwells and began his investigation, intending to check on the condition of Unwin's corpse before confronting the madman responsible for his death. However, there was a problem. Unwin's lair was quite large, and while the lady steward had helpfully pointed him in the right direction, there was no clear indication as to which door led to the omega's bedchamber, forcing Bertram to check each one as he passed by.

What he found was unremarkable.

A napery here, a ewery there, and then closets stuffed full of linens.

A curious amount of them.

More than a castle of this size should ever need.

Bertram stowed that strange observation away and advanced, coming to a corner which he rounded cautiously. There was no sign of the omega, but he did take note of something else—a few of the doors in this section of the hallway had been left open. He made them his priority. It stood to reason that, in their panic, the servants wouldn't have thought to shut the door behind themselves while fleeing, and if Bertram was correct, their blunder would be his gain.

He stepped through the nearest open door and into the room beyond it. At first blush, it was commonplace—nothing more than a normal, if somewhat uninspiring bedchamber complete with a neatly made bed—but the more Bertram saw of it, the less convinced he became that this place had ever been used for sleeping, for hidden away out of sight of the door were oddities.

Disturbing things the likes of which he'd never seen.

Clamps and tweezers and medical saws decorated the wall behind the bed like trophies. Interspersed between them were other medical instruments, some of which Bertram had no name for, and some which he didn't care to name, knowing all too well the pain they caused. Several of them had been hung up dirty, crusted from use.

They were not purely decorative.

The scratch marks carved into the headboard agreed.

Bertram remained on the spot in silent, sober observation for a moment, then rounded the bed to see what else he could find. The cobble there—great swathes of it—was discolored. Unlike the medical equipment, it did not look rusty, but Bertram had shed enough blood to know what it looked like when it seeped into porous stone, and this was it.

This place was no bedroom; it was a torture chamber, and Unwin was its executioner.

But why?

Bertram pursed his lips, running through the things he knew about Unwin Drake as he studied the scratch marks in the headboard. Of all his uncles, Unwin was the least present and the most mysterious. He seldom, if ever, attended family functions under the pretense of being busy. There were too many patients for him to see, was the claim. Too much medicine to practice. Always so much to do.

Was this what he'd really been up to?

Bertram dropped his gaze to the cobble. Beside it sat a basin filled with pink-tinged water. Rags hung from its sides, now crisp and rigid from drying without having been properly cleaned. One of them had tumbled off the side and solidified into a stiff heap on the floor close to the room's end table, on which had been left a knife similar to the one Bertram's brother Everard kept in his medical bag.

It had been used.

Perhaps, Bertram thought as he eyed the thing, his first impression was incorrect. Unwin was an odd duck, but he had never seemed capable of violence. It could be his obsession with medicine had inspired him to display a collection like this, and after going mad, the omega had taken advantage, using Unwin's own tools to do the poor dragon in. The blood could very well be his. The staining. The scratch marks.

It would explain why the lady steward had been too terrified to disclose the details of his death.

A mad omega with access to tools like these could do terrible things indeed.

But then there came a sound from elsewhere in the castle—a scuff of a shoe, maybe, or the sound of someone dropping to their knees. Bertram turned his head to look, expecting to find the omega standing in the doorway, but there was no one there.

Not entirely, at least.

For on the wall to either side of the door were rows and rows of wooden shelves, stretching from floor to ceiling, upon which were crowded dusty, mismatched bottles filled with clear liquid.

Body parts were suspended inside.

In one, an eye. In another, a nose. A third held a cube of flesh, dragon's scales covering one side.

There were several teeth, the tip of a tail, and more than one chunk of bone. Bertram was no doctor, but he knew enough to be certain none of these samples had been taken from animals, and there was no mistaking the piece of jawbone—a human molar had been left inside.

His first instinct was that he was looking at Unwin, but that thought quickly gave way to reason. The bottles were dusty, some of them to such an extent they had almost gone opaque. Unwin had only been dead for a matter of days. He was not the one who had been dismembered and stuffed inside.

But then, why had the lady steward not mentioned this?

Was it that she didn't know, or that she had been conditioned to hold her tongue out of fear that she'd be next?

Bertram pushed the question out of his mind and focused on the task at hand. Despite the gruesome discovery, his objective had not changed. He needed to find Unwin and investigate his body, then track down the omega who had slaughtered him and put an end to his life.

So Bertram turned away from the bottles.

There was another door in this room that seemed to lead into the next, in front of which was a single bloody footprint made in a hurry, like someone had fled into this nightmarish place to get away from the horror next door.

It seemed his search was over.

Bracing himself for what lay in wait, Bertram went through the door.

The lady steward had not been lying. Unwin Drake was a frightful sight indeed. Bertram found him on the floor in the next room in a lake of his own blood, stiff and twisted in death, so pale that in many places, he'd gone blue. It seemed the blood had been entirely drained from his body, but a quick visual investigation revealed no puncture wounds. He had bled out from his orifices— his nose, his mouth, his...

Well...

Suffice it to say his blood had not been choosy on its preferred avenue of escape.

For his continued sanity, Bertram was happy to leave it at that.

Upon taking stock of the body, Bertram pursed his lips in

displeasure and pulled the bedsheet—itself splattered in blood—off the bed to drape over Unwin's corpse.

So Unwin had died by poison, then. Or by some other creeping substance that could destroy a body from the inside without leaving a mark. But how could an omega taken from the Pedigree, with no ties to Unwin's scullery maids, have tampered with his food and drink? It seemed an impossibility. There was no way the omega could have acted alone. The servants would have to be interrogated. No doubt one would crack under pressure and expose the traitor who'd helped end a dragon's life.

In any case, it was now clear that the omega did not, and would not, pose a threat. Content with this discovery, Bertram took his time with his final investigation of the room. Unlike the one before, this one wasn't as overtly horrific. For a bedroom in a dragon's lair, it was bare and uninspiring, but there were a few personal items in it that led Bertram to believe it had been used for its intended purpose.

For one, the chest of drawers in the corner. It had been left open, and inside was a pair of shoddily constructed hose and several threadbare tunics embroidered with the sigil belonging to the Onyx cloister in Constantinople. For two, a mug of water, partially consumed, and left by the bedside. In addition, the chamber pot, while clean, seemed to have been recently used. It was partially dragged out from beneath the bed, where it had been kicked over. Bertram couldn't be sure if it had been an accident or the result of a struggle. With how much blood there was between the bedsheet and the floor, he thought he knew, but he'd learned long ago that things were not always as they seemed.

The question was, did the blood belong to Unwin, the omega, or both? He would likely never know. He'd been tasked with eliminating the threat, and such details didn't matter. A pity, though, that it had all gone so wrong. By dint of the blood-crusted tools in the neighboring room, it seemed the omega had not had an easy life and was, perhaps, right to have done the things he'd done. But orders were orders, and Bertram would follow them to completion. All that was left to do was find the poor creature and put an end to his misery.

Heart heavy, Bertram turned, intending to leave and start his search anew, but to his surprise the doorway was occupied.

In it stood the omega.

3

BERTRAM

The omega was a young man, perhaps in his eighteenth or nine-teenth year, with long black hair that fell pin-straight to his jaw. He was not especially tall, his head barely coming up to Bertram's shoulder, and was built delicately, beautiful in a way befitting a member of the Pedigree. If it weren't for his frailty, Bertram might have described him as regal, but nothing so bony had ever worn a crown. It would only be a matter of time before the poor thing starved to death.

A true pity indeed.

The young man, however, was not interested in pity. Not from others, and not from Bertram. He glared at Bertram through one inky eye, the other bruised and swollen mostly shut. "Who are you?" he demanded in a voice that shook with fear and indignant rage, then drew a knife from the sash tied around his waist and pointed it at Bertram. "And what have you done with my eggs?"

Bertram considered the knife. It appeared to have been taken from the kitchen—a cleaver, by the looks of it. Perfect for butchering meat. Blades didn't frighten Bertram, and neither did the trembling creature in the doorway, but he stood very still all the same. He'd received little information about what had transpired here in Unwin's lair, and even less about the omega responsible, but the pieces were starting to fall into place.

"My name is Frederich," he said simply, offering the omega the name he used to differentiate the heartless agent he became while doing work for the council from his true self. "And my business is not with your eggs, but with you. For the murder of Unwin Drake of the Amethyst clan, you will die by my hand. Is there anything you wish to say before you draw your final breath?"

The cleaver began to shake. Bertram looked from it to the omega's face to better get a read on his next move, figuring he would launch an attack now that he was being threatened, but found nothing to suggest that would happen. In fact, tears had begun to pool on the omega's lash line. One of them, having gotten too fat, tumbled down his bloodied cheek.

"I did not kill Unwin Drake, but I don't regret what happened to him," he said, and lowered the cleaver. "He was a monster. *All* of you dragons are monsters. You take, and you take, and you take." He bared his teeth, but his expression was strained, as though he was struggling to hold back a violent sob. "I've given you three clutches already. Thirteen eggs I'll never get back. Thirteen children I'll never have the chance to meet. But I feel them." He shut his eyes and brought his free hand up to cover his mouth, his brow furrowing in sorrow and rage. "I *feel* them," he snarled between his fingers, opening his eyes to set his sights on Bertram, "and I hear them. They *scream* for me. I can't let it happen again. I can't let these eggs go. You will not have all seventeen. The Pedigree is a lie, and you know it. All of you know it." A sob made sharp by anguish escaped him. "Taking the eggs away does nothing to save an omega. You dragons only insist upon it so you don't have to watch us descend into utter madness, and I won't stand for it anymore."

Four clutches?

It was a lie.

It had to be.

The poor creature was deep in his madness. No omega in Bertram's lifetime, Pedigree or not, had ever produced multiple clutches. Most failed to produce one. The few who did lay—as rare as they were—were all sent far away to lead lives of luxury after their eggs were delivered, and were not ever bred again.

It was how it had always been.

Or at least, so he'd been told.

But the conviction in this omega's voice planted a seed of doubt where there had been none before, and worse, it woke an old, long-forgotten pain that resonated in Bertram like heartbreak.

It came from his dragon, and try as Bertram might, it would not be ignored.

Gritting his teeth in frustration, Bertram summoned his claws, intending to end the omega before he could tell any more hurtful lies, but his claws would not come. He tried again, straining from his efforts, but his dragon, typically eager to manifest, refused to surface. It ached for the young man in the doorway.

"I will be taking my eggs," that same young man told Bertram, his voice shaking as badly as his hands, but determined all the same, "and I will leave, and one day, when my babies are old enough, they will help me end this. All of this. This… meat market you call the Pedigree. If it takes my entire life, I will free every last omega you've enslaved, and I will kill every dragon who stood idly by while we suffered and died and lost ourselves for your selfish gain. It doesn't matter how long it takes, and if I die along the way, so be it." He winced and shook his head, then raked a hand through his hair and tugged it to the point of pain. "At least in death, I won't have to hear them scream."

Calm, Bertram's dragon demanded. *Comfort. Protect.*

Kill, Bertram chided in turn.

But his dragon didn't care for his orders. It huffed and curled up on itself like a petulant house cat, paying Bertram no heed.

Claws, of course, were not the only tools capable of killing a man. If Bertram's dragon didn't want to participate, it didn't need to. He could just as easily wrest the cleaver out of the omega's hands and end him with his own blade.

And yet...

Bertram did not let the emotion play across his face, but his heart tightened painfully at the thought of slaughtering this poor creature. Yes, the omega had done the unspeakable and killed a dragon, but not without reason. Unwin had done the unspeakable to him first, and had Bertram been in the omega's place, he would have done the same.

"How far do you suppose you'll get after you take your eggs?" he asked, buying himself time as he tried to come to a decision. "You must know that if you leave, there will be other dragons like me who will follow you—dragons who won't hesitate to run you through with their claws."

"I don't care."

"You should." Bertram took a step forward to see if the omega would run, but he didn't. He held his own, knife at the ready. "If you die," Bertram reminded him, "the eggs could perish as well."

The omega's fierce expression faltered, but only for a moment. A quick second later, he scowled and took an accusatory step toward Bertram, cleaver-first. "You're only saying that to get in my head. What do you care about what happens to my eggs? They're *mine*. Not yours. They will *never* be yours."

Protect, Bertram's dragon urged. *Recover. Raise.*

Bertram eyed the cleaver and took another step forward. They were close now. If the omega wanted, he could plunge his knife right between Bertram's ribs—but he wouldn't. Bertram could see it in his eyes. For as fierce as the omega was, he was afraid. Afraid of what would happen should he kill another dragon, and afraid of the things it might mean for his eggs.

"After you die," Bertram went on, ignoring what the omega had said, "the eggs will be given to another Amethyst—a family member of Unwin's who will raise them to be proper dragons, the kind who might one day pursue a Pedigree omega of their own in the hopes they might produce a clutch."

The omega hissed as if he'd been struck, but when Bertram took another step forward, he didn't step back.

"Nothing will have changed," Bertram told him. "You will be forgotten and the world will go on without you, the same as it ever was."

"Why are you telling me this?" the omega asked through gritted teeth. "Go on and kill me if you must, but don't taunt me. Haven't I suffered enough?"

"I'm telling you this because I'm giving you a chance to change the narrative. Forget your eggs and run."

The omega's eyes flashed with anger. "I would rather die."

"Then you truly are mad." Bertram took a final step forward and caught the omega by the wrist, squeezing until the cleaver tumbled from his hand and clattered to the floor. The omega shut his eyes in pain but didn't make a sound. He was strong, this one. Or stubborn. Maybe both. "The best chance your eggs have to survive is if *you* survive. Run now and escape with your life. Allow your whelps a chance to hatch and rid themselves of the bond. Be as reckless as you'd like after that, but until then, be careful. Don't let your actions put them in harm's way."

Wide-eyed, the omega tried to tug his wrist free, but Bertram held it firm. He squirmed and struggled, but then eventually gave up hope and stopped, looking into Bertram's eyes. "Why are you doing this?"

"I do it," Bertram said firmly, returning his gaze, "because while I may be a dragon now, I was a whelp without a mother once, a long, long time ago. Now leave. Seek exit through the larder. Not a soul is stationed there. Once you have made it out of the castle, seek employment at the Gilded Orchard Inn and tell them Frederich sent you. The work will not be glamorous, but they will feed and shelter you until you've amassed enough wealth to travel outside of Amethyst territory. Once you've reached that point, leave and never return."

"You're daft if you think I'll go without my eggs."

"There are sacrifices we all must make when we set out to change the world." Bertram pushed the omega into the hall, not hard enough to trip him, but with enough force that he stumbled. "I know it better than most."

It took the omega a few steps to find his balance, but once he did, he glowered at Bertram. "I will find them," he said in a warning tone. "I will find my eggs, and I will take them back, and there is nothing, *nothing* you can do to stop me."

"I know. Which is why I'll be placing them with the only dragon I trust to keep them safe—myself." Bertram nodded in the direction of the servant's stairwell. "Now off with you. Go. This is your last chance. I will tell my clan head I picked the meat from your bones and pitched the rest of you into the midden, and as long as you keep a low profile, he will believe me. Live your life. Find what happiness you can in knowing that your children will live and be cared for, and should one day you find yourself in want of revenge, seek me out, wherever I may be. I cannot promise you mercy, but I swear your death will be as quick and painless as you'll allow me to make it."

The omega scowled, but a moment later he shook his head and took a few stumbling steps back before breaking into a run. Bertram stepped into the hall to watch him go.

It was not like him to show mercy, and should his father discover what he'd done, there would be repercussions, but it was a risk he was willing to take. For the omega had woken something in him. Old pain. Heartbreak long forgotten. A memory of a voice that screamed, and screamed, and screamed for a mother who'd never been there... and later, had wept into nothingness. A void where an atrophied bond had once been.

It would not be the same for these eggs.

Not if he could help it.

Ours, his dragon grumbled, and despite it all, Bertram found it within himself to smile.

"Ours," he confirmed, and set off for the eastern wing to rescue the napery maids.

———

It took next to no time to overpower the barricades and force the doors in the eastern wing open, then escort the panicked maids to safety. Once rescue operations were complete, Bertram sought out the lady steward and asked to be taken to the eggs. They'd been removed from the castle immediately following Unwin's death and hidden away at the local blacksmith's shop, owned and operated by the husband of the lady steward's sister. There, they had been kept warm and safe by the forge while waiting for help from the Amethyst clan to arrive.

The muscular blacksmith and his missus—a round-bottomed lass with a babe on her hip—showed Bertram into the shop and stood by the door as he approached the forge. The eggs had been laid in a nest of scrap cloth, four of them in total. Two were as dark as midnight with purple undertones, the others a shade or two deeper than aubergine, and all of them stunning in their dark radiance. Bertram dropped to his knees beside them and went to touch one, but stopped his hand a fraction of an inch away.

What was he doing, claiming responsibility for them? Such an arrangement could never work. He was an agent of the council and his father's right hand—a deadly tool used by the Amethyst clan to keep their world neat and orderly. He did not have time for children. He didn't even have time for himself.

Ours, grumbled his dragon, and through all of his uncertainty, Bertram knew it was true. He remembered that time, all those hundreds of years ago, when he had cried into the dark in want of a love that had never been there. And while there was no going back to change the fact that his mother had been sent away and his father had always been too preoccupied with matters of the council to be present, the same couldn't be said about these eggs.

He would find a way to care for them.

He would find a way to make things right.

"You may touch them, my lord," said the blacksmith's wife. She had approached on silent footsteps and taken up a space slightly behind Bertram and to the side. "Heaven knows the poor babes need it. I'm no dragon, of course, my lord, and I mean no disrespect in any way, but they seem awfully lonely to me, don't you think? It would do them good to know one of their own is there, looking out for them."

Bertram thought they looked a little lonely, too, but said nothing. Rather, he steeled himself and laid his palm flat against the darkest egg. It was warm compared to his skin. Surprisingly so. Gradually, that warmth rose up inside of him, twining its way up his arm. It was impossible, of course, owing both to the young age of the eggs and the fact that he was not their biological father, but it seemed to him as if the developing dragon inside was seeking comfort in him. Like it wanted closer. Wanted him to keep it safe.

Without thinking, Bertram gingerly lifted the egg and tucked it into the crook of his arm, where it could be near his beating heart. The dragon inside of him purred, and that strange warmth from the egg vibrated in response, like it was learning to purr, too.

"I have you now," he whispered to it. "I understand you might feel as though you are alone, but you are not. You are mine, and I am yours, and I will care for you. You do not have to be afraid."

The warmth vibrated again, then seemed to settle, so Bertram put the egg back into its nest and picked up the next. Like the one before, it reached out with its warmth, and his dragon purred for it. It purred back.

"Is everything in order, my lord?" the blacksmith's wife asked after Bertram finished repeating the process with all four eggs. "Have we done well?"

"Yes. Thank you for your service. The Amethyst clan is in your debt. We shall see to it that your family—and all the families who served under Unwin Drake—are handsomely rewarded."

The blacksmith's wife hesitated, then asked in an uncertain and worried tone, "Do you suppose the clutch will pull through, my lord? I fear the eggs may not hatch."

Bertram's gaze lingered on the four eggs in their makeshift nest, and after a moment of stillness, he nodded. "They will," he vowed, laying his hand on the nearest one. "I'll make sure of it."

4

SORIN

Sorin disregarded the dragon's orders. Heart in his throat, he fled down the servant's stairwell, shut himself in the scullery, and pressed himself into the corner, tugging his knees to his chest to make himself as small and compact as he could.

The eggs were screaming for him.

Their voices cut above the echoes of the ones that had come before, filling his head so full of heartbreak, he could barely think. He willed it to stop, but it would not. Their anguished cries continued, and so too did one recurring thought—*that dragon has your eggs.*

That dragon.

Sorin drew a jagged breath and squeezed his eyes shut, committing his appearance to memory.

Dark hair down to his shoulders.

A charming face.

Deep purple eyes.

A body average enough to be a handsome everyman, yet robust enough to easily wield a blade.

He had said his name was Frederich, and Sorin repeated it

over and over until he was certain he'd never forget. Frederich. Frederich. *Frederich.* The one who had taken everything from him.

And the first one he would destroy.

It took hours, but eventually, the panicked cries of his eggs diminished, then stopped altogether. Echoes of them bounced through Sorin's mind, but they were tolerable now—tolerable enough he was able to stand, legs wobbling, and leave the scullery.

From there, he went straight to Unwin's hoard.

A purse full of coin and a few small, sellable trinkets later, he left the castle.

The dragon—Frederich—did not give chase, but that was fine. He didn't need to.

Because as long as he had the eggs, Sorin would be coming for him.

5

BERTRAM

With James III restored to power, Scotland was once more safe for travel, and travel through it Bertram did. He brought the eggs with him on his journey, swaddled in blankets and secured in a large basket, all the way to Castle Beithir, which was located outside of Braemar—the place Bertram called home.

It was a lonely place, gorgeous with its rolling green hills and pristine lochs, but isolated. By decree of the nine clans, the Highlands belonged to no dragon and were outside draconian jurisdiction and, as such, had been selected as the place where all prospective agents of the council—regardless of their clan—came to train.

But those times were few and far between.

The rest of the time, their training grounds near Braemar stood empty. Seemingly abandoned. Every now and then, a curious human would come across them and try to make a home of them, and while they seldom succeeded, the few times they had proved inconvenient enough that the council had passed a decree ordering one of their agents to establish a full-time residence nearby to keep it from happening again.

Upon his father's insistence, Bertram had volunteered for the position.

He hadn't wanted to, but with Amethyst territory in such close proximity, it had only made sense.

So he'd said goodbye to his brothers and hello to bitingly cold winters and heather-rich glens.

To loneliness.

But such was the life of an agent of the council. They were tools designed to accomplish the objectives laid out for them, not individuals meant to think, and so emotion was trained out of them from the earliest opportunity. Agents did not act of their own volition, even in matters of the heart, and Bertram had been fine with it.

Or so he'd thought.

But then he'd met that omega and his eggs.

Castle Beithir had never felt so desolate as it did when he returned that day.

Clutching the basket to his chest, he made haste from the stables into the central-most room of his lair—the one belonging to his hoard. It was windowless and had been built with reinforced walls to make sure that even should a dragon attack, it would remain standing. There was no safer room in the castle, and no better place for his eggs.

He set them down on a mound of golden coins, its top leveled to assure the basket stayed in place, then began poking around the room to see what he could find. A ruby here. A sapphire there. A golden headpiece from distant lands. An opulent golden mirror. He fitted each piece into the basket, surrounding the eggs with riches until his dragon was purring in satisfaction.

Perhaps it had been a blessing that he had been made to come here—a secluded castle would be the perfect place to nest with his new eggs.

"I beg your pardon, my lord," came a voice from the doorway. It belonged to Agnes, one of the castle's few permanent staff. She was Bertram's steward in everything but name and, despite her old age, was just as sharp and fastidious as she had ever been.

Smiling, Bertram turned to look at her. She was in one of her favorite aprons, the front lightly stained by old kitchen work, beneath which she wore a warm but practical dress. Her long gray hair was pinned up and out of the way, and there was a flush to her cheeks like she had made great haste to come see him.

"Agnes," he said warmly, his smile growing into a grin. He stepped forward and gestured at the basket with a hand drenched in treasure, fine gold necklaces dangling from his fingers. "Come meet my new eggs."

Agnes looked wide-eyed at the basket, clutching a hand to her mouth in surprise. "Oh, dear."

"Oh, dear?" Bertram frowned. "Whatever is the matter, Agnes? Are you not pleased?"

"That's not it." Agnes crossed her arms over her chest, mirroring his expression. "I came as fast as I could to warn you that your father is on his way, my lord. Hamish spotted him on the horizon, approaching our location. He seems to be in a hurry —and now I think I know why."

Bertram's heart sank.

He looked over his shoulder at his unsanctioned clutch and thought he knew why, too.

"Thank you, Agnes," he said, and set down the last of his treasure. No sooner had it left his hand than he was back in his agent mindset—unfeeling Frederich once again. "I will go greet him. Would you mind fixing some refreshments? I'm sure he'll be parched and ravenous from his travels, and I myself could do with something to eat."

Agnes nodded, but even as she attended to him, her eyes kept moving back to the eggs.

"They will be fine," Bertram told her, steadfast in his certainty. "But if you find yourself with a spare moment, would you do me a favor on their behalf?"

She dragged her gaze back to him. "Aye. Anything for you, my lord."

"Would you look into bringing on some new servants?" Bertram shrugged out of his traveler's cloak and folded it over his arm. "We'll need nursery maids, cooks, and scullery maids at the very least, but please feel free to bring on others if you believe there are other positions that should be filled in preparation for the hatching of the whelps. A year should give us enough time to make sure all of them are trained and feel at home in our castle. Please feel free to extend the offer to anyone you think might be a good fit. Money is no object, and you've no need to seek counsel with me over your decision. I trust your judgment entirely."

"I shall see to it," Agnes promised, exiting the doorway to give Bertram passage. He locked the door and tested it, then followed her down the hallway, matching her slower gait all the way to the great hall. "It is good to see you home in one piece, my lord," she said before they parted ways. "And congratulations on your clutch. When your father leaves, you'll need to tell me all about it —I'm sure it's quite the story."

The eggs, glittering like jewels by the forge.

The astonishment he'd felt at the sight of them.

The *happiness.*

The corner of Bertram's mouth twitched into a smile. "Yes. Quite the story indeed."

Grimbold dismounted from his horse upon reaching the castle grounds, his boots impacting the ground beneath him with enough force, they stirred dust up into the air.

"Hello, Father," Bertram said in greeting. He stood a respectful distance away, giving his father room to breathe and space for the groom to rush in and lead the horse away. "I suppose you're here regarding my report following my last mission. I understand my behavior was, in some ways, unorthodox, but—"

"Where are they?" Grimbold cut in, his voice as inflexible as iron.

Bertram flattened his expression. "In my hoard, but—"

"Take me to them. I must see them at once."

Grimbold's tone did not invite further conversation, and Bertram knew better than to push his luck. Right now, they were not father and son—they were clan head and dutiful operative—and that meant it was not Bertram's place to argue.

It was his place to obey.

To shield himself from the hurt that caused, and to keep his true feelings from shining through, Bertram put himself aside and stepped into his role as Frederich. Adopting his persona's easy-going smile, he inclined his head and brought his father to his hoard, where he showed him the eggs.

Grimbold observed them without touching them, his expression unreadable. He did not move, did not look up, did not so much as acknowledge Bertram for several long moments, then shook his head and cussed under his breath. "I had hoped they were fake."

"I beg your pardon?"

"The eggs." Grimbold flicked his gaze to Bertram, eyes as dark with untold emotion as a stormy night out at sea. "Unwin did not seek sanctions, and there is no record of him having taken an omega from any cloister, Amethyst or otherwise. The council is unaware this clutch exists, and with tensions as high as they are right now, it would be in our best interest to dispose of these eggs before that changes."

Bertram wore Frederich while he worked to shield himself against emotion, but even Frederich was not enough—Grimbold's words pierced him deep, like he had taken his claws to Bertram's heart. "I hardly think that is the only way," he said, struggling to keep Frederich's upbeat impartiality in place. "They are only eggs,

Father, and freshly laid. There is time to concoct a cover story that will explain their existence. These are Amethysts—we should do everything in our power to protect them."

Grimbold's temple ticked. "Do you challenge me, child?"

Bertram did.

He never had before, but with the well-being of his eggs on the line, he could not be silent. "I do not, Father. I never would. But I am an agent of the council." He paused, choosing his words carefully, knowing one mistake could mean the destruction of his eggs. "And as an agent of the council, beneath your instruction, I serve all of dragonkind. Are these eggs not dragons, Father? Fertility is low, and within our lifetime, our species could very well go extinct. Should we not do everything we can to prevent that? To keep these eggs alive so a new generation of Amethysts will be there to take our places when we turn to dust? No one need know their true parentage. No one need know they were unsanctioned. I will submit the appropriate paperwork to the council, and I will take an omega from an allied cloister and have them play along. Don't tell me you don't think it would work— you and I are the only souls who would ever know, and that omega will not be able to tell anyone the truth, as he or she will be sent far away to live luxuriously off my coin. The plan is foolproof."

"The plan is flawed." The storm in Grimbold's eyes flashed as though with lightning. "You are an asset to our clan—whelps will only distract you—and beyond that, do you know how vulnerable having children will make you? Should an enemy seek to do you harm, they need only look as far as your nursery."

"I understand." Dodging Grimbold's gaze, Bertram fixed a piece of jewelry that had begun to slip off one of the eggs. "But would you prefer the alternative? Four dead Amethysts in exchange for a single asset? In my opinion, that is no fair trade. Don't you agree?"

Grimbold did not reply, but Bertram felt him simmer.

Hoping to cool him down, he advanced the conversation, allowing his father space by needlessly rearranging the coins nestled in with his eggs. "The whelps will not be young forever. In little more than a short decade, they will be independent enough that I will be able to reprise my duties as though I had never left. In another decade after that, they will be capable young men able to defend themselves against enemy attacks. The window of time in which I would be vulnerable is so short as to be laughable. I see no disadvantages. If we do this, our clan would be four Amethysts stronger, and only one agent short for a few brief years. Osbert and Merewin will gladly pick up my slack, I'm sure, and our family will be the envy of all—one of the very few to have been blessed with eggs."

The tension began to drain out of the air. Bertram turned to see the storm had gone out of his father's eyes. Thought flickered there in its place. "You would have no issue raising them as if they were your own?"

"I swear it."

Grimbold gave the basket—and the treasure in it—a long look. "I will make sure you are given sanctions," he said at length. "In addition, I will give you ten years following your whelps' hatch date to make a show of being their father. When that time is over, you will return to your duties without excuses. Do you hear me?"

"Aye." For the sake of appearances, Bertram didn't smile, but on the inside, he was glowing. "I do."

"I do not like this," Grimbold added, folding his arms over his chest. "But I see the reason in it. This will be the first clutch Amethysts have managed to produce since you boys were hatched, and to destroy it would be a waste. However,"—his tone sharpened—"I will not abide you using this as an excuse to go soft. The ten years you have to father these eggs must also be spent in maintenance of your abilities. I will not have you return to your duties a shadow of the agent you once were. You owe it not only to me, but to the clan you serve, and beyond that, to all of dragonkind."

Bertram inclined his head. "Understood."

"Then I will trust you to concoct the finer details that will sell this lie." Grimbold nodded in the general direction of the eggs. "Nobody must know the truth—the safety of these eggs and the reputation of our clan depends on it."

"You have my word."

There was more Bertram wanted to say, but he knew the value of silence, and let it set in while he stepped around his father and toward the door. Like he'd hoped, his father followed, and they exited his hoard together. Bertram, not wanting to risk his eggs for even a single moment, waited for Grimbold to cross the threshold, then closed and locked the door.

They reconvened in the great hall, where Agnes brought them food and drink, and spent some time in silence while they filled their bellies and warmed themselves with wine. They did not speak. Grimbold brooded and drank quite heavily, and Bertram watched him, ruminating, as he waited for color to rise in Grimbold's cheeks or nose, or for his expression to lighten—signs the alcohol had done its job.

He wanted Grimbold as pliant as possible for what he was about to say.

"When I arrived in Unwin's lair to dispose of the rogue omega," Bertram said a short while later, once Grimbold's cheeks were flushed. As he spoke, he pushed his plate aside and folded his arms on the table, leaning in toward his father conspiratorially. "I discovered things, Father. Atrocities I did not include in my report that would have made any dragon's skin crawl. I do not claim to know the full story of what went on in that castle, but I don't need to have all the facts to know that Unwin Drake was in defiance of the law beyond his unsanctioned clutch, and I am worried as to some of the things I saw, especially after what I found out from you today. There was evidence in Unwin's lair suggesting the omega he impregnated had been taken from the cloister in Constantinople—are you sure there are no records of Unwin having acquired one of the Pedigree?"

Grimbold set his goblet down. "Does it matter? Unwin is no longer with us, and you yourself disposed of the omega. Whatever atrocities Unwin did or did not commit are now irrelevant. We cannot punish the dead."

A cleaver clutched in a shaking hand.

Anger and fear in eyes dark as pitch.

Bertram's heart clenched.

"I suppose not," he said dully. "But it does not explain the presence of clothing branded with the crest from that cloister. With the clans all self-governing the comings and goings of their Pedigree omegas, surely there might be some records being withheld from the council—do you not think it time to revise how the process works? To set in place a system to keep such deceptions from happening, in case dangerous dragons like Unwin prey on the vulnerable or, heaven forbid, the whelps born to them in secret when these illegal dalliances occur?"

The wine was not enough.

Grimbold's lip pulled back in a silent snarl, his eyes darkening with anger. "Do you question the council?"

"I would never."

Grimbold looked him over with a critical eye, then sighed and combed a hand through his hair. It seemed to Bertram as though he were tired, although whether it was of Bertram or of something else entirely was impossible to tell.

"I have brought it up on several occasions," Grimbold said after some time, "but there is too much opposition for any change to occur. The argument goes that there are so few clutches being laid, imposing any kind of new restrictions on any of the clans could lead to extinction, and no matter what it costs, we cannot have that."

Bertram's dragon did not care for that explanation, and

41

showed it by superseding Bertram's will, sending a cascade of scales down his neck. He shrank back in his chair as soon as he felt it and closed his eyes while he strained to fight it back, but the damage had been done.

Grimbold sighed.

He'd seen.

"My power is not absolute, child," he said. "Change can only occur when the majority of the council agrees to it. You should not worry of such things. That is my burden to bear."

"But as an agent of the council—"

"You are bound to the council's word," Grimbold finished for him. "No matter what it may be. I understand your eagerness to change the world, but it is not as simple as voicing your opinion. If it were, much would be different. Both for better, and for worse."

There was truth in those words, but it didn't make them any easier to swallow. Bertram dipped his chin in recognition, but said nothing, causing his sire to sigh again. "You shouldn't be so stubborn," Grimbold said. "You've been trained better than that. This is a fight you cannot win. Divert your focus from the impossible to that which is within your reach. Your whelps will need you, Bertram. Their care is now your priority."

"But what shall become of the whelps who are not as fortunate as my own? Or the eggs laid for sires who will fail them?"

"They shall persevere, as they always have," Grimbold said with a note of finality. "It is how it's always been, and perhaps how it shall always be."

It seemed to Bertram to be more of an excuse than an answer, but it wasn't his place to say so. He was a tool of the council, not a member of it, and had no more say in what was right than any other dragon alive.

6

SORIN

Spurred on by the call of his clutch, Sorin wasted no time. The moment he left Unwin's castle, he put a plan into motion to guarantee his safe passage, and with it in place, he set off to find his eggs.

Out of necessity, he was frugal with his money. He did not know how long it would take to track Frederich down, and as an omega, he knew he would have trouble finding work should he need to earn more coin. So, with just a few meager possessions to call his own, he obtained a pilgrim's badge and traveled from pilgrimage to pilgrimage, moving through Amethyst territory slowly but surely.

He had thought he would need to ask around for information about the dragon, Frederich, in order to track down his whereabouts, but as it turned out, that was not necessary. Sorin could *feel* where he was.

Or, perhaps more accurately, he could feel the eggs.

They tugged on his soul when they called for him, and when he wandered farther from them, they let him know. With them as his compass, he made his way north. Progress was slow, but it was better than being locked up in a dragon's lair, unable to do anything, and while the screams of the whelps he had not been able to save echoed through his mind with every new step forward, he found some solace in knowing it would not be the same with this clutch.

Frederich could not hide from him forever.

Not as long as he had the eggs.

The temperature plummeted. Daylight hours grew short, and night became miserably long. Sorin had come far, and knew he was getting closer, but months had passed, and it had begun to feel like he might never catch up with Frederich. Was he even going in the right direction? It occurred to him—not for the first time—that the pull he felt toward the eggs might not be real. Not once had he heard about such a thing during his time in the Pedigree.

But then again, no one had laid a clutch in hundreds of years.

Not until him.

Still, those feelings of self-doubt lingered. Worsened. Made the screaming louder.

How could he trust himself with a track record like his own?

Thirteen eggs taken from him.

Three clutches he would never meet, who would never know his name.

It was insanity to think it would be different with these four eggs.

Yet even at his most defeated, when it all seemed to be for naught, he kept walking.

He didn't just owe it to his eggs—he owed it to himself.

One sleepless night huddled by the campfire for warmth bled into another, until the call of the eggs encouraged Sorin to break from his pilgrimage and travel Scotland alone. Winter arrived. One short day led to another, and with every step, something in Sorin's soul told him he was getting closer to his eggs.

He traveled through rugged country, up frozen hills and across frosted plains. The cold was unforgivable. It seemed no matter how many layers he wore, it still ate him through to the bone.

But the pull on his soul kept him moving.

Closer and closer he came.

And then one day, upon cresting a hill, he saw it—a lonely castle in a sprawling valley.

The dragon's lair.

The place where he'd find his eggs.

The darkness, the self-doubt, the screaming—all of it evaporated. Joy took its place. Tears in his eyes, Sorin half ran, half staggered down the slope, kicking up clouds of loose snow as he went. At one point, his foot crashed through a rabbit hole, causing him to stumble and fall, but he popped right back up and carried on at his hurried pace as if nothing had happened.

The moment he arrived in the safe, flat land of the valley, he stopped walking and *ran*.

The castle came closer.

Closer.

The call of his clutch brightened. Became energized. Filled with joy.

They knew he would see them soon.

Knew he would take them away.

Within the hour, he would have them, and everything would be right again. He would take his eggs, he would rescue them from Frederich, that vile dragon, and he would—

His foot came down, and the ground beneath him snapped and gave way. With nothing there to support his weight, he pitched forward and fell, smacking face-first not into snowy grass, but a sheet of ice that shattered instantly upon impact. There was nothing beneath it but water.

Deep water.

Water that sucked him under and knocked the breath out of his lungs.

On his way down, he looked up and saw the sun, bright and round, gleaming on its surface—an egg-shaped patch of light surrounded by growing darkness, slipping further and further out of reach.

7

SORIN

The pop and crackle of a fire brought Sorin out of the darkness. He opened his eyes to see he was not at the bottom of a lake, but in a cozy—if somewhat sparse—bedchamber. He occupied the only bed and had been tucked under a veritable mountain of warm blankets and furs, made warmer yet by the fire that burned cheerfully in the stone hearth across the room on the opposite wall. A stack of conditioned wood was piled next to it, and near it, a leather bellows, a shovel, and a broom adorned a brass fireplace organizer. The only missing piece—the poker—was held loosely by an old woman in a drab woolen frock. Her back was to Sorin, and as he watched, she squatted down and prodded the wood in the hearth, making space for another piece.

Sorin's instincts warned him to be wary, but he was so stiff and sore from what he'd been through that all he wanted to do was sink into his comfortable bed and sleep. When was the last time he'd been warm? Four months ago? Five? He couldn't remember. It had been such a long time, and he had come such a long way.

It wouldn't be wrong to rest. He deserved a little downtime after everything he'd been through.

Once he'd slept, he'd get back to it.

He'd track down the dragon and—

His eggs.

Realization struck Sorin like an open palm across the cheek. He blinked his drooping eyelids open and sat up in a rush, knocking away his blankets. The eggs were here, and they were close. Even now, they called to him. He couldn't sleep. He had to find them before Frederich realized he was here.

The old woman, having tossed another log onto the fire, turned. "Ah," she said, her voice cracking with age. "I thought I heard you wake. Lay yourself back down, bairn. You needn't be afraid—you're amongst friends here."

The woman seemed nice enough, but Sorin didn't have time for conversation. The only way he'd be able to best a dragon was to catch him by surprise, and that meant he had to act fast. Ignoring the woman, he sprang out of bed, fully intending to rush the door, but as soon as his feet hit the ground, his knees buckled and he fell gracelessly, only just managing to snag the bedside table on his way down.

"What on earth are you up to, bairn?" asked the old woman as she hobbled over. "You've been ill for quite a spell, and it's a right miracle Hamish found you when he did, or you very well could have died. You're not strong enough to go haring about."

Objectively, she was right. Sorin wasn't strong enough.

But strength had little to do with it.

He would not lie here and let himself be taken prisoner by another dragon.

He had to get up, and he had to keep going.

He had to do it for his eggs.

Gritting his teeth, he lurched forward, using the bedside table as a crutch to get him to the door. With every passing second, his strength came back to him, and as he took his first wobbling steps through the doorway, he knew the worst was over.

He was not fully recovered, but he was in good enough shape to navigate the castle and escape with his eggs.

The old woman shouted fearfully after him, but Sorin did not stop. He ran, stumbling and disoriented, down the hall, following the tug in his soul that had brought him from Unwin's castle all the way here, to Scotland. The woman gave chase, but even as unsteady as he was, he was faster and more agile. Eventually, he lost her, and alone, he pushed on until he found the place that felt right.

A hallway lined with doors.

He was close—*so close*—but Sorin did not stop running. He sprinted down the hallway on unsteady legs, the muscles in his thighs twitching in complaint, in search of the door that felt right.

"Hey!" shouted the old woman from somewhere down the hall, frightening him so much, he lost his footing. Gasping, he staggered forward while trying to keep himself upright and caught his foot on a tented section of rug, which sent him crashing off to the side.

And straight into a lit candelabra.

It toppled upon impact, and as it struck the floor, all of its candles scattered.

Several landed on the rug and set the thing ablaze.

There came a gasp from behind him. The old woman had caught up just in time to see the fire ignite.

"*My lord!*" she screamed. "Oh, my lord! The rug is on fire!"

But the rug was not the only thing burning. Sorin was on fire, too.

The flames spread rapidly. Relentlessly. They ate through the carpet like it was made of straw, and treated Sorin's clothing no differently. Pain—all too familiar—consumed him, but it came secondary to his panic.

His eggs were here.

If the fire spread, they would be cooked alive.

"Bairn!" the old woman cried. "Oh, bairn! What are you doing?"

Sorin answered by showing her.

He pulled himself on top of the carpet fire and used his own body in an attempt to smother the flame.

For a second, it seemed like he'd succeeded, but then flames licked out from beneath him on either side. It was instant agony. Sorin shrieked, rearing back as his skin blistered and burned.

Don't stop, urged a voice in his head—the same darkness that had rejoiced upon seeing Unwin bleed. *The pain doesn't matter. We must protect the eggs. Above all else, they are our priority.*

It was true, but the pain was debilitating, and Sorin did not know what else he could do.

He would die here, he realized.

After everything, this was how it would end.

But then, something strange happened.

His hands moved of their own volition, beating down on the fire to stomp it out, and as they did, his pain disappeared. It was as though his consciousness had been separated from his body, which was now being controlled by someone else.

"What is going on here?" demanded a new, familiar voice right as Sorin put out the last of the fire.

Sorin, still detached from his own body, could not turn to see who it was, and it seemed whoever was in charge had no interest in doing so, either. Now that the job was done and the eggs were safe, it collapsed flat onto the rug and let go of its hold on him, allowing Sorin back in.

Sensation returned.

The pain was unbearable, and it all hit at once, but all Sorin could do was whimper. He was too tired to cry, and too hurt to move. His vision grew increasingly blurry. Knowing he didn't have long left for this world, he focused on the one thing that mattered—the strange connection he shared with the eggs—and pushed as much love and comfort as he could in their direction, not knowing if they would ever feel it, but feeling better for having tried.

As he said his goodbyes, footsteps approached. They were heavier and surer than those of the old woman, and carried an unmistakable kind of gravitas that gave the individual's identity away.

"He's badly burned," said Frederich. "Agnes, fetch Hamish at once. Tell him what has happened. Hurry!"

"Aye," the old woman—Agnes—replied.

Her shuffling footsteps faded into the distance, and Sorin heard her no more.

In the quiet that followed, a dark blur entered Sorin's field of vision. Frederich. The wretched dragon who had taken his eggs away. He squatted next to Sorin, hovering there for a moment before sighing and lifting Sorin into his arms. There was pain, and Sorin squeaked, but then warmth rushed through him and the pain abated.

His vision began to clear.

Sorin tilted his chin, looking up beyond Frederich's chest to his face. He had a proud jaw, he realized. A prominent nose. Strong cheekbones. Moody eyes the color of vine-ripened grapes you might find in a vineyard in France—the kind that, from the very first taste, left the tongue eager for more. Had Sorin not been aware Frederich was a dragon, he might have thought him an angel come to usher him into death, but that was the way of the devil, wasn't it? Always hiding behind appearances to seduce the righteous.

It had to be the same with this dragon.

There was no other way to explain why the sight of him gave Sorin butterflies.

"You aren't supposed to be here," Frederich admonished, but there was no real anger in his voice. "I gave you a second chance. You were supposed to run away."

"Not without my eggs," Sorin managed to rasp.

After everything that had happened, it was that which made Frederich sigh. He shook his head and, looking down upon Sorin with great sympathy, admitted, "I was afraid of that."

8

BERTRAM

It was a truth universally acknowledged that a villainous omega intruding in a dragon's lair must be looking to end his life, and such certainly seemed to be the case for the poor creature Bertram scooped off the charred remains of the area rug. The skin on his arms and sides had burned to the point where it seemed like it would slough right off were any pressure to be put upon it, and while the injury wouldn't kill the omega immediately, it would fester and rot if left untreated, and that would be more than enough to do him in.

It would be a mercy to run a claw across his neck and end his life before his true suffering began, but there was a complication —the eggs had yet to hatch. Under different circumstances it wouldn't have mattered, but the omega was clearly suffering from egg madness, and that meant he had touched the eggs, bonding himself to them. If he died, he could very well take the eggs with him, and Bertram could not let that happen.

His dragon grumbled in agreement and paced, worried, in the confines of Bertram's mind as he rushed their injured guest into one of his spare bedrooms.

The poor thing was so weak, he didn't put up a fight.

"Do not mistake my hospitality for weakness," Bertram muttered as he entered the guest room his father had recently vacated. "I have not changed my mind about you. After the eggs hatch, I will end your life."

At that, the omega opened one of his eyes and fixed his simmering gaze on Bertram as if to say, "I'd like to see you try."

The little thing was spirited.

Bertram admired that.

He set the omega down on the bed, careful of his injuries, then summoned fire from the air to light the hearth, and again to ignite the fat beeswax candles by the bedside. Once the room was sufficiently lit, he very gently extended the omega's arms to get a better look at the damage done.

The omega hissed in pain.

"I can't say I understand your motive," Bertram said as he observed the injuries. "Did you intend to set fire to the castle in order to end my life? You must be aware the eggs are here, and while they are resistant to fire, they are not impervious to it. They would have burned to ash much sooner than I."

"I would have saved them."

"Is that so?" Bertram found a place on the omega's wrist the fire had left untouched and held on to it firmly, making sure his hand was wrapped all the way around and his palm was flush with the omega's skin. "I suppose you know where they are, then, and how to gain access to them."

The omega's expression flattened with irritation, but he said nothing. While he tried not to make it obvious, Bertram noticed that his focus was on his arm. He was afraid, no doubt, that Bertram would use the wound to his advantage and torture him into revealing his plans—and truthfully, had he been anyone but the father of Bertram's eggs, he wouldn't have been wrong. But torture was so often messy and unnecessary, and he had no stomach for it today. Especially not with his dragon pacing like it

54

was, restless and overly concerned for the villain who had tried to steal their eggs.

"I should look into increasing security," Bertram mused as he gently squeezed the omega's wrist, directing what little magic he possessed into him. Slowly—very slowly—his skin began to heal. "News of my clutch has begun to spread, and if an omega can so easily infiltrate my lair, I shudder to think of what my enemies could do should they be so inclined."

The omega flinched. "What are you doing?"

In a panic, he tried to pull his arm away, but Bertram's grip was strong, and he was not willing to let go.

"*My skin.*" The omega pulled again, harder this time, almost thrashing. "My skin is—"

"Healing," Bertram finished for him. "Your skin is healing. I won't be able to restore it entirely, but I'm confident I can relieve some of your pain. It won't be perfect, but I should have enough magic in me to keep the rot at bay until my brother Everard arrives."

"*Stop.*" Despite his poor condition, the omega continued to struggle, fighting him with the same kind of bone-deep fear Bertram had seen in men who knew they were about to die. "I don't want this. I don't want it. Stop. *Stop!*"

Bertram wanted to assure the omega he would do no harm, but at that moment, something strange happened—needlelike pain burst in his head and a trickle of something wet slid down his upper lip. The taste of copper filled his mouth. He touched the wetness, and when he pulled his hand away, he saw that it was blood.

Had he reached the limits of his magic already?

Strange. He'd only just begun.

Frowning, he stopped pouring magic into the omega and let go of his wrist.

His nose stopped bleeding at once.

Having gotten his way, the omega sagged onto the bed with a

withering sigh and closed his eyes. His injuries were only marginally healed, but there was nothing more Bertram could do.

"It seems I've overexerted myself," Bertram said as he stood and took one of the candles from the bedside. "I will try to heal you again tomorrow, after a full night's rest."

"Why not just kill me now and get it over with?"

"It is as I told you. The eggs have yet to hatch. Until then, you will live here with me."

"You intend to keep me as your prisoner, then?"

"Yes." The answer came so easily, Bertram didn't have to think about it. "Once the whelps are born, I will dispose of you, but until then I'll have to keep you in my custody to make sure you don't harm yourself. Or them. I gave you a chance to stay away, but you didn't. You've given me no other choice."

Bertram expected snarls of protest or loud belligerence, but the omega remained silent. All he did was smile. It was a pity to see him so lost to egg madness. If only Unwin had done a better job at keeping him from his eggs. But Unwin was dead now, and there was no going back to fix what had happened. The omega was the way he was, and Bertram would show him what mercy he could until the time to forever end his suffering arrived.

"The door will be barred from the outside," he told the omega as he made his leave. "I will be back tomorrow with clean clothes and breakfast. There is a chamber pot beneath the bed, should you need it, and wood by the hearth should it get cold. I will warn you that if you choose to set fire to this room, you will be the only one to die. There is no escape. The fire will stay contained within these walls and it will eat you alive. It will not reach me or the eggs."

"I won't need fire to kill you," the omega murmured, then sighed and closed his eyes. Bertram left him to his own devices, snuffing the candles by the bedside with a curl of his fingers before closing and locking the door. He would need better barricades soon, but not tonight. With the omega weakened from his injuries, the flimsy lock would hold until he could have a better one installed. Bertram had seen for himself the damage the omega had caused to Unwin's castle, and he would not have the same happen here in his own lair.

In any case, it was a problem for tomorrow. The omega was contained and the eggs were safe, and that was all that mattered for today.

"My lord?" came a nearby voice. It was Agnes, who stood down the hall next to her husband, Hamish. She wrung her hands nervously, an awful look of guilt on her face. "Does he live?"

"He does. My magic was enough to take away his pain for tonight, but I wasn't able to fully heal him. I'll send for Everard on the morrow."

"Did he injure you?" Hamish asked. "There's blood all down your face."

"Ah." Bertram touched his fingers to his upper lip. "It was my own fault. I poured all my magic into him, and this is the result."

Agnes and Hamish nodded, appeased by the answer, but Bertram's own words stuck in his mind. Something about them didn't feel quite right. Whatever it was, it prickled while he explained to Agnes and Hamish that the omega was not to be let out of his room no matter how much he begged or pleaded, and that unless otherwise directed, no one but Bertram should ever venture inside.

It was only when he said goodnight to them and went to wash up that he figured out what was bothering him.

He'd extinguished the candles in the omega's room with magic, but how? He'd drained all of it away to heal the omega. He shouldn't have been able to use his magic at all.

Curious as to how that could be, Bertram passed the blade of his razor over the back of his hand, only pressing hard enough to draw out a few pinpricks of blood. As they swelled, he channeled healing magic through himself, and the cut disappeared.

His nose did not bleed, nor did he feel any pain.

So why had things been different while tending to the omega's wounds?

Troubled, Bertram finished rinsing the blood from his face and retired to his chambers, but sleep was elusive, and when he did find it, it was fitful at best.

There was something unusual about the omega.

Something wrong.

But he supposed it wouldn't matter soon, as once the eggs hatched, the problem would take care of itself.

———

"What's your name?" Bertram asked the next morning as he sat on the omega's bedside, balancing a tray with a bowl of porridge topped with wild raspberry jam on his lap. The omega's injuries looked worse this morning. They had gone an awful shade of pasty red overnight, and looking at them, Bertram couldn't be sure that rot hadn't already set in. Everard would be able to tell, he was sure, but it would be several days before his brother received his correspondence, and several days after that until he arrived.

The omega's shoulders stiffened at Bertram's question, and he set his lips, saying nothing.

"I can't go about calling you omega forever," Bertram said as he set the tray on the omega's lap. "If you won't tell me your name, I'll have to give you one myself."

The omega eyed the tray.

He did not reply.

"All right, then. Keep your secrets." Bertram pinched off a mischievous smile. "Bran it is."

"Bran?" the omega squawked, eyes narrowing to bore angry holes through Bertram. "Why would you want to call me that?"

Bertram shrugged, eyeing the porridge. "It was the first thing that came to mind."

Bran exhaled his frustration, then picked up the spoon beside the porridge and jabbed it into his breakfast. "If that is your will, so be it. You may call me what you wish. Names mean nothing to me, anyway." He glanced pointedly at Bertram. "No matter how terrible they are."

"I happen to like the name Bran."

"And I happen to think you have awful taste."

Bertram arched an eyebrow and took a long look at the young man before him. The murderer, he had to remind himself as his gaze lingered. The creature who had managed to kill a dragon. It didn't matter that the dragon in question had been a monster—no omega had the right to take a dragon's life. Bran could not be forgiven.

But murder did not change the fact that he was astonishingly pretty.

All delicate angles and glossy hair, he carried in him all the poise and radiance of a Pedigree omega even when badly burned. It was easy to imagine why a dragon might want to drape him in gold and bury him in jewels, adding to his beauty until there was no other earthly creation as gorgeous. An omega of his quality deserved to live a long life of luxury, not one cut short by Bertram's claws.

But there was no helping it now.

Bertram had told him he would not show mercy, and he never went back on his word.

"Taste matters little outside polite conversation," Bertram went on to say, happily distracting himself from golden fantasies by carrying on the conversation at hand. "You should consider yourself lucky I'd entertain your opinion at all."

"Why?"

"The wants of a dead man matter little in the land of the living."

Bran shoved a mouthful of porridge into his mouth and said nothing, but the look in his eyes said it all.

The conversation was over, so before a certain omega

distracted him again, Bertram got down to business and took Bran gently by the wrist. Bran's back went rigid, but it wasn't until Bertram began pushing magic into him that his eyes widened with fear. At that point, all hell broke loose. Bran's spoon dropped out of his hand, clattering onto the tray, and with a strangled cry, he thrashed wildly onto his side so his back was to Bertram, spilling his porridge onto the sheets. "*Stop.*"

Bertram stopped at once.

Magic did sometimes burn when it healed, especially when wielded by a novice such as himself, but it shouldn't have hurt this badly. There was something else going on here. Something beyond pain. And as Bertram thought back on the horrors he'd seen in Unwin's lair, he feared he knew what it might be.

"Do you think I'll hurt you?" he asked, but Bran did not reply. He was breathing as though he'd run a race, his chest heaving and his skin pallid. "I have no intention of disposing of you before the eggs have hatched," Bertram assured him, "and that includes letting you die from your injuries. Your wounds will start to rot if left untreated. My magic will keep that from happening, and while it is far from perfect, it will be enough to keep you well until my brother arrives and heals you in full."

Bran did not move, and his panic didn't ebb—he drew one shaking breath after another as though his lungs couldn't get their fill. Bertram reached out a hand, intending to lay it on Bran's shoulder, but stopped a few inches short of contact.

A niggling thought told him Bran would be better off without his touch.

"I am not of the same ilk as Unwin," he murmured, his fingers curling slightly before he took his hand away. "Yes, I will one day be your executioner, but I take no joy from the suffering of others. You will be treated well until the day you die."

"How am I supposed to trust you?" Bran shielded his head with his arms. The raw layers of skin left loose by his burn wrinkled and folded as he moved, but the pain didn't stop him. Fear was too powerful a motivator. "I was told to trust, and I trusted, and trusted, and trusted, but all they ever did was *take.*"

"Your eggs?" Bertram asked.

"My *everything.*"

Bertram contemplated that for a moment, then shook his head. Bran was in the midst of egg madness. It was hysteria and nothing more. The rot wasn't only in his skin, it was also in his brain, and unfortunately, no magic could save him from that.

Still, it complicated matters.

Forcing magic into the boy would do him no good, but leaving him to rot would be worse. Bertram would need to find another way to heal him—a way that didn't cause Bran to panic, like he was doing now. Whatever way that was, it would likely require a great deal of stealth and cunning...

Which was fine by Bertram, as he was well-versed in both.

9

BERTRAM

The solution was *aqua vitae,* which Bertram had imported from the isle itself. It was one of the rare treasures not kept in his hoard, but in kegs in the wine cellar, and despite his initial reluctance to trust a dragon, Bran took to it readily. Bertram had only intended to use it to lull him into a deep sleep, during which he could work his magic without the omega being any the wiser, but the drink had an unintended side effect—it loosened Bran's tongue.

"The first dragon who took me was an Onyx," Bran told Bertram two nights into his captivity, his first glass of *aqua vitae* drained, and a second well underway. "Rumors had spread through the Onyx clan that there was a Pedigree omega who greatly resembled the dragon lord Rustaham, and as it turned out, that omega was me." He wrinkled his nose and scowled at his drink, but his expression lacked its usual venom. Bertram found it quite fetching. "Lord Rustaham was rich, but he was not a popular dragon within the Onyx clan, and he had many enemies. He'd gained his fortune by lying and using underhanded tactics to trick other dragons out of their coin, but nothing he did defied the law, so he was never punished for it. When word got around there was a younger, prettier version of him in the Constantinople cloister, one of the dragons he'd wronged sought sanctions not because he wanted a clutch, but because he wanted to work out his frustrations on a version of Rustaham that couldn't fight back. The eggs came as a surprise. There were five of them in total. I was blindfolded and shackled while I laid, so I never got to see them, but for years after that, I heard them cry out in want of me. Desperate, heartbroken little screams. Even to this day, I can't shake the sound of it. Their pain echoes inside of me, and it won't leave me alone."

Bertram arched a brow and sipped at his drink but said nothing. The story was remarkably cohesive for an omega suffering from egg madness, but he supposed it was to be expected—Bran had been given months to concoct a believable lie while journeying to Scotland. Anything to tug on Bertram's heartstrings and get him to show mercy. Bertram knew the ploy all too well.

"I'd been taught that Pedigree omegas who laid clutches were sent away to live off the riches of their dragon lord," Bran went on to say, "but such was not the case for me. From what I can gather, word spread quickly through the grapevine that I had conceived a clutch, and offers to purchase my services began pouring into my cloister. I suppose one of them was too good to refuse, because as soon as I finished laying, I was shipped off to another hateful dragon and given some foul mixture to induce my heat. I conceived with him after only one attempt. Three eggs, that time. I saw them." Bran's voice hitched, his eyes shimmering with tears. "They were dark jewels as stunning as the endless night sky, but they were taken from me before I could tell them how beautiful and loved they were." Bran cleared his throat roughly and drained his glass, setting it on his knee. "I never saw them again."

Bertram was not naïve—he was aware that not all cloisters were lawful. Some masters and matrons, seeking to fatten their pockets, used their cloisters like brothels and sold their omegas for coin. There had been a few cloisters with similar issues under

Amethyst jurisdiction over the last few hundred years, although none that matched the insanity of the one Bran described. If he had only edited down his story a little, Bertram would have believed him, but his claims of laying multiple clutches pushed it over the top.

It was simply too much.

No omega had ever laid more than one clutch, and no omega ever would. Those rare few who did lay eggs were sent to live in paradise in lands far away, where they spent the rest of their days in luxury, living off their dragon lord's coin. Clutches were such big news that there was no way an omega could slip through the cracks—dragons were always sticking their noses into the business of others, and with news as exciting as that, there were simply too many eyes watching for trafficking to occur.

And yet...

Something troubled Bertram enough that he reached for the decanter, pouring Bran another drink.

He knew the story had to be fake, but all good lies grew from kernels of truth, and he found himself yearning to follow this tall tale down to its roots to see how deep it would go.

Bran considered the drink, sipped at it halfheartedly, then sighed and set his glass on the bedside table. "There was another clutch," he said as an aside, and settled into bed, where he nestled into the pillows. "I would tell you about it, but I can see you don't believe me, so I won't waste my breath."

"Why would you say that?"

"Don't play dumb." He looked up at Bertram impartially. "Your expression reveals nothing, but I can see the way your mind turns behind your eyes. You can look engaged and interested all you'd like, but I know better. I've been the property of so many dragons, I know how you operate—even the pretenders, like you."

"Pretenders?"

"The ones who pretend they're innocent." Bran seemed to

consider something, then reached for his glass and sat up just enough to drink from it heavily. He winced upon swallowing, then set it aside and flopped back into bed, seeming oblivious to his own pain. "They act as though they are friendly and benevolent, incapable of doing wrong, but you—all of you—allowed this to happen to me, and others like me. It wasn't just the Onyx clan—dragons in every clan knew things like this were happening, and no one thought to stop it. You've enslaved us. Shut us into pretty prisons where we're taught to be faithful whores. And even then, it isn't enough for you. You take, and you take, and you take, and you don't care who you hurt as long as you get what you want in the end. All of you are the same. Some of you just show it more than others."

"That isn't true."

"Then will you abolish the Pedigree?" Bran demanded, piercing Bertram with his gaze. "Will you let us go?"

What Bertram wanted to say, and what he almost said out of instinct, was "No," but that didn't sit right. The situation was more nuanced than that. But before he could explain, Bran sighed in frustration. "I thought as much," he said, and turned his back on Bertram. "Goodnight."

Bertram remained seated for a few moments longer, considering the small but fierce omega he'd taken prisoner, then rose without a word and left the room. How was he to make Bran understand that the Pedigree gave omegas otherwise destined for manual labor pampered and privileged lives? The Pedigree was a kindness, not a curse, and the few instances of abuse within the system did not mean the whole thing was corrupt. The checks and balances in place were not perfect, but Bertram had already spoken to his father about putting more stringent regulations in place. It would take time, but eventually the opposition would wane and conditions would improve. The unlucky few who suffered during their time in their cloisters did not change the fact that to serve a dragon was a blessing, and of all those who attended to their dragon lords, those who entered the Pedigree were the most blessed of all.

Those thoughts haunted him for several more hours, giving chase as he paced his lair, never lingering long in any one spot, the lantern he carried all that kept him from the shadows of the night.

Bran, he decided, was misguided.

That was all.

The evils he'd suffered were not typical, and they had shaded his perception of reality. Had he been raised in an Amethyst cloister, he wouldn't have entertained such outlandish thoughts. After all, what were dragons supposed to do if the Pedigree was abolished? Clutches were rare enough as it was—they might never be laid again should the cloisters be shuttered. Then what were the omegas to do? Live as peasants? It made no sense.

Life would be far worse for everyone without dragons there to oversee it, and the Pedigree was the cornerstone of that hierarchy —the foundation of draconian society itself, from which all clutches were produced. It was essential. Abolishing it would mean the end of dragonkind, and that simply could not be allowed to happen. There was no other way.

As wrapped up as he was in his thoughts, Bertram didn't notice that he'd wandered in the direction of his eggs until he found himself in front of the nursery door. It was late, and he was better off in bed, but his hand was already in his pocket, and then the key was in the lock. His dragon stirred as he entered the room and purred with longing as it spotted the eggs, and as one, they moved to the egg bed and wrapped themselves around their clutch, gathering each egg to them as closely as they could so they would feel Bertram's beating heart.

Dark jewels as stunning as the endless night sky.

Did they scream, too?

"You are beautiful and loved," Bertram whispered to them, his heart breaking and his mind somewhere far away. "You don't have to be afraid. I will do anything to protect you."

The eggs did not reply, of course, but a tender kind of love warmed Bertram's chest. He wasn't sure if he should ascribe it to the eggs, but he and his dragon lay with them a while longer anyway, soaking up the feeling until there was nothing left of it—until it felt like the eggs were asleep.

Sometime later, not wanting to leave, but knowing he must, Bertram said his goodbyes to them and locked them up safe, then wandered back through the dark and lonely halls of his castle to heal the young man who would one day die by his hand. Bran did not wake up when he entered the room, so Bertram pushed all the magic he had into him, then sat silently by his bedside while he processed his regrets and stored them away one by one.

It was not easy being an agent of the council, but it was harder yet to be a father.

And if tonight was any indication, this was only the beginning.

It would only get harder with time.

It was a week and a half before Hamish spotted the carriage as it crested a distant hill. In that time, Bran's injury had not gotten any worse, but it had also not gotten better.

"There are horses on the horizon," Hamish said upon entering Bertram's study, where Bertram was penning a letter. "It shan't be long before your brother arrives."

"Wonderful." Bertram set his quill in its holder and left his letter where it lay. He'd finish it later. In all likelihood, it would go unanswered, just the same as the last time he'd written to his father about implementing changes to the Pedigree, so time was no issue. "See to it that his horses are cared for and ask our new cook to arrange for a hot meal to warm his bones. I will greet him in the great hall, where we'll dine."

"Of course, my lord."

"Thank you." Bertram offered him a smile, which Hamish

returned. "Oh, and do ask Agnes if she'll tidy the guest bedroom in the opposite wing from our new resident omega. I don't anticipate he'll cause much of a fuss, but he might should he know another dragon has come to pay us a visit."

"I'll be sure to get it done."

"You're a good man, Hamish." Bertram clapped him on the shoulder. "Thank you."

Hamish nodded stiffly. Behind his eyes, Bertram could tell he was not looking forward to serving Everard, who had a sharp tongue and knew expertly how to use it, but he was a loyal man, and he would do his job.

Bertram admired him for that.

"I'll be in the great hall," he said in parting, then went to wait for his brother, reminding himself on the way of all the white lies and half-truths he'd need to tell about Bran in order to keep the eggs safe.

10

SORIN

Burning magic crashed through Sorin's veins, and he woke up screaming out in pain. He thrashed and kicked, trying to make it stop, but it was futile—he'd been bound sometime during the night, and no matter how hard he struggled, he could not escape.

A shape moved in the shadows.

A dragon.

Unwin.

Trapped like an animal and frightened out of his mind, Sorin struggled harder, crying out in fear and pain. He would die here. He would die helpless and alone, so close to his eggs, yet not allowed to touch them. Not allowed to be with them. Another failure. Another heartbreak.

Even now, they screamed for him.

But he was not enough. Had never been enough.

He was useless.

Nothing more than a womb to breed—a dragon's pretty plaything.

The utter anguish of it all built up inside him until it felt like he would explode. He wailed, gnashing his teeth at the air, and as he did, something flexed in his head like a muscle, and something strange happened—the scalding magic stopped, and the dragon who had been pouring it into him cried out in surprise. "What the devil?"

"It happened to me as well," said Frederich from nearby. As he spoke, all the candles in the room lit and the logs in the hearth burst into flames. "I can't explain it. I thought I'd pushed myself too hard and drained my magic, but now it's happened to you as well. What could be the cause of it? I haven't suffered a nosebleed in centuries."

"I haven't the foggiest."

"Well, take some linen. It will staunch the flow."

The strange clenching feeling in Sorin's head let go, and he slumped onto the bed exhausted. As he caught his breath, his mind cleared, and reality set in.

He was not in Unwin's castle.

He had been bound, yes, and he was unable to move, but he was not at that evil dragon's mercy.

He was with Frederich now. The great pretender.

But what about that other voice?

Sorin peered at the newcomer, wanting to know who it might be.

The newcomer, by the looks of him, was a dragon. He stood near enough to the bedside that Sorin was able to see his unmistakably purple eyes. Unlike Frederich, who could pass his eye color off as black or some unusually deep shade of brown, this dragon's eyes were a touch lighter in color, and while they were pretty enough, they lacked intrigue. There was a look of superiority about them that suggested the dragon thought very highly of himself.

A faulty devil.

Too full of himself to be seductive, and too conceited to care.

The dissimilarities between the two dragons ended there. Like Frederich, the newcomer had dark hair and stood at approximately the same height. The shape of their noses and ears was similar, and while the bottom half of the newcomer's face was largely concealed beneath a wad of linen, what Sorin saw of his jaw suggested the rest of him would echo Frederich as well.

Brothers, then.

Clutch-mates.

Only where Frederich was sophisticated, this dragon was sardonic and prickly.

Sorin didn't trust him in the least, and made his inner feelings known by scowling at the dragon as menacingly as he could. The newcomer noticed, eyed him suspiciously, then turned his attention to Frederich. "You didn't warn me that healing him could very well endanger my life, B—"

"Frederich," Frederich insisted firmly.

The newcomer flattened his brow. "It seems to me as though there is something going on, my dearest *brother Frederich*." He spoke the last two words with emphasis, almost like they were a threat. "Remind me again why you wanted me to come out all this way for the sake of one unknown omega?"

Frederich's expression remained pleasant, but a glint of something lit behind his eyes.

"I was the one dispatched to look into Unwin Drake's sudden passing," he said in an aggressively cheerful tone of voice. "You apprenticed under Unwin, didn't you? So I assume you must be aware of at least a few of the oddities I came across while investigating in his lair."

Frederich's brother blanched. "I might be."

"Then it should come as no surprise to you that amongst Unwin's possessions, I came across this omega, still alive, but in a sorry state. I had no choice but to rescue him."

It wasn't just a lie—it was a lie told seamlessly.

If Sorin hadn't been the omega in question, he wouldn't have thought twice about it... but knowing what he did, it begged the question: what other lies had those lips told?

"I found him in one of the bloodier parts of Unwin's castle,"

Frederich went on to say, "and could not release him to the public for reasons I'm sure you'll understand. Discretion is essential, which is why I've called you here. There is no other doctor I trust with the secrets of the council. You've patched me up enough to know the deal."

A look of comprehension dawned on his brother's face. "Was he... ah... a specimen?"

"A specimen?" Frederich tucked his hands into his pockets. "I suppose you could call him that."

A haunted look pulled the newcomer's lips tight. He shuffled his feet uncomfortably and crossed his arms over his chest. "When I was little more than a whelp," he said, "not long after you left the family for your own training, Father sent me off to Unwin in the hopes he would help me hone my healing magic. He was considered to be the best healer the Amethyst clan had ever had, and I was determined to best him."

Sorin stiffened with fear—he couldn't imagine what horrible things someone would have to do to "best" Unwin—but as his heart started to race and panic began to set in, Frederich put a reassuring hand on his arm, careful not to touch where it was injured. "You aren't in danger, Bran. You needn't worry. My brother is nothing like Unwin."

"You're right," the other dragon bragged, grinning wide. "I'm *much* better."

"*Everard.*"

The dragon—Everard—rolled his eyes. "Yes, yes. Fine. My apologies for spooking your new pet. If you'd just have let me finish, I would have told you I am better than him not because I learned from him, but because of all the research I did on my own. I was with Uncle Unwin for less than a week before I removed myself from his tutelage. The man was unhinged even back then —cut my ear clean off one time without warning and grew it back while I bled all over my perfectly good doublet, and all for the sake of demonstrating how powerful magic can be. Needless to say, I returned home that same day and never went back. If I'd had any inkling that he would continue those experiments, I would have said something, but I assumed he would never try such a thing on anyone who couldn't heal himself—let alone an omega." Everard reached down and, to Sorin's great horror, touched him, healing a portion of his arm. "See, little blackbird," he said gently, "I heal. I only heal. Any pain I cause is for the necessity of healing and not for any other agenda. I am not Unwin."

Sorin didn't trust this dragon any more than he trusted Unwin, but it was pointless to resist. Whether he put up a fight or went along with what Everard wanted, the result would be the same—the dragon would do what he wanted, and Sorin wouldn't be able to stop him. It was better for both of them if he allowed this to happen. Perhaps, if he was calm and compliant, they'd release him from his bindings, and he'd have a chance to escape.

"There." Everard smiled, and it was surprisingly genuine. "Much better. It shan't take long. There will be discomfort, but know that in the end, it will be worth it. Be strong. I know you have it in you."

Sorin braced himself, and soon enough, Everard pushed his warm, healing energy into him. It flowed up his arm and through his body, heating until it seared, but even as the discomfort edged toward unbearable, Sorin felt the difference—the parts of him that had been burned stopped throbbing with pain, and his skin, so tight and sensitive, relaxed as the damage was repaired.

The procedure was over quickly, leaving Sorin unmarked by injury and entirely pain free.

"You called him blackbird," Frederich said casually once the last of Everard's magic had ebbed. "Why?"

Everard looked at him as if he were daft. "Bran means raven."

Surprisingly, Frederich soured. "Do not give pet names to my omega."

"*Your* omega, brother?" Everard smirked. "That is news indeed."

"You know what I mean." Frederich went over to the hearth, seized the nearby poker like a sword, and poked the fire a few times. He made it all look so casual, but it seemed an awful lot to Sorin like he would rather be poking something much more purple-eyed and reptilian. "You always twist my words about. It's a wonder Father didn't have you take Geoff's place after your apprenticeship with Unwin failed."

"Alas. Had I only been born without a sense of humor, you might have had your wish."

Frederich poked the fire again. Several times. Until one of the logs fell to pieces.

Seemingly pleased with this turn of events, Frederich smiled and put the poker away.

"In any case," Everard continued, "*your* omega has been healed, and my job here is done. I would love to stay and chat about all of your mysterious escapades, but I'm afraid London calls. Make sure he stays away from fire next time. Surely you've enough magic in you for that?"

"It was Unwin's doing, not mine," Frederich said stiffly.

Everard arched a brow but didn't reply. Sorin assumed, from their short acquaintanceship, that this was a rare occurrence—one which Frederich took full advantage of by sweeping forward and planting his hand on Everard's back.

"Come," he said, pushing Everard gently forward. "Now that you're done here, I'll bring you to meet the eggs. It would be a shame if you left without having seen them."

Everard met Sorin's gaze as he was pushed forward, biting back on a grin that made his boring eyes sparkle. "Alas," he said. "It seems our time together grows short. Fare thee well, omega. Until we meet again, do be sure to keep my dear brother in line."

"Out," Frederich said with finality.

He marched Everard out of the room.

Before the door closed, Everard poked his head back through the door and wiggled his fingers. The locks on Sorin's restraints released. Everard gave him another wink and opened his mouth to say something, but Frederich grabbed him by the back of the doublet and pulled him away before he could get it out.

Without injuries keeping him bedridden, Sorin quickly grew bored of his small and uninspiring bedroom. Apart from poking at the wood in the hearth as it burned, there was nothing to keep him entertained, and worse, nothing to distract him from the call of his eggs. Wise men often claimed that idle hands were the devil's workshop, but Sorin didn't agree. In this case, he intended to turn his idle hands into the devil's undoing.

He would find a way to escape if it was the last thing he ever did.

And once he succeeded, he would take his eggs and leave this place, and one day, when they were grown, he would come back and slay Frederich for all the wrongdoings he had done.

Breaking out, however, was no easy endeavor.

Frederich had installed several locks on the door to keep Sorin in. They were tricky things, but no lock was truly infallible, and Sorin was persistent. He observed the way they worked when Frederich came and went, and began testing them at night when the castle was quiet and the servants had all gone to bed. It was slow going, but finally, after a few days of refining his techniques, he was successful.

The locks came undone, and the door swung open.

Sorin was free.

He blinked at the empty darkness before him, giving his eyes time to adjust before stepping out of the light of his room and into the unknown on the other side of the door. Instinct took over. He heard his eggs, could *feel* the way they wanted him, and followed that tug on his soul through the quiet castle.

Frederich would not stop him this time.

His persistence had paid off.

It had taken far too long, but finally, he'd won.

There was nothing extraordinary about the door in front of Sorin. It was made of sturdy wood and wasn't ornately carved or otherwise embellished, but despite how plain it was, it was the most beautiful door in the castle, for it was the last obstacle standing between him and his eggs.

For a moment, all Sorin could do was stare at it.

It seemed impossible that he'd come this far, and honestly, he wasn't prepared for what would come next. He had been a dragon's property for so long that freedom no longer felt real. He couldn't imagine what life would look like on his own, raising his babies in peace…

Yet here it was.

He would finally be free of dragons.

He would finally be happy.

He grounded himself with a steady breath and put a trembling hand on the door. It had been left unlocked and slightly ajar, and swung inward with the slightest push.

Beyond it was the nursery.

It boasted three irresponsibly large windows that overlooked the snowy loch. They weren't shuttered, which meant there was nothing to keep out the blustering winter winds, though the room was far from cold—a roaring fire in the hearth did away with some of the chill, but the primary heat source came from something far stranger.

Stranger, and impossibly beautiful.

Globes of fire the size of pearls hung overhead, suspended in midair like stars in the night sky. They were tiny, but heat radiated off them as if to challenge the winter weather, daring it to see what would happen if it was foolish enough to come inside.

Sorin had known dragons were capable of magic, but hadn't realized they could do things like this.

Was it Frederich's work?

Had he done it solely for the benefit of the eggs?

Enchanted, he stepped into the room to get a better look, only to be distracted by something that hadn't been visible from the door.

The bed.

It was piled high with soft furs, quilts, and blankets, and boasted more pillows than any one person could need. Amongst the bedding, something twinkled—treasure. Jewelry, gemstones, and strings of pearls that seemed to loop into infinity. Gold chains tumbled off the sides of the bed like bed skirts, emphasizing its round shape.

Like a nest, his inner voice remarked, and he shivered in pleasure.

It would be the perfect place to spend the day safe and warm in the company of his clutch.

With his eggs.

The eggs.

Sorin snapped back to his senses. What was he doing, wasting time? It didn't matter how much Frederich had spoiled the clutch, because the eggs would not be staying here. Sorin was leaving tonight, and he was taking them with him.

He hurried to the bed and pulled back the topmost blanket, sending coins flying. They clinked prettily on the floor as they fell, making noise that rang bright like bells.

Noise that awakened something huge that had been hidden under the pile of furs and quilts on the bed.

A bedraggled Frederich appeared, shedding bedding like sheets of water. He was nude except for the dark purple scales that tumbled down his neck and shoulders, and while he wasn't armed, a quick glance below the belt revealed he was in permanent possession of a truly lethal-looking club.

Sorin froze, but Frederich did not. He exited the bed with far more grace than was fair and smoothly picked Sorin up by the back of his tunic, carrying him out of the room.

"Release me!" Sorin squeaked the moment he found his tongue. It didn't come out anywhere near angry enough, so to up the ante, he snarled and twisted and squirmed, doing everything in his power to escape Frederich's grip.

"No," Frederich said, holding Sorin away from his body like one might an angry kitten. He was not in the least impeded by Sorin's efforts, and carried him unfalteringly away from the nursery. "You are not to be released. You are my prisoner, and will be until the clutch hatches, at which time I will properly dispose of you. You are not—and never will be—at liberty to walk free in my lair, and under no conditions are you to see the eggs."

"*Why?*"

"Because egg madness has made you careless." The next few sconces along the way lit themselves with a showy flash—Frederich's doing, no doubt. "I saw the way you were in Unwin's castle —how unhinged you became while hunting for your eggs—and even now, right in this very moment, you are carrying on like a wild animal. It is clear you have gone insane."

A wild animal?

If that was what Frederich thought of him, then that was what he would get.

With a snap of his teeth, Sorin aimed a kick at Frederich's ribs, but Frederich caught his legs before the kick could land and swung him up into a bridal carry.

"No," he admonished. "We do not kick. Do you think this is helping your case, Bran?"

Sorin scowled. "There isn't a case to begin with. You're not giving me a chance."

"And perhaps there's a reason for that."

They arrived at the door to Sorin's bedchamber, which Frederich bumped open with his hip. Six steps later, he dropped Sorin gently on the bed, but didn't immediately leave. Instead, he looked down upon Sorin with an infuriatingly neutral expression, like he wasn't angry that Sorin had broken out of his room—just greatly disappointed.

"Do not patronize me," Sorin grumbled. "I am not a child."

"You've the sense of one."

"Is that so?" Sorin glanced down Frederich's body to the partial erection between his legs. "One part of you doesn't find me child-ish, at least. I can work with that. Let me make a bargain with you."

"Absolutely not."

"At least hear what I have to say."

Frederich's lips thinned. He crossed his arms over his chest, but he did not say no, and Sorin didn't give him a chance to reconsider—he launched into his pitch straight away.

"One touch," he said, no longer feral, adopting instead the seductive tone he'd been taught to use during his training while in his cloister. One so golden with desire, no dragon could resist. "One touch, that's all. A single brush of my fingers on each egg. I won't ask for any more than that. Give it to me, and in exchange, I will be yours—all yours—to do with as you please."

"No."

"You could have me, dragon." Sorin rose slowly onto his knees, letting his tunic slip down his shoulder. "You could have me as much as you'd like, as many times as you'd like. Do you want to know what they teach us in the Pedigree?" He angled his head, looking up at Frederich with bedroom eyes, knowing at these angles, he was beautiful. Coyly, he sank his teeth into his bottom lip and let the suggestion percolate in Frederich's mind.

Plump lips, soft and pink.

A wet, warm mouth for the taking.

Like he'd hoped, Frederich's gaze dropped to his mouth, eyelids drooping just slightly. He was weakening to Sorin. Wanting him. And Sorin welcomed that desire by tugging gently on Frederich's arms until they dropped away from his chest. With them gone, Sorin put his own hand there, laying his palm on Frederich's pectoral just shy of his nipple.

His free hand, meanwhile, dipped inward.

Slowly—achingly slowly—he ghosted his fingertips along the base of Frederich's cock.

"I could show you," he whispered, leaning in to breathe the warmth of his words along Frederich's collarbone. "I could make you feel *good.*"

Hunger darkened Frederich's eyes. His half-hard cock twitched.

Sorin, grinning to himself, pressed a kiss to Frederich's bare skin.

"Fuck me," he whispered, and kissed him again and again, soft sweetness meant to mask his bitter lies. "Knot me. Come in me. Rut in me all night if you want to. I want it. *I want you.*"

It was that that did it.

Those words that ensnared the dragon and made him Sorin's slave.

Shuddering with lust, Frederich took Sorin by the wrist and tugged him close. Heat poured off him like there was fire burning in his chest, and quite suddenly, all Sorin could think of was how happy the eggs must have been with him curled up around them, keeping them warm as they all slept under the blankets. Peaceful. Paternal. Content.

He had not expected his own cock to stiffen.

Had not expected the sudden thrill of pleasure that ran through him, like a chill along his spine.

He thought he would be repulsed the first time Frederich touched him, but as Frederich's curled fingers found their way beneath his chin and lifted his head up so they looked eye to eye, Sorin found himself practically panting from the urgency of his own desire.

His heart fluttered.

It was supposed to be a lie, but he *wanted* Frederich to kiss him. To breed him. To knot him.

Drunk off his own lust, he no longer envisioned himself running away—he could only imagine himself nesting with Frederich, kissing and touching as they kept watch over their eggs.

Frederich leaned in to kiss him, and Sorin closed his eyes, lips parting, knowing if he did this, he was sealing his own fate.

But the kiss never came.

"No," Frederich whispered a hair's breadth away from his lips, then pushed Sorin off balance, causing him to fall onto the bed. There was no time for him to react, not even time enough to think, before the door swung shut and the lock clicked into place.

Frederich was gone.

In his absence, Sorin lay on his bed and stared at the ceiling, heart racing and cock half-hard.

He had never wanted a dragon.

Never found sex enjoyable. Never tingled in need of it.

Never felt like this.

Closing his eyes, he took his cock in hand and milked an orgasm from himself. Then another.

He did it thinking about Frederich, imagining him instead of Unwin as the father of his eggs.

Afterward, sweaty and out of breath, he found the strength of will to push those impossible fantasies aside. Frederich was a dragon, and like every other dragon, he was heartless and evil. He was not doing what he had done because he cared about Sorin's eggs—he was doing it for his own benefit. For the prestige of having a clutch. When the whelps were born, he would abandon them to grow up on their own, just like all dragons did.

His heart would not change because Sorin wished it.

He was a dragon, and dragons were monsters. Point final.

But this attraction between them—as unwelcome as it was—did come with some benefits. His attempts at seduction had failed, but he had learned something valuable tonight. Deny it all he liked, Frederich was attracted to him, and that meant one day soon, he would give in. Sorin would give him his body, and Frederich would let him touch the eggs, and even if Sorin never got to escape with them, he would at least have a chance to tell them they were loved, and that he would never abandon them. Hopefully it would calm them and stop their screaming, allowing him to live what little time he had left in peace.

It was as perfect a plan as it could be, all circumstances considered.

After all, Frederich was just a dragon.

But Sorin?

He'd been training for this his whole life.

BERTRAM

The next day, a tray of breakfast in hand, Bertram entered Bran's bedchamber to find the omega posed on the bed entirely in the nude. The only thing keeping him from total immodesty was a thin linen draped over his upturned hip, but it hid very little, and was positioned quite precariously. It seemed to Bertram the slightest movement would make it fall, but that did not stop Bran from full-body stretching as Bertram stepped into the room.

Bertram froze.

As expected, the linen tumbled, pooling quite lewdly over a concealed part of Bran's anatomy.

Stretch complete, Bran made a little noise of contentment in his throat, then opened his eyes and looked up at Bertram from his place on the bed, feigning innocent surprise.

"*Frederich*," he said, a blush rising in his cheeks. "I didn't expect to see you here so early. I, um..." He glanced down at the protruding part of himself concealed by the fallen linen. "I'm always a little worked up in the morning, but usually I have time to take care of it before you arrive. Do you... do you want to help me?" He flicked his gaze up to Bertram, hazy-eyed with lust. "All I need is one thing..."

Bertram remained motionless another moment longer, indulging in the angles and curves of Bran's body. The softness of his skin. The peachy blush of his cheeks. He'd put on a little weight since arriving at the castle, and he was gorgeous. A true jewel of the Pedigree.

But a treasure best enjoyed from afar.

Not taking his eyes off him, Bertram set the breakfast tray on Bran's bedside table, then leaned in and tenderly brushed a wayward stand of hair behind Bran's ear. Bran's eyelids drooped upon contact, and he pressed his cheek into Bertram's palm in a way that promised he would be Bertram's perfect pet, if only Bertram gave in.

Innocent seduction at its finest.

Even Bertram, who had been trained to resist temptation, felt a pulse of desire.

Buzzing from it, he tilted his head and brought his lips against Bran's earlobe, lingering there a selfish moment before he whispered, "You'll have to try harder than that."

He left before Bran could try anything else, his heart beating hard in his chest.

Bran was good, he'd give him that, but he would not succeed.

Bertram's training would not fail him. He was much too good of an agent for that.

Bertram did not serve Bran dinner that evening. He passed the chore off to Agnes and stood watch at the end of the hallway.

"Look at you," tutted Agnes as she passed by, Bran's dinner tray on her hip. "Hiding around the corner, spying on the poor young thing. He is an omega, my lord, not a manticore. There's no need to be afraid. He's likely more scared of you than you are of him."

Bertram made a face. "I'm not afraid."

Agnes eyed him disbelievingly.

"I'm not! I've been to see him plenty of times. He poses no threat to me."

"Then why do you keep him locked up?" Agnes had a look about her that made Bertram think she very dearly wanted to smack him with a dishrag. Or perhaps a wooden spoon. "Bran seems like a lovely young man. You'd see so for yourself were you to give him a chance."

"Perhaps."

Agnes, unaware of the truth behind what had brought Bran to Castle Beithir, shook her head like a disappointed nursemaid and unlocked the door. She afforded Bertram a last withering look, then into the room she went.

Bertram counted the seconds in silence.

One.

Two.

Three.

On four, Agnes shrieked.

Bran shrieked.

A tray clattered.

Bertram was impressed. Three whole seconds had elapsed before chaos erupted. How unexpected.

He'd had his money on two.

After a fair bit more screaming and the clattering of dropped silverware, a ghostly pale Agnes raced out of the room and slammed the door shut.

"Agnes," Bertram said, abandoning his post to approach her. "Are you quite all right?"

Agnes jumped a mile high and spun around. Her frock was soaked through with beef stock, and a carrot medallion clung to her skirt. "My lord! Oh, I..." She thinned her lips, then strained a smile. "I'm fine, my lord. Our guest wasn't expecting company and, um, well, it seems we spooked each other. I'm afraid I dropped his dinner."

"A shame."

"Quite." She cleared her throat uneasily. "I'll fetch another tray."

"Would you like my assistance?"

"No. No, I'll..." Her tight-lipped smile curled into a frown. "Well, I suppose perhaps I would, my lord, but not for some time. The boy is in need of his privacy right now, you see."

"I expect he is, yes."

"*Quite* a bit of privacy." Agnes wrinkled her nose. "Enough privacy, in fact, that I suspect I'll be quite busy in the scullery by the time he's ready to receive guests. Would it be permissible for Hamish to serve him dinner in my place?"

It was no easy feat to hold back his laughter, but somehow, Bertram managed. "He may."

Agnes nodded curtly and scurried off, not once looking behind her. Bertram couldn't say he blamed her. He'd hoped better of Bran, but it seemed the young man had much to learn in matters of manipulation. With another few years and some tutelage, he might truly have been something, but alas, Bran did not have years. He had sentenced himself to death by coming here, and his innate talents would not save him. It was simply not meant to be.

Leaving the thought behind him, Bertram followed after Agnes. It was a shame she had been spooked and the soup had gone to waste, but all wasn't lost. One good thing had come out of tonight—he suspected that after this, Bran would not try to seduce him again.

Several minutes and a flight of stairs later, it occurred to Bertram that Agnes had not locked Bran's bedchamber door. The second the thought registered, he turned on his heel and ran not for Bran's bedchamber, but for the nursery. If the omega escaped the castle, so be it—it was a negligible price to pay to ensure he did not harm the eggs.

In a flurry of footsteps, Bertram emerged at the top of the stairwell and bolted down the hall. The nursery wasn't far, and not much time had passed since Agnes had left Bran's room, but even still, Bertram catastrophized.

What if he was too late?

What if, in his madness, Bran destroyed the eggs?

The thought of bursting into the nursery to find the omega cuddled up on the egg bed, laughing, arms full of yolk-covered, fragmented shells haunted Bertram all the way to the nursery wing. Full of a fear his training had long taken from him, he rounded the corner at full speed, the nursery door now in sight. The area was dark, but Bertram's eyesight was sharp, and he spotted it right away.

The humanoid shape in the shadows, making haste for the nursery door.

The sight of it sparked anger in him like struck flint.

Nostrils flaring, he shot down the hallway and slammed the figure—Bran—chest-first into the wall.

"*Villain*," he seethed in a whisper just short of Bran's soft hair.

"Don't speak so fondly of yourself," Bran hissed in return. "You give yourself too little credit. You are more than a villain to keep an omega from his eggs, dragon. You are not just monstrous—you are *evil*."

Bertram's dragon snarled and sent a cascade of scales down his neck. It wanted him to be reckless, to lash out, to *punish*, but Bertram was too well-trained to act on impulse. Swallowing his fury, he grabbed both of Bran's wrists and restrained them with one hand, then used the other to grab Bran's shoulder, intending to pry him off the wall and march him back to his room.

But Bran was not interested in cooperation.

As soon as Bertram grabbed him, he thrashed and kicked blindly backward, cussing, no more seductive or innocent than a viper poised to strike, teeth out and dripping venom.

"Fighting won't help you," Bertram ground out through his

teeth, tightening his grip on Bran's wrists. "All you'll end up doing is hurting yourself. Why not walk calmly back to your room with me? You'll save us both the struggle."

"Eat shit and die."

Bertram laughed, mostly out of surprise. "The mouth on you."

"When overpowering your enemies is an impossibility, words become the only weapons you have."

"And what says it of the wielder when those weapons are crass obscenities?" Bertram, now more intrigued than angry, somewhat loosened his grip on Bran's wrists. He'd been told omegas in the midst of egg madness were mindless creatures who lacked common sense, but Bran's wits were sharp, and his tongue was sharper. This was a far cry from the desperate, wailing creature he'd encountered in Unwin's castle, and while it was not his place to question the order of things, a curious part of him wanted to know how that could be. "You could do better," he said, purposefully goading Bran on to see how he would respond. "Why throw sticks and stones when you could be nocking arrows?"

"Because sometimes," Bran growled, not missing a beat, "sticks and stones are all you have."

"Fair enough."

Silence lapsed, and Bertram's curiosity grew.

Why was Bran not acting like an omega with egg madness? It made no sense. There was no remission from a thing like that, no reprieve, no cure. He should have been in hysterics now that he'd been caught, or reverting to the doe-like, seductive state he'd slipped into that morning.

What he shouldn't have been doing was trading verbal jabs.

Omegas who'd lost their mind did not have the mental fortitude to engage in metaphor.

Or at least, so he'd been told.

Could it be there was some mistake?

Surely not. Yet here was evidence to the contrary.

Whatever the truth, it was clear something odd was going on

here, and as an individual whose sole use in life was sniffing out suspicious business, Bertram made it his mission to figure out what it was.

"You're not going to let me go, are you?" asked Bran after the silence had set in, looking over his shoulder at Bertram in utter contempt.

Bertram shook his head. "No. I'm afraid not."

"You do know if you bring me back to my room, I'll only break out again. I won't stop. I won't give you a moment's peace. If you won't accept my offer, I will be your waking nightmare. I will make you wish you had killed me when you had the chance. And one day, when I've exhausted you, I *will* get what I want. I *will* have my eggs."

"Is that so?"

"Yes." Bran's eyes narrowed with furious determination. "It is."

"Well, I suppose there's no helping it, then." Bertram peeled Bran off the wall and guided him a few steps back, not releasing his wrists but allowing him some space. "Let's go."

The fury blinked out of Bran's eyes.

"Do you mean it?" he asked in an excited rush. "You'll take me to see my eggs?"

"No." Bertram clamped his hand down on Bran's shoulder and moved him in the opposite direction from the nursery. "But if you and I are to be mortal enemies, then I have some work to do. You see, I take no joy from besting rivals who are so clearly at a disadvantage, and I heard that Agnes spilled your dinner—let me take you to the great hall so we can get some food in you. You'll need your energy if you want to stand a chance at beating me, and you'll feel better after you eat."

Bran did not try to hide his confusion—he looked upon Bertram as though he were the one who had gone insane—but he did not resist as Bertram led him through the castle in the direction of the great hall. Perhaps it was a mistake to trust him like this, but if Bertram knew anything for certain, it was that there was no better way to figure out who a man truly was than to spend time in his company.

Perhaps Bran was simply masking his insanity.

Perhaps not.

But the only way he'd know for sure was if he took the time to figure it out for himself.

So off they went so he could do exactly that.

With Agnes and Hamish's whereabouts unknown, Bertram brought Bran into the kitchen, where the soup pot was bubbling over the central fire. Bran, who seemed suspicious of his sudden charity, hopped up onto the nearby counter and sat, distrustfully watching as Bertram searched the cabinets for a soup bowl and a spoon.

"Are you to tell me you're unfamiliar with your lair, dragon?" he asked as Bertram closed one cabinet and opened another.

"I'm not often home."

"Why not?"

"The reasons don't concern you." Bertram found a bowl and, victorious, began the hunt for a spoon. A ladle had been left in the soup pot, thank the lord, so it was all he had left to find. "Although you'll be glad to know I've made arrangements and won't be called away for the next decade so I can raise the whelps."

Bran crossed his ankles and swung his feet. "You speak as though I won't spirit them away."

"You won't."

"How can you be so sure?"

"Because I do not intend to lose to you. Once they hatch, you'll be dead."

Bertram found a spoon and struck it in the bowl, then ladled out a generous portion of soup and handed the bowl to Bran. He braced himself to have its contents dashed down his front, but

Bran didn't try any such thing. He set the bowl on his lap, wincing a little. "It's hot."

"I'll carry it for you and set it on the table."

"No." Bran scowled. "I'll take care of it myself."

Bertram shrugged and said, "As you wish," which earned him an indignant glare from Bran. The omega then hopped off the counter and, bowl in hand, allowed himself to be led out of the room and into the great hall.

The great hall wasn't far—only a short walk from the kitchen —but it was large, and Bran's bowl wasn't getting any cooler. Bran put on an unaffected air, too stubborn to ask for help, but was clearly suffering. He adjusted his hands over and over until finally, ten paces from the table, he hissed in pain and dropped the bowl.

Bertram caught it with a flourish.

"It is quite hot, isn't it?" He wrinkled his nose in displeasure— the bowl was already starting to burn his palm. To remedy the situation, he summoned forth a claw and sliced open his doublet, which he then ripped from his body. The thing had seen better days, and he wasn't sad to see it go, especially when he caught the look on Bran's face. The omega stared at him wide-eyed in astonishment.

"Here." Bertram balled the doublet beneath the bowl and handed it back to Bran. "The fabric should help insulate against the heat."

"Are you mad?" Bran asked. "That doublet was made of velvet. It was precious."

Bertram shrugged and adjusted his undershirt. "After all that's gone on tonight, I'm beginning to think I might be."

Bran gave him a long look, then shook his head and carried the bowl to the table. He freed it from the velvet and piled the tatters to the side, eyeing them suspiciously, as though they might bite. Bertram sat beside him and poked the pile farther away, into a spot he hoped Bran found less intrusive. It did the trick. Bran picked up his spoon and cooled the soup in it, then started to eat.

There was no conversation. Bertram didn't expect there to be. But there was something quaint about the silence—something almost soothing. It felt an awful lot like the battle was over and the war was won, and though he knew deep down this peace was only temporary, he let himself enjoy it.

The truth was, he *liked* Bran.

He had never met an omega so spirited.

If things were different...

Bertram tightened his lips, the memory of Bran's tunic slipping down his shoulder on his mind.

If things were different, he told himself in a chiding voice, he never would have met Bran in the first place, and he never would have adopted the eggs. There was no point imagining a world like that—no point in playing make-believe.

The world was as it was, and that was that.

He had no space in his heart for flights of fancy or pretty dreams.

Bran was a few spoonfuls away from finishing his meal when there came a scurry of footsteps. Agnes entered the room. She charged forward, all business, then came to a screeching stop.

"My lord!" she gasped. "I didn't expect to see you here. Oh, and... young master Bran." Her cheeks went as red as her nose. "I'm glad to see you've been served a proper dinner. I do apologize for earlier. It was my mistake. You gave me quite a fright when you... well..." She flapped her hands about. "Never mind."

"Agnes?" Hamish called from beyond the door.

Agnes craned her neck and looked over her shoulder. "In a moment, Hamish. You stay where you are. I'll be there soon." With Hamish dismissed, she focused on them once more. "Hamish and I were just getting ready to bring young master Bran his dinner, but since you've seen to it already, my lord, would you like us to clean the mess in his room instead?"

"Yes, please."

"With pleasure." Agnes curtsied—which she rarely did—then

left in a hurry, her skirts swishing. It seemed she was on her best behavior for "young master Bran." Bertram watched her go, smiling to himself, until he heard the clink of a spoon set in an empty bowl.

Bran, finished with his meal, pushed the bowl away and folded his arms on the table, giving Bertram a careful look. "I take it you won't be bringing me back to my room, then?"

"No. Not until they've finished cleaning, at least."

"Then where am I to go?"

Bertram didn't have to think on it hard. "Come with me," he said, "and find out."

12

BERTRAM

Bertram led Bran from the great hall and through the castle's darkened corridors to a spiral stairwell. Unlike many in the castle, its sconces were lit, and the stairs in good repair. No cobwebs lurked here, not in the forgotten corners where the wall met the ceiling, and not in any of the arrow loops along the way.

"A spire?" Bran asked as they began the ascent, Bran first with Bertram trailing behind. "Where exactly are you taking me?"

"All will be revealed in time."

"You test my patience."

Bertram chuckled. "Funny—you test mine."

It took some time to reach the upper landing. Bertram was used to the climb and thought nothing of it, but Bran, having been recently injured, was breathless by the time they made it to the top. Bertram stood with him while he recovered, then pushed open the heavy wooden door before them, revealing the wonders within.

"Welcome," he said, "to my chambers."

Bran opened his mouth—likely to argue—but whatever biting remark he'd intended to make never made it past his lips. His eyes widened. "Is this a trick?"

"I don't see how it could be."

"It's magic, surely. An illusion... a spell meant to deceive me."

"Had I such power, do you think I'd squander it like this?" Bertram stepped into the room. "I can assure you there is no magic here. What you see is real."

Bran pursed his lips, then shook his head wildly and followed him through the door.

The room was small in comparison to most, and circular in shape. It was well-furnished, boasting—amongst other things—an impressive bed and a luxuriously upholstered chaise longue, and kept warm and bright thanks to a fire burning in its welcoming hearth. But its most striking feature was its wide glass window, which, during daylight hours, offered an excellent view of the loch.

"Impossible," Bran muttered as he stood before the glass. The pane extended far above his head and stretched out a meter in each direction from his sides, framing him in starlight. "You can't tell me this isn't magic."

"It isn't."

"How is it possible?" Bran touched his fingertips shyly against the glass, then drew them back as if he'd been stung. "It's cold."

"It's meant to be."

"I don't understand." Bran clutched his cold fingers to his chest, staring transfixed at the window. "Glass windows are small and never this clear. Where are the bubbles? The ripples? The distortions? How did you manage to curve it to fit the wall, and how did you make it so big?"

"There is a glassmith in Westminster," Bertram revealed. He took a seat upon the chaise and joined Bran in his observation of the window. "He was called to the profession after leaving the Pedigree. I learned of him following a visit with my brother, Everard, who had paid him quite handsomely to install glass in his favorite sitting room, where he could best show it off. It was quite beautifully done, and I found myself jealous, so I journeyed to

Westminster to speak with the glassmith and see if he wouldn't be willing to work with me on an ambitious project—the one you see before you. We forged the glass here, in this room, using my dragon fire to turn the raw materials molten. Our first attempt shattered, but the glassmith was not deterred, and he came up with a solution that strengthened the pane and resulted in the window you see here." Bertram paused to cross an ankle over his knee, watching Bran hesitantly touch his fingertips to the glass anew. "It's the pinnacle of human achievement, elevated by magic. What the glassmith learned from the process may help him produce similar marvels, but never will there be another piece like this. Not without a dragon there to oversee the process. Together, we made something that will never be made again."

Bran grunted in disgust and took his hand away.

"You injure me, Bran," he said lightly, as if in jest. "Humanity is cunning and clever, but its true potential can only be reached with the help of dragons. We complete you just as you complete us. The good we do for you outshines the bad. Your hatred is misplaced."

"You tell yourself that to dismiss the truth."

"I could say the same about you."

Bran balled his hands into fists. "If you think I am the only one who has suffered at the hands of a dragon, you are wrong. The system is broken. It doesn't matter if some cloisters treat their omegas well if the rest of us are being made to suffer, and to weaponize the success stories of the lucky few who emerge unscathed is cruel. You choose to ignore our struggles and trick yourself into believing nothing is wrong because you see some of us doing well, but if you truly cared about us, you would listen when we tell you that we are being mistreated. You would believe us. You would help us. You wouldn't tell us that everything is fine. You can support our successes all you want, but that does not forgive what you are doing to us—you are a pretender through and through, and your silence screams your guilt."

An unpleasant feeling rose in Bertram, one he found difficult to contain. Instinct told him to lash out at the stubborn omega who refused to see reason—to snap and snarl until he understood that he was wrong. Yes, the Pedigree was not without its flaws, but this? It was a step too far.

However, emotion did not define him.

He took a moment to calm himself, relying on his training to keep a level head, and said as evenly as he could, "You are mistaken. I've been visiting cloisters near and far as an emissary of the council for longer than you've been alive, and in all my travels, there have only been a few instances where I was forced to take action due to the mistreatment of the omegas housed within. In all but those cases, every omega I've met during my travels has been cared for, given food to fill their bellies and a bed to call their own. None have ever spoken of mistreatment or told me they'd rather be elsewhere."

"Why would they?" Bran seethed. "It's not as though you've given them a choice."

Bertram's expression did not change, but his hands tightened into fists. "I would think that if any of them wished to be elsewhere, they would have said so."

Bran had the audacity to laugh. "Is that right?"

"Yes, it is."

"You're delusional." Bran shook his head and sat on the floor in front of the window, his back to Bertram and his chin tipped upward, eyes on the stars. "Nothing I say will change your mind, so I shan't say anything more. You and I will never see eye to eye. I shouldn't have wasted my breath."

Bertram sucked in a calming breath and released his fists. Anger was weakness. Its unpredictability made men sloppy and senseless, and he could not afford to be either. Not as an agent to the council, and not now as father of a clutch. "Your madness has twisted your mind, Bran," he said softly once he'd recovered. "Your world is different than the one the rest of us live in."

Bran stayed silent for a long while—long enough, Bertram thought he wouldn't reply—then in a voice thin with fury, he muttered, "Grigore Răzvan."

"I beg your pardon?"

"Grigore Răzvan."

Bertram sat straight, alarmed. Grigore Răzvan was an Onyx dragon who'd fathered a clutch five or six years back—the first dragon to have successfully fathered offspring in around four hundred years.

"Avranos Malas," Bran continued, his voice now shaking with anger. "Adalwolf De Vries. Unwin Drake. Tell me it's the madness. Tell me I'm imagining things." He rose and spun to face Bertram, danger in his eyes. "I know my truth. I know what happened to me, and I know what's happening to omegas like me. I will not lie to make you comfortable. You can pretend all you want, but what happened to me is real."

It was a punch in the gut.

The dragons Bran had named were the ones who'd fathered clutches within the last five years. It was a miracle, some said. Others claimed it was a sign the infertile times were over, and that there was hope dragonkind would not go extinct.

It was not the kind of thing a Pedigree omega should know.

"Did Unwin tell you?" Bertram uncrossed his legs and leaned forward, resting his elbows on his thighs as he looked Bran over, scanning him for signs of deception.

"Tell me what?"

"Their names."

"No. All Unwin ever spoke of was himself."

"Then where did you learn them from? Someone must have told you. The matron at your cloister? Or one of Unwin's servants, perhaps?"

"No one told me anything." Bran laughed, but it came out bitter. "Heaven forbid the omega speak the truth. Do you wish me to describe them to you, my lord dragon?" The mockery in his voice was cutting. "I shan't go into detail about Grigore or Avranos since they're from the Onyx clan, and it wouldn't be unusual for them to have stopped by my cloister. But Adalwolf is not an Onyx dragon. He belongs to the Sapphire clan."

Bertram said nothing to confirm or deny, but Bran was right. Adalwolf was a Sapphire dragon. According to his paperwork, he had conceived his clutch with a Pedigree omega from the Ruby clan who was now living a comfortable life of luxury abroad, but it did not escape Bertram that he, too, had lied and claimed something similar.

"Adalwolf," Bran said, "has hair like hay when it catches the setting sun—golden with reddish undertones. He wears it long and drawn back with a leather band. He favors blues and greens when he dresses, and has a fondness for gold, as most dragons do, with one exception—the silver pendant he wears around his neck. He never removes it, not even to sleep, and fiddles with it sometimes when he's deep in conversation. Upon first glance you might think there is nothing odd about him, but he has a secret." Bran crossed the room and came to stand in front of the chaise, leaning in to whisper it into Bertram's ear. "He wears shoes with tall soles to hide how short he is. Without them, he's barely any taller than I."

Bertram sat frozen, too stunned to act or speak. It was madness, all of it, but against all odds, Adalwolf was as Bran described.

He was telling the truth.

Sickness twisted tight in Bertram's gut, and he sucked a breath in through his teeth to chase it away. It didn't work. It only curled tighter.

How long had this been going on?

How many other omegas had been spirited away to be sold to the highest bidder?

How many were suffering right now, without hope their pain would end?

As an agent of the council, it was not Bertram's place to decide how the world should be—he was to do as he was told, and nothing more—but this… this was the kind of wrong he'd be sent to stop, were whispers of it to reach the right ears. But how did one stop something that went on unseen?

Something so well hidden, no one knew to look for it.

It made sense now why Bran would kill Unwin. Why he'd commit the villainous acts he had. He had known no one was coming to save him, and he had been forced to take matters into his own hands.

But there was a detail amiss, and it niggled.

"I don't understand," Bertram said as Bran stepped away, putting some distance between them. "If what you say is true, then why did you not dispose of Grigore upon the first signs of mistreatment? Why wait until four dragons had harmed you before killing one?"

"You think I killed Unwin Drake?" Bran laughed. "I don't know how Unwin died, only that he did."

"All of the blood drained from his body. It was not a natural death. Someone had a hand in it—he did not bleed himself to death on his own."

"Then I owe whoever did it my thanks." Bran's expression didn't waver. "But I wasn't involved."

Bertram let the statement sit between them while he picked it over. It didn't seem to him as though Bran was lying, but Bertram found his story hard to believe. There was more to it than Bran was letting on, that much was certain, but the truth would need to be unraveled some other day. Bertram had learned too much tonight as it was, and it was best he digest it all fully before he went back for more.

After a prolonged silence, Bertram leaned forward and clasped his hands between his knees, looking Bran in the eyes. "Let us not talk any more about that for now. There is something else I want to know. Were I to take you back to your cloister, would you be able to point me to where you were being held, and to the parties responsible for your suffering?"

Bran's eyes widened. "You believe me?"

"I believe there is something strange going on, and that you have been wronged. As to whether I believe you entirely, I've yet to make up my mind, which is why I'll ask again—were I to take you back to your cloister, would you be able to show me where they took you, and where they might be keeping the others?"

Bran's bewildered look sobered, leaving him quite serious. "Yes, I would."

"Then it sounds like, for the present, it would be best if we put our rivalry aside." Bertram slotted his fingers together and pushed his hands out until his knuckles cracked, then sat back and looked Bran over with his most easygoing expression. "As I told you earlier this evening, I have been given leave from serving the council, and while I had intended to spend my time raising the whelps, I can't ignore the call of duty. Once the eggs have hatched and everyone is settled, I will depart for Constantinople to investigate your claims. If it is as you've said, there is much work to be done, and whether the council wants to hear it or not, I will see that all is made right."

"Is this a trick?" Bran asked suspiciously.

"No." Bertram cocked an eyebrow. "I am many things, but I am not a liar. I have a sworn duty to protect my kind and those who serve us. If siding with the enemy will allow me to save countless innocent lives, then I am not above putting our differences aside. We can pick up where we left off after we get this sorted—until then, I shall call you a friend."

"How do you expect me to trust you?" Bran took a step forward in what Bertram assumed was an attempt at intimidation, but the omega was so small, it didn't frighten him in the least. "You dragons are all the same—rotten, selfish monsters willing to do or say anything to get your way. If you want me to believe you, it will take more than just your word."

"Would a show of good faith do?"

"A show of good faith?" Bran laughed. "I'm not sure there's one large enough."

"There is." Bertram paused to make sure Bran was listening, then said, "If you will agree to be my ally, I will take you to see the eggs."

13

SORIN

"I accept," Sorin said in a rush, the words flying out of him before Frederich could come to his senses and rescind the offer. It was, more than likely, a trick—no dragon was so charitable—but even so, he had to take his chances. At this point, he would have made a deal with the devil himself if it meant there was even the slightest possibility of being reunited with his eggs.

Frederich, seeming surprised by his sudden cooperation, had the gall to raise an eyebrow at him. "Do you not want to hear my terms first?"

"Which terms would those be?"

"First and foremost, I require your discretion." Frederich rose and stepped around Sorin to stand in front of the window, his hands clasped behind his back. "There is a chance my father or brothers could come by to visit, and on the off chance any of them meet you, you are not to breathe a word to them of what I plan to do. You must understand that I am overstepping my authority to look into this claim of yours, and should anyone find out before I am able to take action, it could mean catastrophe. Is this agreeable?"

Sorin nodded. "Yes."

Frederich was silent for a moment, his expression unreadable as he looked out into the night. "Next, I must ask that you stop causing me so much grief. No more breaking out of your room, no more sneaking into the nursery, and no more attempts at seduction, including greeting me in the nude. We are allies now. When you want to see the eggs, you simply need let me know, and we will find a way to make it happen. But that said, I will have you know"—he hesitated, and when he spoke again, there was a strange weight to his words—"even when I was your enemy, I never would have accepted your body in trade for what you wanted. I am not that kind of dragon. I want to know what's mine is mine willingly. Do you understand, and do you agree?"

Sorin looked Frederich over carefully, disbelievingly, but did not find any evidence to suggest he was pretending. After a thoughtful moment spent reflecting on that discovery, he carefully said, "I do."

"Lastly," Frederich went on to say, eyes ever fixed on the stars as they twinkled beyond the window, "while I will grant you access to the eggs as a sign of good will, there are some stipulations you must agree to. As omegas who touch their eggs go mad and become susceptible to carelessness and clumsiness, during each visit to the clutch, you shall be restrained. I will be there with you, supervising, to keep the worst from happening."

"I would never hurt them. Egg madness is a lie."

"So you claim, but you must understand that when it comes to the eggs, I cannot take any risks. I love them far too deeply to gamble with uncertainty."

Sorin's heart panged.

The eggs were his, not Frederich's, but his mind wandered back to the nursery—to a bewildered, naked Frederich rising from a treasure-drenched bed. Any nursemaid could have taken his place, yet there had been Frederich, curled around eggs he himself had not sired, keeping them warm with his own body heat, *nesting...*

His cheeks flushed.

It was not within a dragon's nature, but perhaps Frederich really did love the eggs.

"All right, then," Sorin said, and ducked his head, glad Frederich was looking elsewhere. "I agree."

Frederich looked over his shoulder at Sorin, smiling charmingly. "Then it sounds as though we have a deal. Are you ready for me to uphold my end of the bargain?"

It was a pointless question.

Sorin had never been more ready for anything in his entire life.

Using rope fetched from a stash of travel supplies, Frederich restrained Sorin's arms and legs, binding them separately, but tightly, so he could not move. Sorin had anticipated a level of discomfort, but there was none—Frederich took great care in making sure Sorin's restraints did not cut off his circulation, and seemed unusually familiar with the most effective ways to tie up a man, all of which he put to good use.

He had not said, exactly, what kind of work it was he did for the council, but between their rocky introduction and now this, Sorin was fairly sure he had a good idea.

Once bound, Frederich scooped an immobile Sorin into his arms and cradled him to his chest. The warmth of him was intoxicating. Sorin let himself indulge in it, resting his head on Frederich's shoulder as Frederich carried him through the darkened halls of the castle, past a maze of empty rooms, and finally, into the nursery.

Everything was as Sorin remembered it.

The windows. The roaring fire in the hearth. The bed with its furs piled high.

The only thing that was missing were the pearl-like orbs of

fire that had dotted the air. Without them, the room was only passably warm and dimly lit. Cozy. What little firelight there was made the treasure on the bed glitter alluringly, but no trick of the light could ever make it look as good as when it would decorate the eggs.

The eggs.

Sorin's heart leapt at the thought of them, knowing he was finally—*finally!*—about to be granted his dearest wish. There would be no saving him from the heartbroken cries of the clutches he had failed, but these eggs would not be made to suffer. They would know he loved them. They would know he cared. And even though he was destined to die before he ever got to make an impression on them, he would at least be allowed to see them hatch. To kiss them on their tiny heads and get to know their names.

"As you are bound," Frederich said in a near whisper, his head not all that far from Sorin's ear, "I will sit with you to support you. Doing so will ensure you do not accidentally fall, and will also help me prevent you from making any sudden moves that may jeopardize the safety of the eggs. Is this permissible?"

Sorin nodded.

"Then please brace yourself to be moved."

Frederich sat upon the bedside, well away from the central mound of bedding, and positioned Sorin so he was seated on his lap. He kept one arm around Sorin's waist to help keep him upright, and with the other, he reached for the pile of haphazardly assembled bedding.

"Remember our arrangement," he said in a warning tone. "Should you cause a scene, I will not hesitate to return you to your bedroom. The safety of the eggs comes first. Do you understand?"

"Yes."

"Then you may have your wish."

Frederich threw back the blankets, revealing four precious treasures more gorgeous than any of the gold and jewels strewn about the bed. The eggs. They were as beautiful as Sorin remembered, dark amethysts that gleamed like gemstones in the room's low light.

"Babies," he breathed as tears he couldn't wipe away tumbled down his cheeks. He tried his hardest not to move so as not to betray the deal he'd made with Frederich, but it was hard to do when every fiber of his being was begging him to close the distance, to touch them, to curl up around them, to keep them warm in this comfortable nest until their hatching day.

One of his tears dripped from his chin, landing on Frederich's arm. Frederich twitched in surprise, took a second to figure out what was going on, and then tenderly swiped his thumb over each of Sorin's cheeks, clearing his tears away.

"You needn't cry," Frederich murmured, his touch far too tender for a monster masquerading as a man. "As long as you uphold your end of the bargain, you may see them as much as you wish."

Sorin shook his head. "That's not it."

"Then what is the matter?"

"It's just…" He squeezed his eyes shut in defense against further tears. "I didn't think you'd actually do it. I didn't think you'd bring me here."

Frederich stayed silent for a telling beat of time. "I am an honorable dragon, Bran," he said after a moment. "I know the dragons you have met thus far have all fallen short of respectable, but not all of us are monsters. While it's true we are not perfect, many of us have kind hearts and wish the best for others—even those beneath us. I would never make a bargain with you I did not intend to keep."

Despite Sorin's best efforts, more tears fell. Frederich, without being asked, wiped them away.

"You are no longer their prisoner," Frederich added in a whisper, his arm tightening around Sorin not to restrain him, but as though to draw him into an embrace, "you are mine, and even though I cannot grant you your freedom, I can promise you that you will not be forced to endure any more atrocities. Whether you rescind my offer or not, I will still take care of you. I will keep you safe and in good health, warm and fed and worry free." He faltered, and when he spoke next, something resembling regret stole the joy from his voice. "You will want for nothing until the end. Your pain is behind you now. You may not be free, but you have found yourself an ally in me."

The tears came down harder, unimpeded.

Sorin didn't sob, didn't make a sound, didn't so much as tremble out of fear Frederich might perceive it as a sign of madness and take him away, but beneath the surface, he was ruined. It had been almost seven years since he had last known kindness, and after everything that had happened, he had convinced himself he'd never know it again.

Yet here was Frederich.

The dragon—the monster—the one who, with an easygoing smile, had vowed to end Sorin's life.

By all rights, he was a villain, and yet Sorin's heart disagreed.

He knew what evil looked like. What it felt like. How rotten it was.

Frederich was not like that.

He was misguided, yes, but at his core, he was still good.

A gust of wind blew into the room, making Sorin shiver. Frederich, as though on instinct, reached out and covered the eggs with their bedding, shielding them from the cold. He took his time to tuck them in, making sure they were well insulated before leaving them be. Sorin watched him work without saying a word, a lump in his throat.

Frederich was not acting like a dragon only interested in the eggs because of the prestige they would bring him.

He was acting like a father.

And while the eggs called for Sorin, eager for his touch, they did not scream.

They were *happy.*

Even should he never touch them at all, they would be okay.

"They like you," Sorin said, voice wet from his tears. "You've been taking good care of them—they're happy."

"Do you think so?"

"No... I know it." Sorin took a deep, shaking breath to ground himself. "I told you, egg madness is a lie. All omegas who lay are connected to their eggs whether they touch them or not. I can hear them calling for me, but it's not like it was with my other clutches. These eggs aren't screaming in fear and heartbreak. They're content, and I ascribe that to you."

"They're happy?" Frederich asked, a surprising degree of vulnerability in his voice.

"They are. To a degree. They don't understand why I won't touch them, but that pain is minimal compared to what it could be if they knew no love at all."

Frederich hesitated, hand poised in the air as if he was considering pulling back the bedding. Finally, after a long moment, he drew his hand back and rested it on Sorin's thigh. "Do you think," he said quietly, "if you were to touch them, that pain would go away?"

Sorin looked at Frederich's hand.

His heart gave a painful squeeze. "I think it would."

Frederich's fingers curled, the veins on the back of his hand protruding. There was a war going on inside of him, a war that thickened the air with unknown tension to the point where even Sorin felt the heaviness of it. It lasted for several moments before Frederich's fist released.

"I am a fool," he muttered, speaking to himself. Then, without warning, he moved Sorin off his lap and flattened him on the bed.

Before Sorin could ask what he was doing, Frederich was towering over him, hands on his shoulders to keep him locked in place while he looked down directly into Sorin's eyes.

Sorin couldn't help it—his cheeks flushed, and his heart began to hammer as a sudden rush of heat flared through him. He was helpless, yes, and had every reason to be afraid of what Frederich might do to him, but he felt no fear, for the intensity in Frederich's eyes was not rooted in lust or greed.

It came from nervous spontaneity.

From exhilaration.

Sentiments which were echoed in his voice when he told Sorin, "Do not move. Do not so much as twitch. You must remain perfectly still."

"Why?"

In response, Frederich tore back the mound of bedding, exposing the clutch to the world. "Because," he said, picking the first egg up from its nest of gold and linens, "to ensure their utmost happiness, I will be placing the eggs on you."

14

SORIN

Frederich straddled Sorin's hips, cradling the egg to his chest. Once situated, he looked down at Sorin in contemplation, then shook his head and summoned forth a claw, which he hooked beneath the neckline of Sorin's tunic and put to use by slowly and carefully slitting the fabric until his torso was exposed.

"Do not move," Frederich warned again, but he might as well have saved his breath, because Sorin would not move. Not now. Not with his heart in his throat and every inch of him prickling with excitement. He looked up at Frederich placidly, waiting, not daring to breathe, let alone speak, out of fear that if he did, the dream would end.

Because it had to be a dream.

How else could he explain how good Frederich felt on top of him, and how good he looked with their egg, painted marble in the moonlight.

Their egg.

Sorin's heart thudded at the thought.

"I'm ready," he finally whispered, sure that would be it—that he'd wake up in the bed of his glorified prison cell—but nothing changed.

The dream didn't end.

Frederich remained where he was, just as he was, and better yet, he reached out and touched Sorin gingerly, tracing his fingertips down the inside of Sorin's arm.

"I will place the first egg in the crook of your arm," he said in a quiet voice when Sorin stayed still and silent. "I will do the same with the second, but on the opposite side, and the third will go here on your belly."

His fingers trailed along Sorin's ribs, then inward to his stomach, barely missing the dip of his navel, sending pleasure shooting through Sorin that left goosebumps in its wake.

"The last," Frederich said, "I will hold in place beneath the third egg. I will keep them there for as long as you'd like—within reason—provided you do not move. Should you want to get up or readjust your position, you must give me advance warning. I'll need time to put the eggs safely back into their nest. Do you agree?"

"Yes," Sorin breathed. "I do."

"Then let's begin."

Frederich laid the first egg into the crook of Sorin's arm. It was soft and leathery, warm to the touch, and heavy—heavier than such a delicate-looking thing ought to be—but it was perfect. So completely perfect.

And it was *happy*.

A wave of joy suffused Sorin, washing through him until he felt it from the tips of his toes to the very top of his head. The radiance of that feeling clustered in his mind, building and building with innocent excitement until he felt something gently click into place inside of him. At that point, the feeling coalesced into something tangible.

A bond.

It had always been there, but now it was complete.

Tears streamed freely down his face, and he squeezed his eyes shut to try to stop them before they broke him down entirely. He could not risk sobbing. Frederich would see it as a sign he was descending into madness, and then he would never get to touch the other eggs.

So, choking back his tears as best he could, he focused on his breathing until a soft, leathery weight filled the crook of his other arm. The next egg. The second it made contact, a new source of joy flowed through him, filling him, multiplying and better defining itself until finally, another bond was set in place.

When Frederich laid the third egg on his stomach, the same thing happened, and when he put the fourth egg below it, in the space where Sorin's bare skin ended and his hose began, it happened again.

Wet cheeks wetter with each passing second, Sorin reached through each of the new bonds and sent love to his babies he knew they would be able to feel, and as he did, their tiny voices quieted down. They did not cry out for him any longer, because they knew he was finally there.

"They stopped," Sorin said with a sniffle, smiling so hard his cheeks hurt. "They're not calling out for me anymore. They're happy."

"And you?" Frederich asked. "Are you happy?"

Sorin's lips wobbled, and the sob he longed to let out in that moment was the hardest one of all to resist. "Yes," he said. "I am."

Frederich kept his word and sat with Sorin that night, allowing him contact with the eggs. Sorin soaked it in for all it was worth, familiarizing himself with each egg and individually showering them with his love. With so many months spent apart, he had a lot of it to go around.

But as the night wore on and the eggs fell asleep, Sorin's mind began to wander.

The first thing it noticed was that, while the four voices of his eggs had gone silent, the heartbroken cries of the clutches long ago taken from him remained. They were quieter now, and much easier to overlook—especially when he was focused on other things—but reuniting with this clutch had not cured him. While he was not suffering in the same way he had been before, it seemed likely that he would never find complete relief.

It was not great news, but it didn't keep Sorin down for long. He had this clutch now, and he was happy. What pain he did feel was manageable and would not stop him from living a passably normal life. He had endured far worse and still persevered. He would not give up now.

Especially since he had found something new with which to occupy his mind—the dragon currently sitting on his legs.

Unlike Sorin, who had spent his time bonding with the eggs, Frederich had no such distractions. He had been polite about it, but without anything else to occupy him, he had spent the evening in quiet observation of Sorin. Eyeing his bare chest and stomach. Watching him bond with the eggs. It wasn't something he did lecherously, and the attention did not make Sorin feel uncomfortable, but every time he looked up at Frederich, Frederich was quick to turn his head and pretend he had not been looking at all.

Like he felt guilty about it.

Or maybe it was that he had something to hide.

Sorin considered the possibilities as he watched Frederich watching him from the corner of his eye. Was he really paying no attention to Sorin beyond what he considered necessary for the safety of the eggs, or was something else going on? Could it be that the sight of Sorin with the clutch had stirred the same kind of impossible and unwelcome thoughts in Frederich that Sorin had had the night he'd seen Frederich rise up from the bed where he'd been nesting with the eggs?

Surely not.

And yet...

The longer Sorin sat with that thought, the more his cheeks burned.

Frederich was his enemy—the one who had kept him from his eggs—but he could not deny that a part of him wished Frederich would see him that way. With Frederich sitting on his legs, together in the nursery, both of them on the bed, it was easy to imagine nesting down together, curling around their clutch, kissing, touching, unable to keep their hands off each other, sharing more than just an uneasy allegiance.

Sharing gold.

Sharing their bodies.

Sorin practically gilded from how heavily he had been decorated with treasure, and Frederich on top of him, hazy-eyed with lust, thrusting deep, breathless from effort.

But there was no way that could happen. After the eggs hatched and Frederich fulfilled his promise to investigate Sorin's cloister, one of them would kill the other.

They were not meant to nest together.

They were not meant to be a family.

There was no use imagining otherwise, so to distract himself from what could never be, Sorin focused on the eggs. They were sleeping now, so—not wanting to disturb them—he studied what he could see of their shells and imagined what they would look like when they hatched. Would their scales be the same color as their shells? He thought they might, but didn't know for sure. No one had ever told him, likely because no one had ever seen a dragon egg before.

His clutches were the first to be born in a very long time.

Sorin's plan to keep himself distracted worked up until the egg Frederich was holding upright on his lower stomach moved. Alarmed, Sorin lifted his head to see what was happening just in time to spot Frederich laying the egg on its side, supporting it with just one hand so he could use the other to reach into the nest at the center of the bed and take from it a golden necklace—a dainty thing with an elegant design glittering with diamonds and rubies. Frederich scrutinized it, shifting it this way and that until he found the correct angle, then draped it carefully over one of the eggs.

The egg woke just enough to shiver with pleasure before falling back to sleep.

Sorin shivered, too, but for reasons far less innocent.

He watched, lips parted, as Frederich reached back into the nest and repeated the process over again.

It wasn't long until each egg was fully decorated, their shells barely peeking out from beneath all the gold. The excess pooled on Sorin's body, strings of pearls resting in the valleys between his body and his arms while gold chains curled in the crooks of his elbows. A fat diamond pendant bound in gold dripped off one of the lower eggs and tumbled neatly down his belly into the dip of his navel.

Sorin felt it, but Frederich... Frederich watched it happen, and what he saw sent scales rushing down his neck. When he next looked up, desire had darkened his eyes.

He reached back into the nest and fished out a new handful of treasure—not for the eggs, but for Sorin.

With it, Frederich decorated him with coins and glittering jewels that cast reflections of their inner fire on his skin like freckles, and when that first handful ran out, Frederich went back for more. A sapphire-studded necklace came next, which Frederich pooled in the dip of Sorin's collarbones. Then golden ear cuffs, which he affixed in place. Bangles. Bracelets. Rings.

Sorin, heart hammering, too stunned to breathe, watched as Frederich, eyes dark and smoldering, selected two identical coins from the nest to lay over his pebbled nipples. More quickly followed after that, positioned like stepping stones down Sorin's chest and belly all the way to where his bare skin ended and his codpiece began.

A new coin in hand, Frederich eyed the obstacle. He spun the coin between his fingers contemplatively, then placed it flush with Sorin's skin and slowly—deliberately—slid it beneath the garment.

It slid down Sorin's body and bumped shyly against the base of his cock.

Sorin sucked in a jagged breath, lips parting, cheeks burning to the point it felt like his whole face had been set on fire. The coin had barely touched him, but his cock was throbbing like Frederich had wrapped his fist around it and started to pump.

He wanted to move—needed to move—had to flex his hips, and buck, and jerk until that feeling went away, but if he so much as twitched, he'd lose access to the eggs.

"Put them away," he begged suddenly, urgently, rushing through the words like if he didn't get them out all at once, they would never come. "Please, put the eggs away. I swear, it's not egg madness, but I can't stay still any longer. I can't. I—"

Frederich caught him by the chin, and Sorin stopped speaking at once. Their eyes met. Quiet fell. In the stillness, the sound of Sorin's heartbeat was loud. It drummed in his ears at a frenzied pace, drowning out the noise in his head. Still, when Frederich spoke, Sorin heard him with perfect clarity.

"You are not mad," Frederich told him in a voice that was more dragon than man. He traced his thumb over Sorin's lips and dropped his gaze to watch before looking back into Sorin's eyes. "I trust you. I believe you. You proved yourself tonight—you needn't convince me any longer you're safe to be around the eggs."

Lips parted, tugged lewdly open by Frederich's thumb, Sorin could say nothing.

He didn't bother to try.

He was too stunned, too buzzed, too dizzy. Drunk off the things Frederich was doing to his body and paralyzed by his sudden display of trust.

So he lay there, still and silent, sparks of longing zipping up his spine, as Frederich released his chin and honored his wishes, taking the eggs off his body and returning them to the nest, where they'd be safe. He covered them in the bedding and tucked them in to insulate them against the cold, and when he finished, a new coin glinted between his fingers.

He spun it slowly—absentmindedly—as though imagining all the places it could go.

"One word," he said, gaze fixed on Sorin, "and this ends here. I will not put another finger on you, nor will I hold you in contempt for the decision you make. You are not my property. Your body is no one's but your own, and yet…"

The coin stopped moving.

Frederich hesitated, then touched its edge to the bare skin just shy of Sorin's belly button, where a diamond still remained.

"I want you, Bran," he admitted. "I shouldn't, but I do, and if you allow me to place this coin on you, I cannot promise that I will be able to hold myself back."

The coin rolled south, weaving unhurriedly between the others left like golden stepping stones. It stopped just short of Sorin's codpiece, near where the last coin had disappeared.

"Not now that I have seen you in my gold," Frederich said in a near whisper, like he was speaking to himself. "Not now that I have seen you take such good care of my eggs."

His eggs.

His.

Sorin's breath caught in his throat.

He had vowed that he would take his children and—when they were grown—kill every last dragon for what they had done to him. For what they had done to his kind. But at that moment, all he could think about was how good it would feel were Frederich to be on top of him. Kissing him. Nipping at his lips. Slipping rings onto his fingers. Tugging his legs open. Slipping his cock inside.

He did not want vengeance.

He wanted quiet nights in the nursery, body aglow from orgasm, fingers laced, legs entwined.

"I want it," he said breathlessly. Then, "I want *you.*"

The coin fell, decorating him, and Frederich—the monster who was no monster at all—did what he'd warned Sorin he would, and made Sorin his.

15

BERTRAM

Gold scattered. Lips met. A kiss, hot as dragon fire and every bit as all-consuming, began. Bertram was not an impulsive dragon— the urge to give in to temptation was weakness, and had long ago been trained out of him—but he could not will himself to abstain any more than he could will his heart to stop beating.

He needed Bran in a way he had never needed anything or anyone else.

Needed to claim the omega who looked so good wearing his gold, and who had been so gentle with his eggs.

Stirred by those memories, compulsion seized him. Under its control, he carded his fingers through Bran's hair and tugged— not painfully, but possessively. He wanted Bran to feel him every- where, to know there was no part of him Bertram did not want to make his own.

Mine, rumbled his dragon.

And Bertram, with his whole heart, agreed.

Bran gasped as Bertram tightened his grip, breath hitching with arousal, and opened his mouth to trace Bertram's lower lip shyly with his tongue. In response, Bertram opened up for him and met Bran's tongue with his own. He licked into Bran's mouth as Bran moaned for him, and kissed him like that until they were both too starved for breath to continue. Panting, Bran stared up at him with lust-fogged eyes, lips parted and ready for more, and Bertram—self-control shot—indulged them both. He ripped off his shirt, cleaving through it with his claws, then tugged Bran's hose and codpiece down as far as the binding around his legs would allow. Without clothing to restrain it, Bran's hard cock sprang free.

Bertram did not keep it that way for long.

One hot kiss at a time, he followed the length of Bran's body to the base of his cock and introduced it to his mouth.

He did not wrap his lips around it. Didn't mouth it, swallow it, make it *his,* even though he wanted to. Instead, he took his time. He kissed it, teased it, tested it, until finally Bran shivered and sucked in a jagged breath sharp with pleasure. Only then did Bertram run his tongue to the head of Bran's cock, swirling once to lick up the precum Bran had spilled before setting his lips around it and taking it inside.

Bran let out a broken cry. At the same time, his hips snapped up suddenly, involuntarily, to bury himself as deeply as he could in Bertram's throat. He jerked his shoulders, fighting the restraints that bound his arms, and as Bertram dutifully swallowed Bran to the base, he thought he knew why.

Bran wanted to hold his head down.

To fuck into his mouth.

To claim Bertram in the same way that he was being claimed.

And while it was reckless to allow him the luxury of his arms in such close proximity to the eggs, Bertram wanted it, too. Wanted to know that Bran felt the same feral desires.

So, reckless as it was, he groped blindly up Bran's body until he found the rope holding his arms in place. A pass of his claws made quick work of it, and as the final cord snapped, Bran's arms jerked free. He grabbed Bertram by the hair and held his head in place as he thrust into Bertram's mouth.

No lover—omega or otherwise—had ever dared use Bertram like this.

It was unbefitting of a dragon.

And he loved it.

Wanted more of it.

It woke a savage part of him that had him tightening his lips and using his tongue not only to drive Bran toward orgasm, but to encourage him to do it more.

And Bran, panting and gasping, complied.

He used Bertram, fucking into his mouth until his muscles were taut and trembling, and his thrusts sharpened and became erratic. Teetering on the edge of pleasure, he lifted his head, sending loose gold chains tumbling from his hair onto his shoulders, and watched through partially lidded eyes as his cock slid between Bertram's lips.

It didn't take long after that.

A few thrusts later, Bran's fists tightened. Twisted. Pulled. Breathing hard, he pumped himself into Bertram's mouth a final time and made a tortured sound of pleasure that barely made it out of his throat. Orgasm ran through him, twitching and pulsing as it shot through his cock, giving Bertram just enough of a warning to pull back so Bran filled his mouth and not his throat with cum.

One shuddering thrust after another, Bran came and came again. His grip on Bertram's hair loosened, but Bertram chose not to break free of his hold—he remained in place, coaxing pleasure out of Bran with his tongue until his balls were drained.

"Please," Bran said in a small but urgent voice. He tugged gently on Bertram's hair, directing him off his cock. Bertram looked up at him and found that Bran was shaking, his cheeks flushed, eyes as hazy and as lidded by lust as an omega at the peak of his heat, and although Bran was not in season, there was an undeniable, primal hunger in his voice when he next spoke, begging desperately for, *"More."*

Bertram was not one to keep an omega in need waiting. He stripped out of his clothing, then sliced through the rope binding Bran's legs and stripped Bran naked as well. Only one obstacle remained—there was no oil here in the nursery, and Bran was not in heat and therefore was not slick and ready for him—but Bertram was nothing if not a resourceful dragon, and already had a solution in mind.

He spat Bran's cum into his palm and smoothed it over his dick.

Bran watched, lips parted, breathing hard, then glanced up to look Bertram in the eyes.

He didn't speak.

He spread his legs.

Bertram crawled up his body, helping himself to the space between Bran's thighs, and grabbed him by the hips. He lifted Bran up effortlessly into position, causing the copious amount of gold and jewels pooled on his chest and belly to shift, and gave him only enough time to hook his legs over Bertram's hips before Bertram gave them what they both wanted, pushing deep inside.

Bran cried out. He was only half-hard since his orgasm, but it was pleasure, not pain that shaped his voice. His thighs clamped onto Bertram, and with what little range of motion he had, he threw himself into riding Bertram's cock. It was hard, and fast, and messy—selfish in a way Bertram had no idea an omega could be—and it brought Bertram's dragon straight to the surface of his mind.

He had pleased the father of his eggs, and now he was reaping the reward.

With a snarl no human mouth could make, Bertram dropped on top of Bran, folding him into a mating press, and mirrored Bran's intensity, thrusting hard and fast inside. Bran cried out in pleasure and threw his head back, stretching his delicate neck in an invitation Bertram could not refuse. He latched on, kissing, sucking, nipping, knowing Bran would wear his bruises just as beautifully as if they were jewels.

"Knot me," Bran begged, almost babbling, a hint of an accent—his mother tongue—peeking through his polished English. He rolled his head to the side, the golden ear cuff Bertram had clipped onto him glittering in the dim light. "Put it deeper," he pleaded breathlessly. "Put eggs in me. *Make me yours.*"

It was wrong.

They weren't sanctioned, and worse, Bran was a criminal. If anyone found out what they were doing, the consequences would be severe.

But Bertram's dragon did not care for that thought.

It roared in triumph—in *pride*—and fucked Bran into the mattress as the thought of Bran, swollen with their eggs, drove Bertram feral with need. Scales swept down his neck and over his shoulders, and without warning his wings burst free, fanning out with such intensity, they extinguished the fire burning in the hearth.

The room plunged into darkness as Bertram's knot swelled.

He came deep inside of Bran, hips pumping, driving his seed farther, pushing it as deep as he could.

Bran moaned quietly beneath him, shivering and catching his breath as Bertram's knot locked them together. He tightened rhythmically around Bertram's cock, squeezing his knot, coaxing it to its full potential, and as Bertram came down from his high, he realized it was because Bran had come a second time. A meager spattering of semen dappled his stomach—pleasure Bertram had chased out of him.

Without thinking, Bertram reached between them and rubbed the mess gently into Bran's skin.

He wanted Bran to wear that pleasure just like his bruises—to carry it, knowing it had come from him.

After a while spent panting, after Bertram's knot had swollen to its maximum size, Bran collapsed bonelessly on the mattress.

He looked up at Bertram, eyes just as lidded as they were before but no longer quite as hazy, and cupped Bertram's cheeks, gently dragging him down for a slow and passionate kiss. They made out as Bertram's balls emptied, sometimes grinding on each other, sometimes lying still. In his post-orgasmic clarity, Bertram was able to push his dragon back into the recesses of his mind, but he kept his wings out, wrapping them possessively around Bran.

He knew Bran would not conceive outside of his heat, but every now and then, as he shot more cum inside of him, he imagined with a shiver that it would be the load that filled Bran with his eggs.

"Is this how you treat all your allies?" Bran asked, laughter in his voice, as their kiss ran out of steam. He took Bertram's bottom lip between his teeth, not even enough pressure behind the gesture to call it a nip, and tugged just slightly before letting go. "All you had to do was bring me to see the eggs. This was truly above and beyond."

Bertram chuckled. "Consider it a show of good faith."

Bran hummed and turned his head, unknowingly exposing a piece of golden jewelry woven into his dark hair. Even without firelight, it glimmered alluringly, enhancing Bran's natural beauty in a way that made Bertram's heart skip a beat. Before he knew what he was doing, they were kissing again. Slowly. Passionately. Bran's fingers winding through his hair and Bertram's hands on Bran's hips, holding him in place as he began to thrust again. It was slow, and it was lazy, but it was *good*. Bertram could not recall the last time he had felt so at peace.

Never mind so happy.

They made love another time that night, the moonlight painting Bran with its alabaster light, their body heat providing warmth to their clutch. Bertram did not see Bran back to his room, and Bran did not attempt to flee, nor did he succumb to madness and try to harm the eggs. When Bertram woke early the next morning, Bran was curled around them protectively, the perfect picture of a father, so obviously in love with them even while asleep.

Bertram did not lock Bran's bedchamber door when he returned him to his room later that day, nor did he chase Bran away that night when he opened the unlocked door to the nursery and slipped into bed with Bertram, riding him until they were knotted together before, exhausted, they broke apart and fell asleep cuddled up with the eggs.

His father had been right to worry. The eggs really would be his undoing.

He had dared to defy the council for them.

And now, with the enemy sharing his bed, he remorselessly did so again.

16

BERTRAM

Castle Beithir was not the same after that night. At first, Bertram was convinced it was all in his head—an effect of having bedded a Pedigree omega—but in the months that followed, he witnessed a change not only in himself, but in the servants as well.

Levity.

It followed him wherever he went, from the nursery to the kitchen, and even out into the castle grounds. Whereas before the castle had been silent, now Agnes hummed while wringing out the linens, and more than once, Bertram heard Hamish snort with laughter when the old man thought himself alone. The new maids seemed happier as well, giggling amongst themselves, especially when they happened to catch sight of him. It seemed to him as though their cheeks were rosier and their eyes brighter. Curiously, they also began to rouge their lips and wear their hair in fanciful braids.

Bertram didn't mind it, of course, but he did find it rather odd. All of it had come from nowhere. If he hadn't known better, he'd have thought a curse had been lifted from the castle, but he knew there was no such thing. The truth was far less mystical than that.

And there was no surer sign of it than one morning when,

upon entering the nursery, Bertram discovered Bran seated on the egg bed, framed by the rising sun. He was dressed in well-tailored hose and a richly dyed purple tunic, so dark it was almost black.

A nursemaid sat at his feet.

It seemed she'd been there a while—her skirt was billowed out around her and her eyes were closed, her posture loose and relaxed. Bran was braiding her hair.

Bertram stopped in the doorway, not wanting to interrupt, but the nursemaid must have heard his footsteps, for her eyes fluttered open. It took her a moment to clue in to who was standing at the door, but when she did, she gasped and flew to her feet. Her braids spiraled open over her shoulders, quickly coming undone.

"I'm so sorry, my lord dragon." She brushed her skirts down in a hurry. "Please, forgive me. I swear it won't happen again."

Bertram crossed his arms loosely and leaned against the doorway, an eyebrow raised. "Forgive you? Whatever for?"

"I shouldn't have been idle. I do apologize."

"Nonsense. Come, sit back down where you were before." Bertram pushed off the doorway and came to sit next to Bran. "The eggs don't need constant tending—the whelps will, but they won't be here for some time. Before they arrive, we should take advantage of the peace and be as idle as we can. Bran, would you redo that braid for her?"

Bran raked his teeth over his lip, biting off a smile. "Of course."

The nursemaid looked between them nervously, but soon enough, her tension eased. She approached the bed without a word and sat at Bran's feet. Once she was settled, Bran combed his fingers through her hair and separated it into sections, then began to braid. He worked with quick and nimble fingers, turning her loose blonde locks into an artfully woven crown.

It was lovely, but it was missing something, and Bertram was fairly sure he knew what that something might be.

He craned his neck to look upon the treasures spilled across the egg bed and selected a simple string of pearls previously draped over one of the eggs. "Bran," he said, holding it out. "Do you think you'd be able to thread these onto the pins you're using?"

Bran looked at the string of pearls and popped a brow. "Are you really giving up your treasure?"

"Only one piece of it. It should be enough to decorate all the maids, don't you think?"

Bran took the necklace from him and nudged one of the pearls to get a look at the size of its hole. He shrugged. "I could make it work."

Bran's hands were soft—untouched by physical labor—but with a quick twist of the silk thread and some force, they tore the necklace apart. Each pearl was secured on either side by a knot, but the pearl on the very end dropped onto Bran's lap. It rolled into the valley between his legs, its milky luster stunning against Bran's darkness, and woke an urge in Bertram.

Something fiery and familiar.

It felt a lot like his dragon.

"Will you press down here for me?" Bran asked the maid, indicating a part of the braid he'd previously been holding in place. When she did, he set the string of pearls on his lap and picked up the one that had fallen loose, fitting it with some difficulty onto the maid's plain hairpin.

Bertram watched until Bran put the pin in her hair, at which point his attention shifted to the pearls strewn across Bran's thighs.

The fiery feeling in him flamed.

The maids weren't the only ones who deserved decoration. If Bertram could, he would pin pearls in Bran's hair and fit his fingers with rings until there wasn't space for more. The compulsion made his fingers twitch, but he refrained. Such a thing wasn't proper to do, especially in polite company.

But that didn't mean he couldn't compromise.

With the deftness befitting an agent of the council, Bertram sneaked a hand across the bed and discreetly gathered up all the nearby coins and little treasures he could, piling them up by Bran's thigh.

One day, perhaps, he'd see Bran drenched in gold again.

One day, but not now.

Not with the nursemaid there to see.

While Bertram worked, Bran continued to pluck pearls off the string, oblivious to what the dragon next to him was doing. He fitted each onto its own hairpin and placed it in the nursemaid's hair, as meticulous about its placement as any artist would be. There was nothing clumsy about him, and certainly no sign that his frequent exposure to the eggs was causing him to go mad. Could it be that there was something special about him that was helping him stay sane?

Bertram glanced from his hands to the small mountain of gold coins stacked next to Bran's thigh.

He sneaked a few more coins into the pile.

A short while later, Bran had just one hairpin left to decorate. He tugged at the next pearl, but the knot holding it was stubborn, and the string refused to break. Bran grunted in frustration and put the pearl behind his teeth, leaving the rest of the necklace to dangle over his lips and down his jaw. The sight of it caused Bertram's heart to leap into his throat, and, unable to help himself, he slid his hand onto Bran's thigh.

Bran's eyes widened and he startled, the pearl finally popping off its string. The necklace slipped out of his fingers and pooled on his thighs, but the pearl—that single pearl—remained in place behind his teeth. It glinted in the light, teasing, tempting, until Bertram could resist its siren's song no more. His hand slid inward, feigning pursuit of the dropped necklace, but stopped short so he could brush his fingertips against the front of Bran's codpiece and the hardening cock beneath.

It was reckless to tempt fate here in front of the nursemaid, but with Bran surrounded by treasure, Bertram didn't care. He leaned in, closing the space between them, and brushed his lips against Bran's, asking for—but not taking—his kiss.

It made it all the sweeter when Bran gave it readily.

It only lasted a second, but when their lips parted, there was a pearl in Bertram's mouth. Bran, red-cheeked, gave Bertram a hazy-eyed, lingering look, then ducked his gaze and went to pluck another pearl from the necklace before the nursemaid could realize what was going on.

"That's all of them," Bran said upon securing the last hairpin in place. While he spoke, Bertram, too enamored to care if he was caught, allowed his hand to slip higher up Bran's codpiece and caressed him through his hose. Bran's red cheeks went crimson, and he shot Bertram a warning look, but at the same time, he shifted his hips to better press himself into Bertram's hand, wanting more. Bertram smirked at him, which earned him an elbow to the side.

Composing himself—but not pulling away—Bran said to the maid, "Come see me again tomorrow and I'll braid your hair over again."

"Thank you," said the maid, unfolding from where she'd been sitting. She rose daintily, and before she could turn, Bertram snatched his hand away and folded it inconspicuously on his lap.

Ah, the perfect crime.

He smiled at the nursemaid, who smiled back uneasily before her gaze drifted to Bran... and the obvious bulge behind his codpiece. Her cheeks colored and her eyes snapped back to Bertram.

"And what of the pearls, my lord?" she asked in a hurry.

"What of them?" Bertram asked, hiding the pearl in his mouth in his cheek.

"Shall I return them to you on the morrow?"

"Keep them."

Her eyes widened. "You... wish for me to keep the pearls?"

"I do." Bertram glanced at Bran, who seemed a little grouchy from the embarrassment he'd been subjected to, but who was still flush with pleasure. "And should you see any of the other maids, let them know that should they come to Bran to have their hair done, they may keep the pearls he gives them as well."

She bowed her head and curtsied so low, it was a wonder she didn't tip over. "Thank you, my lord."

"Think nothing of it." Bertram paused. "Although if you would like to show your thanks, I wouldn't mind if you closed the door on your way out."

The nursemaid did, the sweet thing that she was, and no sooner was she gone than Bertram's hand slid over Bran's thigh and back to where it belonged.

"You're incorrigible," Bran chided, but he straddled Bertram's lap and threaded his fingers through his hair all the same. "I should walk out of this room and leave you right here on the bed, alone. What were you thinking, touching me with someone present?"

"I'll give you three guesses."

Bran pinched his lips in irritation, but the color in his cheeks deepened. "Brute."

"So you claim." Bertram arched a brow and produced the pearl from his cheek, pinching it between his fingers. "But shall I remind you which one of us it was who pushed this into my mouth?"

Bran's fingers tightened in his hair. "It was an attempt to choke you, I assure you. Nothing more."

"You will be the death of me, do you know that?"

"I did promise that, didn't I?" Bran leaned forward and nipped Bertram's earlobe. "But what is it that you always tell me? Not until the eggs hatch. When that day comes, we'll see which one of us bests the other. Until then, we should enjoy what time we have left. What do you say?"

Bertram said nothing. Instead, he dropped the pearl onto the bed and seized Bran's ass, flipping them around to pin Bran in the gold forgotten between the sheets. Coins scattered. Bran's tunic rode up, exposing the dip of his navel and a flash of his hip, and Bertram could take it no longer. He grabbed treasure—fistfuls of it—and scattered it over Bran's body, putting it in contrast with his skin.

Bran gasped when the metal touched him. It was cold. The perfect balm for an omega's heat, and the perfect nest for a mate. Bertram dipped down, kissing the soft skin right above Bran's navel, then set a coin there. Then another. For each new breath Bran drew, the coins toppled, but Bertram carried on unperturbed. Jewels joined the mix, and with them, Bertram filled the spaces left by the fallen coins until what little was exposed of Bran's skin was entirely covered.

Still, it was not enough.

Bertram teased Bran's tunic up his stomach and over his chest, eventually taking it off him completely and tossing it to the floor. With each new inch of skin revealed, he piled more coins and jewels until a vision of a gold-drenched Bran stretched out before him.

Treasure suited him—Bertram had never seen anyone wear it better.

It made him want to comb through his hoard for all the best pieces so he could see how they looked on Bran.

"You really are an odd dragon," Bran muttered, lifting his head to look at the finery covering his body. "When I suggested we should enjoy ourselves, this wasn't quite what I had in mind. What are you doing?"

It was a good question—what was he doing? He did not know what had possessed him. Dragons did not share their gold, especially not with omegas they would one day need to slay.

"I was… attempting to crush you beneath the weight of all that treasure," Bertram said lamely, not bothering to put effort into masking his lie.

Bran cocked an eyebrow. "Like I was trying to choke you with that pearl?"

"Yes. Quite."

"Right." Bran let his eyes wander down Bertram's body, not attempting to hide what he was doing in the least. "Well, if you want to try crushing me to death, I know something else you can use that's far more likely to get the job done."

"Is that so?"

"Yes." Bran's gaze flicked up, meeting Bertram's. "Let me show you."

He grabbed Bertram by the tunic and tugged him down on top of Bran, pressing upward with his hips so his stiffened cock pushed against Bertram's thigh.

Coins tumbled and clinked.

Jewelry shifted.

Bran, having brought Bertram down, wrapped his arms around Bertram's neck and brushed their lips together in a not-quite kiss that drove Bertram wild.

"Your own body weight will be much more effective," Bran whispered, teasing Bertram with the movement of his lips as he spoke. "If you really want to give it your best shot, I would suggest pinning me down and pounding your body onto mine. Often. While leading with your hips. And preferably naked. I've heard it's a foolproof way to do an omega in. Do you want to give it a try?"

The dragon inside of Bertram reared up at the invitation, and the next thing Bertram knew, his claws were out and Bran's hose was lying around him in tatters.

"Wretched dragon," Bran admonished, but in the same breath, he ran his fingers down Bertram's neck. Scales had formed there, slotting one against the other in haphazard patterns that dipped over his shoulders and down his back, where they surrounded newly manifested wings.

Bertram flexed them. Fanned them out. Brought them back in. If the council knew he'd become so emotionally volatile that he

couldn't contain his own dragon, they'd have his hide. But Bran...
Bran brought Bertram back to the days before he'd been Frederich, when all the best parts of himself had not yet been whittled away.

"*Mine,*" he rasped. It came out in his dragon's voice, but it rang true in Bertram's heart all the same.

Bran made a sound—a gasp of pleasure—and kissed him, and the last of Bertram's walls fell. His wings fanned with a sudden snap, then curled around Bran protectively, keeping him close.

They made love there, amongst their eggs.

Made love while Bertram's dragon soared.

It was wrong to want Bran like he did, and worse to act on his forbidden desires, but with him, Bertram did not feel like an expendable pawn in someone else's game. With Bran, he was just himself. A dragon, a father, a lover.

With Bran, he was more than he'd ever been before, because with Bran, he was free.

"Who taught you to braid hair like that?" Bertram asked one morning in the nursery after the last maid was done up for the day. Sunlight streamed through the windows onto the bed, warming the eggs. Bran had been spending all his free time with them lately, rarely leaving them, even to eat.

"Hm?" Bran wriggled his way to the center of the bed. He was in the midst of taking off his tunic when Bertram spoke, and had been caught off guard. "What was that?"

"Who taught you to braid hair?" Bertram asked again.

"Oh." Bran stripped his tunic over his head and set it aside, moving their clutch carefully into place against his body. "One of the girls in my cloister. She was older than I, and aged out a few years after I arrived. In her absence, I became the one the other omegas turned to when they wanted their hair done."

"Do you miss it?"

"Sometimes." Bran stroked the egg resting against his stomach. "But I would not go back. Not to that cloister or to any other, regardless of how well they treat their omegas. I am sure your investigation will flush out the worst of the corruption, but it does not change the fact that the system is fundamentally abhorrent. I will not be made to reprise my role in it, and when I am able, I will liberate the omegas trapped within it, starting with the ones from my old cloister."

"You know that isn't possible."

"Neither were these." He gestured to the eggs. "Yet here they are, and here I am, no madder than anyone would be, considering the circumstances." Bran met Bertram's gaze and held it, expression unwavering. "I *will* free them, Frederich. You may not wish it, but I am not beholden to you. Until I draw my last breath, I will do what's right for my kind."

"You—"

Bertram had intended to argue, but stopped short when there came a crisp noise from somewhere on the bed, like porcelain cracking in twain. Bran went very still, his eyes wide with shock.

"What's the matter?" Bertram asked. "What was it that made that noise?"

Bran said nothing.

He didn't need to.

For the noise happened again, and this time Bertram saw what had caused it.

A tiny egg tooth had burst through the shell of one of their eggs.

17

SORIN

A black talon swiftly followed the egg tooth, punching a new hole through the shell of the hatching egg. Cracks formed, rushing outward from the site of impact, and in a few places, the shell chipped, sending jagged little purple pieces raining down onto the bedding.

Sorin watched it happen from the bedside. He'd scrambled away as quickly as he could once he'd realized what was happening, and now perched awkwardly half on the bed, half off it, not sure what to do with himself. A very vocal, emotional part of him wanted to be right there with his babies, stroking their shells in encouragement as they freed themselves from their eggs, but dragon law strictly prohibited any kind of interaction with a hatching clutch, and while Sorin didn't care for dragons or their customs, Frederich was right there, and he was much stronger than Sorin would ever be. He could easily restrain Sorin if he were to try and defy the law, and worse, he might lock Sorin up like a prisoner in his bedroom.

So Sorin ignored his instinct.

It was better to honor Frederich's customs and get to see the clutch hatch than to defy him and be taken away.

While he reasoned all of that out, Frederich approached the bedside. He collected Sorin in his arms and sat them both more comfortably, with Frederich on the bed and Sorin in his lap, wrapped loosely in Frederich's embrace. No sooner had they settled than a second egg rocked and shook, and with a *crack!* an egg tooth pierced its shell.

The two other eggs showed no signs of life.

They remained eerily still.

"Are they all supposed to hatch at once?" Sorin asked uneasily, eyeing the motionless eggs.

"Aye."

"Then why haven't those ones begun?"

"It's still early." Frederich held him closer. "Give them time. My youngest brother, Alistair, was believed to be a dud, but pulled through at the last second, just before all hope was lost. Some eggs simply take longer than others. Do you still feel a connection to all of them?"

Sorin looked inward, focusing on each distinct cord of the egg bond. He nodded.

"Then we needn't worry. The whelps will come when they are ready—there isn't anything we can do."

Sorin frowned. The egg bond told him that all was well, but the stillness of the two eggs worried him. Why weren't they as active as their brothers? His fingers twitched, and he had to ball his hands into fists to keep himself from reaching out.

"Must we really not touch them?" he asked, impatiently dragging his nails across his palm. "I won't help them hatch—I only want to hold the ones that haven't started to move. It seems unfair to ignore them simply because their brothers were eager to be born."

"I'm afraid such is the way of things. The rules stipulate that once the first egg begins to hatch, the clutch must be left alone so each whelp may come into the world on his own terms."

"The rules are barbaric and outdated."

"Perhaps." Frederich chuckled. "But they are the rules all of us are bound by, and they have been put in place for a reason."

"And what reason is that—to make us suffer?"

"It certainly feels that way, doesn't it?" There was a tone to Frederich's voice that suggested this would be the end of the conversation, but to Sorin's surprise, he continued onward. "I've heard it said by dragons far more knowledgeable than I that many of our rules and customs date back to before the war, when the world was a different place. At that time, when there were so many dragons that resources were scarce, it must have made sense to let nature sort itself out this way. Strong whelps would have been an asset to the survival of their clan against enemy aggressors. Weak whelps would have been a detriment, taking food out of the mouths of the capable. To some extent, I can understand."

"But resources aren't scarce anymore," Sorin argued. "There are hardly any dragons left."

"And hardly any clutches, either. Why go through the effort of changing the rules when there is rarely reason to use them?"

"Because the clutches that are being laid deserve better."

"Are all omegas as stubborn as you?" Frederich asked in good humor.

"No," Sorin said, giving him a look. "But I'm beginning to wish they were."

Frederich started to say something, but cut himself short when one of the eggs that had previously been still wiggled so violently, it toppled onto its side. Sorin winced, wanting badly to swoop in and make sure it was fine, but Frederich held him securely in place and would not let him go.

"One day," Frederich went on to say as they watched the three eggs shake and wiggle, "the rules may be repealed. There's no telling what the future could hold. But dragons are exceptionally long-lived, Bran, and we are not creatures who embrace change.

Tradition is important to us. Our world is the way it is for a reason."

"And if those reasons are wrong?"

"You think too much," Frederich scolded, but it was half-hearted at best.

He held on to Sorin as though for comfort.

The fourth egg began to rock.

The second egg beat the first, splitting open a good ten minutes later to reveal a dark purple whelp. The whelp blinked, shook all over to rid himself of the remnants of his shell, then stepped out of the mess he'd made and spotted Sorin. A shiver ran through him, and with an excited chirp, he scurried at top speed across the bed and scaled Sorin's chest with ease.

Sorin, laughing, caught him in his arms and held him close. The whelp was too small to reciprocate, but he showed Sorin his love in the best way he could, purring and butting his head under Sorin's chin as his happiness flooded their bond.

It was perfect.

He was perfect.

Sorin rocked him gently, blinking mist out of his eyes.

His heart had never been so full.

The next egg hatched not long after that, and out tumbled another whelp just as perfect as his brother. He wasted no time in running over to Sorin and perched on his shoulder, where he delighted in chewing on Sorin's hair. Frederich tsked him, and he stopped for a moment only to start right back up again.

The third egg took longer to hatch. An hour after the birth of the second whelp, he finally struggled free of his egg and, shaking himself, skipped across the bed to Sorin, curling up on his lap.

It would have been a perfect moment if not for one thing—the fourth egg. It rocked intermittently, but never all that much, and then went still. Sorin watched it uneasily while he bonded with his babies, stroking their small scaly heads and toying with the spines along their backs. They purred and chirped and flapped their wings for him, and while he was truly and deeply happy, he was devastated as well.

What was to become of the fourth egg?

Would it make it?

He leaned against Frederich for support, and as though Frederich knew what was on his mind, he whispered, "It's not over yet. All will be well. Have faith."

Sorin had learned to never trust a dragon, but Frederich made him want to believe. He closed his eyes and focused all of his love into the connection he shared with the last egg, hoping all it would take was a little extra love to set him free. It was foolish, but bound as he was by tradition, it was all he could do.

Another fifteen minutes passed, and then another fifteen after that. The whelps had fallen asleep, tired from having hatched, and still the fourth egg was still and silent. The only sign it was alive came through the bond, through which Sorin was able to feel a subdued glow.

"Perhaps it is simply not meant to hatch," Frederich admitted regretfully a short while later. "Some whelps simply do not thrive."

"He's alive," Sorin insisted. "I *feel* him. Please—please will you let me help him? He will not steal food from the mouths of our other children. We have more than enough here to care for him, and I can't sit here and watch as the worst comes to pass. If I do nothing, I fear he will die."

Frederich's arms tightened around him, only to loosen, and then fall away.

He took each sleeping whelp dutifully from Sorin, releasing him, and before Frederich had time to change his mind, Sorin crawled away. He came right up to the unhatched egg and sat on his legs, hesitating. How was he to break into the shell? Was there a knife nearby, or some other piece of sharp treasure? He glanced at the gold scattered about the nest and found nothing.

The only sharp thing within range was...

"Lend me your claw," he said abruptly, looking over his shoulder at Frederich, who was more handsome than he'd ever been with his arms full of baby dragons. "I need something with which to puncture the egg, and it's the only thing nearby that will do."

"I am bound by the law," Frederich argued. "I won't stop you, but I cannot help you, either."

"The law is *wrong*."

"You may be right, but it is not our place to decide."

"Do you mean to tell me you would let the whelp die, then?" Sorin's bottom lip began to tremble—not with sorrow, but with rage. "Lend me your claw, Frederich. Or does tradition truly mean more to you than the life of another living being?"

Frederich dropped his gaze. He watched the whelps as they slept in his arms, then slowly shook his head and laid them in the bedding before crawling to Sorin's side. "I have sworn my life to the council," he murmured, lifting up a hand, his fingers spread. "I am a champion of justice whose purpose is to obey. I do not make the rules, Bran. I do not have any more say than you do. I simply do as I am told, and by doing so, I serve my people." Frederich hesitated, and a claw, curved and razor-sharp, emerged from his nail bed. "I was taught to be heartless, to distance myself from my emotions, as justice is rarely tidy. But these whelps deserve better of me. When it comes to them and their well-being, I am not a tool of the council, I am their father, and I will defy death itself should it mean they will stay safe and happy."

He held his hand out for Sorin to take.

"You may have my claw," he said. "Together, we will save this egg."

Sorin's anger vanished. Stunned, he looked at Frederich dumbly for a few seconds, then took Frederich's hand and brought the sharpened tip of its claw toward the egg. He held it a fraction of an inch away from making contact, neither of them moving, neither of them breathing, both all too aware they were on the threshold of committing an unthinkable taboo.

If Frederich allowed him to do this…

If he allowed him to use his claw and open the egg, there would be no going back. He would be betraying his kind. Heart racing, Sorin searched Frederich's face for any sign of regret or hesitation and was surprised to find none. Frederich's expression was somber, but it was also determined.

He was ready.

He wanted to do this.

For all of his shortcomings, he truly was not like other dragons. He was in no way perfect, but he was learning, and his willingness to listen would save their whelp from certain death.

Sorin's heart panged with raw emotion he did not care to name. To distract himself from it, he took a steadying breath and moved Frederich's claw into place, positioning it against the egg. One curl of Frederich's finger would pierce the shell, and once that happened, Sorin would pry it open.

But before he could instruct Frederich on what to do, the egg wiggled and toppled onto the bedding. A tiny egg tooth pierced the shell, disappeared, and then pierced it again. Without a word, hand in hand, Sorin and Frederich watched as the final whelp hatched all by himself. He split his egg open one punch of his egg tooth at a time, then tumbled clumsily out of his shell, shook himself off, and looked up at Sorin with sweet and innocent eyes.

He was a dark and dreamy purple, like the color of a raven's feathers when bleached by the sun.

With a little chirp of joy, he butted his head beneath Sorin and Frederich's clasped hands and nuzzled their palms, soaking up their love.

"Hello, baby," Sorin whispered. He took his hand from Frederich's and stroked the whelp's head, blinking tears out of his eyes. "We're so glad you're here. We were so worried about you."

The whelp purred and bopped his head first into Sorin's hand, then Frederich's, as if to say they needn't worry—that he was okay. Sorin followed him with his hand as he moved, stroking his tiny scales and playing with the spines down his neck and back, but he was such a small whelp that there was not enough space for both him and Frederich to pet without getting in each other's way. Their fingers brushed, each time electric.

Was it his imagination, or did he see Frederich shiver in pleasure when they touched?

Cheeks heating, wanting to know if it was all in his head, Sorin hooked his pinkie delicately over Frederich's the next time their hands met. The briefest flicker of a smile lit Frederich's face as he did, and Frederich curled his pinkie around Sorin's in return.

They sat together, pinkies linked, and showed their love to their new whelp until at last, the whelp fell asleep. Only then did Frederich take his pinkie away, picking up the sleeping whelp to put him to bed with his brothers. When he finished, he turned to Sorin and brushed his knuckles gently down Sorin's cheek.

Sorin shivered.

He did not resist the kiss that followed.

Rather, he looped his arms loosely around Frederich's neck and let Frederich pull him onto his lap. The kiss deepened but didn't become greedy or possessive. It wasn't a seductive kiss. It was steeped in emotions both of them felt, but neither of them wanted to say.

Almost like they were in love.

But that couldn't be. There was no space in their hearts for that. Frederich had vowed to end Sorin's life, and Sorin had vowed the same. Their alliance was but temporary. At their core, they were, and always would be, enemies.

Yet Sorin did not stop kissing him.

Did not stop himself from curling his fingers in Frederich's hair, or from feeling the lofty, weightless happiness that Frederich's touch instilled in him. He kissed him until there were no more kisses left to give, at which point Frederich dragged him down onto the bed and gathered Sorin to his chest. Sunlight poured down upon them, warming them, and Sorin basked in it. He had never been so blissfully happy.

But even at the peak of his happiness, he knew it could never last.

His lot in life wasn't to bed a dragon or raise a family. He had been given a chance to change the world, and even if it broke his heart, he had to take it. He could not sit by and be happy while others like him suffered. He could not allow dragons to sentence other innocent omegas to lives of pain—lives spent tormented by the memory of frightened, heartbroken screams.

So while he basked in the sunshine, safe and happy in Frederich's arms while their children slept nearby, he worked on pulling back on those unreasonable expectations, laying out the facts to himself over and over so he would never forget.

The happily ever after he wanted was impossible.

For his own well-being, he had to convince himself of it and stop dreaming of a life that could never be and a love he would never have.

Sorin spent the day in the nursery with the whelps, trying to make good on his promise to himself, but come nightfall, his will grew weak, and he found himself in Frederich's bed. With the whelps under the supervision of a nursemaid and down for the night in the nursery, they made love without worry of interruption, slowly and passionately, Frederich thrusting up into him with purpose and stealing the moans from Sorin's lips with one searing kiss after the next.

It won't be forever, Sorin tried to tell himself as Frederich buried his cock inside of him, rutting, lighting Sorin up with pleasure brighter than the stars in the night sky. *It can't be forever. There's too much work you have to do.*

Frederich's knot swelled, and his cock pulsed, unloading hot cum in Sorin that Sorin instinctively worked deeper. Whimpering, he grinded himself on Frederich's knot until he came and let his orgasm milk Frederich's cock dry.

They kissed and grinded and groped each other until Frederich's knot dislodged, at which point Frederich dismounted and lay beside him, partially covering them with the bedding to guard them against the cold. With a lazy swirl of his hand, a dollop of flame popped into existence above Frederich's index finger. It hovered there idly, flickering and sputtering. "Are you planning on sleeping now?" Frederich asked. "Or will you stay up a bit longer? The boys will be up at first light, I'm sure—I've heard it said whelps are quite active. These sunless hours may be the only ones we get to spend alone together for quite a while."

Sorin's gaze drifted from Frederich's face to the ball of flame above his finger. It shuddered, pulsing upward, as Frederich poked at it. "How long is a while?" he asked.

"About three years, I'd imagine." Frederich gave the fireball a particularly spirited poke. "That's around the time whelps first begin to transform into boys."

"Is that around the same time you'll be ending my life?"

Frederich made a noncommittal noise.

He flicked his index finger against his thumb and sent the fireball into the air. It hovered high over the bed, then exploded into starlight that spread throughout the room.

"I've been meaning to ask you something," Frederich said, dodging the question. He tucked his arms behind his head and watched the tiny points of light that hung suspended overhead. "Normally I would have waited until daylight to ask this, but I'm afraid it's been weighing on my mind for quite some time, and if I don't get it out now, it might get stuck there forever."

"What is it?" Sorin came to lie on his back next to him, resting his head on Frederich's arm so they were looking up at the lights together.

Frederich said nothing for a while, then took a steadying breath and untucked his free arm, swirling his finger through the air. The lights began a slow orbit, like flower petals caught on the surface of moving water. "When we were intimate for the first time," he said as those petals swirled, "you asked me to put eggs in you."

Sorin stared past the lights at the ceiling. "Yes. I suppose I did."

"Were you being serious?"

Sorin said nothing.

He didn't know if he could.

"I figured it was bedroom talk and nothing more, owing to your past, but..." Frederich pinched his fingers together, gathering all the glimmering lights back into a singular flame. It flickered, then popped out of existence, leaving them in the dark. "If one day it were to happen, would it please you to bear my clutch? Or would it only hurt you more?"

Sorin simmered in the darkness.

It was a long while before he admitted, "I don't know."

"That's fair." Frederich pushed air through his nose—a humorless attempt at a laugh. "You owe me no answer. Truthfully, I shouldn't have asked. The council would never grant me sanctions to have another clutch, and even were they willing, my next window of opportunity would be well outside your lifetime."

Something in Sorin's chest clenched. "Oh."

"I'm sorry." Frederich really did sound repentant. "I didn't mean to hurt you. It was just... something I needed to know."

Sorin pressed his lips together, struggling to fight off a frown. It shouldn't have bothered him. He was destined to leave this place and never return. There was no future for him here.

And yet...

"Were I to live forever," he asked, "would you want me to give you another clutch?"

Frederich did not hesitate. "I would like that very much."

Sorin closed his eyes. He didn't acknowledge the tear that fell down the side of his face.

What a pretty dream forever would be, if only he had more time.

BERTRAM

Time heeded no master, and did whatever it saw fit. As it marched onward, it brought snow and took it away. Sprouted grass. Made wildflowers bloom.

Bertram failed to notice.

He had eyes only for his boys.

The whelps were active and healthy, bright-eyed and curious in all they did. Every day they learned and grew, and while they caused trouble wherever they went, they were too pure of heart to ever do so maliciously.

Waryn was the boldest of the bunch. Nary a day went by when Bertram didn't hear the telltale skitter of his claws in a hurry, seeking out adventure in all corners of the castle, whether he was meant to be there or not.

Edmund was the clever one. He followed Waryn endlessly, allowing his brother to take the lead so he could learn from his mistakes. When the whelps got into trouble, it was rarely Edmund at the helm, but by Bertram's estimation, it was almost always his idea that caused the mess in the first place.

Owyn, while every bit as curious and rambunctious as his brothers, would rather be affectionate than adventurous—he spent most mornings curled against Bran's bare stomach on the egg bed while Bran basked in the sunlight and stroked his scales. Out of all of the whelps, he purred the loudest.

Then there was Piers.

Piers was independent. He loved his brothers and regularly joined them in their pursuits, but he also enjoyed spending time on his own, quietly exploring parts of the castle where Waryn never thought to look. Like Edmund, he was clever, but he was also cunning. Whereas the other whelps never thought to hide after causing a mess, Piers quickly learned how to spirit himself away to avoid detection.

Of all the whelps, he was the one who worried Bertram the most, as he was the one who reminded him most of himself.

"Is this what you were like as a child?" Bran asked one sunny day that spring. He stood knee-deep in the loch outside the castle, Bertram an arm's length away, as the whelps roughhoused in the water. Owyn, seemingly summoned by the sound of his father's voice, broke free from his brothers and waded over. Bran scooped him out of the water and cuddled him to his chest, prompting Owyn to push his head affectionately up under Bran's chin. He allowed himself to be cuddled for a good ten seconds before springing out of Bran's arms and into the air, his wet scales flashing in the sunlight. He beat his wings with everything he had, straining to stay airborne…

And promptly dropped like a stone into the loch.

He'd made an excellent effort.

The rest would come with time.

"Not quite." Bertram widened his stance as Piers and Waryn darted through the water toward him. Both arrived at the same time and clawed their way up his legs to his shoulders, where they readied themselves to jump. "I was raised next to a rushing river," he explained as both whelps launched themselves into the air. "Any whelps who jumped into its waters were quickly swept away. As such, I became a strong swimmer long before I dared any attempt at flight."

"And did you enjoy it? Swimming, I mean."

"I thought I did." Bertram glanced at Bran, whose hose had soaked through to his upper thighs, and whose hair was bejeweled with water droplets that shone like diamonds. "But I've reason to believe I never quite knew what enjoyment was until recently."

A blush rose in Bran's cheeks, and he hurried to collect Edmund from out of the water. Edmund, who was more than capable of scaling Bran on his own, thrashed and flopped like a fish until he finally wriggled free. On the way down he spread his wings, and to everyone's surprise, he caught the air in such a way that he glided—not fell—into the loch.

All was still for a moment, then Bran gasped and scrambled to him, sinking to his knees and pulling Edmund to his chest. He squeezed Edmund tight, then looked up at Bertram. A smile wobbled onto his lips. "Did you see? Did you see what our baby just did?"

Bertram's heart fluttered. *Our baby.*

He squeezed Bran's shoulder. "Aye. I did."

"You did so well, baby." Bran, sounding close to tears, kissed the top of Edmund's head again and again. "So, so well. How are you so big and strong already? You're supposed to stay little forever."

Edmund, looking awfully proud of himself, purred, but he wasn't able to enjoy his victory for long. All three of his brothers scampered up Bran and descended upon him, dragging him out of Bran's arms and into the water to play.

Bertram stood by Bran's side and watched them, unable to keep himself from smiling. It was true, what he'd said before—he'd never known enjoyment like this. But that wasn't the full story. What he'd left unsaid, but felt down to his very marrow, was that he'd never known love like this, either.

One quiet morning on a lazy day, while Bertram and Bran cuddled in the egg bed as the whelps roughhoused around them, there came a commotion from down the hall. Curious, Bertram lifted his head. It was Agnes, by the sound of it, squawking about something or other.

Perhaps Hamish had gotten into the pie again.

But that hardly seemed a reason to storm the nursery. There had to be something more serious going on.

Bertram thinned his lips and braced himself for trouble, and just as he'd suspected, trouble came trundling down the hall.

"You mustn't!" Agnes insisted, now close enough for Bertram to overhear. "Allow me to escort you to the great hall so that I may tell my lord dragon of your arrival. It shan't do to burst in on him unannounced, my lord. Please. Consider the whelps!"

There were exceptionally few people who would intrude on Bertram's lair unannounced, and fewer that Agnes would see fit to call lord. Bertram sat up in a rush, dislodging Owyn from his chest, but it was too late. Before he could separate himself from the forbidden omega in his bed, the nursery door flew open, revealing Grimbold Drake.

"Father." Bertram put on his easiest smile despite the unease in his stomach. He slipped out of bed, grabbing a robe from a nearby chair. "Your visit comes as a surprise. I wasn't expecting you for another two weeks. To what do I owe the pleasure?"

Grimbold cast a withering look at Bran, who was decorated from head to toe in gold and flushed from kissing, then caught sight of the whelps who now hid behind him. The ice melted from his face, and Grimbold—the mightiest and most powerful of all Amethyst dragons—dropped without a word to his knees.

The whelps, curious as ever, surveyed him for a moment, then sprang off the bed and came to meet their grandsire. Waryn took the lead, bumping his head against Grimbold's thigh before forcing his way beneath the elder Drake's hands, like a house cat looking to be petted. Grimbold remained frozen in place, watching, then a smile cracked his stern face, and he laughed. He scooped Waryn into his arms and held the whelp to his chest.

Waryn licked his cheek.

"They are just as you described in your letters, Bertram," he said as Piers and Edmund clawed their way to his shoulders. Owyn contented himself with curling up against his knees. "Healthy, all of them. Bright-eyed and full of life. Four fine young dragons, every one of them energetic and strong. You've done a fantastic job."

"Thank you, Father."

"Have they learned to summon flame yet?"

"Not yet, no."

"Ah." Grimbold's smile grew. "So the worst is yet to come. You'll want to stow your tapestries before it happens—today, if you want to ensure they stay safe. While I can't speak for these four, I can tell you that your brother, Hugh, was quite the mischief-maker when it came to fire. I lost many a good piece of furniture to his antics. The nursemaids told me he was fascinated by the flicker of his flames. I imagine one of yours might be, too."

Owyn purred. Smoke poured from his nostrils.

Grimbold set a hand on his head, and it stopped.

"Duly noted," Bertram said.

"Now," Grimbold set all the whelps down and stiffly rose to his feet, "I am parched from my travels. Will you join me in the great hall? I would appreciate your company."

"Of course."

Bertram bowed his head and showed his father out of the room, but behind his easy smile, his apprehension grew. Grimbold Drake was not the kind of dragon to visit on a whim. He was here for a reason, and knowing what he did of his father and the council, Bertram dreaded what that reason might be.

Out of an abundance of caution, he did not acknowledge Bran on his way out of the room.

The dainty footsteps that tailed him all the way to the great hall were much more difficult to ignore.

"There has been an incident in Ruby territory," Grimbold said solemnly once Agnes had brought them both tankards of Bertram's finest ale. "No dragons have died—thank god—but by François's estimation, half a dozen Pedigree omegas are missing from the Parisian cloister."

"Runaways?"

Grimbold shook his head. "We're not sure. François claims they have been stolen, but I find that hard to believe. An operation of that size would have required a considerable amount of stealth and coordination—someone would have gotten clumsy and let word slip—but so far, there are no leads. In my opinion, the omegas have fled. Regardless, with so many missing, this has become a matter of public security. The council has no choice but to step in."

Bertram swore under his breath. "When am I to leave?"

"You're not to leave. The other agents have been dispatched, and the clan heads have agreed to assemble. I came not to collect you, but to see the whelps before I go, as I will not be able to visit during our agreed-upon date in two weeks' time."

"You're not planning to travel into other clans' territories alone, are you?"

"No. Sebastian will accompany me."

"Sebastian." Bertram slumped into his chair, relieved. "A worthy choice."

"What he lacks in charisma, he makes up in muscle." Grimbold chuckled. "I've half a mind to pair you two upon the completion of your sabbatical. If nothing else, he would be an asset on missions where diplomacy is not an option." His mirth ebbed, and he looked pointedly down the slope of his nose at Bertram. "Perhaps he would keep you from playing house with wild omegas."

"I haven't the foggiest what you're on about."

Grimbold arched a brow and drank.

He did not bring up Bran again.

From there, the conversation moved on to other things—the whelps, mostly. Grimbold was quite taken by them, and the more Bertram told him of their exploits, the more love shone through in his eyes. Bertram had always known his father to be an impersonal and somewhat cold man whose life revolved around matters of the council, so this new facet of him came as a surprise. It had not been like this when he was a whelp.

Perhaps Grimbold was making up for lost time.

But whatever the case, Grimbold listened intently to all Bertram had to say, then spent the rest of his time at Castle Beithir in the company of his grandwhelps, who took to him immediately.

He stayed but a day.

On the morrow, after sunrise, he whispered something into each whelp's ear, then stepped into his carriage and was gone. All in all, it had been a painless visit—perhaps the best Bertram had ever had.

But he did not make it out of it scot-free. Trouble found him later that night when a fiery-eyed Bran entered the bedroom. He headed straight for Bertram, slamming the door shut in his wake.

BERTRAM

Bertram frowned. "I take it you're not here to cuddle?"

The look Bran gave him could have slain an entire army of dragons. "This is no time for jokes. The council will kill those runaway omegas. You know it as well as I."

"They fled knowing what would happen should they be caught."

"And? Do you truly think death is an acceptable punishment for the pursuit of freedom?" Bran clenched his fists. "Tell me they deserve to die, Frederich. Say it out loud. Look into my eyes and tell me you would feel no guilt were you their executioner."

Bertram looked into Bran's eyes and said nothing.

He could not bring himself to say that on behalf of the council, he'd done far worse.

"You know it's wrong." The anger dropped out of Bran's voice. He crossed the room and climbed up onto the bed, straddling Bertram's lap. Bertram expected violence, but instead, Bran pressed his palm against Bertram's chest, right over his heart. "You know it is, so why let it happen? Why not do something? Say something? They would listen to you."

Bertram closed his hand around Bran's, shamefully lowering his gaze. "I don't have the kind of power you think I do."

"You only tell yourself that. You're one of them—a dragon. Your opinion would at least be considered. All I am to them is an omega. They would never listen to me."

"Bran..."

"No." Bran wrapped his arms loosely around Bertram's neck, eyes wet and expression miserable. "This isn't time for excuses. Not now. Not with six lives on the line. All those omegas want is a chance to reclaim what was stolen from them. To live happy, normal lives. Help them. Help *me*."

"It's not as simple as you make it sound."

Bran recoiled like he'd been struck. He looked Bertram in the eyes, his own wide with shock and vulnerable with betrayal, then pinched his lips into a wobbling frown and turned his head to the side. In a quiet, mournful voice, he murmured, "If you will do nothing, then I will be the one to go."

"No." Bertram caught Bran by the arm, anchoring him in place even though he'd made no attempt to move. "You cannot. You must stay. The whelps need you. *I* need you."

Bran dug his shaking fingers into the front of Bertram's tunic. The wetness in his eyes gathered in his lashes, and when he spoke, his voice was choked with tears. "Do you remember what you told me when I first came to the castle? You said once the eggs had hatched, you would put me to death for my crimes. Only one of us was ever going to make it out of this—you know it as well as I. If you don't want me to leave, then you'll need to kill me. I won't stop you. I'm a threat to your kind, and by all rights, I deserve to die... just as you and your kind deserve death for what you've done to me and mine."

"No." Bertram tugged Bran to him and buried his face in Bran's soft hair. "It doesn't have to be like this. You don't have to go. Society will not be like this forever, but change takes time."

"Change takes *action*," Bran croaked. His fingers tightened.

Tears soaked through Bertram's tunic, wetting his shoulder. "The ones in power need to see that change is necessary. That it is not only wanted, but needed. They need to *hear* us. Those omegas who escaped are my allies. Alone, we're weak, but together our voices will rise up, and we will be heard."

"Bran..."

"No." Bran sniffled, then lifted his head and looked Bertram in the eyes. "There are sacrifices we all must make when we set out to change the world... and I know it better than most. Our game has come to an end, Bertram. Frederich and Bran were fun distractions, but you know as well as I that they aren't who we really are." The tears that had previously soaked Bertram's shoulder now fell freely down Bran's cheeks. "My name is Sorin," he said, "and I am your enemy. Until my dying breath, I will fight for the omegas your kind has enslaved... and so help me, I will free them. I will leave the world a better place than I found it, and I will kill anyone who tries to get in my way."

"I know." Bertram slid a hand behind Sorin's head and guided it back to his shoulder. "I understand."

"I wish things were different."

"I wish it, too."

Sorin sucked in a shuddering breath and rested his full weight on Bertram. It wasn't much.

"I leave tomorrow," he said. "Please... will you be my Frederich just one last time and help me forget?"

Bertram nodded and kissed the top of his head.

They made love that night, as they had so many nights before, but it wasn't the same.

It couldn't be.

Because this time, it was goodbye.

Sorin left when the sky turned red at dawn, stopping only to slip into the nursery and hold each of the whelps one last time as they slept. Bertram watched from the doorway, heartbroken, then followed him to the stables, where a sleepy stablehand readied a reliable gelding and helped Sorin into the saddle.

He looked small on the horse, Bertram thought.

Too small to take on the world.

But this was the same omega who'd risked his life to reclaim his eggs. The one who, despite all odds, had slain a dragon. If there was anyone who could accomplish this impossible task, it would be him.

Bertram led Sorin's gelding out of the stables and across the grounds, coming to a stop not all that far from the loch where they had spent their days playing with the whelps. Sorin looked past it and out across the darkness into which he was headed, then at Bertram, who was framed by the rising sun. He said nothing, and Bertram fared no better. He dared not speak around the lump in his throat, so instead he took Sorin's hand and pressed his knuckles to his lips.

A final kiss.

When it was over, Bertram took his hand from Sorin's, but not before pressing something into Sorin's palm. "A token to remember me by," he said. "Something that will always make me think of you."

"Bertram…"

"No objections." Bertram wrapped his hand over Sorin's, making him curl his fingers around it. "Take it. If you do not wish to keep it, use it to brighten the lives of those you meet on your journey, and know that whenever I see a pearl, I will think of you."

The pearl necklace in Sorin's hand glinted in the light of the rising sun in the moments before he stowed it in his saddlebag. When it was secure, Sorin wiped his arm across his eyes then shook his head as if it could chase his heartbreak away.

"Should we meet again," he said, "I will endeavor to show you the same mercy that you have shown me."

"Don't," Bertram objected. "If we are to meet again, it will be on the council's orders. Show me no mercy. I won't deserve it. Protect yourself, not me."

"Then I suppose this is it, then." Sorin's lips wobbled, but despite his struggle, he was able to maintain a smile. "Goodbye, Frederich."

"Goodbye, Bran."

Sorin hesitated, looking into Bertram's eyes a final time, then guided his horse into the dark and was gone.

20

SORIN

Sorin did not travel into the darkness alone. An old foe waited for him there—the noise in his head. After such a long time spent in remission, it came roaring back as if it had never left and followed him out of Scotland, through England, and into France. Some days, it was tolerable... others, not so much. He could muddle on through throbbing headaches and deep-rooted feelings of guilt, but those surface-level symptoms weren't the worst part of his condition. That honor was reserved for the dark thoughts that came with them.

Thoughts that, on his worst days, he found difficult to ignore.

Why did you ever think you could do this?

You've failed every last one of your children, and this will be no different.

Those omegas would be better off without you.

You aren't going to get there before the dragons do. By the time you arrive, everyone you're trying to save will be dead.

He knew in his heart those thoughts weren't entirely true—that he was capable, and that doing something was better than doing nothing at all—but the more they swirled around his head, the more they wore him down. By the time he arrived in Paris, he was more than discouraged. He was defeated. Why had he ever thought he could do this? He was but one omega, and a damaged one at that. He hadn't the brawn nor the mental wherewithal to defeat the council. He should have stayed in Scotland, with Bertram and the children. The guilt would have been crushing, but at least he would have had his boys to keep him happy.

Out here, he had nothing but regrets.

Who was he to think he could help those omegas when he couldn't even help himself?

Exhausted from the effort of fighting with his own brain, he barely noticed when the foot traffic on the street thickened. He was in a poorer part of the city—a place dragons would never deign to visit—and as it was in any city, there were always plenty of people around. The hustle and bustle did not stop, and so it was not inherently suspicious when a few people came close enough to brush up against his leg as the crowd spewed out onto the street.

What was suspicious was the glimmer Sorin saw when the crowd receded.

It was coming from a young man.

He was short enough to disappear within the crowd, and slender—not even the baggy peasant's clothing he wore, nor the heavy cloak he wrapped around himself, could hide how malnourished he seemed. His hood was drawn, blocking the details of his face from Sorin's view, but Sorin cared not what he looked like.

He cared for the glimmering thing clutched in the young man's hand.

His pearls.

"Hey!" Snapped out of his spiraling thoughts, he made a mad grab for the young man, but it was useless—he easily slipped away. "Stop!"

The young man, of course, did not stop. He took off running, weaving through the crowd in a way Sorin's horse could not. It would only take a few seconds before he put so much distance between them, Sorin would never find him again. He should have accepted the loss, moved on with his life, and continued his search for the omegas, but at that moment, Sorin wasn't thinking clearly. His dark thoughts had pushed him to his breaking point, and this was more than he could take.

Those were *his* pearls.

The ones Bertram had given him.

The last token of affection from the dragon he considered the father of his eggs.

He could not lose them.

Could not let them go.

So as the pickpocket ran, Sorin leapt off his horse and followed. He shouldered through the crowd, feet pounding the cobble, zeroed in on the little glimpses he got of the pickpocket along the way. Without stopping, without thinking, he followed those glimpses beyond the main street, down darkened alleys, and finally through a residential courtyard where they spooked an elderly napery maid hanging clothes out to dry. The courtyard was fenced off by stone walls, and the only way out was the way they'd come in, but that did not deter the pickpocket. He increased his speed and leapt at the wall, scrambling up to the top with ease. He perched there for a gloating moment, looking over his shoulder, smirking, to watch Sorin lose, but unfortunately for him, Sorin was the father of four rambunctious whelps, and could scale walls like this in his sleep. He launched himself up, finding his footing on a jutting stone, and scrambled up the wall with such speed, he nearly took flight.

The pickpocket gasped, but it was too late—Sorin lunged and grabbed him. The force of impact knocked them both off balance, and they toppled off the wall onto the unevenly paved street below.

Sorin maintained his death grip through it all.

He was *not* letting the pickpocket go.

"Let go of me!" the pickpocket snapped, speaking in French.

Sorin had learned the language—alongside several others—while being trained to become part of the Pedigree, and was not only able to understand, but reply. "Not until you give back what you took from me."

The pickpocket hissed and thrashed, but it was useless. Sorin had him, and he would not let go. Finally, the pickpocket seemed to realize it, for he stopped struggling and twisted at the hip in order to glare at Sorin with hatred that cut through to the bone.

But no sooner did he see Sorin's face, than his anger fell apart.

He blinked, astonished, and rolled over so they were face to face. "You're like me," he said.

Sorin did not know what to make of this sudden change in behavior. Had the pickpocket not known he was stealing from an omega when he'd looted Sorin's saddlebag? It had to be a trick, he thought. Something meant to get him to drop his guard so the pickpocket could break free and escape.

"You won't trick me," Sorin shot back, unwilling to give in to the pickpocket's game. "It doesn't matter that we're the same. You stole something from me, and I want it back."

"Your French is magnificent," the pickpocket remarked, ignoring everything Sorin had said. "You barely have an accent. I'm impressed. It's not often I meet an Englishman with such a talented tongue."

Sorin wasn't English, and was about to say so, but the pickpocket continued.

"Come. My friends stole your horse and the rest of your abandoned belongings while you were chasing after me, and the only way you'll get them back is if you do as I say."

His horse.

The reality of the situation crashed into him, and Sorin felt suddenly sick at having left his poor horse behind. He hadn't meant to abandon him, but in the heat of the moment, getting his pearls back had seemed so important that he hadn't considered what might happen to everything he'd left behind.

"Why are you helping me?" he asked the pickpocket, experimentally loosening his grip. If it really was a trick, he figured the pickpocket would bolt if given even a little freedom, but he didn't. He separated himself from Sorin and stood stiffly, cracking his back and rolling his shoulders to work out the ache caused by his fall before offering Sorin a hand.

"I'm helping you," he said as he dragged Sorin to his feet, "because you and I are the same, and were our situations reversed, I would hope you would help me in just the same way. Now, come. We shouldn't stay out much longer—we've attracted too much attention as it is. The streets aren't safe right now for people like us."

Sorin didn't argue. He knew it all too well.

Instead, he gave the pickpocket a thorough look.

His hood had been knocked off when he'd fallen off the wall, revealing a pretty heart-shaped face with a cute button nose and full, pink lips. His eyes were clear and blue, and his hair was an auburn rat's nest. With some good grooming, Sorin imagined it would fall into lovely loose curls, but the pickpocket didn't seem concerned with his appearance. He hiked his hood back up, obscuring his face, and gestured for Sorin to follow him.

"Where are you taking me?" Sorin asked as they walked.

The pickpocket looked over his shoulder at him, a twinkle of mischief in his eyes. "Where do you think? I'm taking you home."

The pickpocket led Sorin through a labyrinthine network of streets, oftentimes so narrow, they could not walk side by side. It seemed an entirely different world from the Paris Sorin had seen from the Left Bank, which was sparkling and modern. Here, there was no such luxury—every other step over garbage or the rancid puddles left by spilled chamber pots—and the farther they went, the worse the conditions became. Entire buildings stood abandoned, their walls visibly crumbling, and the streets were in shambles if they were paved at all. A sour sewage taste clung to the air, and beneath it, an undercurrent of smoke. The longer they breathed it in, the more Sorin found himself missing castle Beithir.

It lacked the amenities of a city, but at least the air there was clean.

He was in good shape, but the thickness of the miasma made him feel like he was always short of breath.

Eventually, they arrived at a cluster of decrepit buildings. At one time they had been quite fetching—perhaps even owned by nobles—but as with everything else in this place, they were decaying after years of disuse. Someone had taken the time to board up the windows and doors, but exposure had begun to eat the wood away. The pickpocket took advantage of it, going right up to one of the doors where only one moldy wood board remained. He waggled his eyebrows at Sorin, shouldered the door open, and ducked under the board, disappearing inside.

Not wanting to be left behind, Sorin followed suit and found himself in the dark and ransacked foyer of a nobleman's abandoned home.

"Your horse is in the courtyard," the pickpocket said. He was already on his way up a creaky set of stairs to the left. "The rest of your belongings are up here. Watch your step. The sixth step is rotted and could collapse under your weight. It's best to skip it entirely."

Sorin blinked, allowing his eyes time to adjust to the dim light.

By the time he was able to see clearly, the pickpocket was gone.

He remained where he was a second longer, taking stock of what little he could use to defend himself if this turned out to be a trap, then followed the pickpocket up the stairs.

The sixth step was indeed rotten, and no one was waiting to ambush him upstairs.

He emerged on the landing to discover a central hallway down which were several rooms, only one of which still had its door. It hung askew on its hinges like it hadn't quite given up on life, but wasn't sold on it, either. Beyond it, Sorin caught a glimpse of the pickpocket, and beyond him, he spotted several crude and dirty mattresses pushed together to form one large nest which occupied the center of the room. It was sparsely outfitted with understuffed pillows and threadbare blankets, and was being used by a pretty young woman. Like the pickpocket, she was malnourished, and had a lively sparkle in her eyes. Her long blonde hair was pinned up in a rushed and messy updo little better than the pickpocket's rat's nest.

She was seated on the very edge of the nest of mattresses, rifling through—

"Hey!" Sorin cried, jolted out of his thoughts by what he saw. "That's my saddlebag!"

The young woman stopped what she was doing and scowled at him.

"What is he doing here, Jacques?" she asked as the pickpocket took the saddlebag from her and carried it to the room's only piece of furniture—a dusty table positioned beneath a boarded window. "You were supposed to lose him in the streets, not bring him home."

"Change of plans," the pickpocket said. "Look at the clothes he is wearing."

The young woman glanced down Sorin's body, and the scowl dropped off her face. "Purple, and of exquisite workmanship, too. Not the clothes you would typically find on an omega." Her eyes darted up to Sorin's, and she said very matter-of-factly, "You are of the Pedigree."

The distinction took Sorin by surprise. No one knew the world of dragons existed—no one but those who were a part of it

—and that could only mean one thing. "And you're the omegas who escaped from the Parisian cloister," he said, not bothering to hide his surprise.

"Took you long enough," the pickpocket said, smirking in good humor. "I'm Jacques, and this is Amélie. The others must still be outside, tending to your horse. Who might you be?"

"My name is Sorin."

"Are you not English?" Jacques wrinkled his brow. "You are wearing Amethyst colors, but have a foreign name."

"I'm from the cloister in Constantinople."

"You were chosen by an Amethyst dragon, then?"

A memory of Bertram lounging in bed, stirring fire through the air, squeezed painfully in Sorin's heart. "Yes," he said after a pause, "… something like that."

Jacques' expression softened. He seemed to consider something quietly, glancing up and down Sorin's body with a measure of somber sympathy, then waved him over to the table.

"I'm sorry about what happened to you," he said to Sorin privately once Sorin had arrived. "Only one of us has ever been chosen, but seeing how the light was gone from her eyes when she returned to us affected us all, and ultimately led us to plan our escape. We may not know each other, but you need not feel alone. All of us are here for you. We may not know your pain, but our shared experiences make us family, and you can rest easy knowing that you are safe with us here. If all you want is silence, we will not say a word, but if you want to speak, you have our ears."

Sorin dropped his gaze. It didn't feel like it was enough, but swept up by so many conflicting emotions, all he could manage to say was, "Thank you."

The brief silence that followed was cut short by the distant sound of many unhurried feet climbing stairs, then voices in the hallway. Conversation. Laughter. They ushered three young men and one young woman, all of them in plain and threadbare clothing, into the bedroom. Upon entering, one of them was playfully tossing Sorin's coin pouch in the air.

They all stopped when they saw Sorin.

The coin pouch landed with a jingle in the cupped palm of the young man.

"Jacques?" he asked uneasily while the other two stepped in front of the young woman, blocking her from view. "What's going on?"

"It turns out today's target was not a target at all. Meet Sorin of the Pedigree, raised in the Constantinople cloister. He was chosen by an Amethyst dragon and escaped, and now has found his way to us."

The two young men blocking the young woman visibly relaxed, but the one with Sorin's coin pouch did not trust as easily. He narrowed his eyes and looked Sorin up and down with overt scrutiny, then flicked his attention over to Jacques. "How can you be so sure he is not working with the dragons?"

"I can't." Jacques shrugged. "But since no dragons came to his aid when he was in pursuit of me, it stands to reason he is working on his own."

The young man grumbled something, which Jacques ignored.

"I told him we would give him back his things, by the way," Jacques said, eyeballing Sorin's pilfered coin pouch. The young man sighed in annoyance, but tossed Jacques the pouch anyway. It landed with a merry jingle in Jacques' outstretched hand.

"Here are your things, as promised," Jacques said to Sorin, setting the pouch on top of the saddlebag, then the pearls on top of that. "I apologize for the inconvenience, but you must understand that when you enter certain parts of Paris looking as you do, you paint a target on your back. We do not enjoy living as thieves, but we left our cloister with nothing more than the clothes on our backs, and have had to do what is necessary to survive. I hope you can forgive us."

"I forgive you," Sorin said, taking back the pearls. He closed his fist around them, watching as they disappeared, and added, "It was an honest mistake."

"So, what brings you to Paris?" Amélie asked from the bed. She folded her arms on her knees and leaned forward, tilting her head inquisitively as she looked up at him. "You seemed to have heard about our escape from our cloister, so I take it you came to find us?"

"I did. I knew the council would be after you, and I wanted to make sure you were safe."

"The council will never find us," the young man—now sans coin pouch—scoffed. "We are much smarter than dragons. We know everything they know, and more on top of that. You, on the other hand." He arched a brow, gesturing at Sorin's clothing. "You wouldn't have stood a chance. You look like you belong to a dragon. Had one passed you on the street, you would have been immediately spotted and killed."

Sorin looked down at himself.

He hadn't thought twice about the clothing he was wearing, but the young man was right. Bertram had spared no expense with his wardrobe, dressing Sorin in quality fabrics colored with expensive dyes. The seam work was flawless, and the other small details on his garments, while subtle, were expertly done. Distracted as he had been with his suffering, he had been careless, and made a target of himself for thieves and dragons alike.

"I believe what Therron means to say is that, perhaps, it would be safest for all of us if you stayed with us for a while," Jacques said, smoothly taking over the conversation. "We do not look like much right now, but we have a roof over our heads, enough to eat so we don't starve, and a strong drive to survive. Once the council's efforts to recover us have ended and it is safe for you to travel again, you would of course be free to go, but until then, why don't you lie low with us? We will teach you everything you need to know to survive on your own."

"Where were you planning to go next, anyway?" Amélie asked.

She seemed earnestly curious, and while Sorin didn't know her, he couldn't help but trust her. She—and the rest of these omegas —had been kind to him when they could have taken advantage of him, and he had no reason to doubt their intentions.

They were family, after all.

Born into the same world and shaped by the same kind of suffering.

"Well…" He spent a moment studying them, searching one face after the next, looking upon the strangers who understood him perhaps better than anyone else.

Strangers who were allies.

Who were becoming friends.

He had felt hopeless and alone since leaving Bertram behind, but now, though there was still pain, there was hope. He was not the only one who thought the way he did, nor was he the only one who had seen the evils in dragon society and done whatever it took to get out.

Absentmindedly, he twisted a pearl between his fingers.

"Where I go next will depend on you," he said at last, "and if you'll join me on my quest to change the world."

BERTRAM

On a dreary summer morning, while the whelps splashed around in the loch, a desolate Bertram observed a rider crest the nearby hill. He watched silently from where he sat, on alert but not alarmed, and summoned forth his claws as a precaution.

As it turned out, he needn't have worried.

It was only the local courier bringing him a piece of mail.

Bertram accepted it with a small word of thanks, and off the courier went. When he was out of sight, Bertram opened the letter to find it contained but a single word.

Safe.

There was no signature, but pinned to the parchment was a pearl threaded onto a raven's feather.

It spoke for itself.

The next letter Bertram received came not from Sorin, but from his father. The Onyx cloister in Constantinople had fallen, and its omegas were nowhere to be found. All agents of the council had been dispatched to aid in recovery efforts, and the clan heads had agreed to meet in Onyx territory while an investigation took place.

Surely, wrote the most senior Drake, one of the clans had to be behind this. Likely the Topaz clan, in a bid for territory. Since they'd lost Frisia to the Sapphires, they had been far more aggressive, and it would not be a shock for them to lash out like this.

In any case, Grimbold warned, it would be wise to keep a close eye on the whelps. It seemed likely the villainous dragons behind the attacks would target other vulnerable members of dragon society, and if it really was the Topaz clan behind it all, Amethysts in particular would need to watch their backs. Those bronze bastards were an unstable lot—thank god Bertram and his brothers had nothing to do with them.

Grimbold concluded the letter by stating that the Onyx agents were reasonably sure the ne'er-do-well who had stolen the omegas away was still within city limits, and with some luck would be discovered soon. Quick action from the Onyx clan had blocked all outbound routes save the trade route to Persia, which was guarded, but still open out of necessity. With the Onyx clan's constant vigilance, no villainous dragon would slip through the cracks.

But an omega might, Bertram thought as he set down the letter and picked up his quill, and if that was the case, he had no time to waste. The fact that Sorin was alive after pulling off a stunt like that was nothing short of a miracle, and Bertram did not intend to squander it. The boys needed their father, and Bertram...

Bertram needed Sorin, too.

He never should have let him go.

So he would bring him home before the council realized their mistake.

An extremely aggrieved Geoffrey arrived at Castle Beithir before the week's end, summoned to Scotland by Bertram's letter. He was to help the nursemaids with the whelps while Bertram stepped out on business.

"Between you and Father," Geoffrey grumbled, "I shan't have a moment's rest. What in the world is going on out there, Bertram? Father hasn't deigned to tell me."

"It's confidential, I'm afraid."

"It always is." Geoffrey turned up his nose. "Yet somehow I still end up getting involved. I really would rather the two of you stay here, in Amethyst territory. Whatever is happening out there can be addressed by the appropriate clans. We needn't stick our noses into everything."

"I agree with you," said Bertram, then promptly left for Constantinople to do exactly that.

22

BERTRAM

By the time Bertram arrived in Constantinople, a strange feeling told him Sorin had left the city, but he didn't let it deter him, as there was only one way he could have gone. With all other routes blocked off, the wayward omega fled across the desert, and the Amethyst agent followed.

Passage wasn't quick, nor was it easy. From pilgrimage to caravan, from carrack to litter, Sorin slipped from group to group, never lingering in any place for long. Bertram followed the rumors of him like perfume on the breeze through towns so small, they had no name, and into the campsites of those who wandered, but who were never lost. Every time Bertram left empty-handed and heavyhearted, but he pushed ever onward, fueled by his drive to correct the wrong he'd done, until his persistence brought him all the way to the sprawling city of Beirut, where the air was spiced and the sky was so blue, it made the ocean jealous. There, in the heat of the midday sun, Bertram glimpsed what he thought was a flash of Sorin's hair as someone hurried down an alley, but when he charged around the corner in pursuit, there was no one there.

The chase continued, and would continue until he brought Sorin home.

With the trail having gone cold, Bertram scoured the city, searching for clues as to Sorin's whereabouts. It seemed hopeless at first, but then the owner of a local inn confided in him that he'd declined service to a strange young man several hours ago—one with dark hair and travel-worn clothes who'd tried to pay for his lodgings with gold coins. It seemed to him, the innkeeper said, that the young man was a thief, and not worth housing. How else could an unaccompanied omega come into the possession of such wealth?

Bertram didn't comment on the coin, but he did press for further details.

According to the innkeeper, the young man had been quite irate, but calmed upon seeing another omega, one who was traveling in a small group headed for Damascus. While he wasn't sure, it seemed to him as though the young man had followed them as they left.

It was all Bertram needed.

He began the journey to Damascus that same day.

Most made the journey by camelback, but camels weren't creatures known for agility or stealth, so Bertram set off on foot. He followed the road at a distance, navigating uneven and sometimes difficult terrain, but despite his progress, he saw neither hide nor hair of Sorin.

Hours passed.

Day wore into night and still there was nothing.

His omega was nowhere to be found.

By the time the stars were at their brightest, Bertram's hope had dwindled. Perhaps the innkeeper had been wrong, and Sorin hadn't come this way at all. There was a chance—and a good one at that—that Sorin had doubled back to Constantinople. It would make much more sense to have returned now that time had passed and travel restrictions had likely eased than to set off on a fool's journey to Damascus, where he knew not the lay of the land or the ins and outs of its cloister.

But just as Bertram convinced himself to turn around, he spotted it.

A light on the horizon.

A campfire.

Could it be?

It was a long shot, surely, but Bertram's heart believed.

He hurried down from the hillock on which he was perched and cut through the desert in the direction of the campfire. It was housed in what seemed to be the remnants of an ancient sandstone ruin. The walls—what was left of them—had been eroded by time to such an extreme that it was hard to tell what kind of building had once been there, but Bertram didn't care to know. He rounded the outcrop, keeping to the shadows, and spied upon the campfire.

It had not been left unattended. Sorin was on his knees in front of it, frantically rooting through a satchel.

And he was not alone.

Next to him was a painfully slender omega. The poor thing looked half-starved, but there was a glimmer of intelligence in his eyes that told Bertram he was not as helpless as he appeared. Could he be from the cloister in Constantinople? Bertram took a closer look. The omega's fair, curly hair told him it was unlikely, but why, then, would Sorin have followed him out all this way?

He decided to stay hidden for now.

It was better he get a clearer picture of what was going on before making himself known.

"I'm sorry," Sorin said as he rifled through the bag. "Sorry. So sorry. I... I didn't mean to. I really didn't."

"It barely hurts," said the omega, touching a shallow wound on his neck, which was bleeding slightly. "I will be fine."

"Here." Sorin pulled a strip of tattered fabric from inside the satchel and brought it to the omega. He moved strangely—stiffly. The last time Bertram had seen him so tense was in Unwin's lair, when he'd been soaked in blood and threatening Bertram with a knife. "Use this. Pressure will stop the bleeding."

"Thank you."

Sorin grunted in acknowledgment, then sat heavily in front of his companion. It was unlike him to be so graceless. What had happened in the time they'd been separated? Bertram feared the worst.

"Which cloister are you from?" Sorin asked as the omega tended to his injury.

"I am from the Sapphire cloister in Frisia."

"You've come far. It won't be hard for you to escape."

"Escape?" The omega frowned. "I haven't a clue what you mean. I have been contracted to a dragon, and am now under his care. No one is pursuing me—I've done nothing wrong."

"No, it's…" Sorin's shoulders tightened as though in pain, and he shook his head wildly before continuing. "You're in danger."

"Danger?"

"It's all a lie." Sorin leaned forward, eliminating an uncomfortable amount of space between himself and the omega. "What they teach you in the Pedigree is wrong. There isn't such a thing as egg madness. It's—"

At that exact moment, Bertram's weight dislodged a hunk of crumbling sandstone from beneath his feet. The noise it made as it tumbled into the sand was slight, but in the quiet of the night, with just the crackling of the fire and a hushed conversation to mask it, Bertram may as well have shouted out that he was there.

Sorin sprang to his feet and pulled the omega up with him. The poor creature was so startled he dropped the scrap of fabric he'd been holding to his neck, but it was of little consequence, because as soon as he was on his feet, Sorin rushed behind him and held a knife up to his throat. "Who's there?"

Bertram winced, but chose not to step out of the shadows, lest Sorin spook and harm the omega. "It's me. Bertram."

"*Frederich.*" Sorin relaxed, but only for a moment. A blink of an eye later, the tension returned to his shoulders, and he held the knife that much more tightly against the poor omega's throat. "What are you doing here? Where are the whelps?"

"Safe at home. You needn't worry. I've made sure they will be well cared for in my absence."

Sorin shook his head like he was chasing away a fly. "You can't be here. You need to go."

"Why?" Bertram took a step forward, approaching the glow of the campfire. "You liberated the cloister in Constantinople and walked away with your life. What more could you want?"

"You know *exactly* what I want."

"It's impossible and you know it."

"You only say that because no one has tried it before, but I've succeeded once, and I'll do it again. If you knew what it's like in my head, you'd do it, too. On your life, you'd never let another omega suffer like I have. Even if you had to walk away from everything you knew. Everything you *loved.*"

The word hung heavily between them.

Too heavily.

It felt as though it had torn the bottom out of his chest.

"You love me?" he asked quietly, looking into Sorin's eyes. They were fearful and wild, but they were tempered with longing. Heartbreak. Desire for something both of them wanted, but that could never be.

"Of course I love you." Sorin's voice shook, and in a moment of weakness, he dropped his gaze. "If the world was different, I never would have left. I would have stayed with you. When I was with you, I was happy. Everything was *good.* But how could I live with myself if I did nothing? I couldn't. You don't understand, Frederich—I *want* to go home. I *want* to be with you and the whelps, but there are thousands of omegas who need my help. Who need to be saved. If I don't do this, no one will. How can I abandon them?"

The frightened omega Sorin held at knifepoint whimpered.

Sorin winced and eased the blade away from his neck.

"There are other ways," Bertram said softly. "What if I told you I would help? That I could give us what we both want? Because I can't stand to be without you, Sorin. The days since you've been gone have been as dark and lifeless as if the sun had vanished from the sky, and I can't take it anymore. I love you, too. I love you more than I thought I could love anything. With you, I feel like me again."

Sorin winced again.

Bertram wanted to go to him, to hold him, to heal his broken heart, but he dared not approach in fear of what might happen to the omega held at knifepoint should Sorin spook.

"I should not have let you go," he said instead, speaking softly, hoping beyond hope that his words were getting through to Sorin and he might reconsider. "Please. Please, let me make this right. I love you, and I will do better. I swear it. Just… let me bring you home."

In the firelight, the tears in Sorin's eyes were easy to see. He urged the captive omega forward, approaching Bertram, when suddenly he stopped. Above the crackle of the campfire came a sound.

Something whirred overhead.

Sorin jerked his head upward to look at it, and Bertram followed suit.

There, circling the skies of the campsite, was a dragon.

When it saw it had been detected, it stopped spiraling and cut toward Sorin at a staggering speed. Sorin stumbled backward, bringing the omega with him, only to bump into something that hadn't been there a second before—Bertram's brute of a brother, Sebastian.

Before Bertram could react, a growling Sebastian pried the

knife out of Sorin's hand and brandished it against his throat. *"Let my omega go."*

Bertram's training couldn't save him—the moment the knife bit into Sorin's skin, a violent fury rose up inside of him that could not be repressed. The next second, the world went black.

His dragon had taken control.

23

SORIN

Bertram stepped out of the shadows as the knife the dragon held to Sorin's neck slipped, breaking his skin. The cut wasn't deep, but it stung enough that Sorin hissed through his teeth in pain.

Wet heat pooled on the blade.

Blood.

Sorin's gaze shot up to Bertram's face just in time to see his nostrils flare.

Murder lit his eyes.

As blood trickled down Sorin's neck, Bertram's lip pulled back in an ugly snarl, and with no other warning than that, he bolted across the campsite and toward the villainous dragon holding Sorin captive, his claws out and raised, ready to kill.

"No!" cried the omega captive. He was a delicate thing, little more than skin and bones, but he was fierce. With a surprising display of strength, he threw his whole weight into escaping Sorin's grasp—and succeeded—but he did not run away from the fight. He threw himself into it instead, jumping in front of Bertram right as he was about to tear into the dragon who had stolen Sorin's knife.

Unable to stop in time, Bertram's claws sliced into the omega like blades.

The poor thing shrieked in agony, and the dragon behind Sorin let loose with a strangled cry that rang in Sorin's ears. Bertram reared back, eyes wide with horror, but it was too late. There was nothing he could do. The damage was already done.

It was too much.

All of it was too much.

The noise in Sorin's head—echoes of his lost babies—flared up, ringing in his ears. His head throbbed. His whole body felt like it was falling apart, but his skull was the worst offender. It threatened to split open from the force of the dark thoughts ricocheting in his mind.

You are the one responsible.

The omega is hurt because of you.

Who do you think you are, tempting fate like this?

You were lucky in Constantinople, and now that omega is paying for your hubris.

A scream ripped out of Sorin's throat that shook with panic and pain and primal fear. He hadn't wanted this. He had wanted to do good—to help the omega escape a dragon who would pillage his body at best, and sentence him to a life of suffering at worst. But wanting something was a hollow gesture. Want never changed anything. It had not changed the council, it had not changed society, and it would not change this.

If he wanted to fix this, he had to *do* something.

So although it could mean his life, he gritted his teeth and tugged on the dragon's wrist to try to get out from under the knife.

To his surprise, it worked.

The dragon released him and pushed him away.

Sorin stumbled to catch his footing, then scrambled desperately toward the omega, nearly tripping over his own feet in his haste, but at that very moment, the dragon that had been circling overhead landed clumsily right next to him, thumping out the campfire and plunging them all into darkness. Chaos followed. Voices screaming. Confusion. Panicked footsteps through shifting sand. Sorin turned, not sure where to go, as the noise in his head grew louder.

The omega.

Where was the omega?

He had to save him from the dragon.

He had to set him free.

"Omega?" Sorin shouted, but his voice was lost beneath the commotion of everything else going on. He stumbled forward, lost but desperate. "*Omega?*"

Someone grabbed him from behind.

"*No!*" Sorin hissed, twisting, struggling. He beat his fists against the arms around him, but they were strong, and they held fast. They would not let him save anyone. Perhaps not even himself.

The screaming in his head reached a fevered pitch, and Sorin screamed with it, clawing at his hair as he was dragged away. A hand clamped over his mouth, silencing him, but he screamed regardless. Screamed for what he feared might happen to the delicate omega. Screamed for what he couldn't fix, and for the future that might be. He fought until he was worn out and screamed until he'd gone hoarse, but by then, it was too late. He'd been carried through the desert to somewhere new—a place where the crumbled remains of ancient pillars rose up through the sand and a stretch of eroded rubble no more than two feet tall was all that remained of a great wall from long ago.

Wherever it was, he already knew it was too far from the campsite to ever dream of finding his way back.

He'd never free that poor omega now.

"Let me go," Sorin croaked when at last the hand removed itself from over his mouth. His throat burned from overuse, but the effort of speaking through the pain proved to be worth it—the arms let him go. Sorin broke away violently, wanting to run, to hide, to find a way back to save that doomed omega, but he only managed to stagger a few paces before his knees buckled and he fell. The sand caught him, roughing up the palms of his hands, but it did nothing to stop his stomach from turning.

He felt like he would be sick.

Not from the pain, but from the anguish of it all.

He couldn't get the omega's scream out of his head.

As he fought to hold back his nausea, there came a sound from next to him—the shifting of sand as it gave way to substantial weight. Sorin glanced in its direction from the corner of his eye and saw his assailant had dropped to his knees beside him.

It was Bertram.

His enemy, come to capture him. His lover, who couldn't stay away.

"Leave me be," Sorin muttered. He pushed stiffly off his hands and sank onto his haunches, giving Bertram a withering look neither of them believed.

Bertram blinked at him in wonder.

It was an odd and somewhat innocent gesture—almost as though he'd never looked upon an omega before.

"Leave me be, Bertram," Sorin repeated, more firmly this time.

Bertram blinked and cocked his head.

His pupils were reptilian—elongated swollen slits. Why were they still that way? Sorin could have sworn he heard him speaking to the others during the chaos at the campsite. He had been human enough then, but now...

"Bertram?"

The name did not register.

The dragon came round and sat in front of Sorin, and Sorin frowned, looking from the scales on his cheeks, to his claws, to the sharpened tips of his fangs as they peeked out over his bottom lip. When Bertram blinked again, a clear second eyelid swept over his eyes.

"You're not Bertram, are you?" Sorin asked quietly.

Bertram did not reply.

It seemed the monster in him had taken over.

The man Sorin loved was gone.

SORIN

"Have you come to kill me?" Sorin asked the beast.

It looked at him curiously through Bertram's slitted eyes and shuffled closer, but showed no signs of hostility. It sat where it was, watching him quietly, and after a moment of thoughtful—almost nervous—hesitation, it laid its hand on Sorin's thigh.

Shyly, it started to stroke.

Sorin looked at the offending hand, then at the creature. Dragons were all teeth and fire—selfish, destructive things that only took and never gave. There had to be an ulterior motive behind this kindness... and though it churned Sorin's stomach to think about it, he was fairly sure he already knew what it was.

To test what he believed to be true, he laid his hand on top of the dragon's and pushed with just enough pressure to force the dragon to stop.

The dragon would not stop, of course.

It would ignore what Sorin wanted and keep touching him, growing bolder and bolder until it finally forced itself upon him just like every other dragon had before. He had foolishly let himself believe that Bertram would be different, but in the end, he was a monster just like the rest of them. He would take what he wanted and make Sorin his, and the cycle would start all over again.

But as Sorin stilled the dragon's hand, the unexpected happened.

The dragon did not fight him.

It stopped.

"Bertram?" Sorin asked cautiously.

The dragon gave him a toothy grin far removed from Bertram's typical brand of suave, then leaned forward and rested its head on Sorin's shoulder.

Sorin's heart stood still.

It could tear into his neck if it wanted to—it was close enough Sorin felt the puff of its breath on his skin—but murder didn't seem to be on its mind. Rather than rend flesh, it turned its hand so its palm was against Sorin's and, ever careful of its claws, wove their fingers together.

Gently, very gently, it squeezed.

"You shouldn't have come," Sorin whispered, but he did not take his hand away. He didn't know if the dragon understood, or if Bertram could hear him, but it didn't matter. He would not die docile and submissive. If these were to be his last moments, he needed to speak his piece. "I was doing fine on my own, even when the screaming got bad again. I found those runaway omegas, and we freed my friends together."

The dragon made a chirping sound and touched its nose to Sorin's neck. Sorin's jaw went slack, and he closed his eyes, leaning into the touch.

Why did it feel so good?

"I would have saved that traveling omega, too," he went on in a quiet voice, shivering in pleasure as the dragon nuzzled beneath his jaw. "I was so close. If you hadn't distracted me, we would have gotten away. I could have changed the course of his life."

The dragon whined shamefully, stirring a paternal part of Sorin that only made the screaming worse. He winced and squeezed his eyes shut against the pain. It was only after the flare subsided that he noticed he'd tangled his free hand in the dragon's hair tightly enough to hurt it.

But the dragon didn't retaliate.

It let go of Sorin's hand and gathered him in its arms, drawing him onto its lap.

"Mine," it said in a voice that wasn't quite Bertram's. It cupped the back of his head and guided it down to its shoulder. "Mine."

"I'm sorry," Sorin choked out in a whisper. Tears flowed freely down his cheeks. He let go of the dragon's hair and stroked it, desperate to apologize.

How could he hate something and love it so much at the same time?

Why couldn't things be easier?

All he wanted was to be free.

"I shouldn't have blamed you," Sorin said. "I should have been more careful. If I'd been paying attention, tonight never would have happened. I wouldn't have been taken by surprise, and you... you never would have..." A lump formed in his throat, and Sorin buried his face against the dragon's shoulder to stave off a sob. "I wanted to save him," he admitted in a thin and tear-strained voice. "I thought if I took him away, he'd be safe, but now he's... he's..."

The dragon wrapped him up in its arms and nuzzled its scaled cheek against the side of Sorin's head.

Sorin broke.

He didn't just sob—he wailed.

What good was he if he couldn't save the one who needed him the most? Whether he lived or died, that omega was doomed, and it was all Sorin's fault. All of it.

Why had he ever thought he could do this?

Dragons were vicious, powerful creatures, and he was but one man.

It took a long time to cry it all out, but the dragon held him through all of it, never asking for anything in return. When

Sorin's sobs devolved into whimpers and he had no more tears left to cry, it pressed a very human-feeling kiss into his hair and nosed affectionately against his scalp. "You did well, Sorin," Bertram—not the dragon—whispered. "You did so incredibly well finding those Ruby omegas and setting the Constantinople cloister free. I am proud of you. One failure doesn't change that. What you've accomplished has done the world good, and it would be a shame if you were to give up on it. If you must blame someone for what happened tonight, don't let it be yourself —blame me."

"I hate you," Sorin whispered, voice quavering beneath the weight of the lie.

"I know."

"You've ruined everything."

"I know that, too."

"Will you take me home?"

Bertram pushed air through his nostrils—a humorless laugh. "Only if you promise not to give up."

Dragons really were merciless, weren't they? Always wanting precious things.

But just this once, Sorin indulged that bestial instinct and gave Bertram his word.

BERTRAM

They spent the night huddled together for warmth, Bertram keeping Sorin safe from the desert's unforgiving chill, and continued on the next morning. Bertram wished he could have stayed to help heal Sebastian's poor injured omega, but with Sorin now in his custody, it was impossible. He had already lost control once, and with disastrous consequences—if he stayed, he feared it might happen again.

No wonder agents of the council were trained to detach themselves from their emotions.

As cool and collected Frederich, such a thing never would have happened.

But Bertram had not been Frederich for some time, and he feared that when it came to Sorin, he might never be Frederich again.

They arrived in Beirut around mid-afternoon. Bertram secured them lodging at an inn—not the same one Sorin had been spotted in before—and Sorin took immediate advantage of the bed, falling asleep as soon as his head hit the pillow. He was not well, and the sleep was needed. Bertram had not imagined it when he'd spotted Sorin at his campsite—during their time apart,

Sorin's condition had deteriorated, and he was just as paranoid and tense as he had been while searching for his eggs in Unwin's lair. Bags had formed beneath his eyes, and he had lost noticeable weight.

It was worrying.

Bertram would have to keep an eye on him to make sure he was eating. Hopefully a full belly would help him shake the grip his madness had on him. It seemed a plausible remedy—he had been doing so well before.

In any case, there was nothing he could do about it now. Sleep came first, and everything else would follow. In the meantime, Bertram occupied himself by planning their travel back to Scotland. He had taken a risk going through Constantinople with his father and the other Amethyst agents on the scene, but now that he was with Sorin, he could not afford to take a risk like that again. They would have to go another way. By sea, perhaps. It seemed the most feasible alternative.

But there was an issue.

What had become of the liberated omegas?

It was clear Sorin was connected to them, but they had not been with him at the campsite, and Bertram did not know if they were waiting for Sorin to return.

He worked around the variable, plotting a few possible routes to account for the most likely scenarios, then ate a light dinner and tried to sleep without much success. His mind was racing, his conscience heavy.

He recalled all too well the pain he had accidentally inflicted on that omega—what should have been a warning for his brother had turned into a near fatal blow.

It was not like an agent of the council to feel guilt.

Like every other emotion, it was trained out of them during apprenticeship, as it was a detriment to their line of work. A point of weakness. Not befitting of any dragon who was to be the council's tool.

Yet Bertram felt it—the knot in the pit of his stomach.

The sense he had done wrong.

He sat at the foot of the bed, not wanting to disrupt Sorin, and curled and uncurled his clawed fingers, watching them gleam in the dying light.

He had never lost control like that before. Most times, his dragon was relegated to the back of his mind, a lurking presence and nothing more. It—like unchecked emotion—was dangerous. Too reactive. A hazard.

But it had never been an issue before.

Not until Sorin.

Darkness crept through the room and suddenly, it was night. Bertram, who had sat far too long with his thoughts, stood and stretched the stiffness out of his body. He could not change what had happened, but he could make sure it never happened again.

He would keep Sorin safe from others, and by doing so, he would keep others safe from himself.

———

Sorin woke terrified in the middle of the night, gasping as though he was drowning. He bolted into an upright position and snatched at the blankets wildly, no doubt to try to throw them aside, but froze when Bertram spoke.

"You're safe," Bertram said. He sat by the window, watching the stars as he idly flicked a flame in and out of existence. "You're with me. We're in Beirut. There is nothing to fear."

It took Sorin a moment, but he did manage to relax. "I thought it was a nightmare."

"Some of it, perhaps." Bertram did away with his flame. "But not all."

The silence that followed was heavy, and Bertram broke it as soon as he could.

"We must return to Scotland quickly," he said. "My brother

Geoffrey is with the whelps, and he no doubt wishes to go home. But you have business to tend to, don't you? The liberated omegas weren't with you in the desert. Are they waiting for you? We can take an extra few days to go to them so they know you are safe and well. If you do not want me involved with it, I understand, but I would be glad to offer my assistance in helping them secure lodging somewhere the council would never think to look for them."

"No." Sorin paused, and after a moment of consideration, said, "The omegas from the Ruby cloister are adept at hiding in plain sight, and have secured lodging with the coin you gave me that should keep them safe indefinitely. They don't need help. Even were I never to return, they would continue to be well, and I'm sure they will train the omegas from the cloister in Constantinople to be just as self-sufficient."

"But surely they will want to know what happened to you."

"Maybe." Guilt troubled Sorin's face, and he stared dejectedly at his blanketed knees. "But if I am going home with you, what difference does it make? My time with them is over."

"I wouldn't be so sure."

Sorin glanced up at him, studying him through the darkness. "What do you mean?"

"I told you I would help," Bertram said, flicking the sphere of fire he'd been toying with back into existence. "I told you there was a way we could both get what we want, and I am a dragon of my word. If you believe your friends will be fine on their own, then let us return to Scotland for now while I think things through. I have a plan, and should it withstand the scrutiny of my idle mind during the trip home, you shan't be saying goodbye to your friends forever."

Sorin eyed him. "I would question you if my head didn't feel like it was about to fall off, but I am in too much pain to interrogate the truth out of you." He dropped onto the bed and draped his arm over his eyes. "Will you come to bed? You don't have to sleep if you don't want to, but I rest easier when you're near."

Bertram rose and crossed the room, unlacing his clothing as he went. He was naked by the time he arrived at the bedside, and climbed up onto the bed carefully. Straddling Sorin on his elbows and knees, he laid his forehead atop Sorin's arm.

"Do you trust me?" he asked quietly, not needing much volume with their faces so close.

Sorin puffed out a soundless laugh. "I probably shouldn't, but I do."

"Then trust me." Bertram pressed a gentle kiss to Sorin's arm before flopping onto the bed by his side. "I will make things right."

Sorin hummed noncommittally and tucked himself under Bertram's arm. He fell asleep, but Bertram stayed up a while longer. There were too many thoughts he needed to entertain, and things he needed to do.

26

SORIN

Time dulled the sharp edges of Sorin's guilt, but it did not take them away. He dwelt on the fate of the fair-haired omega all the way from Beirut to Braemar, feeling miserable to have failed him and unable to forgive himself for it, until Castle Beithir appeared on the horizon and gave him something else to think about—the boys.

Did they know he was coming home?

He pictured the four of them at play, tumbling over each other in a bid to nip each other's tails, all stopping at once upon spotting him. There would be a moment of shock, then a sudden rush of clicking claws and a chorus of tiny chirps and purrs.

Would they all still be able to fit in his arms?

He didn't know. Couldn't know. But his heart swelled near to bursting with the desire to find out.

As those thoughts took hold, Sorin craned his neck and peered at the castle from his place on the saddle behind Bertram, watching as the sunrise unveiled it from the shadows. Would the boys even be awake when they made it home? If they rode quickly enough, perhaps he could surprise them by being there as they woke up.

Unless they hate you for leaving, said the darkness. *You didn't only fail that omega—you failed them, too.*

As though in agreement, the cries of his lost children grew sharper. Shriller.

Sorin winced and pressed his forehead against Bertram's back.

In an attempt to calm himself, he closed his eyes and breathed.

The air was full of Bertram's scent—sweat, and dust, and horse, with a note of alpha beneath—and beyond that was the smell of the Highlands. Of home. Wildflowers and tall grass. The crisp chill of the morning. It was familiar, and it was good, and in it, Sorin found some reprieve. The cries faded, the pounding in his head lessened, and the dark thoughts drifted away.

He was home.

He was here with Bertram, and while he was not perfect, he was loved—and no matter what his mind told him, that was enough.

Bertram let their mare set her own lazy pace, and by the time they reached the castle, the morning was well underway. A young stablehand appeared as if by magic upon their approach and helped Sorin down from the saddle before taking the mare from Bertram. With her reins in hand, he offered his dragon lord a polite bow of his head, then turned to lead the mare away.

The sunlight glinted off something in his hair—a pearl, stuck on a hairpin.

"Are you Beatrix's sweetheart?" Sorin blurted out.

The stablehand stopped and looked over his shoulder at Sorin, color high in his cheeks. "Pardon?"

"I apologize—I do not mean to pry. It's just... Beatrix tends to the whelps in the morning, and I thought perhaps you might know when they wake these days, if only through conversation with her. I've been gone for quite some time, and I fear by now their schedule has changed from the one I knew."

The stablehand glanced nervously at Bertram, and upon finding him engaged with a very harried-looking Hamish, guided the mare around so he was facing Sorin. "Aye," he said in a hushed voice. "Should you hurry, you might find them asleep."

"Thank you."

The stablehand nodded, then left with the mare, cheeks blazing.

Hamish was less easy to dismiss.

When Sorin came up to Bertram's side, Hamish was in the midst of describing an incident in the garden involving the heather and a sudden surplus of "reptilian fertilizer" that had *not* been there before. Hamish, who took great care in tending to the grounds, was none too pleased about it, but even as he ranted, Bertram wore an easy smile that made it seem like at any moment, he might laugh.

He was glad to be back, Sorin realized.

Glad for the castle, as quirky as its servants could be, and happy to be home.

Heart warming, he put his head on Bertram's shoulder and wove their fingers together. It would not be like this forever, but what mattered was that it was like this for now. What sense was there in worrying what would happen in the months to come?

He was home, he was safe, and he was *happy*.

It had been such a long time since he'd last felt that way.

As he clasped hands with Bertram, Hamish stopped speaking mid-sentence and stared at them with wide eyes. He mumbled something about the primrose, excused himself, and took off in a hobbling hurry, not once looking back.

"Scoundrel," Bertram accused Sorin lightheartedly. "You spooked Hamish. Have you forgotten our game of pretend? Dragons are expected to have their dalliances with betas. We mustn't flaunt ourselves in front of the servants lest they tattle and inform my father."

"The servants are already well aware," Sorin retorted. "We have not been subtle. And besides, your father knows. He discovered us in bed together. But enough of that." He squeezed Bertram's hand, then let it go. "There will be time for us to bicker later. Would you come with me to see the children? If we hurry, we might be able to be there with them as they wake."

A softness came over Bertram's eyes. "Let's hurry, then."

Together they left the courtyard, and Bertram took Sorin home.

Sorin had been away longer than he cared to admit, but he still knew the corridors of the castle by heart. With Bertram on his tail, he hurried from the grounds to the nursery, passing by several of the nursemaids, who all seemed shocked by his return. They must not have expected to see him again.

Sorin waved to them in passing, but didn't stop to talk. His feet moved of their own accord, knowing only a few walls separated him from the children.

Not oceans.

Not countries.

Walls.

In minutes they'd be reunited.

Leaving them had been the hardest thing he'd ever had to do.

Hands trembling, Sorin opened the nursery door and led Bertram inside. The whelps—all four of them—were asleep on the bed. Owyn had buried his head under a small hill of golden treasure, while Piers slept atop a pillow, the sun shining on his dark scales. The other two were hidden under the blankets, but Sorin would have recognized those bumps anywhere. He approached the bed while Bertram closed the door, and was a moment away from climbing up to join his babies when Piers lazily lifted his head and blinked open his eyes.

Sorin froze. He didn't even breathe. Pulse pounding in his ears, he watched Piers watching him.

"Hello, baby," he said at last, voice quavering. "I'm home."

Piers squawked a frantic note of delight and half ran, half flew across the bed, nearly bowling Owyn over in his haste. Sorin laughed and opened his arms, catching him, but was not nearly as ready for the other three whelps, who all sprang out of bed and rushed over to him, eager for his touch. Their combined force knocked Sorin over, and he fell onto the bed laughing as they licked his face and butted under his arms. They were indeed bigger now than when he'd left—too large to sit on his shoulder, and certainly too big to fit on him all at once—so they made a game of pushing each other off him and tussling for his love.

Through their bond, they showered him with joy.

"Piers, be nice, now," Bertram warned as he joined Sorin and the whelps on the bed. Piers had taken to nipping at Waryn's toes in an attempt to get him to leave Sorin's arms—a tactic Waryn was none too fond of. He shook his small foot in the air like it stung while ribbons of smoke poured from his nostrils.

"Have they learned to summon flame?" Sorin asked as Piers climbed over him to Bertram, who took him into his arms.

"Aye." Bertram gave Piers a cheeky look. "And it seems they've learned to use their teeth, too."

Piers butted his head under Bertram's chin in apology, then made way as Edmund joined him on Bertram's chest. The two settled down quickly, allowing Bertram to hold them, and oh, was it unfair how handsome he looked as a doting father. Sorin's heart skipped a beat and, unable to help himself, he laid a tender hand on Bertram's thigh.

Bertram looked up from the boys as Sorin touched him, smiling from the depths of his soul, and in that single perfect moment, the anxiety and heartbreak Sorin had endured during his time abroad melted away. There were still battles to be waged and wars to be won, but in this moment, there was peace.

If only it could last forever.

For it was only blissful moments like these that ever seemed to hush the screams that pounded like war drums in his head.

A sound woke Sorin far too early the next morning. He groaned and cracked open an eye, and there was Bertram by the bedside, tugging on his hose.

"It's still dark," Sorin said through a yawn. "What are you doing getting dressed at this hour? Have you been called away?"

Bertram fastened his hose and with a final tug to make sure it was properly in place, turned to face Sorin. He curled his fingers through the air, and just like that, dragon fire popped into existence overhead, allowing them some light.

"Not quite," he said, holding his hand out to Sorin, "but I am an honest dragon, and I intend to keep my word."

Sorin looked at Bertram's hand, then lifted his gaze to look him in the eyes. Bertram smiled at him—a genuine smile—and offered his hand again.

"Come, Sorin," he said. "The morning is already well underway, and we have much to do."

"I don't follow," Sorin admitted hesitantly. "I wasn't aware we'd made plans."

"We didn't. But I did make you a promise." When Sorin was silent, Bertram elaborated. "I told you I would help you in your quest, and that there is a way to get what you want without having to be apart from me. I did not say it just to placate you. I truly did mean it sincerely, and now, I intend to show you how."

"You'll help me?" Sorin asked, surprised, but hesitantly hopeful.

"Aye. I promised I would."

"How?"

Bertram lifted Sorin's hand to his mouth and kissed his knuckles, love shining in his eyes. "I've had plenty of time to think it over," he said, "and the longer I dwelt on it, the clearer the solution became. As with the glassmith from Westminster, the only way to achieve the impossible is to come together and enhance your human ingenuity with my magical might."

A shiver ran through Sorin.

He squeezed Bertram's hand and let the dragon pull him out of bed. Bertram brought him close, then curled his finger beneath Sorin's chin and lifted it to steal a kiss from his lips.

"Get dressed, love," Bertram said when the kiss concluded, alight with an excitement that truly made him come alive. "When you're ready, come meet me in my study, and together we'll change the world."

27

BERTRAM

Change came one mindful step at a time, and it started that morning in Bertram's study not with any kind of heroic gesture, but through the simple act of listening. Too much time had been wasted on disbelief. It had been easy to pretend that Sorin was delusional—much easier than to admit the terrible truth—but that ended today. The society Bertram had been born into was not the utopia his people made it out to be, and if he was to see it for what it truly was, it was his responsibility to hear what the ones failed by it had to say.

It was not a short conversation.

Sorin spoke of his past in detail, from his upbringing in the Pedigree up until Unwin's death, and spared no detail as to how he had been mistreated. The claims he made were so far removed from what Bertram knew that they seemed outrageous at best, but he did not interrupt. He held his tongue and listened, reminding himself that he did not always know best. Sorin had proved him wrong about egg madness, after all, and it stood to reason that was not the only lie Bertram had been raised to believe was the truth.

So he stayed quiet and receptive, and when all was said and

done, rather than tell Sorin that he knew nothing and that he was mad, Bertram looked him in the eyes and said, "What do you think must be done to prevent other omegas from suffering like this?"

Then let him speak again.

It was noon by the time Sorin finished, and by then the whelps —all four of them—had stolen into the study. Owyn curled up on Bertram's lap and the others settled by his feet, watching as their father paced the room and explained in no uncertain terms his plans to liberate every last cloister.

When finally he stopped pacing, the three whelps on the floor went to him. Edmund weaved around his legs and Waryn lay across his feet. Piers vied for his attention in a different way—he climbed onto Sorin's abandoned chair and stood on his hind legs to look imploringly over the back of the chair at his father.

His plan worked.

Sorin leaned over and kissed him atop his head, prompting the other whelps to scramble up onto the chair beside him, little claws digging into the top of the chair back and necks craned in hopes of kisses.

"Would you give me a day to think on what you've said?" Bertram asked as Owyn hopped off his lap and went to join his brothers. "I came into our meeting this morning with an idea as to how to proceed, but having heard all you've had to say, I want to make sure I factor what I've learned into my plans before I bring them to you for consideration. Is that acceptable?"

Sorin's dark eyes found him from across the room.

They warmed with happiness.

"I'll give you more than a day if you promise not to wake me at such an ungodly hour again."

Bertram chuckled.

He could work with that.

"The plan," said Bertram the next afternoon, unrolling a marked map of the world across the desk in his study, "is an ambitious one, but regardless, I am of the opinion that it is within our means."

Sorin pinched his brows together and craned his neck to get a better look at the map. Owyn sat on his lap, anchoring him in place. "What are all of those red dots?" he asked.

"Cloister locations." Bertram tapped one of them. "The ones the council has been made aware of, at least. It is possible there could be secret cloisters being operated by some of the less savory clans, and should that be the case, I will update this map as we learn of them."

"And this black dot?"

"It's the location of Castle Beithir, in which we currently reside."

Sorin sank back in his chair and idly stroked the spines on Owyn's back. He frowned. "I didn't realize there were so many cloisters."

"Aye. There may not be many dragons left, but the Pedigree has not suffered a similar decline. Some cloisters contain but a few omegas, but they remain operational. Do you see now why it would be impossible for one omega to liberate them all?"

"I suppose I do."

"Which is why our focus must shift from total liberation to something more manageable and discreet. You said the Ruby omegas who escaped their cloister are resilient and resourceful, not only able to survive in your absence, but capable enough to teach the omegas from the Constantinople cloister how to do the same. These omegas... do you consider them allies?"

Sorin's eyes sharpened. "I do."

"Then here is what I propose." Bertram moved away from the table to the chess set he kept in the corner. From it, he took several pawns, but placed only one of them on his return to the table—a black pawn he positioned over the dot representing

Castle Beithir. "Alone, we are limited in what we can expect to achieve. In your lifetime, you have already accomplished the impossible twice, and while I have tremendous respect for you, I am not foolish enough to believe you'll be able to do so again."

Sorin frowned in resignation.

He wouldn't admit it, but the troubled look in his eyes revealed he agreed.

"And even were your luck to hold," Bertram added, "with each new cloister you dismantled, the more your infamy would grow until every dragon would have heard of you... and unlike me, they would not hesitate to spill your blood. Especially should they catch you in the act. But together"—Bertram placed the other pawns near the dot marking the Constantinople cloister—"we are no longer bound by such limitations. Feats previously beyond the reach of a sole agent become possible. Our reach expands. Our power grows. One loss would not spell the end."

Sorin's gaze flicked up to meet his. "Are you suggesting we liberate omegas from one hell only to entrap them in another? I won't stand for it. They deserve freedom. If they don't want to fight, they shouldn't have to."

"I agree." Bertram fanned two pawns—one white, one black—between his fingers. "Which is why we will give them a choice. Every omega rescued will need to be rehabilitated in order to gain the skills they'll need to survive on their own. Those who wish to disengage from our society will be welcome to do so, and will be given all the support they need to help them on their way." The white pawn landed on the map with a clink, far from any red dot. "But those who wish to stay and fight, perhaps like those Ruby omegas you mentioned..."

"Would join us," Sorin murmured. "Of course."

Bertram nodded, eyes on the black pawn between his fingers. He turned it slowly round and round, then set it silently with the others clustered around the dot in Constantinople. "With my coin and my cunning, I can make this endeavor a reality. But Sorin, I must be honest with you. If we are to do this—if we are to involve the lives of many in this unseen war—a compromise must be reached. I understand your wish is to liberate every cloistered omega, but it is simply not possible. We must learn to pick our battles in order to protect the lives of our allies. They deserve our compassion as well."

Sorin did not argue, but he visibly prickled. "What do you propose?"

"For the safety of all parties, I propose we target only the cloisters committing wrongdoings. Those in which omegas are abused and illegal operations are uncovered."

"And what of the omegas who yearn for freedom, but who are trapped in cloisters that don't meet those criteria?"

"Provided their quality of life remains unchanged, they would be left to age out of the Pedigree as intended."

"Absolutely not." Sorin sat up in his chair so abruptly, Owyn hopped down and scurried out of the room. "Why should they be left to suffer, imprisoned despite having committed no crimes? All cloisters must be investigated, and the omegas in them who wish to leave must be freed. It is only right."

"I agree with you," Bertram said as levelly as he could. "And if we had the resources to do so, I would see it done in a heartbeat. The issue is, we don't. One day, perhaps, we might, but even should we, how are we to investigate every cloister without arousing the suspicion of the council? We must be strategic about the choices we make. I will not endanger the lives of the omegas who plead fealty to us, and I will not endanger you."

Sorin pinched his lips and stared stubbornly into Bertram's eyes, but Bertram would not be cowed.

"I am willing to commit treason for you, Sorin," Bertram murmured. "I am on your side. But if we are to succeed at this, we must find a way to compromise. We cannot scorch the earth and expect not to get burned."

"Says the dragon."

Bertram sighed. "I understand your disappointment. I wish there was another way, but I can only do so much. I am a dragon, not a god, and should we be discovered, I will not be spared any more than you will be. The punishment for betraying the council is death, and I will not be exempt simply because I am Grimbold Drake's son."

At that, Sorin frowned and looked away.

Slowly, he relaxed against the back of his chair.

"Ultimately, the decision is yours," Bertram said once Sorin had settled. "There are two ways this can go. Either we focus our efforts on saving the omegas who desperately need help right this very second, or we make them wait while we comb through cloisters one by one to save those who are unwilling participants in the Pedigree, but who are otherwise fine."

"Fine until a dragon breeds them," Sorin said despondently. He lowered his chin, ducking his gaze. "How can I leave them knowing there's a chance they'll suffer like I have? I don't want anyone else to have to hear the screaming of children they'll never have a chance to meet. All cloistered omegas must be freed."

Bertram's fingers curled around nothing.

He took a tentative step forward, wanting to reach out a hand, but knowing better. Sorin didn't need his platitudes—he needed him to stay strong.

"Clutches are rare," Bertram said softly, dropping his hand to his side. He glanced across the map, at the cluster of pawns surrounding Constantinople, and frowned. "Your experience leads you to believe otherwise, but you are not the norm. Most Pedigree omegas who are selected by a dragon will never produce an egg in their entire lives. If it weren't for you, there wouldn't have been a dragon born in centuries."

Sorin's expression grew distant, then became small and sad. He touched his fingers to his temple as though he was in pain, and without looking at Bertram, said, "Promise me you speak the truth."

"On the lives of our whelps, I swear it."

Sorin curled his fingers in his hair. It looked like he wanted to lash out, to spring forth, to let his madness go, but after a tense moment, all he did was draw a shaking breath and close his eyes.

He set his hand back on his lap.

"I accept," he said, and opened his eyes, meeting Bertram's gaze. "We will focus on the omegas who need us—those who are trapped in horrific conditions, and those who have slipped through the cracks and no longer have hope, like me all those years ago. But before we proceed, there are two conditions you must agree to."

"Name them, and we shall see."

"Firstly, should we come across another omega like the one I failed to rescue in the desert—one clearly in need of our help—we will find a way to help them. We will not leave them to suffer, for even though you claim clutches are rare, there is damage done when you are forced to share a dragon's bed."

Bertram pursed his lips, but after a moment spent in thought, he nodded. It was likely that in Sorin's short lifetime, they'd never come across such an omega again.

"Secondly..." Sorin took a deep, stabilizing breath. "If you ever betray me, you must understand that whatever agreement we come to will be rendered null and void. I agree that with our current resources, it would be a death sentence for me to forge out into the world and dismantle cloisters on my own, but in the future, that may change. At that time, I will not hesitate to do what I think is right if it means keeping omegas safe. Do you understand?"

Bertram said nothing.

He held Sorin's gaze.

Sorin did not look away, nor did he back down. He pierced Bertram with his eyes in a silent challenge, daring him to refuse, far braver than any human should be.

"I accept," Bertram said at last, and came around the table to shake Sorin's hand. "I won't betray you. Not now and not ever. For as much as you are mine, I am yours, Sorin. Your lover, your partner, and your co-conspirator. Other dragons may not listen to you, but I have heard you, and you have changed my mind. For you, I will betray the council, because what we do, we do for good."

"For good," Sorin said, and clasped his hand.

Business concluded, they left the room, but even in their absence, their pawns remained in play.

SORIN

There was a degree of risk in transporting escaped Pedigree omegas through dragon-owned territory, but with Bertram's knowledge of the council and the movements of its agents, it was a risk worth taking. Bertram orchestrated the journey from his study, plotting the safest paths and securing shelter at each checkpoint along the way, and even arranged for a generous sum to be sent to their future guests.

Were something to go wrong, he explained to Sorin one day while he and the whelps lounged next to him in the study, it was essential the omegas have the coin they'd need to survive on their own.

Sorin did not argue, but he did not entirely agree, for if something went wrong, coin would not be necessary. The council and its agents would show no mercy. Any captured omega was as good as dead.

But Sorin needn't have worried.

Weeks turned into months, and all continued to be well. Slowly but surely, the omegas drew nearer. According to Bertram's estimation, they would arrive at Castle Beithir any day now, and with their imminent arrival on his mind, Sorin found himself watching the horizon while he went about his daily routine, eager to be the first to spot their riding party plodding a steady path toward the castle through Braemar's hilly countryside.

What he was not expecting was for a dark shape to appear in the sky.

Sorin had been in the loch, playing with the boys, but when he saw it, he stopped.

His heart leapt into his throat.

The shape grew larger. Came closer. Became more defined.

It was heading straight for them.

Sorin gathered the boys in a panic and rushed them into the castle. He did not know if he had been spotted, did not know if this was the end, but he did know that if he did not hide, there would be no hope for him.

"*Bertram!*" he shouted as he dove out of sight of the doors, but it was far too late—his voice was swallowed by the *thump!* of a massive Amethyst dragon landing on the castle grounds. The game was over. All he could do was keep running and find a place to hide in the hopes that somehow, as impossible as it seemed, everything would be okay.

BERTRAM

"Brother," Bertram said cordially as his hulking battering ram of a brother burst through the front doors of the castle. "What business brings you here today?"

Sebastian answered by slamming his fist into Bertram's face.

The blow connected with a sickening, meaty sound and the *crunch* of crumpling cartilage. It knocked Bertram off balance, forcing him to take several steps back in order to find his footing.

Something wet slid over his lip.

He touched his hand to his face and discovered the something was blood.

"Ah." He looked from his bloody hand to his brother, who was advancing upon him in quite a menacing way. "That business. Yes. I should have known. Would you like to come up to my study to discuss what went on?"

Sebastian snarled and grabbed Bertram by his doublet, easily lifting him off his feet. "*You could have killed him.*"

Bertram had suffered fates far worse than mild strangulation, and as such, only choked a little when he replied, "Harming him was not my intention."

Sebastian did not care for that answer.

The corner of his lip curled back in contempt, and he pitched Bertram across the room like a rag doll. Bertram slammed into the wall shoulder-first, and with a *pop!* the joint gave. When he hit the ground, his arm flopped uselessly to his side.

"Bugger," he said through gritted teeth, taking hold of his lame arm with his opposite hand. "I quite liked that one."

"And I quite liked my omega," Sebastian seethed, "but that didn't stop you from flaying him alive."

"I stopped as soon as I realized what was happening."

"Your claws almost split him in half." Sebastian crossed the room as dark and brooding as a storm cloud and sank to his knees in front of him. Bertram braced for pain, but Sebastian had not come looking for blood. He grabbed Bertram's limp arm and shoved his shoulder back into its socket. "He is human, Bertram. He is small and weak. He almost died."

"It was an accident, and I am very deeply sorry that it happened."

Sebastian's eyebrow twitched, but otherwise, he kept his anger contained to his voice. "If you are truly so repentant, then why did you run? And in the company of a villainous cur, no less. Tell me why you would protect that villain over me, or I will not believe your apology sincere."

For strong and silent Sebastian, it was quite the speech. There was more at play here than hurt feelings. Bertram couldn't help but wonder if, perhaps, Sebastian had fallen in love with his Pedigree plaything, and searched his eyes for any hint it might be true, but Sebastian was not an expressive dragon, and all Bertram found there was quietly simmering rage.

"I was on business," Bertram said simply after a beat of silence. "You know I am not at liberty to discuss the work I do."

"Business that involved the protection of an omega holding my mate at knifepoint?"

"Your mate?" Bertram's eyebrows popped up in surprise. "Surely you jest, brother."

"I do not. Peregrine is my mate, and will be mine forever." Pride shone for a moment in Sebastian's eyes, but it was gone a second later, locked away behind his steely resolve. "Which is why you must tell me why it is you protected that vile creature. I must know so I can keep Peregrine safe."

"I am not at liberty to discuss the details of my mission."

Sebastian's eyes darkened with anger, but even as they did, Bertram held his gaze. He would not back down. No one could know what had happened that night, lest his secret come to light and his family be torn apart before his very eyes.

"But I will tell you this," he said. "Your mate is in no further danger. The situation has been resolved."

Sebastian pierced him with his cold, steely eyes, then reached out a hand, which Bertram took with his good one. With a yank, he pulled Bertram to his feet.

"One day," Sebastian said once Bertram was upright, "you will need to decide where your loyalty lies—with your duty, or with your family. When that day comes, I pray you remember that you are a Drake first and foremost, and Father's puppet second."

Bertram had nothing to say to that. He took the kerchief from his pocket and dabbed at the blood on his face.

Sebastian didn't stay for much longer after that—message delivered, he hurried back to his mate—but the ghost of him haunted Castle Beithir long after he'd left, whispering his parting words in Bertram's ear whenever his mind was idle.

I pray you remember that you are a Drake first and foremost, and Father's puppet second.

The line was impactful, but it was flawed.

Because when the time came, Bertram prayed that first and foremost, he would remember to be true to himself.

30

SORIN

Sorin bolted, fleeing far from sight before the dragon came through the castle doors. The boys scrambled after him, squeaking, anxious, not knowing what the matter was, or why their father was so afraid.

How could they?

They were too young to understand treason, too young to know what would happen to those who dared defy dragon law. They were innocent. And if this dragon was here to destroy them all for what Sorin had done, it was his duty to protect them. To hide them. Even if it meant his own life.

"Lord Sorin!" Agnes called anxiously from the doorway to the scullery, her voice thin and fearful. She had poked her head out and spotted him, no doubt having heard his pounding feet and the clamor of claws on stone. "In here, bairn," she bade him. "Come, now. Shan't no dragon think to look in here."

Sorin went to her instantly.

She barely had enough time to hobble out of the way before he barreled into the room, the whelps right on his heels.

"We need to hide them," he told her in a rush, breathless from having run and hoarse from fear. "I do not care what becomes of me, but we cannot let anything happen to them."

"In here," Agnes urged as she beckoned, throwing open the doors of a base cabinet in which scrap cloths and other cleaning supplies were kept. The whelps scurried over, piling in, and while it was a tight squeeze, they did all manage to fit inside. Agnes closed the doors on them, then gestured for Sorin to follow her. As the scullery maids looked on in fear, she brought Sorin deeper into the scullery to a back corner out of sight of the door. It was sectioned off from the rest of the room by a freestanding shelf used to store dishes, creating a small alcove in which buckets and basins were stored.

Agnes moved them all unceremoniously out of the way, and Sorin took their place.

He huddled in the corner, making himself as still and quiet as he could be, terrified but alert, listening for the footsteps he knew would be coming. If Agnes was wrong and the dragon did think to come in here, he would not hesitate. He would give his location away to save the boys. All it would take was one kicked bucket. His death would distract the dragon, and as long as the boys didn't make a peep, the dragon would move on, and they would stay safe.

"Out," Agnes bade the scullery maids, waving them off with a washcloth. "Everyone out, and don't breathe a word of what is happening in here to anyone, do you understand?"

The maids exchanged worried looks, but left quickly and without argument.

In their absence, the room was still and quiet.

Without the hustle and bustle, there was nothing to distract Sorin from the noise in his head.

The inescapable screams.

Since returning to Castle Beithir, they hadn't been bad. Most days, they were hardly louder than a distant ringing—easy enough to overlook, and often forgettable entirely. It wasn't difficult to function when the screaming was at that level. Sorin had never had a problem staying focused during those times and found himself full of energy.

But the voices were not distant now.

As he cowered, heart pounding, sure that death was near, they grew bolder and more demanding. They shrieked. They wailed. The pain was overwhelming—like someone was driving a blade through his skull—and his dark thoughts had taken control.

You failed.

You failed.

You failed.

Sorin squeezed his eyes shut, tugging his knees to his chest. He pressed his forehead to his knees and tried to breathe—tried to squash the screaming down so he could listen for the dragon—but it was like trying to hold back the ocean with his hands. It would not be contained.

He did not know how long he struggled, only that he did.

Gasping, panting, heart rattling his ribcage like a trapped bird, he did his best to listen to what was going on around him. Tried to hear the footsteps he knew were coming, so he could protect his boys.

And when they did come, although he was a wreck, he braced himself.

If they came into the scullery, he would kick the bucket.

But oddly, the footsteps stopped.

"You are safe, love," said Bertram from the doorway, prompting Sorin to lift his head. The whelps, hearing their father's voice, spilled out of the cabinet and came skittering over to Sorin, showing Bertram the way.

Bertram approached cautiously and stopped a respectful distance away. The whelps, who had taken it upon themselves to surround Sorin, chirped and purred as though inviting him to join them. Owyn, affectionate as he was, went over and butted his head against Bertram's leg.

"It was my brother, Sebastian," Bertram explained, bending down to pick up Owyn, who had plopped down across Bertram's feet. "He came to express his displeasure over what happened in Beirut. I apologized, and he is gone now. He does not know what we are planning, and does not know about the liberated omegas. He did not come for you."

Sorin drew a shaking breath and raked his hands through his hair. "I thought..."

"I know." Bertram held Owyn to his chest, idly stroking his spines. "I did, too, but that is not the case. If he knew, he would not have held himself back, and we would not be having this conversation."

Sorin closed his eyes.

His head *throbbed.*

He had been so sure that he would die, yet somehow, he was alive.

"Are you well?" Bertram asked, quietly concerned.

Sorin opened his eyes and realized his jaw was clenched, and he was pulling his hair. The three whelps not in Bertram's arms watched him anxiously, expressions just as heartbroken as the screaming in his head. It was clear they wanted to help him, but they were young and scared, and they didn't know what to do.

One look at them brought Sorin to tears.

He unclenched his jaw and let go of his hair, opening his arms, and they raced into his embrace, all of them somehow managing to fit despite how large they'd gotten. Sorin held them as tightly as he could, kissing their heads and stroking their scales as tears streamed down his cheeks.

"No," he choked out through a sob. "No, I'm not well at all."

Bertram was at his side in an instant, dropping without hesitation to his knees. He set Owyn down, sat next to Sorin, and tucked himself against his side. As soon as he had settled, Owyn draped himself across Bertram's chest and rested his chin on Sorin's arm, purring comfortingly.

They huddled in the corner together, all six of them, a family, and stayed there until Sorin had no more tears left to cry—until the screaming no longer made his head pound—but there was no amount of time long enough to let Sorin forget how close he had come to losing them.

Or how someday, his ambition might steal his happiness away.

The liberated omegas arrived a short day later, and while Sorin was not better, he had recovered enough that upon spotting their caravan on the horizon, he had the energy needed to step into his role as host and mentor. In time he knew he would be fine, but it would not be today.

"Now I know why you were so cagey about your connection to the Amethyst clan," Jacques remarked in good humor as they sat to dine that evening. The great hall was packed, every seat at its long table filled. Some of the omegas around it were quiet and exhausted from the journey, but others—like Jacques—were invigorated by their arrival and had become quite chatty. The room was abuzz with conversation. No longer was Castle Beithir stale and stagnant; with their guests there, it had come alive. "I never would have trusted you had you told me you were allied with a dragon. One you've had whelps with, no less! Are you his mate?"

Sorin felt his cheeks color. "No."

"Curious." Jacques clicked his tongue and raised an eyebrow. "I didn't think a dragon would be willing to hear our side of the story unless he had a mate putting thoughts in his head, but I suppose I was wrong. You must have excelled at your training to have convinced him to go against his own kind like this." He smirked. "You'll need to teach the rest of us your technique."

Sorin's red cheeks burned. "No," he mumbled, diverting his gaze to Bertram, whose arms were laden with bowls of stew as he helped Agnes bring dinner into the room. "That life is behind you now. You'll never have to bed a dragon against your will again."

Jacques chuckled and raised his goblet, toasting the air in Sorin's direction, and drank deeply. Those closest to him—unabashed eavesdroppers—smirked at each other and toasted him as well. Soon, the whole table followed, omegas both bold and timid raising their glasses to the dawn of a new age, and while Sorin had no way of knowing how this would go, even in the low place he was in, he felt the power behind it.

Together, they could do this.

It was terrifying, but as long as they were united, everything would be okay.

Some omegas were not fighters. They yearned for simple, quiet lives in places dragons would never find them. For them, rehabilitation was straightforward—by day, they apprenticed under the servants in Castle Beithir, learning a skill or trade that could sustain them, and by night, they rested.

Those who wished to join the fight for liberation did not have it as easy.

By day, they learned the skill of their choice, but by night, they trained.

Bertram taught them all he knew, from espionage to swordplay and all things in between, and despite how difficult the training proved to be, they excelled.

Amongst those he trained was Sorin.

Yes, Bertram had begged him to come home—had promised they could change the world from right here in the castle—but

Sorin was not naive. Nothing in life was ever truly promised. There could come a day when he would need to take up arms to defend their cause, and he would rather be prepared for it than leave his life—and the lives of his children—up to chance.

Those years passed in flashes of blunt blades swung at sunset and the clashing of harmless steel. In exhaustion. In frustration. In blisters that turned into calluses, and bruises that scattered like wildflowers in shades of black and blue and green.

But they also passed in lingering looks. In Bertram's quiet smiles as he watched Sorin when he didn't think Sorin was looking. In hushed "I love yous" between the sheets, legs tangled, breathless and knotted together as they prolonged each other's orgasms. In the children getting older, growing bigger. In laughter around the long table. In camaraderie. In love. In family.

By the end, Sorin had not only become a better fighter—he had become a better version of himself.

Perhaps there was some merit in the concept of humans and dragons working in tandem to better one another, he thought to himself one day while Bertram taught them all a final lesson—the secrets of successful impersonation, as had been taught to him during his apprenticeship many years ago. Like the glassmith in Westminster who had achieved the impossible with dragon fire, something miraculous was taking place here—something no dragon would ever believe.

Under Bertram's tutelage, their perfectly cultivated omegas had shed the mantle of the Pedigree.

They believed the lies they'd been taught no more.

Sorin followed along with the lesson, but his mind was elsewhere. He had been so quick to dismiss the potential benefits dragons might bestow on human society, but now that he was seeing it in action, the results were undeniable.

He could not have done this without Bertram.

They were stronger together than they ever could have been apart.

"We should find a new name to call ourselves," Sorin said after the lesson had concluded and everyone had gone their separate ways. He had just finished putting the children down for the night —no easy feat, now that they were able to transform—and was now back in Bertram's bedroom, undressing so he could go to sleep as well.

Bertram watched him strip from the bed, back propped up by pillows, his arms folded casually behind his head. Muted desire flickered in his eyes. "Switch accents," he said. "Say it again."

"Are you serious?"

"You did great during today's lesson, but that doesn't mean you shouldn't practice."

"It's barely been an hour." Sorin shoved down his hose and shot Bertram a playfully scalding look, but did as asked. "We should find a new name to call ourselves," he said in a Scottish accent, poking fun Bertram's way. "We are no longer Pedigree, but we are still bound together by a common goal. Warriors, the lot of us. Capable and determined, intelligent, dedicated to our cause." He finished undressing and climbed onto the bed, crawling on his hands and knees up Bertram's body until they were nose to nose. "It won't be long before our first mission, and I cannae in good faith send our friends out to change the world without a respectable title to call them by."

Bertram chuckled, turning his head so their lips brushed. "My accent isn't that thick—I've only lived here in Scotland for a few hundred years. Are you sure you aren't impersonating Hamish?"

"Nae," Sorin whispered, eyes closing, lips brushing Bertram's in a not-quite kiss. "All you. Only you."

Bertram sucked in a breath and chased Sorin's lips, but Sorin denied him. He kept himself just far enough apart from Bertram so that their lips were touching, but a kiss would be awkward.

"Answer my question before you kiss me," he purred, slipping into an Irish accent. "You were the one who came up with this plan—you should be the one to name us."

Bertram made a noise of complaint and took Sorin by the hips. "You are the force behind this movement," he countered. "The organization of our efforts may be my doing, but the heart and soul in what we do is all you."

"Are you trying to charm me into bed?" Sorin asked with a laugh, reverting to his normal voice. He leaned forward, capturing Bertram's lips in a quick kiss that promised more to come. "Because it's working."

"Not until you answer your own question," Bertram fired back, mirth in his voice. "Name us, love. Who are we?"

"We are warriors," Sorin said thoughtfully, choosing his words with care. He changed positions, sitting on Bertram's lap both to be more comfortable, and to enjoy the feeling of Bertram's erection pressing up between his legs. "We are champions of justice. We are strong, courageous, and resourceful. We will give voices to those who have not been heard, and those afraid to speak."

He thought on it as he ran his hands through Bertram's hair and delighted in the way Bertram shivered.

"We are the Vanguard," he said at last, "and we will always fight for what is right."

"Excellent choice, love," Bertram said, and kissed him.

Not long after that, Bertram's cock found its way somewhere far more pleasurable than between Sorin's legs, and they christened the birth of their movement together—exactly as it should have been.

"Do you think they'll be fine on their own?" Sorin asked. He stood in front of the glass pane window in Bertram's chamber, watching their companions ride south. The rehabilitated omegas who did not want to join the fight had left the week before, having been given modest dwellings in villages of their choice and enough coin to keep them fed and happy until they had settled into their new lives, and the rest were leaving now, bound for Diamond territory. According to Bertram, there was a Diamond cloister in the lower Volga region that was notorious for the mistreatment of its omegas, but due to strict border policies, the other clans had been able to do very little about it. Politics had kept that cloister's omegas suffering for years—decades, if not centuries.

But help was finally coming.

The Vanguard would set them free.

"I do," Bertram said gently, coming up to stand behind him. He smoothed a hand across Sorin's lower back and over the globe of his ass before taking him politely, but possessively, by the hip. He had been especially generous with his affections in the last few days, hardly able to keep his hands to himself and insatiable in bed. That morning alone, he had knotted Sorin three times, and while Sorin was *not* complaining, it was a strange turn of events.

He had chalked it up to the excitement of the day, but now he wasn't so sure.

Especially when Bertram nosed into the place behind his ear, kissing chastely but suggestively.

Wanting more.

"They are strong, love," Bertram whispered, his words hot on the back of Sorin's ear. He nipped gently, toying, teasing, causing Sorin's cock to twitch and start to stiffen. "More than that, they're cunning. Nothing will stop them. All will be well—you'll see."

"I should be out there with them," Sorin countered, but there was no heart in his argument. He leaned back, fitting himself against Bertram's body, wanting to know if he was erect, and more than that, wanting contact with Bertram's erection. Wanting it on. In him. Sliding up between the cheeks of his ass and frotting —slowly at first, but with increasing need—until it found purchase and pushed inside.

Stretching him.

Filling him.

Reshaping his tight body until it was perfectly molded to his cock, and then knotting him once he'd worked himself in deep.

Sorin's heart fluttered. Suddenly winded, he braced a hand on the window to support himself and grinded himself on Bertram's cock, panting. It felt like if he didn't get a cock inside him *now*, he would be done for.

Recklessly, he yanked down his hose.

It didn't matter if anyone saw—he needed Bertram's cock inside him.

He needed to be bred.

"You want to be out there with them?" Bertram asked, sounding just as wildly horny for Sorin as Sorin was for him. He reached around, pushing Sorin's codpiece out of the way to grab his cock right at the base. "If you joined them, you couldn't have me. Or this."

He thrust forward with his hips, driving his clothed erection against Sorin's ass in a way that suggested he would have sunk himself into Sorin down to the base had he not been wearing clothes.

Sorin gasped, thighs trembling.

He planted both hands on the window, spread his legs, and perked his ass.

Deep down, he knew he shouldn't—that something wasn't right—but that voice of concern was so small and distant, it was barely a whisper. Like the screaming of his lost children, it dwindled down to nearly nothing and was promptly forgotten.

It didn't matter if it was wrong—he *needed* to present himself.

It felt like he would die if he didn't get Bertram's cock.

"It's normal to feel unsettled or guilty when seeing those you love off on a dangerous mission," Bertram said amidst a rustling of fabric. "But your place is here, with me. There is value in being a strategist. In being a leader." The hand around Sorin's cock began to pump. The other seized Sorin by the hip. "You do not need to be in the field to be helpful. Our work keeps them alive, and will bring them home safe."

Bertram's bare cock butted between Sorin's cheeks, and Sorin's knees went weak. He threw his weight forward, trusting his arms to hold him up, and stood on his toes to lift his ass that much higher.

Whimpering.

Begging Bertram without words to fuck his hole.

"*Sorin,*" Bertram groaned. He pumped his hand slowly and steadily, but the pleasure of his touch was overshadowed by how *good* it felt to have Bertram's bare cock on him. It thrust lazily over his hole, gliding, already so wet. Practically soaking.

It would feel so good slipping inside of him.

It would breed him *deep.*

"Put it in," Sorin begged, barely managing to choke out the words. "Put it in, *please.*"

The head of Bertram's cock snagged his hole.

Pushed.

Sank in.

Sorin gasped.

Trembling, he held his position.

Just a little more and he would feel *so good.*

Don't do this, a small voice inside of him whimpered. *Don't let it happen. You don't want this. Please, no.*

Bertram pushed deeper, the first few inches of his cock stretching Sorin out. He loomed behind Sorin, so large and warm. Heat was pouring off him, his presence alone sweltering.

Sweat dripped from Sorin's brow.

He dropped his head, panting.

What was happening to him?

It was wrong. All of this was wrong.

"Stop," he croaked. Pleasure crashed through him, making him want to sink down on Bertram's cock and take it all the way, but then the pleasure twisted. Soured. It filled his stomach with a rotten feeling tinged with dull dread. "Bertram, *stop.*"

"Sorin?" Bertram asked uncertainly. He pulled out right away and stepped back to give Sorin space. "What's wrong?"

"We can't," Sorin croaked. Slowly, not trusting his legs to hold him, he braced his arms on the window and stood upright, but even that was a struggle. "*I* can't," he clarified, and looked over his shoulder to lock eyes with a stunned-looking Bertram. "I'm going into heat."

31

BERTRAM

There was talk, sometimes, amongst the agents of the council. Conversations that only happened late at night in remote camp-sites, far from the ears of polite society, in places where the chill of cold night air bit the insides of Bertram's nostrils and the only sound outside their own ruckus was the trill of reed and sedge warblers.

On nights like those, between swigs of sour alcohol straight from the flask and bouts of easy laughter, tales were told. Tales of agents who'd stormed cloisters and come across omegas in heat, thighs glossy with slick and eyes glazed over, so beside themselves with lust that at the first sight of an alpha, they put their asses up and their heads down, begging to be bred.

"The scent of an omega in heat is unlike anything you've known, and unlike anything you'll know again," warned one of Bertram's fellow agents, Siroslav, on one of those nights. "It's been five years since I came across the boy, and I still fixate on him. On the way he looked at me with those big, pleading eyes. I would give every coin in my hoard for the chance to bury my face between his cheeks. To lap up his slick. To *taste* him."

At the time, Bertram had laughed and admonished Siroslav for his lechery, but he hadn't understood.

He did now.

Nothing compared to the scent of an omega in heat.

Sorin seemed to know it, too. He looked at Bertram from over his shoulder with eyes much like Siroslav's omega—wide and pleading, innocent. But with a certain undercurrent of uneasiness, as if he trusted neither Bertram nor himself.

He was right to worry.

If Bertram hadn't been trained to disregard his baser impulses, he would have pushed Sorin onto the bed, stripped him naked, and bred him until he couldn't anymore—and this was just the start of Sorin's heat. How much stronger would that impulse grow in a few days, when his heat reached its peak?

The thought made Bertram's cock throb.

Take, his dragon demanded. *Mine. Breed.*

"I don't want to have another clutch right now," Sorin whispered in a panic, disrupting Bertram from his thoughts. He had—with some difficulty—pulled his hose back into place well enough to conceal himself, but a stripe of his hip remained visible. Temptation incarnate.

He wanted his mouth on it.

Propelled by desire, he took a step forward only to stop dead in his tracks as Sorin shrank back, pushing himself fearfully against the window.

"Don't," he begged Bertram in a small voice. *"Please."*

There was fear in Sorin's voice, but there was something pained in it as well—something under tremendous pressure being worn thin that might at any moment break. Bertram felt the tension of it.

Felt it stretch thin within him, as well.

If either of them made a wrong move, it would snap, and it would all be over. One of them would tumble headfirst into desire and drag the other down with him. There would be no more polite veneer of self-control.

They would give in to their bodies, and they would breed.

Breathing hard, Bertram yanked his hose back into place in an effort to stave off the inevitable, but the damage had been done. He wanted Sorin. Wanted to knot him through his heat and fill him with eggs. It was what any dragon would want.

But it would also be their undoing.

Bertram had explained one clutch away by the skin of his teeth —he would not get so lucky a second time. There would be an investigation when word got out, and the council would discover he was harboring the fugitive he'd been sent to kill. Sorin would be neutralized, and the eggs destroyed or left for dead.

And Bertram...

He feared he would not do much better.

What would become of their whelps then?

He couldn't let it happen.

The boys needed their father, and Bertram...

He needed Sorin, too. More than he could say.

"Please," Sorin repeated, heartbroken, begging. A feverish flush spread across his cheeks. "I need to go."

Bertram's dragon hissed in disagreement, but Bertram pushed it down. Silenced it. Made it small and still until he had full control.

He would not harm the mate of his heart.

He would not harm his family.

"Let's go," he said, grabbing Sorin by the arm and leading him out of the room.

"Where are we going? The guest wing is the other way."

"The guest wing," Bertram said, "was good enough for the Ruby omegas, but I know a better place for you. Somewhere safer, where you'll feel more comfortable."

"Where is that?"

They reached the end of the spiral staircase and hurried down the hall.

"The only place I know with absolute certainty will keep you safe," he told Sorin as they went. "My hoard."

Bertram's hoard was hidden within the fortified walls at the very center of Castle Beithir. It had been built before the rest of the castle under the supervision of a dragon much older than Bertram, and had been designed to be near impenetrable, resistant to both attacks by hostile dragons and war machines. Even now, hundreds of years later, those walls endured, and so too had the sole set of sturdy wooden doors leading to the hoard within. They creaked on their ancient hinges as Bertram muscled them open, letting out a rolling wave of cold air that weaved around his ankles.

Bertram shivered, but Sorin rushed forward, nearly crying in relief. "*Cold.*" He said it like a prayer, and no sooner was he through the door than he sank to his knees in worship, a tithing of coins spilling onto the floor around him from one of the piles of treasure he'd disturbed. "So cold." With a sigh, he sank belly-down into the riches. "*Good.*"

While Sorin acquainted himself with the floor, Bertram summoned flame and set the room's candles alight.

The hoard room went from a dark nightmare to a gilded dream.

Compared to most Drakes, Bertram's hoard was rather meager. Unlike Alistair, who ferreted away books as though one day words might cease to exist, or Everard, who claimed he had no penchant for any treasure in particular, but who owned a suspicious amount of rare and exotic spice, Bertram had no head for anything outside the traditional. His hoard contained nothing but gold and jewels. It spilled out of chests and lay in shimmering piles stacked so high, it rivaled Beinn Nibheis itself. The most sentimental pieces—those Bertram had acquired early in life, before he'd been in a position to get what he wanted when he wanted it—were on display on open-shelved cabinets, or stowed away in locked drawers to which only Bertram held the keys. In times of indulgence, he visited those nostalgic treasures—lifted them from their velvet-lined drawers and let his mind wander back to simpler times.

The only objects on display in his hoard that didn't fit that description were the ones that Sorin had sent him when they were apart. Bertram had artfully arranged the pearl, the feather, and his letters as centerpieces out in the open, where they could be easily seen. Of all his possessions, they were the ones he valued the most.

But with Sorin there, even they had lost their luster.

Bertram had eyes only for him.

"Sorin," he began, but stopped in his tracks. Sorin's heat carried in the air, and he *tasted* it. The sweetness of it. The flavor of deep, unyielding need.

One taste and all sense fell out of his head. The suppressed dragon inside of him clawed its way to the forefront of his mind, urging Bertram into action with a single word: *breed.*

The demand was incontestable.

Bertram's jaw went slack. Arousal ripped through him like fire through tar, and as it sizzled, he took a step toward Sorin, who stopped looking at the treasure and started looking up at him. A beat passed, and with it, a moment of understanding.

Sorin's eyelids drooped and his lips parted.

The feverish flush in his cheeks began to creep down his neck.

"Will you give me your knot?" he asked in a hot whisper, backing slowly into the nearest mound of treasure so he could recline upon it. His breathing was labored from the weight of his arousal, and the sound of it—god, the sound of it—drove Bertram mad with want of him. He would stuff Sorin full of his knot forever if only he could hear his voice next to his ear. All those hitched little whines of pleasure.

The sounds of an omega who had been given it all, but who still wanted more.

The sounds of an omega greedy to breed.

Possessed by the thought of it, Bertram dropped to his knees in front of a heat-drunk Sorin, who looked him over appreciatively, then suggestively spread his legs. He caught Bertram by the front of his doublet and pulled him forward, but the gesture was symbolic at best, because Bertram crawled to him willingly.

Crawled between those legs.

Butted Sorin's thighs farther apart with his knees as he came close.

And when he had come as close as he could, he kissed Sorin like he was starved for his lips.

Like without them, he might die.

Sorin kissed him with equal fervor, and soon they were tumbling back into Bertram's treasure, Sorin fumbling with Bertram's hose while Bertram pulled off his doublet.

He *would* fill Sorin with his eggs.

He would take his omega's heat and make Sorin his forevermore.

"Please," Sorin urged, barely breaking long enough from Bertram's lips to speak. "Please. I need it. I need you inside me. Your knot. *Please.*"

A wild look glimmered in his eyes—the look of an omega gone mad. It reminded Bertram of the scared stick of a boy he'd met in Unwin's castle—the feral thing who'd threatened him with a knife, as fierce as he was determined, but scared out of his mind.

Knowing what was coming, and not wanting it.

Fearing it.

And while Sorin wasn't scared for his life anymore, it was enough.

Bertram remembered.

He could not do to Sorin what those other dragons had done.

He would not injure him with another clutch.

"I'm sorry," Bertram murmured as he scrambled back, putting quick distance between them. More coins scattered. Cold metal bit into his palms, but he didn't let it deter him—bracing his palms on the floor, he pushed up onto his feet. "I'll have Agnes bring food and water," he said, backing rapidly toward the door. "She will care for you this week and see to all your needs."

"Please," Sorin croaked, reaching out for him. "Come back."

"I can't."

"*Please.*"

"One day," Bertram told him from the doorway, his heart beating itself near to death with desire, "but not now. Not until you tell me while you're in your right mind that this is what you want."

"It's what I want," Sorin said instantly, but even as he said it, tears ran down his cheeks. "I won't be mad. I swear. I want this more than anything. I want *you.*"

But that look was in his eyes.

The glimmer.

The fear.

Bertram's heart twisted.

He shook his head and shut the door, but it could only do so much.

Like Siroslav, Bertram feared he wouldn't easily forget what he had left behind.

32

SORIN

Sorin's heat consumed him, and as it did, his sense of time and space melted away. Only the here and now remained, his reality defined by the heaviness of his body and the throbbing need between his legs.

The burning urge to be stretched and filled by a knot.

To bury his nose in his lover's neck.

To grind his hips and surrender himself to the cock that was breeding him.

Shuddering, Sorin dug himself into Bertram's treasure and took his length in hand. In his mind's eye, Bertram was there with him, eyes turning into slits as his inner monster emerged. Codpiece bulging, teeth sharpening into fangs, he tore his clothing to shreds, revealing the beautiful purple scales all down his neck and shoulders, then dropped down on top of Sorin.

Cock hanging between them, glossy and leaking precum, he took a moment to look into Sorin's eyes.

Then, with the ferocity of an animal, ripped Sorin's hose open and yanked his hips into position, crudely pushing inside.

Sorin's hand pumped wildly. Breathless, he thrashed to the side, sending coins scattering, as pleasure bolted through him, crackling like lightning. The beast inside of Bertram was fucking him. Ruining him. Pounding into him with such brutish force all Sorin could do was cling to him and take it.

His cum burned when finally, it filled him.

And his knot...

Sorin cried out in despair as the fantasy came crashing down around him.

There was no knot.

He was empty and alone.

"Bertram," he cried brokenly, but Bertram wasn't there. In agony, Sorin bucked into his hand, but the pleasure he received was fleeting. It would never be as good as being filled by Bertram's cock.

As being come in.

As making eggs.

As being bred.

A sudden surge of pleasure crashed through Sorin, and he came hard into his own hand only to immediately start pumping himself again.

Where was Bertram?

He needed him.

He wanted to get pregnant.

He missed the way eggs made him feel *full.*

But do you really? asked a voice inside his head. Sorin tried to ignore it by plunging deeper into his fantasies, but it followed, refusing to let him go. *You are more than your heat wants you to believe. This isn't who you really are.*

Sorin didn't want to hear it. In his mind, Bertram's mouth was planted on that slick spot between his legs, his tongue as hot as it was relentless, preparing Sorin for another breeding. Working him until his thighs quivered and his eyes were rolled back in his head.

Don't let yourself be tricked like this, the voice insisted, horrified. *Don't let them breed you again.*

The burning arousal eating Sorin up from the inside suddenly went cold, shocking him back to his senses.

What was he doing?

He didn't want to have another clutch.

Not now.

Maybe not ever again.

Terrified that Bertram had heard him calling out and was on his way, he scrambled up and looked around the room in a panic. It was shadowy, poorly lit by candlelight, but it seemed empty. The only sound was his own labored breathing and the clinking of the coins and jewels he'd knocked out of place.

Bertram was not coming.

He'd locked Sorin in his hoard to keep him safe, and until Sorin's heat was over, he would stay away.

It's because he loves you, the voice whispered, and despite his panic, Sorin knew it was true. He had been used by dragons since he was old enough to go into heat, but his life was different now. Bertram was not like the others. He would not take advantage of Sorin, even though doing so would have been easy.

Sorin was safe with him.

A sob rattled its way out of Sorin, coming from a place so deep, he felt it shake his ribs.

Dragons had taken, and taken, and taken from him until he was destroyed both inside and out, but Bertram—*Bertram!*—the one who should have ended his life, had given him another chance. He'd shown Sorin what it was like to love, and be in love, and if Sorin did nothing else with his life, he would show Bertram that love was reciprocated.

He would love him with all his heart, as broken as it was and as dark as it could be.

He would give him everything.

And one day, maybe, when he was ready, they could have a clutch together. More babies. Eggs to snuggle up around. Brothers for their boys.

But only when he was ready.

How lucky he was to have found the one dragon who would let him choose for himself.

No longer afraid, he settled back into his bed of jewels and closed his eyes, feeling the onset of his heat creep up on him. Hand around his cock and Bertram on his mind, he let it consume him, knowing it wouldn't be like it had always been.

He was safe now, and he was loved.

He would never be made pregnant against his will again.

———————

Sorin knew for sure his heat was through when Agnes brought in a tray of steaming porridge and his stomach rumbled loudly in response.

"You seem yourself today, bairn," she remarked, setting the tray on a small dinner table that had been brought into the hoard early into Sorin's heat. "Has it gone?"

"I think so."

"It's certainly been long enough."

"How long have I been here?"

"A good week." Agnes finished fussing with his breakfast and turned to look at him, gesturing at the table. "Come eat. While you do, I'll have the girls draw you a bath. I'm sure after sleeping on gold for so long, your poor back will appreciate it."

Sorin glanced at the pile of treasure he was lying in. It had felt heavenly when he'd been burning up with heat, but now that he was in his proper frame of mind, it was a bit uncomfortable.

Careful not to push himself too far, too soon, he got up slowly and let Agnes help him to the dinner table, where he discovered a meal fit for a king. In addition to the porridge, Agnes had brought him a bowl of fat gooseberries and another of currants. Generous amounts of butter and honey had been portioned in separate ramekins, and after Sorin sat, he added them to the porridge and ate with great relish.

It tasted heavenly, and not just because Agnes knew how he preferred to fix his breakfast—he couldn't for the life of him remember when he'd eaten his last meal.

While he ate, Agnes and the servant girls brought in a wooden tub and heated water for his bath. They finished their work before he finished eating and left quietly to give him his privacy, allowing Sorin to finish his meal at a leisurely pace before going to bathe.

He scrubbed himself clean with the sweet-scented soap Agnes had provided, then dried off and dressed in the garments left out for him. It was nice to feel somewhat human again. Thank goodness heats only came twice a year—he didn't think he'd be able to handle it if they came any more frequently than that.

Sorin was twining his wet hair into a braid to keep it off his shoulders when there came the sound of someone clearing their throat from across the room. He looked in the direction of the noise to find Bertram standing in the doorway, lips quirked and one eyebrow playfully raised.

"Am I interrupting?" he asked. "I can come back some other time."

"Don't you dare." Sorin secured his braid and, grinning, hurried over to Bertram, popping up onto his toes to wrap his arms around Bertram's neck. "I've missed you."

Bertram's expression mellowed, and he had never looked more in love than when he took Sorin by the hips and pulled him close, admitting in a whisper, "And I, you."

A thrill of pleasure shot through Sorin, and as Bertram seized him and brought their bodies together, he kissed Bertram's mouth hungrily.

"Are you sure you're over your heat?" Bertram asked in a husky voice when their lips next parted. His hands had strayed to

Sorin's buttocks, where his palms greedily took their fill. "Perhaps we should wait another day or two for certainty's sake."

"There's no need," Sorin said, and kissed him again. "The fire inside me is gone. I missed you, is all. A week is a painfully long time to spend apart from the one who has your heart."

He felt Bertram smile, but if he had something to say, it remained unspoken—Sorin's lips claimed his again, and they kissed until Sorin was hot-cheeked and flustered, his erection pressing into Bertram's. If only their clothes weren't in the way.

Bertram seemed to think the same, as he had taken to toying with the hem of Sorin's tunic, teasing it up slowly to run his fingers over his skin beneath. Shivering, Sorin laid his head on Bertram's chest and let himself enjoy that small but simple pleasure.

"We shouldn't," he murmured without really meaning it. "It's been a week since I've seen the boys. We should go to them— spend time together as a family."

Bertram squeezed his ass and pulled him closer, and for a panicked moment, Sorin feared he'd been mistaken about his heat —or worse, about his dragon—but after a quick kiss, Bertram let him go.

"The children are in the garden," he said, offering Sorin his hand. "Will you allow me the pleasure of escorting you to them?"

Another thrill ran through Sorin, and smiling, he took Bertram's hand. "There's nothing I'd like more."

The boys, predictably, were trying to set the garden on fire. Fortunately, their flames were small and the garden was quite damp from a recent rain.

When they sensed his approach, all four stopped what they'd been doing and clumsily made a mad dash for him, chirping and trilling and tripping over their feet. Waryn was in the lead, having discovered that if he beat his wings furiously enough, he'd gain extra speed. He was the first to make it to Sorin, leaping at him from a short distance and letting his wings carry him the rest of the way. Sorin caught him mid-jump and cuddled him close, and to his delight, Waryn purred and ducked his snoot under Sorin's chin.

"Baby," Sorin whispered, blinking back tears. "I missed you, too. I'm so happy to see you again."

The other three whelps were on him now, which was an issue, as they were not as small as they had once been. As they scaled him, Sorin began to topple under their weight, but Bertram stepped in silently to support him, holding Sorin up and relieving him of two of their whelps with ease.

"Hello, babies," Sorin cooed, kissing each of them on the head. "I missed you all. Were you good for your father while I was away?"

They replied all at once, chirping over each other, until at last they grew tired of being held and scrambled out of Sorin's and Bertram's arms to resume their games.

"No setting fire to anything," Sorin ordered as they scampered through the garden, leaving Beatrix to give chase.

"Do you think they'll listen?" Bertram asked, amused, as he slipped his arm around Sorin's waist.

Sorin shook his head. "No, but it makes me feel better to have said it."

"Fair enough. Do you want to follow them? You said you wanted to spend time together as a family."

Sorin craned his neck to get a look at the children to find they had already begun roughhousing with each other. Only half of them were still dragons. The other half had transformed into boys, and were trying to ride their brothers like small, scaly horses.

"I think," Sorin said, "we should wait until they've worn themselves out."

"Then would you like to visit the orchards with me?" Bertram asked. "The last of the apple trees are blooming."

In answer, Sorin tilted his head back and leisurely kissed the corner of Bertram's mouth, deepening the kiss only when Bertram turned his head and brought their lips fully together.

"Only if you won't take me to bed," Sorin whispered when the kiss broke.

There was as much dark desire as there was playfulness in Bertram's voice when he answered, "I don't see why I can't do both."

33

BERTRAM

There in the orchard, while apple blossoms rained down around them, Bertram parted Sorin's thighs and kissed his way slowly inward, making sure to take his time. Sorin, whose back was to the tree, gasped in muted delight and carded his fingers through Bertram's hair as Bertram kissed his way upward.

By the time Bertram arrived, Sorin was already half-hard.

"A week without you," Bertram breathed, letting his lips brush the base of Sorin's shaft, "was torture of the cruelest degree. I would rather be taken captive and have my scales plucked from me one by one than suffer your absence again."

Sorin's breath hitched, and his fingers tightened. "I wish you could have been there with me."

"One day," Bertram said in a low voice, "perhaps I will be."

Sorin shivered and perked his hips in a silent plea which Bertram eagerly answered. He took Sorin into his mouth, teasing his tip with his tongue until Sorin's thighs were trembling, then took him deeper.

And deeper.

Working his mouth, his tongue, and his lips until the sound of Sorin's breathing grew labored and desperate. Not long after that,

Sorin let out a plaintive cry and shot his load onto Bertram's tongue.

"*Bertram*," Sorin gasped, releasing Bertram's hair to let his arms drop lamely to his sides. Bertram glanced up to make sure he was okay and discovered he'd gone hazy-eyed with lust. A few flower petals had landed in his hair—white against black, a stark dichotomy.

Perhaps it was their time apart, or perhaps it was because the stress of Sebastian's unexpected visit was finally fading, but the image of Sorin like that—rosy-cheeked from sex and haphazardly decorated—struck Bertram in the same way that seeing treasure did.

His heart clenched, and his spirits lifted.

He was compelled to kiss the inside of Sorin's thigh one more time.

"I love you," he said simply, letting the words heat Sorin's skin. "Mate or not, you own my heart. I know it to be true."

"Is that so?" Sorin said with an exhausted laugh, dragging Bertram up to him and bringing their lips together for a fierce kiss. "I'm glad to hear it, for I find myself in need of a replacement for mine—a villainous dragon stole it long ago."

Beaming, Bertram kissed him, and they sank into the soft grass at the base of the apple tree together.

What an impossible but wonderful thing it was to be in love with a man he had sworn would die by his claws, and to have that man love him back.

They made up for their time apart with every spare second that week. When not otherwise occupied with the children, Sorin found his way into Bertram's arms, and together they'd find a quiet place to make love.

In Bertram's study.

In the larder.

In the stairwell near the great hall.

It was passion like Bertram had never felt before. An unyielding, inescapable fire that lit beneath his skin whenever Sorin was near—and it seemed he wasn't the only one who felt it. Sorin took pleasure from him greedily and often instigated their dalliances, gleefully dragging Bertram off to bed.

In fact, Sorin was the one who'd been unable to keep his hands to himself that morning. Bertram had still been stirring when he'd felt Sorin snuggle up behind him and reach across his body, grasping his half-hard cock in his hand.

Now, ten minutes later, that cock was fully hard and buried in Sorin's ass.

"Do you remember what I told you when we first met?" Sorin asked, voice thin with pleasure, as Bertram inched them toward orgasm. "How I told you I'd kill every last dragon? After the Vanguard succeeds in abolishing the Pedigree, I think I very well might see my plan through and put an end to the tyranny of your kind."

"Is that so?"

Sorin moaned as Bertram rolled his hips, sinking in deep right as orgasm caused his knot to swell.

"*Yes.*" Sorin wrapped his arms around Bertram's neck and curled his fingers in his hair. "God, Bertram. It feels so good. *So good.*"

"Will you spare me, then?" Bertram said through a laugh. "It would be a shame were I to die by your hand, for I'd take my knot with me."

"Not you." Sorin's back arched, and he let out a choked cry. "You aren't one of them."

"So you concede that some dragons are good."

"*Only you.*" Sorin's grip on his hair tightened, and Bertram heard his orgasm in the desperate pitch of his moan as much as he felt it in the way Sorin squeezed around him. A few uncontrollable bucks of his hips later and Sorin grinded against him, milking his cock, bringing Bertram to come a second time.

For a while, conversation gave way to strained gasps, quivering moans, and the scuffle of feet seeking purchase on smooth bedsheets, then Sorin fell still, and Bertram did, too. They lay together silently, catching their breath and holding on to each other tightly, until Sorin added, almost offhandedly, "And the children. I will let them live as well."

"How charitable."

Sorin shoved Bertram's shoulders, but it was more playful than anything. There was laughter in his eyes. "I am not a monster." He hesitated. "You know that, right?"

"I do." Bertram nosed along Sorin's jawline, placing firm kisses where his heart told him they belonged. "But I do think you are misguided."

"Not enough to keep me out of your bed."

"No." Bertram came to a spot under the ridge of Sorin's jaw near his pulse point, where his scent was strongest. He lingered there a moment to breathe it in. How strange yet wonderful it was that behind sweet notes of honeysuckle, Sorin smelled like home. "But I am not delusional," he said once his heart was filled with the unique scent. "I know myself to be misguided, too."

"Then let us be wrong together."

Bertram's lips twitched.

He liked the sound of that.

For years, they did just that.

Under a shroud of secrecy, Sorin raised the children by day and helped Bertram oversee matters of the Vanguard by night. The work they did was not easy, but through Bertram's connections with the council and Sorin's hands-on experience with matters of the Pedigree, they mobilized the Vanguard from afar and began the slow work of rescuing and rehabilitating the omegas who'd fallen through the cracks of an imperfect system.

But as heavy and as important as the work was, they weren't always on the job.

The whelps made sure of that.

As they grew, they became as independent as they were curious. The speed with which they mastered their transformations didn't help. Opposable thumbs were the devil's work. How did anyone keep young children contained?

Bertram became quite used to locking every door behind him.

Coincidentally, the whelps became used to lock-picking.

They were a mischievous bunch. A handful. Under Waryn's leadership, they terrorized the Highlands in ways only young boys could—hunting bugs and spooking rabbits. Creeping up on oblivious, grazing ewe.

But there was innocence in what they did, too.

On warm days, they took to their scales and splashed about the loch. On colder ones, they bundled themselves in layers of woolen clothing and chased snowflakes with their tongues. Youthful mischief aside, they were good boys. Polite and pleasant. Eager to please. Charming.

Especially Piers.

It worried Bertram how much of himself he saw in that boy, but he did his best not to let it get to him. The current Amethyst agents were young enough that they would not be retiring anytime soon, meaning Piers did not risk getting selected as a potential replacement. Not until well into his adult years, at least.

Unlike Bertram, he would not be taken from his brothers.

He would get to enjoy his childhood in its entirety—Bertram would make sure of it.

When the whelps were old enough, Bertram taught them to read and write, and once they knew their letters, he introduced them to foreign languages. Sorin sat in on the lessons, and took to them with such voracity that Bertram soon had nothing left to teach.

"How else am I to communicate with the omegas I save?" Sorin replied when Bertram asked him about it. "If I truly wish to change the world, it's in my best interest to be able to speak to everyone I meet—and not just speak, but speak well."

Bertram couldn't fault his logic, but he did question his motives. They could lead the Vanguard from the safety of their home, so there was little reason to venture out and risk discovery. Perhaps, when the whelps were older, Sorin might join their men in the field, but even then, human lifespans were short. Sorin would only have so much time. In fifty short years, he could very well be no more.

It bothered Bertram tremendously to think about it, and so he did his best to put the thought to rest, but it would not be settled. It reared up on him in quiet moments when his mind was idle, and plagued him when he noticed Hamish and Agnes slowing and changing with age.

Sometimes, to escape it, he let himself pretend that Sorin was his mate and that he would live a long and happy life, blessed with prolonged youth, but if Sebastian really had found his mate in that curly-haired omega, they didn't stand a chance. Mates were so rare, they might as well not exist—two brothers from the same clutch would never be so lucky as to find theirs at the same time.

Sorin would keep his normal lifespan. He would grow old and die while Bertram stayed young, and there would be nothing either of them could do about it.

It was easy to be discouraged by the hopelessness of it all—to know that this love he'd found was temporary, and would last for but a short portion of his long life—but rather than dwell on his heartbreak, Bertram threw himself into enjoying what time he did have.

To the whelps, he was the best father he could be. Firm, but kind. Attentive, but not overbearing. Quick to laugh, and unashamed to show his love.

To Sorin, he was a devoted lover and a steadfast partner. He made love to him each night as though dawn would never come, and in the morning held him close and whispered sweet things against his earlobe before pledging his love between his thighs. He vowed not only to listen, but to follow through. When there was something wrong, he fixed it, and when there was something right, he made sure it happened again.

And for a while, it was enough.

For a while, he threw himself into changing the world and loving his whelps and his should-be mate.

Then one day without warning, Grimbold came, and everything fell apart.

3 4

BERTRAM

Grimbold arrived in the way any unhurried dragon might—by horseback—and proceeded to spend an inordinate amount of time in the stables, up to lord knew what. Bertram would have been unaware had Hamish not noticed and come hobbling up to his study, leaning heavily on his gnarled cane, to let Bertram know that his father had arrived.

"Father?" A chill swept down Bertram's back. "He did not write to say he was coming to visit."

"It's him, all right, my lord," Hamish said. He sounded slightly winded from climbing the stairs. "My old age may be catching up to me, but I haven't lost my mind yet."

To illustrate, he tapped a finger to his head.

Bertram frowned.

Hamish and Agnes were in retirement now, not that either of them had accepted it. Agnes still puttered around the kitchen, clucking at the new servants like a mother hen, and Hamish lurked in every corner of the castle like a persistent, if helpful, shadow, overseeing every bit of handiwork and groundskeeping that went on. Bertram had tried to stop them—had tried to ply them into rest and relaxation with chests full of coins and the promise that all would be well—but it had been pointless. Men and women could not be swayed by gold when their hearts were made of it.

And so, much to Bertram's consternation, they stayed.

"Where is Sorin?" Bertram inquired. "Has Agnes gone to inform him of my father's arrival?"

"Lord Sorin has yet to return home from adventuring with the boys, my lord." One heavy tap of his cane at a time, Hamish shuffled over to the armchair in the corner of the room and sat, wincing as he did. "There's no telling when they'll be home."

"And Father—has he said how long he plans to stay?" While Bertram spoke, he capped his inkpot and tucked the letter he'd been writing to the Vanguard into his desk. "Or if not, has he disclosed what urgent business he has that prompted him to visit unannounced?"

"No, my lord."

"I see." Bertram took a small key from another drawer in his desk and used it to lock the letter away. "Is there any way we can send one of the servants to alert Sorin to his presence?"

"We could." Hamish's lips thinned. "But there's little chance it will do us any good. You know the boys—there's no telling where they've gone off to. We could send every last one of us out on the hunt and still turn up empty-handed."

He was right.

Bertram pushed a sigh through his teeth.

This was an issue.

His father was not stupid. He'd seen Sorin wear Bertram's bruises like strings of pearls and glimpsed the blush high in his cheeks during his prior visit, and while one quiet indiscretion with an omega could be seen as a simple lapse of judgment, the same could not be said were Sorin to be seen acting paternally to the boys a decade after he'd been caught in Bertram's bed.

An old memory dredged itself up from the riverbanks of

Bertram's mind: *Perhaps he would keep you from playing house with wild omegas.*

Grimbold knew.

But if he were to see how far Bertram had taken it...

Bertram could not allow it to happen.

"Send someone," he said. "If they are unsuccessful in their search, so be it, but I would rather try than leave things entirely up to chance."

Hamish bobbed his head. "Yes, my lord."

"While that's underway, I will do everything within my power to keep my father from running into Sorin. Please inform the servants that should they see Sorin, they are to inform him that my father is here."

"They've already been told."

"Good man, Hamish. Thank you." Bertram gifted him a smile, then cast a jaundiced eye over his desk for any last tells. When he saw nothing, he crossed the room and offered Hamish a hand, helping the man to his feet. "You should have sent one of the servants to tell me the news—it's a long set of stairs to climb to come all the way to the study."

Hamish, now on his feet and leaning heavily on his cane, waved Bertram off. "Nonsense."

"Would Agnes think that, were she to know?"

Hamish went rather pale.

"I shan't tell her," Bertram clarified, "provided you allow me to help you down the stairs."

"But your father—"

"You told me that Father is in the stables," Bertram said, interrupting Hamish before he could argue his point further. "As far as he knows, I'm unaware he's here. He won't begrudge me not dropping everything to see him."

"And should Lord Sorin return home with the boys?"

"Then he shall return home. It's as simple as that. A few extra moments spent with you won't change what will or won't happen." Bertram came around to stand next to Hamish instead of in front of him, and placed a gentle hand on the man's back. "Come, now," he said. "The quickest way to be rid of me is to let me help."

Hamish grumped and grumbled, but allowed himself to be helped out of the study and down the stairs. For his age, he was still quite spry, and while Bertram was glad for it, he thought all the while of Sorin, and how little time they had left together before this would be their life—Bertram, young and unchanged, while Sorin's body betrayed him until eventually…

They arrived at the landing, and Hamish hobbled off.

Bertram wished the ache in his heart would go, too, but it persisted. It was little wonder why Sebastian had held on to his anger for all that time—if this was what it was like to love someone without being their mate, Bertram could only imagine how devastatingly painful it had been for his brother to watch as the one to whom his soul was tethered was put in danger. Had he been in that position, he would have held on to that anger, too. Would have let it simmer. Fester. Grow. It wouldn't have mattered that the damage done had been by accident—all that would matter was that it had been done at all.

It was a testament to Sebastian's heart that he hadn't come after him with teeth and claws. Come at him like Bertram had back then, on that night outside of Damascus, when Sorin's life had been in danger.

When he'd been so terrified of what might happen that the weight of his fear had crystallized into jagged, cutting anger. Rage so sharp, it had severed his senses. Shut off his brain.

Made him turn on his own brother.

Bertram understood it, now.

He did not envy Sebastian, having to survive a love like that.

Perhaps that was the reason mates were so rare.

But the truth of it all didn't matter. Like so many other dragons, Bertram would not find his mate, and worrying about the ins and outs of what life might be like were that to change was pointless. There were more important matters at hand.

Like wrangling his father.

By the time Grimbold left the stables, Bertram had gone back to being Frederich. It had been an uneasy switch. At one point in his life, before Sorin had come and stolen his way into his heart as surely as he'd stolen into the castle, Bertram had never had an issue distancing himself from his emotions and slipping into that role, but over the last decade, that had changed. Now, putting himself in Frederich's mindset was like trying to squeeze into clothing several sizes too small.

But Bertram still managed a charming smile when Grimbold strolled into the room, and didn't let his discomfort bleed into his posture. He would not give him a reason to suspect anything was amiss.

"Father," Bertram said, amiably enough, when Grimbold entered the great hall. He set down his wine glass, filled with an expensive and deceptively tart wine imported from a Vanguard-run vineyard in Bordeaux. "What an unexpected surprise."

"Unexpected?" Grimbold sat opposite Bertram. "Surely you jest, child. There is nothing unexpected about this."

A creeping cold filled Bertram's stomach. "Is that so?"

"Quite." Grimbold folded his arms on the table and leaned forward, his dark eyes piercing Bertram with unreadable intent. For a moment, Bertram was sure he'd been found out—that one of the servants had betrayed him, or perhaps that one of the children had said something careless—but then Grimbold arched a brow and said, "It's been ten years," putting Bertram's fears to rest.

Bertram mirrored Grimbold's expression, arching a brow in understated astonishment, and gave himself a second to process what he'd heard by sampling his wine.

Tart, like he'd remembered.

He didn't hurry to set his glass back down.

"The council is deploying all agents into Diamond territory," Grimbold explained as Bertram idly swirled his glass. "You will join them. Siroslav has suspicions that there is something afoot in Crimea and has requested a full investigation. The other agents will fill you in when you arrive."

Bertram's wrist stilled. The wine swirled to a stop.

Crimea.

Of all places, Crimea.

His stomach tightened.

It seemed he would be able to personally deliver his letter to the Vanguard.

"Osbert and Merewin—have they already been deployed?" he asked.

"Yes."

"Then I assume that I am to be deployed immediately as well."

Grimbold nodded. A quiet kind of pride shone in his eyes. "The others will welcome you there," he said. "They've set up a base of operations near the Crimean cloister. Accommodations have already been made."

"Will I have until the morning?" Bertram asked, setting down his wine. "I'd like to say goodbye to the children."

"Of course. You leave at dawn." Grimbold searched Bertram's face for a long moment, then sat heavily back in his chair and seemed to relax. "Speaking of the whelps, where are they? I expected I would be rushed upon my arrival, yet they never came. Are they well?"

"The boys are fine," Bertram assured him. "They're enjoying a day off from their studies, out exploring the Highlands with one of their nursemaids." The lie tasted bitter, but it came out sounding as plain as the truth. Just as plainly, he shifted his gaze toward the door. "Why don't we get you situated in one of the guest bedrooms while they're gone?" he asked. "It's safe to say that once they come back, you shan't have a moment's peace."

He'd expected Grimbold to agree—maybe rap his knuckles on the table as he stood stiffly, sore from travel.

But he did no such thing.

He sat still and silent, and not just for a moment—he kept it up long enough that the cold dread in Bertram's stomach turned to ice.

He knew, didn't he?

He had to.

If not the whole truth, then enough that he'd puzzled the bulk of it together and was now trying to ferret out the final pieces using silence as his weapon, waiting for Bertram to panic and fill in the blanks. It was what Bertram would have done, were he in his father's place. Hell, he'd done it thousands of times before while interrogating unsuspecting parties. Did Grimbold really think so little of him to believe such a simple tactic would work? Or was it that he knew what Bertram had only discovered today— that Frederich was a mask Bertram was outgrowing now that he'd turned traitor, and that his sabbatical had made him weak.

Weak enough to be susceptible to tricks like these.

Not fit to be an agent anymore.

Those thoughts spun at dizzying speeds in Bertram's mind and stirred up panic that gripped him and would not let go. If he were caught, what would become of the children? Of Sorin?

He feared he knew the answer... and it was that fear that propelled him into action.

Feeling as though he would fall apart at any second, he put on his easiest, most charming smile and looked boldly into his father's eyes. "Shall we go?"

Grimbold paused, seeming to assess him, then nodded.

He said nothing.

And while one of the servants was able to intercept Sorin before he set foot in the castle, Bertram wasn't sure it mattered. A dragon as important as Grimbold had not come all the way to Scotland on a whim. The conversation they'd had could have been penned into a letter.

It was the conversation left unsaid that was the real purpose of his trip.

Stop playing house with wild omegas.

Grimbold was here to make sure of it.

The children took the news of Bertram's imminent departure in stride. Owyn, who was still the most expressive of the bunch, allowed his bottom lip to tremble, but upon a quick elbowing from Piers, pulled himself together. The rest of the boys managed to maintain a degree of stony stoicism, but that night, before scampering off to bed, each of them came to say a private goodbye to their father that proved far more soulful.

The first visit happened that night while Bertram entertained Grimbold in the sitting room.

Waryn, as rash now as he'd been as a whelp, barreled into the room at top speed. He was shirtless, and as he ran, he let loose with his wings. They flapped wildly behind him until, several feet from Bertram, he leaped into the air and batted them wildly, keeping himself airborne.

Bertram had just enough time to plant his feet on the floor before Waryn crashed into him, locking his arms in a death grip around his neck. The chair—thankfully—did not tip over, but it had been a near thing.

"I'll keep everyone safe, Father," Waryn declared, burying his head under Bertram's chin. "I'm big and strong and I'll defeat anyone who dares come here with wicked intentions on the mind! I promise. You needn't worry about us."

Bertram smiled and kissed the top of his head. "I know you will. You're a strong lad, Waryn, and a good dragon. But you mustn't let it all fall on you. Your brothers will help. And your nursemaids."

"And your grandfather," Grimbold supplied. "I shan't be staying in the castle, but should you ever need me, I will be here. You mustn't worry, child. You are loved."

Waryn twisted around to face Grimbold, and Bertram was surprised to see him smile. "I'll protect you, too, Grandfather," he promised. "I'll be brave and protect you all."

Bertram gave him another kiss on the head, and after a brief cuddle, Waryn went away to sleep. No sooner did he leave than Edmund appeared at the doorway and, upon invitation into the room, presented Bertram with a letter. It was sealed with too much purple wax and the stamp had been lifted before allowing proper time for all that wax to dry, but Bertram didn't linger on its imperfections—he focused on the neat handwriting on the front of the envelope and let it warm him.

"You're to read it should you ever feel lonely," Edmund said. "It's from all of us."

Bertram had a feeling the letter was not, in fact, a collaboration, but it only made him love Edmund's kind heart even more. He swept the boy into his arms and hugged him until the nervous tension in Edmund's shoulders relaxed and he let go of his reservations, returning the hug and holding on tight.

"I will treasure it," Bertram promised. "And when I return home, I shall put it in my hoard."

"Do you mean it?"

"Aye." Bertram closed his eyes and gave him one last squeeze. "I do."

The next to seek him out was Owyn. Bertram heard him pacing outside the sitting room door long before the child mustered up the courage to come inside. When he finally did, he did it bashfully, sidling up to Bertram as though he was afraid that he was an unwelcome guest interrupting an important conversation.

The truth was the opposite in all regards.

Bertram very much wished to see his son, and since the other boys had come to visit, his conversation with Grimbold had concluded. There was nothing to interrupt.

"Will you come home soon?" Owyn asked in a timid whisper after climbing up onto Bertram's lap and melting against his chest. "We'll all miss you."

"I'll be back as soon as I can," Bertram reassured him. He gathered Owyn up in his arms and kissed the top of his head. "You needn't worry on that—as much as you will miss me, I will miss you more, and I will do whatever it takes to come home to you as soon as I can."

Owyn seemed satisfied by that. His small body relaxed, and eventually, his breathing slowed and evened out. He'd fallen asleep.

With a quiet word to his father, Bertram excused himself and carried the child to bed. He covered Owyn in his favorite quilts, then brushed his hair back from his brow and kissed him one last time. Of all the children, Bertram worried the most over how Owyn would adjust to his absence, but he knew, deep down, that he would be fine.

He had his brothers, and he had Sorin.

The lad would pull through. It would just take some time.

When Bertram was sure the boy was comfortable, he left the room only to run into a familiar face.

Sorin.

Sometime between Grimbold's arrival earlier that day and that very moment, he'd stripped out of his finely tailored clothing and into the drab garb worn by the servants. Over the last ten years, Bertram had gifted him jewelry—a ring here, a necklace there, a pretty bauble for his hair—and while Sorin had never been the type to drench himself in gold, he did seem to enjoy wearing it in moderation.

Now he wore nothing.

Not so much as a golden hairpin.

Bertram's chest tightened painfully.

How had it come to this?

"Is it true?" Sorin asked in a hushed voice after Bertram had closed their son's bedroom door. He paused only long enough to glance down the hallway nervously, as if expecting to find Grimbold there. "There's been talk amongst the servants that you are to leave at first light."

"Aye," Bertram admitted regretfully. "It's true."

Sorin frowned. He took a moment to be silent, then gave it up to sigh. "We knew it was coming," he said, crestfallen. "I just didn't realize it would come so soon."

"Nor I."

A noise from elsewhere in the castle—the clatter of a loose stone kicked across the cobbled floor—perked Bertram's ears, and for a moment, both he and Sorin stood still while they listened and waited for the worst to come. Bertram, who had been trained to be unflappable, could barely hear over the thundering beat of his heart.

But Grimbold did not rush out of the shadows, and whatever or whoever had kicked that loose stone did not appear. Eventually, Bertram's heart slowed to normal and his muscles—stiff in anticipation of a fight—loosened.

They had not yet been discovered, and as much as he wanted to stay with Sorin, it was in their best interest they conclude their conversation before that changed.

"They are sending me to Crimea," Bertram said in a rush.

Sorin's eyes widened, the whites of them catching the light from the candles burning in a nearby sconce. "Crimea? You must be joking."

"I wish I were."

"Has the council discovered us already?"

Bertram thinned his lips, but despite his apprehension, he shook his head. "I don't know. I don't think so."

"Then why come to visit?" Sorin glanced nervously down the hall, then shifted his weight from foot to foot. It looked like he was getting ready to run. "He could much more easily have written with orders to send you away."

"I think he has come to see for himself that I am no longer consorting with you."

Sorin snorted and shook his head. "Better that than the alternative, I suppose. We cannot risk detection. The work we do is too important to be exposed."

"I know." Bertram took the key to his desk from his pocket and gave it to Sorin, who closed it in his hand without giving it so much as a glance. "And with that in mind, this key is to the locked drawer of the desk in my study. In it are the most recent communications I've received from our correspondent. Word is that an agent of the council has been sniffing around after one of the runaway omegas we were able to rescue last year, and has uncovered our plan to liberate the Crimean cloister. When Father arrived today, I was midway through drafting a response—a strategy for evading the eyes of the council—but now there's no need to write. I'll be delivering my plan in person."

Sorin's hand tightened around the key, and something only a fraction kinder than anger flashed through his eyes. "That's madness. You'll be discovered!"

"I'll be fine."

"Bullshit." Sorin kept his voice hushed, but anger bled into it all the same. "They're setting you up. They know."

"I don't believe that."

"And you didn't believe me sane, either," Sorin said pointedly. "You pretend you know better than everyone, but you know nothing, Bertram. You work with beasts. You are fooling yourself to think they wouldn't delight in the hunt."

Bertram put on his finest Frederich smile. "You wound me, Sorin. I'm a smarter rabbit than that."

"And should you meet a clever fox?"

"Then teeth and claws will do the trick." With a theatrical wave of his hand, Bertram summoned forth his claws, which shone like obsidian in the dim light. "I am prepared for what I have to do, and I am under no illusion that it will be easy—the necessary things in life seldom are."

"And why is it fine for you to take this risk, but not me?" Sorin's voice shook. "When I ran off to do what was necessary, you followed me—begged me to come home with you, so I would be safe. Why is this different? Why are you allowed to run off and risk your life while I must sit here idle?"

"Because of the two of us," Bertram slid the claw of his index finger down the back of his opposite hand, splitting his skin and drawing blood, "I am the one most likely to survive should something go wrong." The cut closed almost instantly, the only suggestion it had ever existed a faint white line where his skin had knit itself together.

Sorin pinched his eyebrows in frustration, but finally gave in and shook his head. "I'm not happy about this."

"Nor am I." Bertram gestured to Sorin's clenched fist, inside which was the key. "Sorin... I want you to know that I am under no illusion that I am invulnerable. I am aware that if things do go wrong, our efforts will die with me. It's why I want you to keep that key. Should I never return home, take the documents you find inside the drawer and use the information therein to continue your efforts, and take whatever gold you need from my hoard to see them through. You may not be able to free every omega, but I know you will make a difference, and I trust you to do what's right and good in pursuit of our ultimate goal."

"Madness," Sorin mumbled, but the edge of anger in his voice sounded awfully close to grief. "You're not allowed to die. No one is allowed to kill you but me."

Bertram chuckled. "I know."

They stood together, too afraid to touch, lovers in strangers' bodies, until Sorin shook his head wildly and took a few hasty steps back, like he'd only just realized the danger they were in. "We need to go."

"I know."

"Do what you must," Sorin said, quickly checking over his shoulder before meeting Bertram's eyes, "but make sure you come home to us. I *love* you."

It looked like he would run, but instead he sprang forward and popped onto his toes, kissing Bertram on the lips before sprinting off into the night. He was gone before Bertram could gather his wits enough to reply, but Bertram didn't let it stop him—he whispered his words into the darkness of the hallway, hoping the castle would find a way to let Sorin hear that Bertram loved him, too.

Piers was the last of the children to visit. He came to the sitting room late that night, long after his brothers had fallen asleep, right when the embers in the hearth were losing their molten glow. Had Bertram not been trained to be perpetually aware of his surroundings, he wouldn't have noticed his approach. The child kept to the shadows and stepped quietly.

It was disconcerting how good he'd gotten at it.

Worse, it unnerved Bertram how Grimbold perked up when his grandson slunk out of the shadows to stand next to Bertram's armchair. There was a telling gleam in his eyes—excitement over untapped potential that Bertram had last seen when he had been young and similarly gifted. It made the hairs on the back of his neck stand on end, and prompted his dragon to hiss a warning. A single, simmering, *No.*

Bertram hadn't realized he'd made the noise aloud until Grimbold looked at him. Their eyes met. The gleam went nowhere, but with an arch of his brow, Grimbold slouched back in his chair.

He said nothing, letting Bertram take the lead.

"Shouldn't you be sleeping?" Bertram asked Piers, a hint of his dragon still in his voice despite his best efforts to suppress it. "I do believe you were supposed to have been in bed an hour ago."

"I couldn't sleep," Piers lied.

He did it well.

Grimbold's lips quirked.

Bertram's dragon seethed.

"I couldn't sleep," Piers repeated, "because I couldn't stop thinking about how different it will be after you're gone. It shan't be the same. Not at all. I'll miss you, Father."

"And I you."

The conversation continued, and Piers said his quiet farewell, but through it all, Bertram was on edge. Grimbold put on quite the act, pretending to occupy himself with a loose thread on his doublet, but even out of the corner of his eye, Bertram could tell the man was scheming.

And he didn't like it one bit.

Piers, who was perfectly polite and well-behaved, eventually excused himself and wandered off for bed... and whatever other dark corners he found along the way. There was silence for a moment after he left, then—like Bertram had feared would happen—Grimbold gave up on playing pretend.

"The whelp has potential," he said. "He's not like his brothers. Have you been training him as your replacement?"

"No." It came out cold, almost snarled, and Bertram didn't regret it. "Piers will not serve the council."

Grimbold grunted in acknowledgment and didn't press the matter further, but with Bertram riled, he became poor company, and their conversation languished and died. In its wake, Bertram excused himself with a mumbled word about how he'd need sleep if he were to fly to Crimea at dawn, and Grimbold let him go. He needed sleep, too, he claimed. There was an urgent meeting he needed to attend in the morning—one he couldn't afford to miss.

Bertram took the long way to his chamber to try to exhaust

himself, but it was no use. He was no less wired when he lay down to sleep than he had been in the sitting room, watching his father scheme. Restless and riled, he lay in his empty bed, in the spot where Sorin should have been, and worried. Not for himself, but for Piers, and the boys, and the not-quite-mate he'd leave behind.

The Black Sea had once marked the edge of the known world, and as Bertram circled its waters, losing altitude as he approached Yalta, he thought he understood why—it was immeasurably vast. Even from on high, there was no sign an opposite shore existed. Its sparkling blue waters stretched past the horizon and well into the realm of the unimaginable.

It was no wonder it had been left unexplored for so long.

But out there, beyond the horizon, beyond hope that the water would ever end, were distant places. Uninhabited shores. A chance to start anew.

Maybe one day, Bertram would visit them.

But for now, he had a job to do, and a family waiting back home.

Once he was low enough to land, he coasted the rest of the way to the shore and touched down on a secluded beach outside the city, where sea-serpent-fearing locals dared not go. Rumor had it that men had been dragged into the water and drowned by the beasts who lurked in its shallow waters, and while it was far from the best lie the agents of the council had spun in order to secure territory, it did in a pinch.

Upon landing, Bertram went through his transformation slowly, giving his body the time it needed to change without significant pain. Once he'd tucked all parts of his dragon back into himself, he stretched his arms high over his head to work the stiffness out of his sore muscles, then crossed the beach for the nearby tree line, where densely packed ancient oaks and Greek juniper trees hid a pea-sized cabin.

Bertram tested the front door.

It was locked.

"Bother," he muttered, summoning forth a claw. Everard, the wily bastard, had mastered some kind of magic that allowed him to come and go as he pleased whether a door was locked or not, but Bertram was not as magically inclined. Luckily, there were other ways around a lock, and he made quick work of the mechanism, manipulating the pins with his claw until he heard the thing click.

The door opened.

Bertram stepped inside.

The cabin was not lit, but light poured in through the open door and showed Bertram the way. He didn't have far to go. The cabin's main purpose was to serve as a dressing room for visiting agents, and its only piece of furniture—a large wardrobe—was positioned opposite the front door.

Bertram strode over to it, dressed, and left the cabin for Yalta.

He locked the door on the way out.

The other agents were not hard to spot—they'd gathered at a tavern near the cloister and were crowded around one of its long tables, conversing over tankards of ale. Bertram took stock of them upon entering, from Adhils' blond curls to Vsevolod's long black plait, and concluded that at least one agent from each clan had assembled.

None of them appeared bothered by today's business.

None of them but Siroslav, who kept glancing at the tavern door and out the windows, almost as if he was looking for someone. Knowing what he did, Bertram was surprised the man could sit still for long enough to enjoy his drink. His omega was the one the Vanguard had rescued after he'd run away a year ago. Had their positions been reversed, Bertram doubted he'd be so calm.

"Frederich," came a familiar voice as Bertram approached the table. It belonged to Merewin, one of his fellow Amethyst agents. He was Bertram's senior by a good four hundred years, but was young at heart, and far less callous than Osbert, who had trained them both. "Come sit," he said, gesturing with a sweep of his arm at the empty chair beside him. "I've saved a seat for you."

"Does Osbert not need it?" Bertram asked as he came around the table.

Merewin rolled his eyes. "Osbert was called away. Apparently something is afoot elsewhere, and he was called in to conduct an investigation. We aren't needed. Not that I feel we're particularly needed here, either." He leaned in close and admitted in a conspiratorial whisper, "Between you and me, I think Siroslav has summoned us here for nothing. Why call in reinforcement from every clan over an escaped omega and a vague suspicion that something untoward is happening? I understand the circumstances, but this kind of response seems irresponsible. Too rash. But I suppose it's to be expected. He hasn't been quite the same since... well, I needn't tell you. I'm sure you already know."

Bertram sat.

He knew.

And if all went well, he hoped to use it to his advantage.

"Anyway," Merewin continued, sliding his tankard of ale over to Bertram while waving down the barmaid to order another, "you haven't missed much. We did some poking around last night, but the cloister seems to be in good condition, and its omegas gentle and pliant things, eager to please. Obedient to their matron, too. Not even Felix could tempt a single one of them out of the courtyard, and you know how good he is at that."

Bertram arched a brow. "Impressive."

"Aye. They breed them right here in Yalta." Merewin snickered. "Perhaps when I next have sanctions, I'll try for a clutch with one

of them. Which reminds me—congratulations are in order."
Merewin's eyes sparkled, and he smiled at Bertram in the easy,
disarming way that all agents did. "Four whelps. Not bad for a
young thing like yourself. I hadn't heard that you were trying for a
clutch."

"It seemed pointless to mention it," Bertram lied, leaning back
in his chair as he slipped into Frederich's easygoing ways. "I
thought it would take me hundreds of years to succeed. Imagine
my surprise when my chosen omega conceived on our first try."

"That's good Amethyst blood for you," said Merewin, beaming.
"You should have seen the look on Kalfken's face when he found
out, the smarmy bastard."

Bertram glanced down the table at Kalfken, who appeared to
be the sole agent from the Topaz clan in attendance. The man was
doing everything in his power not to look their way—all Bertram
saw of him was his back and his long, rust-colored hair.

"The Topaz clan kicked up a bit of a fuss after it happened,"
Merewin continued. "Nothing came of it, but it was a point of
contention amongst us for a while. They kept insisting the paperwork was somehow falsified, and that the clutch should be
disposed of. Laughable. As if you would be so daft."

Bertram arched a brow and drained what was left of
Merewin's tankard.

"In any case, all of it's settled." The barmaid arrived with
Merewin's new tankard, which he drank from deeply before
advancing the conversation. "Now that the initial investigation
into the cloister has been conducted, we're moving on to look into
this suspicious force that allegedly took that one omega. A lot of
bull, if you ask me, but I suppose stranger things have happened."

A thin feeling of dread coiled in Bertram's gut.

It was odd.

He didn't fear discovery, but his anxiety built regardless, piling
higher and higher until he thought he might be ill.

Was it the ale?

He glanced at Merewin, who seemed unaffected, and discounted the thought. If anyone had wanted to poison him, they wouldn't have done it here. Not with so many agents present.

But this fear—this anxiety—whatever it was, he couldn't explain it away.

"Frederich, are you quite all right?" Merewin asked, frowning. "You look peaky."

"I'm—"

Bertram had meant to say that he was fine, but as he spoke, the building fear inside of him spiked, and he found he couldn't breathe. A pain ripped through him. An impossible pain.

Razor-sharp agony.

It was the feeling of a dragon's claws in his chest, trying to tear him apart.

Gasping for breath, Bertram grabbed uselessly at his tunic, sure that another agent—perhaps Kalfken—had sneaked up behind him to flay him where he sat, but there was nothing there.

Nothing but his own uninjured skin.

"Frederich?" Merewin asked, alarmed.

Conversation at the table stopped, and all eyes turned to Bertram, but he was in no condition to pretend that everything was fine. The claws—the ones that weren't there—dug deeper, piercing, tearing, seeking out his heart. One last rush of fear filled him, then everything went black, and it all stopped.

He had closed his eyes.

When he opened them, he discovered that not only had he stumbled out of his chair, but that he'd made it halfway to the door. Merewin was at his side, his hand gripped tight onto Bertram's arm.

"Frederich?" he asked. "What happened?"

"I… I don't know." Bertram slid his fingers over the places where claw marks should have been, but weren't, to his pulse point, which throbbed frantically as though the attack had been real.

But how could something like that be fake?

He'd felt it.

Felt his chest be skewered.

Felt those claws.

And yet, there wasn't a mark on him.

The pain hadn't been his own.

Which meant...

In a rush that chilled him to the core, Bertram realized two very important things.

The first was that the fairy tales were true—a mated dragon could feel his omega's suffering as clearly as if it were his own.

But it was the second realization that had him pulling away from Merewin and running for the door, mission be damned.

Because he knew where Osbert had been sent.

And why.

35

SORIN

"We have a guest, my lord."

Sorin, who had been tending to the children in the southern solar, looked up to find Hamish had joined them. He hadn't heard him come in, but that was no surprise—since Bertram's sudden departure, he had been distracted and melancholy. Worse, his head had started giving him trouble again.

"Is that so?" he asked, putting on a smile he didn't quite feel. "Who is it?"

"One of our lord dragon's clutch mates," Hamish said. "He had hoped to catch Lord Bertram before his departure, but arrived just a moment too late. Regardless, he has traveled quite a way, and hopes to make the best out of his time by visiting with his nephews. Since you are acting as their chamberlain, I told him I would come to collect you."

"Which brother?"

"He did not say."

"Oh." Sorin frowned in thought. Of Bertram's six brothers, he'd only met Sebastian and Everard. He supposed it stood to reason that of the remaining four, one might make the trek out to finally meet his nephews, but what unfortunate timing. If only he'd ventured out a few days earlier and arrived before Bertram's duty pulled him away. "Well, I suppose there's nothing to do but to welcome him into our home. Will you show me to him, Hamish? I only ask that while he's here, you and the other servants treat me as one of your own. No more 'my lord.'"

"Of course, my lord."

Sorin snorted with laughter.

They were off to a great start.

He left the boys to play in the solar and followed Hamish to the great hall, where Bertram's brother would be. The stranger waiting for them there was quite the Drake indeed—tall and with massive shoulders, dark-haired, and with eyes a curious shade of a purple. He lacked Bertram's jawline and his nose was wrong, but there were certainly parts of him cut from the same cloth.

The unnamed brother smiled at Sorin upon his entrance into the room, and Sorin smiled right back and performed a polite bow—one befitting a Pedigree omega.

"What hospitality might I render you, my lord?" he asked.

The dragon shrugged those big shoulders of his. "I want for little. Some food, a bed for the night, and the chance to see my nephews. I'm afraid that without my brother here, it would be improper to stay for long."

Sorin found himself impressed. He had heard from Bertram that his relationship with his brothers was strained due to the fact that Bertram had been separated from them in early childhood to begin his apprenticeship, but this brother was nothing but polite and courteous. Sorin found himself liking him already.

"Of course," he said. "We can arrange for that. But before we do, you must excuse me, my lord dragon—what is your name?"

"My pardon. I am Alistair."

Sorin racked his mind, then came up with it. "You're the last hatched of Bertram's brothers."

Alistair smiled sheepishly. "Never going to live that down, I'm afraid."

Sorin's smile grew.

He went to step forward and usher Alistair into the castle, but before he could, Hamish held out an arm, blocking the way. To Sorin's surprise, he struck his cane quite aggressively on the cobble, almost like how an angry rabbit might stomp its foot.

"Nay," said Hamish. "Who are you, really? For I have met Alistair, and you and he are not the same."

Alistair blinked in surprise, then looked upon Hamish with confusion and gave him a meek smile. There wasn't an ounce of malice in his expression, but there wasn't any warmth, either. There was nothing at all.

"I'm sure you must be mistaken, my good man," the dragon said. "I am indeed Alistair, runt of the litter, as Everard likes to name me. Do you truly not remember me?"

Hamish struck the floor again, his jaw set and his eyes narrowed. "No. No you are not, and I am not mistaken, ye scaly bastard. Begone from here! You're not welcome."

Alistair's smile melted, and his expression became quite pained. He looked from Hamish to Sorin and frowned as though in apology. "Memory does tend to soften over time…"

Hamish prickled. "I'm hundreds of years younger than you, I'll have you know! Do not listen to this villain, my lord. He is not who he claims to be."

"My lord?" Alistair's gaze flicked to Hamish. "You speak to an omega, my good sir. Are you quite sure you're of sound mind?"

The situation was deteriorating, and quickly. If the dragon was Bertram's brother, a slip of the tongue like that might have been overlooked, but if what Hamish said was true, this dragon was not family, and he was not to be trusted.

"I think," Sorin said firmly, "that you should go. You may call again when Lord Bertram has returned, but for now, I do insist you leave."

"I wish you would let me explain," Alistair said, sounding wounded. "There has been a misunderstanding. If we could just sit for tea and talk this through—"

"Over my dead body." Hamish took a step forward, brandishing his cane like a sword. "Out with you. Out with you now!"

Alistair sighed. "I was quite polite, and had sincerely hoped that no blood would have to be spilled today, but it seems we've come to an impasse, and my orders are quite clear." The dragon held up his hand, and as he did, tiny amethyst scales plunged down his fingers, turning them into talons. Claws like knives emerged from their tips. "You," he said, pointing one of his wickedly sharp claws at Sorin, "have been found guilty of the unlawful inculcation of an agent of the council, and for your crimes, shall be put to death. And you, old man," the dragon's gaze flicked to Hamish, "are unfortunately collateral."

Claws out and ready to kill, the Alistair impostor swept forward at frightening speed, headed straight for Hamish. It all happened so fast, Sorin barely had time to think, to react, to breathe—but as the dragon advanced, ready to kill the man who had given his life to Bertram and the castle, Sorin's body knew what to do. On instinct, he rushed in front of Hamish and took the attack onto himself.

"Lord Sorin!" Hamish gasped, grabbing onto his tunic from behind, but it was too little, too late.

The dragon ran Sorin through with his claws.

They sank like knives into his chest.

Sorin gazed down at himself. At the base of the obsidian claws that were still outside his body.

There wasn't much to see.

The dragon had skewered him through.

"Oh," he muttered numbly. Until then, death had never seemed possible, but now it was here, and it would not be made to wait. It would not be like it had been with Unwin, when he'd been sliced open again and again only to be stitched back together.

It was over.

There would be no coming back from this.

The dragon would kill him, and he would die.

Sorin looked at the dragon's face. At the Not-Alistair. He wore an empty but charming smile as he pushed his claws deeper, like he was readying himself to rip Sorin apart.

It was a mask, Sorin realized.

One he'd seen Bertram wear, when they'd first met.

Back when he had been Frederich.

Back before they'd fallen in love.

It was the face he'd hidden behind to put distance between his true self and the work he was asked to do. The bloodshed. The slaughter.

It was a face he hadn't seen for a long time.

"Lord Sorin!" Hamish bellowed, voice trembling with tears. "Get off him, ye cold-blooded devil! You have no right! He did no wrong!"

Sorin heard Hamish's voice, but his mind was somewhere far away, dragged back to that harrowing moment all those years ago when he had last felt agony like this—when he'd been pregnant and willing to do anything to keep his eggs.

It had been torture then, having to fight to save them when it would be so much easier to give up.

But now it was worse, because there was so much more he stood to lose.

The omegas of the Vanguard were depending on him.

The boys, and Bertram, too.

He would die, and they would all suffer.

Would they ever understand why he had left them on their own?

Tears streamed down Sorin's cheeks. Dragons really were monsters, weren't they? Soulless creatures incapable of love. All but Bertram. Bertram, who had been so kind to him. Who had believed in him. Who *loved* him.

And now, because of this dragon, he would be alone.

Sorin's hopelessness swelled as his heart broke, and as it did, the screaming in his head grew louder and louder until it was the only thing he could hear. His temples throbbed. A cruel pressure built up behind his eyes, pushing, expanding, like his skull might split open at any moment.

Then something in his head flexed like a muscle, and the dragon who'd run him through with his claws shuddered and stepped away. He tore his claws out of Sorin's chest, leaving four deep puncture wounds that immediately began to gush blood.

Sorin didn't feel them.

He was no longer at the forefront of his mind.

The thing inside of him, whatever it was, had taken control and dragged his consciousness away.

"What...?" muttered the dragon. He put a hand to his head and winced in pain.

The strange sensation flexed in Sorin's head again, then shifted and—somehow—*squeezed.* The dragon gasped, then choked and gurgled, clutching at his throat. It sounded like he was drowning, but that couldn't be right. There was no water here to drown in.

But there was blood.

Gallons of it.

The first trickle of which dripped from one of the dragon's nostrils only moments before it began to leak from his eyes.

"Lord Sorin?" Hamish asked in alarm just short of Sorin's ear. "What in the heavens—"

The thing inside Sorin flexed one last time, and the dragon fell to the floor.

Blood pooled around him, spreading swiftly.

Mere seconds later, he breathed no more.

In the quiet that followed, Sorin looked down at himself. Blood had soaked through the front of his tunic and continued to sluggishly pulse from his wounds in time to the beating of his heart.

"Oh," he muttered, and collapsed.

The world faded, and as it did, the thing inside him wrapped around him protectively, holding him close as lonesome darkness set in.

36

SORIN

When the darkness finally let Sorin go, he realized he was not alone. Someone was fussing over him. A woman, he thought, from the weight of her footsteps and the small sounds of consternation she made. Agnes, maybe. Her voice was familiar, but as Sorin groggily opened his eyes, he found his vision too blurry to tell. Whoever she was, she dabbed tenderly at his brow, then shuffled across the room and sat on a low piece of furniture. Head down and elbows on her thighs, she slowly slumped forward as if falling asleep.

Not wanting to disturb her and far too disoriented to risk sitting up, Sorin closed his eyes again and worked on remembering exactly what had happened. One minute, he'd been going to meet a dragon, and the next he'd woken here, in this strange, small room that was neither his bedroom, nor the great hall.

Where was this place?

He opened his eyes and blinked hard a few times, clearing the fog away, to discover the room was filled with shelves stacked high with pickling cans, bags of grain, and other sundries. By all appearances, he had been brought to one of the pantries, but that couldn't be right.

Why would there be a pallet bed in the pantry?

And under what circumstance would he have been brought here in the first place?

A knifelike pain cleaved neatly through Sorin's brain, and he lifted a hand to his head, wincing. Not only was the screaming back, but he had a headache from hell. Groaning from the pain, he covered his eyes with his arm to block out the light, and no sooner had he than the woman across the room startled awake with a noisy snort.

"Ah, Lord Sorin," she said, revealing she was indeed Agnes. "Thank goodness you're finally awake."

With some difficulty, she climbed to her feet and hobbled across the room to his bedside, stopping a little more than an arm's length away. Her frock was stained with blood, and the skin on her hands was red and irritated, but beyond that, something else was wrong.

Even though she seemed concerned for his well-being, she refused to come any closer.

"Agnes?" Sorin croaked. His mouth and throat were desert-dry. "What happened?"

She smiled nervously. "I was hoping you might tell me."

How could she not know? Surely Hamish had seen what had happened, and Hamish told Agnes everything. Something else had to be going on. Something he couldn't remember.

In search of answers, he closed his eyes and turned his focus inward, stringing together what fragments of memory he could find into one cohesive image, only to find it incomplete. He'd gone to the great hall with Hamish, met a dragon by the name of Alistair, and then…

Nothing.

His memory fizzled out.

All he could remember was pain.

"I can't remember," Sorin admitted. He blinked open his eyes to find Agnes frowning at him, partially out of concern, but also from another emotion, one far more difficult to pin. Whatever it was, when Sorin met her gaze, she quickly looked away. "What do you know about what went on? Maybe hearing you speak about it will help stir my memory."

Agnes looked across the room nervously, then crossed her arms and shook her head. "Oh, Lord Sorin, I only know what I've been told. My Hamish said a dragon came to the castle, pretending to be someone he was not, and when the deception was revealed, the dragon came at the both of you with his claws out, ready to cut you down."

The scene played out in Sorin's head just as Agnes described it, the dragon's claws glinting as he rushed forward, murder on his mind. But Sorin's memory was not limited to what he'd seen. The terror of that moment came rushing back as well. The helplessness. The pain.

He remembered jumping in front of Hamish.

Remembered the bite as the claws pierced his chest.

He touched the area where he'd been stabbed and found that since the attack, his wounds had been bandaged. Someone—likely Agnes—had packed them with gauze and wrapped them tightly with strips of linen, and somewhere during the process, must have applied some sort of numbing agent, because it hurt far less than it had any right to.

Perhaps that was why she was keeping her distance. She'd seen his wounds when they were bloody and raw, and if Sorin had learned anything from his time with Unwin, it was that a sight like that was enough to spook even the bravest souls.

But still, something wasn't quite right.

"Where is Hamish?" he asked suddenly, bolting upright out of fear and instantly regretting it. Pain shot through him—strangely worse in his head than his chest—and his only recourse was to lie back and let it pass. "Please," he said once he was able. "Tell me he's well."

"He is uninjured," Agnes said, but in such an uneasy way that it was clear there was more to the story. "He told me you stepped into harm's way to shield him from the dragon. We both owe you a great debt of gratitude, my lord. Had you not intervened, Hamish assures me he surely would have died."

"But where is he now?" Sorin attempted to sit up to get a look at the pantry door, but his injury complained when he started to move, and he immediately abandoned the idea. Wincing, he looked to Agnes for answers and found her watching him with pity from where she stood, one hand partially outstretched, like she was warring with herself over rushing to his side.

"Agnes?" he asked, frowning. "What's going on? Is Hamish safe?"

"Aye. He's well enough, my lord. At the moment, he's taking care of some business with a few of our most trusted servants. He will be back soon."

"And what of the dragon?"

Agnes refolded her arms and glanced across the room, where Sorin assumed the pantry door to be. "He's as dead as a doornail." She hesitated, and a truly worried look crossed her face. "Hamish has gone to attend to the disposal of his body. He told me…" Her arms tightened, and she turned her head so her cheek was against her shoulder, her eyes anywhere but on Sorin. "He told me you were the one who killed him, my lord, and that it was a frightful sight indeed."

Sorin, a dragon slayer? It was such an outlandish notion that he would have laughed if he hadn't been in pain. He'd sworn to Bertram long ago that one day he would kill every last dragon, but even he was not delusional enough to believe that an unarmed omega could have done one any amount of harm, let alone end his life.

But the fear shining in Agnes's eyes told another story.

"How could I have done that, Agnes?" Sorin asked, confused. "I had no weapon and no plan in place. It couldn't have been me."

"Hamish swears he saw it, my lord. Saw you cry out in pain, and then…" Agnes dropped her gaze. "Then the dragon began to bleed, and he did not stop, even after he was dead. It came out of him from every place it could until his body was entirely drained."

Sorin felt himself go pale. "He… he bled to death?"

"He did indeed. I cleaned up the mess myself."

"And there were no stab wounds?"

"From what I was told, you were the only one injured." Agnes worried her sleeve, still not brave enough to look him in the eyes. "Hamish would not let me see the body. He said it was too frightful a sight."

Sorin didn't doubt it for a second.

He'd seen Unwin contorted in death, and figured the impostor dragon looked the same.

"Are you a witch, Lord Sorin?" Agnes asked in a quavering voice after a beat of silence, the words rushing out of her as if she could hold them back no more. "Have you been hiding it from us all this time?"

"I…" The sandy feeling was back in Sorin's mouth. "I don't know. I don't understand what happened. There must be another explanation. I am just an omega. I cannot be a witch."

"I want to believe you, my lord. I really, truly do, but… there is another thing." Agnes pursed her lips, expression pained, clearly at war with herself. "When Hamish fetched me and had me tend to your wounds, they were so severe I was sure you would die. Still, I did my best to patch you up just like Lord Everard showed me. 'Twas years ago, before you came here, but once he stayed with us for a fortnight in January and amused himself by teaching me some of what he knew. He said with his brother living at the ends of the earth, he might one day need me to keep him alive until he himself could be summoned, and a good thing he did, for I've had cause to use my small knowledge of healing several times since." Agnes bit her lip. "But I thought to myself, seeing you like that, that even all I knew would make no difference. That all the spiderweb and honey in the world could never staunch your wounds. Yet an hour later, when I went to change your linens, your injury had improved by such a degree I was sure I was seeing things. It was as if you'd been healed by a dragon, my lord..." She eyed him only for a second, and fearfully. "But there are no dragons in the castle. You have been healing yourself."

It was lunacy.

Sorin was not a witch. He did not possess magic. He was an omega who knew more than most thanks to Bertram's insistence he be educated, but he was in no way comparable to a dragon. He'd never grown a single scale.

And yet...

"Will you show me, Agnes?" he asked, touching the bandages wrapped tightly around his chest. "I would like to see it for myself."

Agnes nodded and, despite her fear, stepped forward. With her assistance, Sorin sat up, and while he did still feel pain, it was nowhere as bad as it should have been. He knew the agony that could come from a dragon's claws, and this pain was not the same. Rather, it was dull and strangely warm, like his chest had soaked up the glow of a fire.

Once Agnes had him upright, she unwound his wrapping and helped him off the bed and over to a large basin of water. "Here," she said, gesturing at the surface of the water. "Look and see for yourself."

Sorin gazed down at his reflection. His hair was in a state of disarray and he was pale from having lost so much blood, but otherwise, he recognized himself. With Agnes's help, he leaned over to get a view of his chest and saw that while there were four distinct claw marks where the dragon had ripped into him, they were no longer raw. The lacerations had begun to close, and the shallowest of them was almost entirely healed.

Sorin delicately touched the skin around his injury. It tingled in quite an unusual way. Finding it unsettling, he dropped his hand and stepped back from the basin until his reflection vanished from the surface of the water. Agnes followed, keeping a hand on his arm even as she shook with fear.

"How long was I unconscious?" he asked in a near whisper, terrified.

"A good three hours. When I found you, you were a bloody mess, all torn open and in poor shape. What else could it be but magic's doing, my lord? I cannae say I've seen anything like this my entire life."

"I don't know what to tell you. I'm not doing this on purpose. Any of it. I swear I'm not a witch, but... what else could this be if it isn't witchcraft?" He laid a hand over his injury, hiding the claw marks. "There is magic in me. There has to be. But I have no control over it. I don't know how it works, and I don't know when it might strike again." His face crumpled. "What am I to do, Agnes? *What am I to do?*"

"You've lost your color," Agnes remarked, sounding worried. She guided him back to the bed without answering his question. "Rest, now, my lord. You've pushed yourself too hard, and there's no magic that will save you from that."

Sorin sat, too numb to argue, but how could he rest when his whole world had just been turned upside down? He was not who he thought he was. Not just some defenseless omega who had escaped certain death twice through blind luck. No. There was wild magic inside of him—dangerous magic with a taste for dragon blood—and if he did not take action, it could put his boys in harm's way.

And he could not let that happen.

He had to do something now.

"I have to go," he said, and it sounded just as numb coming off his tongue as it did sitting in his brain. "I can't stay here. Not only is the council after me, but this magic inside of me... it's targeting dragons, and I can't risk losing control of it around the children. For the sake of everyone in this castle, I need to leave." He lifted his gaze, looking Agnes in the eyes. "Tell the council when they come to look for me that I died during the attack, and that you buried me just like you did that dragon."

"Lord Sorin—"

"Promise me, Agnes," he croaked, fighting off tears. "Promise me that when they ask, you will tell them they got what they wanted—that I died bleeding and in pain. It's the only way they'll leave you be... and my disappearance is the only way I can make sure my family stays safe."

"You mustn't say such things! There must be another way."

The pain and fear at war in Agnes's eyes was too much—Sorin had to look away. "Not this time, I'm afraid."

"Lord Sorin..."

"I do not like this any more than you do," he said quietly, staring at his knees. "But what other choice do I have? I am a danger to you in every possible way. A criminal in the eyes of the council. A wanted man. A witch." His voice broke. "The time I spent here with you in Braemar was time I never should have had. Time I stole from a dragon whose soft heart gave me another chance at life when all I deserved was death. But that time is over now. I am a danger to him, and to the children. I cannot stay. Tell me you understand."

Agnes was quivering all over again, but this time not from fear. She grabbed her apron up in her hands and used an unspoiled corner of it to dab her eyes, but it was no use—tears streamed down her cheeks anyway and made her voice sound wet when she said, "I do."

Sorin couldn't stand to see her that way, broken because of him. The guilt was too much, and he knew if he let himself simmer in it that he might be tempted to stay. But he couldn't. Not while he was a danger to the ones he loved.

He could not return until the council thought him dead and he'd found a way to control his magic.

"Do you know where the children are?" he asked while Agnes sniffled. "I left them in the solar when I went to see the dragon, but I highly doubt they're still there. Do you know where they might be?"

"Aye. Beatrix is looking after them." She sniffed a final time and dropped her apron. "When I learned what had happened, I asked her to keep them busy. I believe she's taken them to the stables and put them to work, as far outside of harm's way as could be. Do you intend to head there next? I would like to come with you, if it pleases you, my lord. To see you off, and be with the bairns through their grief."

"Not yet. There are a few things I must tend to first before I leave."

"I will help you," Agnes said, and it was a statement, not an offer.

Sorin wasn't sure how much help she would be, but he could not begrudge her that.

After leaving the pantry-turned-hospital room, Sorin's first stop was his bedchamber, where he dressed himself in clean clothing and selected a few garments to take with him on his travels. Next, he entered Bertram's hoard, where he pilfered a wallet fat with golden coins and selected a few small and easily concealable pieces of jewelry that would be easy to sell at market should the need arise. Lastly, he let himself into Bertram's study, where he hastily wrote two letters, then accessed the locked drawer in Bertram's desk, to which Bertram had given him the key.

It contained the last thing he would need.

With that secret knowledge hidden away, Sorin locked the drawer and gave Agnes both letters and the key.

"This one," he said, holding out the first letter, "must be dispatched as soon as possible. It is addressed to Lord Everard Drake, and is a plea for help. I do not know how long it will be before another dragon from the council is dispatched to investigate the first one's disappearance, but I do know that someone will be coming, and that it will be soon. With Bertram gone, there needs to be someone here—someone who can advocate for you and the children, and send future impostors away. Please, make sure this gets to him as quickly as it can. You have my blessing to take whatever you need from Bertram's hoard to make it happen —I know that when he discovers the truth, he will understand."

Agnes nodded and tucked the letter beneath her arm. "And this one, my lord?" she asked, indicating the letter that remained in Sorin's hand.

Sorin looked down at it.

Ran his thumbs over the parchment.

"This one," he said much more quietly, "is for Bertram. When he returns, please give it to him along with this key on my behalf. It will tell him everything he needs to know about what has happened to me."

Agnes accepted the letter and the key with trembling hands and placed both in the large pocket of her apron, where they disappeared from view. "I will make sure he receives them," she promised. "You needn't worry about a thing."

"Thank you." Sorin gave her his best smile, but it was a small and tremulous thing. "I have one last favor to ask of you, Agnes— will you go into the stables on my behalf and ask one of the grooms to ready my horse for travel? I would do it myself, but with the children there, I don't trust myself, I'm afraid."

"You won't go to see them one last time?"

"No."

"But Lord Sorin..."

"Please don't make this any harder." Sorin's voice cracked. "I wish that things were different, Agnes. I really, truly do. But how can I go to see them when I know that should something go wrong, it could end their lives?"

Agnes lowered her head. "I will ask one of the grooms to fetch your horse," she said miserably. "And Lord Sorin?" A beat of silence passed. "I will look after your family, bairn, and I will make sure your boys grow up knowing the depth of your love. You needn't be afraid."

In his short lifetime, Sorin had suffered, and suffered greatly. He'd been taken against his will, separated from his eggs, and abused. He knew what it was like to shed blood. To lose limbs. To be torn open to the point where he was sure death was coming, only to wake up healed and have it happen all over again.

But of all the hardships he'd endured, nothing hurt like this.

It was too much to take.

A sob wrenched itself out from somewhere deep in his chest, and it broke him.

He would never see his babies again.

He would never get to see them grow.

"Oh, bairn," Agnes cooed, gathering him in her arms. "Bairn, I know. Let it out. Once you do, you'll feel better, you'll see."

Sorin didn't think that was true, but he didn't let that stop him. He buried his face in Agnes's shoulder and wept until he had no more tears left, then headed with her to the stable, where the hardest goodbye would be the one that could never be.

While Agnes went to fetch one of the stableboys, Sorin went to sit by the paddock, afraid that if he came too close, the children might find him. It was late in the day—too late for such an ambitious journey—but the weather was mild and the sky was clear. If his luck held, the road ahead would be easy, and with a few good days of sunlight on his side, he'd reach his destination within a week.

Once there, his new life would begin.

He'd never see Scotland again.

Mournfully, Sorin hugged his legs to his chest and looked out across the grounds. From where he sat against the paddock's fence, he had a clear view of the loch and beyond it, fields of golden, swaying wild grass that would soon succumb to winter's chill, brown, and go dormant or die. He'd seen it happen year after year. Seen the world give life, and then take it away.

He thought he'd broken that cycle when he'd come all this way for his eggs.

But he'd been wrong.

"Papa?" asked a small voice not far from Sorin's ear, startling him so much, he hit the back of his head on the fence post. Cussing, he cupped the site of impact to keep it from throbbing and turned his head to find Piers standing there, no more than an arm's length away.

They made eye contact.

Piers blinked and cocked his head. "What are you doing here, Papa?" he asked, searching Sorin's face for an answer. "It's not like you to want to be alone."

Sorin's mouth went dry all over again.

He wanted to run.

He *should* run.

But this was his baby—his heart and soul.

How could he turn his own son away?

"You need to go, Piers," Sorin said firmly, but even as he did, tears began to roll down his cheeks. "You mustn't be here. You are in danger."

"You're crying," Piers remarked, and frowned. "I'll go get Owyn. He'll know what to do."

"Do *not* get your brother."

But Sorin's command fell on deaf ears.

Piers was already gone.

Sorin scrambled to his feet and cast a hasty look around for somewhere to hide. The paddock was too wide open, and while the fields of tall grass in the distance might do the trick, it would take a while to get to them, and he didn't think he had the time. Returning to the castle was an option, but a poor one—Sorin wouldn't be able to see the groom come out with his horse, and if he missed his chance to leave, it would make things that much worse.

The only option, then, was to sneak into the stables through the paddock doors and hide in one of the stalls until Piers and Owyn gave up looking for him. He'd risk discovery by Waryn and Edmund, who were still at work in the stables, but it seemed to be his only option. It was the only way he'd be able to make a clean break.

The paddock fence was tall and sturdy, having been built to keep horses in. Four wooden boards, stacked horizontally equal measures apart, blocked the space between each fence post, too tight a squeeze for Sorin to fit between, but just barely.

If he wanted to reach the other side, he would have to climb.

It shouldn't have been difficult—the fence was only about five feet tall—but not even an hour ago, Sorin had needed help to walk from one end of the pantry to another, and despite the magic in his blood healing him from inside, he had yet to fully recover, and his body was not happy with what he was asking it to do. His legs shook as he stepped up onto the first board, and his grip was weaker than it should have been as he stepped up onto the next. By the time he'd made it to the top, he was sweating and dizzy, shaking almost as badly as Agnes after she'd learned his terrible truth. Still, he was proud of himself. He'd done it. All that was left to do was lower himself into the paddock and hurry for the doors, and then—

"Papa? What are you doing?" asked Piers, who had appeared out of nowhere.

He'd not only brought Owyn with him, but Edmund and Waryn as well.

His sudden appearance spooked Sorin so badly that he slipped and tumbled gracelessly into the paddock, barely managing to land on his feet. By the time he righted himself, Piers was standing next to him, having slipped through the space between the slats that Sorin had been too large to fit through.

All three of his brothers followed suit.

"And why are you in the paddock?" Piers asked, looking up at him with the same curiosity Sorin often saw in his father's eyes. "I saw the stableboy tacking up your horse—are you thinking about taking her out for a ride?"

Sorin took a step back. He glanced desperately over his shoulder, hoping the groom would be there with his horse, but he was nowhere to be seen.

"Papa?" Piers followed him, and to Sorin's horror, the other boys did, too. All four of them came far too close, and worse, as he backed away, they followed, not letting him go.

"No," he croaked, but his throat was closing, convulsing with a sob. "Don't. Stay away."

"He wants to play tag!" Waryn bellowed, laughing, and suddenly, all four children were on him, rushing toward him, not knowing that they were in danger, thinking he wanted to play.

"*No!*" Sorin cried one last time, but it was too late—the boys would not stop.

So he ran.

He ran as they laughed and whooped and hollered.

Ran as they chased him.

Ran as fast as he could, but still, it wasn't enough.

They caught him easily.

Waryn tackled him, locking his arms around Sorin's legs and bringing him to a sudden stop. On any other day, Sorin would have been braced for it, but he was panicked and weak from his injury, so he lost his balance and fell.

"Look what you've done," chided Edmund as Sorin groaned

and tried in vain to wiggle away. "You big oaf. You hurt Papa. Look, he's crying."

"He was crying before," Piers said as a matter of fact. "That's why I went to get Owyn."

"Owyn will make it better," Waryn agreed.

But Owyn only made things worse.

Upon his brothers' prompting, he came to sit by Sorin's side and wove their fingers together so their hands were palm to palm, then, with great tenderness, he lay down by Sorin's side and tucked himself beneath Sorin's arm so they were cuddled up together, like they often did when Sorin told him stories before bed.

"I'm sorry you're sad," Owyn whispered mournfully. "I'm sad, too. But bad feelings never last forever. Father will come back one day soon, and then we'll all be happy again."

Sorin choked back a sob. He would rather be at Unwin's mercy and be cut open every day than here, knowing that his sweet boys were unhappy, and that he'd only be adding to their unhappiness.

"You can't," he choked out through a sob. "Owyn, you can't. You have to go. Please. Please, *go.*"

"Papa?" Owyn asked, heartbreak in his voice. "Papa, you don't have to be sad all on your own. It's okay. We don't mind if you're sad. You may think we're still small, but we're actually big and strong and powerful, and we will protect you just like Father does. We always will, no matter what, so you don't have to be sad or afraid."

It was a dagger to the heart, and it carved a sob out of Sorin that burst from him violently.

Owyn, not understanding, hummed in consternation and cuddled closer, but Sorin couldn't let him stay there.

Not when there was so much at risk.

Not when he couldn't guarantee their safety.

Heartbroken, he tugged his hand away from Owyn's and wiggled out of Waryn's grasp. Once free, he popped up onto his hands and knees and rose onto his unsteady feet, drunk with fear and misery. It felt like he would fall on his face at any second, but it didn't matter—for the sake of his boys, he needed to get away.

"Papa?" Owyn scrambled up with him, grabbing his hand. "You don't look well. What's wrong? You can tell us. It's okay."

The other boys surrounded him, picking up on Owyn's concern. It was clear they weren't going to leave him alone until they had an answer, so Sorin swallowed what he could of his sorrow and pulled himself together enough to speak.

"Something has happened," he said. He chose his words carefully, not wanting to reveal too much in case the council questioned the boys. "I have done something very bad, and I need to go away."

"Where?" Waryn asked.

"Should we get our horses?" Edmund looked toward the stable. "Beatrix's husband has been teaching us to tack them up, so it won't take us long."

"No." Sorin shook his head, feeling his throat start to tighten. "You won't need your horses, as you won't be coming with me. I need to go on my own. The four of you will be staying here."

The boys quieted down, and all at once, Sorin became very aware that four sets of purple eyes were watching him, some suspiciously, and some with disbelief.

"Why?" Piers asked.

"Yeah, why?" asked Waryn. "We're old enough to go with you, and besides, if we don't, who will keep you safe?"

"I'll be safe on my own," Sorin promised. "I know I am only human, but before you were born, I traveled great distances without assistance and survived plenty of dangerous things. I am not worried about myself, but I am worried about *you*, which is why it's so important I leave. There's…" He paused out of necessity, having to force the words out. "There's something evil inside of me, and I am afraid that it will hurt you if I stay."

"An evil thing?" Piers perked up. "What is it?"

"I will vanquish it!" Waryn declared.

Edmund looked between his brothers, then warily at Sorin. He did not step away, but he didn't get any closer, either. Sorin noticed he kept an eye on Piers, as if waiting to see what he would do.

Owyn, however, seemed not to notice what his brothers had said or done. Frowning, he tightened his grip on Sorin's hand as if to ask him to stay, but Sorin couldn't.

He squeezed Owyn's hand, knowing it would be the last time, then broke contact and stepped away.

"The evil thing inside of me," he told them, "is dangerous. It could kill you if it wanted, and it cannot be vanquished. That's why I have to go away."

"But will you come back?" Piers asked.

Sorin's lips wobbled. He looked down on them, on their four heads of messy dark hair and big, imploring eyes, and said the hardest word he'd ever had to say. "No."

"Never?" Edmund asked uncertainly.

"Never ever?" Owyn warbled.

"Never," Sorin told them, and started to cry all over again.

When the stablehand found them, bringing with him Sorin's travel-ready mare, the five of them were huddled there in the paddock, not far from the fence, all four boys weeping as Sorin held them to his chest. He had wanted to spare them from this goodbye and keep them safe from the wild magic inside of him, but in the end, he was glad for this last moment of selfishness—it was one last chance to commit his babies to memory.

The softness of their hair.

The touch of their sun-soaked skin.

The small hands. Their voices. Their hearts.

And in that moment, Sorin told them everything he wished he could have told his other children—that they were beautiful, and that they were loved, and that even though this was goodbye, he would protect them, and he would do it with all his heart.

Sorin left them when the sun was setting, just before the world went dark.

But day or night, it made no difference. The light had already been snuffed out of his life.

Shadows didn't scare him anymore.

37

BERTRAM

Bertram did not stop—he flew through the night. A cutting western wind fought him, sliced into the nooks and crannies his scales couldn't hide, but the pain it caused him was muted by fear. Even now, hours since the incident in the tavern, the memory of those phantom claws digging into his chest refused to let him go, and even though conditions weren't right for flying, he feared if he let up for even a second, they would rip his soul to shreds.

Sorin wasn't safe.

Was hurt.

Was *dying*.

Comfort would come later, after he had saved his mate.

So, despite the pain, he flew.

He pushed forward and endured, and as night faded and day began, his efforts finally paid off.

Castle Beithir appeared.

It was little more than a gray speck on the horizon, but seeing it gave him hope. The bond had gone dark, but it had not severed, and that meant Sorin was in there somewhere, injured but alive. He would be able to find him and pour his healing magic into him, and all the wrong that had been done to him would be made right.

Just a little farther now, and everything would be okay.

With the castle in his sights, Bertram tucked his wings to his body and shot forward like an arrow, gaining speed while losing altitude. No dragon was allowed to fly below cloud cover due to the risk of being spotted by a human, but Bertram knew the land and the comings and goings of its people, and he would not let the law of the council stop him.

Not after what they had done.

In minutes, the castle was upon him. Bertram dipped lower, so close to the ground now that the long grass brushed his belly, and began his transformation.

As he flew, dragon gave way to man.

Bones snapped. Muscles contracted. Parts of him condensed and disappeared. His fangs gave way to molars and his scales pushed free, leaving stretches of smooth human skin in their place. Transformation was by nature a slow process—the magic required to shed one body for another was immense, and the magic needed to shield those bodies from the pain of transformation was greater still—but Bertram rushed the process. He did not have time to wait.

Well aware of the consequences, he channeled all his magic into his transformation. With none left over to protect him from the reshaping of his body, he felt every bone break and every muscle reform itself.

It was agony.

But for Sorin, he would die this death a thousand times.

Bertram was a few feet from the ground when he lost the last of his dragon—his wings. With them gone, he dropped gracelessly out of the sky. His legs, clumsy from disuse, gave out beneath him upon impact and sent him pitching forward. He toppled to his knees, skinning his palms to keep himself from falling on his face, only to scramble back up and fall all over again.

The exhaustion of flying through the night had drained him, and his painful transformation had done him no favors. His legs couldn't bear his weight, and even as he dragged himself up onto his hands and knees, his arms shook.

If he kept pushing himself, he'd collapse.

But what was the alternative?

Sorin needed him.

The children needed him.

He'd been a fool to leave.

Head hung, breathing hard, Bertram crawled toward the castle. Tears streamed down his cheeks. He'd been taught that emotions were weaknesses that could be used against him by an enemy seeking to gain the upper hand, but he'd never understood how that could be until now—now that it felt like his heart had been ripped from his chest and shredded before his eyes.

Was this what it meant to be mated?

A sob—the first in centuries—tore itself from his throat, and his arms finally buckled. He slumped to the ground, head buried between his forearms, and let loose the pain he'd buried inside himself over the last four hundred years.

He'd been foolish to think he could make this work. His father had been right. It had been irresponsible to take Unwin's clutch. He'd already lost his brothers in service to his clan—why had he ever thought he wouldn't lose his chosen family, too?

In his despair, he barely heard the thud of something small but dense strike the ground nearby. It very well may have been a figment of his imagination, but then it happened again, closer this time, and then another time after that. When he finally did notice, he lifted his head and looked up, bleary-eyed, to see he was no longer alone. Hamish stood before him, leaning heavily on his gnarled cane, and by his side was Agnes, who looked like she might cry. She was dressed for the kitchen, and her apron was dusty with flour, but she must not have been deep into her work, as her hands were dry and clean. They were clutched to her chest over a bulky ball of fabric—some kind of thick-knit garment made of brown wool that Bertram didn't recognize.

"Up now, my lord," said Hamish, hobbling over. He offered Bertram his hand. "Do not mourn. He lives."

"Where is he?" Bertram choked out. His voice was strained and hoarse—gritty—like his throat was made of sand. "Is he safe?"

"Up, now," Hamish repeated, stretching his fingers out with an invitational shake. "Let's get you back on your feet."

Bertram squeezed his eyes shut until the last of his tears ran down his cheeks, then gritted his teeth and took Hamish's hand. The old man pulled him up, and Bertram leaned on him, too weak to support his own weight. Meanwhile, Agnes shook out the garment, revealing it to be a shawl. She swept forward and wrapped Bertram up in it. Her hands trembled as she did up the buttons.

"We don't have all the answers," she said quietly once the last button had been fed through its hole. "But what we do have is this." From the pocket of her apron, she produced a letter, which she held out to him. "He sent word to your brother as well, asking for him to come and protect the children against other possible threats."

A burst of fear turned Bertram's stomach to ice, but his dragon seethed with rage. If any dragon—Amethyst or not—had so much as laid a claw on his children, he would hunt him down and paint the ground with his entrails while he still lived. "Are they safe?"

"Aye, no harm has come to them. But I fear their wee hearts have been broken. It will do them good to see you, my lord." Agnes dipped her chin and dodged his gaze. "But first, please, you must read the letter. You must see what Lord Sorin has to say. Hamish and I—we don't understand what has happened, and we've been worried. Will you please read it and tell us if Lord Sorin is all right?"

Bertram nodded and took the letter from her. It was written in Sorin's hand, but the letters were rushed and the quill strokes uneven—surefire signs he'd been under duress. Casually, Bertram glanced at Agnes and Hamish both, trying to gauge their reactions, but they kept their eyes down and their expressions somber. If they were withholding information, they were doing a damn good job at it.

He would have to follow up with them later, after he read what Sorin had to say.

Bertram—

Read the letter.

I have learned a great deal under your tutelage, but I'm afraid I know no word in any language suited to describe the heartbreak I feel having to write this letter to you. But there is no escaping it. So much has happened, and none of it good. I am sure Agnes and Hamish will tell you what they know of the situation, but there are details they are bound to miss.

Details that pertain to me.

I do not know how to say this other than to state the plain and terrible truth—I have killed a dragon.

I didn't mean to and I do not know how it happened, only that it did. He attacked me, claiming my life was forfeit as per the decree of the council, and as his claws slid into me, something inside me snapped and he began to bleed. Whatever that something is, I believe it killed Unwin, too.

If you, like me, are tempted to pin the blame for this on someone or something else, don't. Whatever this dark and evil magic is, it lives inside of me, and I have proof. Hours after the attack, my wounds healed of their own accord. I remain injured, but to such a small degree that it barely seems the attack happened at all.

What else can we blame but magic?

Magic that does as it pleases, and that has slaughtered not one, but two dragons.

Magic which I cannot control.

Bertram—I cannot put you or the children at risk. My heart is breaking, but I have to go.

I love you more than I thought possible, and I will love you every bit as fiercely until the moment I take my last breath.

Goodbye, my love.

You were everything to me.

Yours forever, no matter the distance between us,

—Sorin

"Sorin is safe," Bertram murmured, heavy-hearted, once he'd read through the letter.

"Will he come home?" asked Agnes. "Will he come back to Castle Beithir?"

Bertram thinned his lips, and it was answer enough. Agnes wrapped her arms around herself and pressed her cheek against her shoulder, but she didn't let grief overwhelm her. After a moment spent in sorrow, she shook her head and came around to Bertram's other side, placing a hand on the small of his back to offer both comfort and additional support. "Let's get a meal in you," she said. "Come now, my lord. There are few woes a hearty stew can't make better."

Bertram nodded, but he said nothing. His tongue felt useless and frozen, and words wouldn't come.

With Agnes and Hamish supporting him, he returned to the castle.

It no longer felt like home.

"To the best of your recollection, tell me what happened here when I was away," Bertram said after Agnes had seated him at the table and served him a heaping bowl of stew.

Hamish sat across from him, his cane resting against the table. Bertram couldn't recall a time when the man had ever looked as tired and stressed as he did now. The dark circles under his eyes were so pronounced, they almost looked like bruises.

It seemed Bertram was not the only one who'd had a sleepless night.

"I don't know what to say, my lord," Hamish mumbled, shaking his head. "A dragon arrived—an Amethyst. He claimed to be Lord Alistair and wished to see the children, but I knew it was a lie. I'd met Lord Alistair during one of his silly Grand Tours, and he and that dragon were not the same."

"Alistair would not have come unannounced," Bertram said with a nod. He dug his spoon into the stew and ate, and while it was delicious, he found he had no appetite. With a frown, he prodded at a piece of potato, then set down the spoon. "Very few of my brothers would do such a thing. We do not have such an easy relationship."

"This dragon would have had me believe otherwise," Hamish said quite gravely. He folded his hands on the table and lowered his gaze, frowning. "When I revealed his lie, he continued his deception and called my memory into doubt. Lord Sorin, bless him, believed me, and when we both insisted he leave, he attacked. He meant to spill my blood, but Lord Sorin intercepted and was wounded in my stead." Hamish's frown deepened. "And then…"

"And then?"

"I cannae say." Hamish wove his fingers together and worried his knuckles, refusing to lift his gaze and meet Bertram's eyes. "It seemed like magic, my lord. The kind of evil you read about in fairy tales. Lord Sorin let out a scream, and the dragon started bleeding. It came from his eyes, his nose, his mouth… everywhere."

"And what happened after that?"

"The dragon died," Hamish admitted in a quiet voice. "Lord Sorin fainted once he did, and I called Agnes in to tend to him. While she did, I disposed of the body. It was a frightful sight. So pale and cold, even though he was so recently deceased. It seemed to me there wasn't a drop of blood left in him." Hamish squeezed his hands together nervously, then dared glance up at Bertram. "How could that be possible? Our Lord Sorin is righteous and just —a kind man, and a good father. Could he really be a witch?"

"Lord Sorin is Lord Sorin," Bertram said firmly but kindly. "What he has or has not done does not change who he is, or who you know him to be."

"Then do you think it to be true, my lord? Do you think him capable of magic?"

"I think," said Bertram levelly, choosing his words with care, "that he, like you or I, is capable of any number of incredible things when it comes to protecting the ones he loves."

Hamish nodded gravely.

He hadn't much to add after that.

In the silence following their conversation, Bertram ate what he could of the stew, then excused himself from the table. There was still so much to do. Everard was on the way, and as soon as news reached his father that he had abandoned his post around the time of Osbert's death, Bertram knew he would visit as well.

But before that—before any of it—he had to see his boys. To

make sure they were all right, and that they knew they were safe and loved.

He spent the day with them out by the loch, trying his best to turn a blind eye to the work Hamish and the other servants were getting up to in the garden.

The flowers would be out in force this spring.

Red Devon daffodils, their trumpets the color of blood.

Everard arrived on the morrow not by horseback, but by air. The heavy beating of his wings heralded his descent onto the castle grounds, giving Bertram just enough time to look out the nearest window and see him land. No sooner had he set claw to earth than the children—all four of them—burst out of the castle and were upon him, scaling him like a mountain. Waryn, the quickest of the lot, sat on Everard's head like one might sit upon a horse.

"Let's go flying, Uncle Everard!" he cried, pointing skyward, before crashing his ankles into Everard's temples. "Up!"

A bit of smoke escaped Everard's nostrils, but he complied and, once all the boys were settled, lifted off and flew lazy circles over the loch. Despite having perfectly good wings of their own, the boys whooped and hollered and punched the air as though they'd never had such fun in their lives.

Bertram watched them, quietly enjoying their antics, until Waryn stood up and dove off Everard's head into the loch, at which point Bertram left his study and went to wait in the great hall for his brother's imminent arrival.

No more than ten minutes later, Everard arrived. He was nude, and his hair was dripping wet. His feet left puddles in his wake.

"What the devil is going on?" he demanded, sounding cross, although not as cross as Bertram had assumed he would be. It was more than likely that had to do with the three sets of eyes peering in at them from the doorway. Piers was the only one missing, but Bertram was not naive enough to think he was absent—the boy was simply better at making himself scarce.

"I received a letter," Everard continued, having stalked right up to Bertram's place at the table. "It claimed the children were in need of protection by a dragon, and yet here you are. Have you given up your scales, brother? Last time I looked, you were a dragon—although I suppose with all of your secrecy, that very well could have changed."

"I am, indeed, still a dragon." Bertram arched a brow and slipped on one of his easiest smiles. "And you, dear brother, are quite naked. Come. Let me find you some linens. While you dress, I'll explain what has happened."

Everard narrowed his eyes. "By explain, you do mean transparently, right? Not some handwavey, vague non-explanation?"

Bertram rose from his chair and fixed the boys with a pointed look. Owyn gasped, and they scattered.

"If you'd like," said Bertram once they'd gone, "I'll keep my hands behind my back throughout the conversation—no hand-waving, guaranteed."

Everard sighed. "Would it kill you to give a straight answer every now and then?"

"No," Bertram said cheerfully, steering Everard out of the room. "But it very well could kill you, and I would rather that not come to pass."

Once Everard was dried and dressed, Bertram took him into his study and shut the door. It wouldn't keep them safe from small ears, but the illusion of privacy made him feel better and seemed to put Everard at ease, for he dropped the cheerful uncle act and glared at Bertram like he'd caught him pinching golden coins out of his hoard.

"What's going on, brother?" Everard demanded. "Have those bronze bastards threatened the children? Annoyances, the lot of them. If this is about their dispute with the Sapphire clan over territory, I would take it to the council. Our ties with other clans should not paint targets on our backs. Their grievances are with the Sapphires, not with us."

Bertram shook his head. "No. Nothing of the sort has happened. I'm afraid you were called here for naught. The letter was a fabrication—an attempt by a disgruntled servant to besmirch my name and reputation, and nothing more than that." The lie grated on the way out, but it sounded smooth to Bertram's ears. "You have my sincerest apologies, Everard. The servant has been released and won't bother you again."

Everard's expression softened somewhat. "Are you lying to me, Bertram?"

"No."

There was silence, marred only by the sound of rustling fabric as Everard loosely crossed his arms. "I do feel as though there is something you're not telling me, but whatever it is, I want you to know that I am here for you. You and the children both. We might not always get along, but we are family. You needn't carry the weight of the world on your own."

"Thank you." Perhaps it was yesterday's vulnerability creeping up on him again, but Bertram no longer had to force his smile. "I truly do appreciate it."

"In any case," said Everard, "I am relieved to hear the whelps are safe and all is well, whether you're being truthful or not." He smiled back. "Now, come. I've traveled a very far way—and at great personal expense, might I add—and I find myself quite peckish. Join me for breakfast. It is the least you could do."

Bertram acquiesced with a nod and showed Everard out of the study. Breakfast was a small price to pay for the comfort of knowing there was one Drake still on his side.

Everard left the next day, taking Bertram's largest source of distraction with him. The boys needed tending, of course, but they were young men now, and learning independence. More often than not, they kept themselves occupied, which left Bertram plenty of time to think.

But his idle mind proved to be a dangerous thing.

Most times, it thought of Sorin. Where he'd gone, and what he was doing. How he'd managed to kill not one, but two dragons, and what this strange magic of his could really be.

Bertram didn't believe him to be a witch.

He didn't believe in witchcraft at all.

Magic belonged to creatures like him, who were born with it in their blood. It did not belong to humans. If it did, the world would be a different place, and human life far less transitory.

But how else was he to explain what had happened?

He'd seen Unwin himself, his body drained of blood, wretched in death, and now to hear that Osbert had suffered the same fate... it couldn't be a coincidence.

Sorin was behind it somehow.

Had caused it somehow.

But even as time marched onward, Bertram couldn't figure out how that could be.

Worse, when he wasn't preoccupied by that mystery, his mind moved on to hurtful things.

He had been betrayed.

Osbert had not come to the castle of his own accord—he had been sent there. Sent by Grimbold. Sent to make sure Bertram had given up his omega.

And now he was dead because of it.

Bertram did not believe his father was an evil man, but the pain of knowing what he had done hurt deeply. There had never been much love between them—Bertram was his puppet, and had accepted it long ago—but over the last decade, Sorin had undone the programming that had made Bertram think such acts of heartless cruelty were okay.

Yes, agents of the council risked too much by being attached.

Yes, the power they wielded could be exploited and turned against their own clan.

And yes, it was better to sever attachments lest they lead to disaster...

But Sorin was his mate, and there was no way to distance himself from that.

Those thoughts stuck with him, digging in like barbs until, a week following Everard's departure, Bertram could take it no more.

While the boys played outside, he shut himself in his study to write. The next day, he did the same. It was not an easy process. He scrapped letter after letter, none of them quite right, but the right words were in him somewhere, so he wrote, and rewrote, hoping they'd emerge.

"You needn't be so hard on yourself," scolded Agnes one day when she came to bring him tea. By then, a pile of crumpled letters littered the study floor, and Bertram's inkpot had run quite low. "Lord Sorin will be thrilled to hear from you no matter what you say—your letter needn't be perfect."

But Agnes was wrong on both counts.

The letter did have to be perfect, because Bertram wasn't writing to Sorin—he was writing to his father.

"Thank you, Agnes," he said politely, setting his quill down to accept her offering. She tutted at him, having known him long enough to tell when he wasn't taking her seriously, but didn't push the matter. Instead, she gave him a hard, lingering look, then hobbled out of the room to cause trouble elsewhere. Likely down in the kitchens. One of the new servants wasn't performing to her standards, and Agnes had taken it upon herself to sort the girl out.

Once she was gone, Bertram set the tea on his desk, picked up his quill, and went back to writing. An hour and three crumpled attempts later, he gave up.

Which was just as well, as no sooner had he than a spooked servant threw open the door and announced in a tremulous voice that an unexpected visitor had arrived—Bertram's father, Grimbold Drake.

BERTRAM

Grimbold did not waste time. When Bertram entered the great hall, his father stopped pacing and turned immediately to face him, his traveler's cape flapping about his ankles as he did.

"We have matters to discuss," he said brusquely. "Come, let us adjourn to your study. We need the privacy of a closed door."

Bertram's blood ran hot and his dragon gnashed its teeth, but theirs was a game of cat and mouse, and Bertram couldn't afford to let it end. Any sign of hostility toward his father would be an admission of guilt, and would only make things worse. He could not let on how attached he had become to Sorin. Not only would it be a mark against his professionalism, but it would lead to further investigations that might endanger Sorin's life. A single misspoken word could ruin everything.

So, even though Bertram would have rather run his father through with his claws, he smiled politely and bowed his head in concession. "Of course, Father," he said. "Please, follow me."

The study door shut behind them with finality. Bertram, playing the role of a gracious host, showed his father to one of the room's armchairs as though nothing was wrong, but Grimbold wasn't interested in hospitality. He sat heavily and sighed, crossing his arms over his chest and giving Bertram a weary look. "Merewin informed me you left Yalta in a hurry. I take it you know, then."

Bertram's lips tightened. He sat stiffly opposite his father. "That you were using Osbert to spy on me?"

"No." An emotion passed through Grimbold's eyes, although which, Bertram couldn't tell. "That I was using him to investigate what I believed to be a potential threat. You should be glad I did. It seems I was right, for now he's missing and presumed dead. It could have been the whelps, Bertram. Osbert gave his life to keep your family safe."

It took every ounce of Bertram's control to keep his dragon from lunging forth and ripping out his father's throat, but Grimbold did not know the truth, and he never could. If Bertram had been in his place, he would have come to the same conclusion.

His father was not a villain.

Not any more than Sorin.

But it was a hard truth to swallow when Bertram had been so deeply harmed by what he'd done.

"Do you know where the omega has gone?" Grimbold asked when Bertram said nothing.

Bertram shook his head. "He fled long before I arrived, and told no one where he was going. The servants observed him taking off toward London, but that hardly means it was his intended destination. It's far more likely he's squirreled himself away in some hamlet. If you intend to look for him, I'd suggest you send your men there first, but I will not be joining them. For now, I need to stay here to ensure the children are safe. You are right—their lives were in danger, and until I know the threat is truly gone, I will not leave them again."

"I'd thought as much." Grimbold sat straighter, mirroring

Bertram's posture. He looked his son in the eyes. "We made an agreement when you claimed the clutch as your own. Ten years of sabbatical, after which you promised to return to your duties without excuses."

"Would you risk the children's lives, then?" Bertram asked, a hint of a challenge creeping into his voice. "I will serve my time, Father, but the boys—"

"You must let me finish, child." Grimbold held out a silencing hand. "I have no plans to deploy you abroad. Merewin can deal with foreign matters for now. You are needed here."

A creeping feeling pricked its way down Bertram's spine. "Please, explain."

"Osbert's death leaves the Amethyst clan vulnerable," Grimbold said. "You will be tasked with training a new agent—one who will swear his life to the council and to his clan, just the same as you have, and just the same as every agent before."

"Who?"

"Piers."

Bertram was on his feet before his brain could register what his body was doing. He caught himself a few steps away from Grimbold, realizing to his horror that his dominant hand was fully clawed. "I won't allow it."

"You have no say in the matter."

"*He is my son.*"

"And you are mine." Grimbold didn't snap, but his lips pursed and his eyes narrowed in irritation. "Do you think I haven't given this any thought? Piers displays all the natural talent you did at his age, and with you there to teach him, he will excel. The Amethyst clan may never know better agents than the two of you."

"He is but a child, Father."

"And so were you."

Bertram had been trained to keep his wits about him regardless of the circumstance, but in the face of this new development, it was as if his mind had turned to peat. "There has to be another candidate," he managed to say when all other words failed him. "Piers can't be the only one. There must be someone just as suitable."

"Do you question me, child?"

Bertram set his teeth. "I do."

The look in Grimbold's eyes went dark, like a storm sweeping in off the sea. A single line of scales tumbled down his neck, but with a grunt and a jockeying of his posture, they disappeared.

"Fatherhood has changed you," he remarked, "and not necessarily for the better. You swore an oath to protect and serve your clan, Bertram. You must understand that part of that includes honoring the choices I make for all Amethysts. Piers is the dragon best suited to become our new agent. Not only does he display natural talent for the profession, but he is young enough that as he grows, he won't just learn our ideals—he'll embody them. As you do." Grimbold paused. "As you *did*. I will not change my mind."

"Does what I want mean nothing to you?" For all his training, Bertram couldn't keep his voice from quavering. "I understand the clan must always come first, but Father, I have given so much for them already. Is it not enough that I was taken from my brothers? That I was made to spill blood and risk my own life? Must I now give up my son, too?"

"You mistake my intentions," Grimbold said, more softly this time. "I do not mean to punish you with this decision. You know better than any of my children that the work we do necessitates sacrifice. What our hearts want is not always in alignment with what the clan needs, and the clan must always come first."

"I see." Bertram's hands shook, and he was sure the rest of him was no better off. To better hide his vulnerability, he went back to sit in the armchair opposite his father, where he balled his fists and dug his claws into the meat of his palms, but even that wasn't distraction enough. He knew what Piers would have to give up to become an agent of the council, and it ate at him.

His son deserved better.

He deserved to be free.

"Our lives are not easy ones, child," Grimbold said gently. "I wish things were different, but this is how it must be. We must not only think as fathers, but as protectors of the people. As leaders. Selfless and brave. Tell me you understand."

Blood beaded where Bertram's claws pierced his skin, but it didn't help. He didn't feel brave at all. "I do."

"Piers will begin his training in a fortnight," Grimbold said. "The other clans have been made aware that a new Amethyst candidate has been selected, and as his training progresses, they will send an agent each to help shape his development, as is tradition. You will remain his primary overseer throughout, and will ensure that his education is in alignment with Amethyst virtues, just as Osbert once did for you."

"I understand."

"Time will take the pain away," Grimbold promised. He rose and squeezed Bertram's shoulder, a reassuring gesture that did nothing to ease the iron grip despair now had on Bertram's heart. "As Piers develops, you will see that this is for the best. I trust in you, Bertram, but you must trust in me, too."

Bertram nodded.

This time, he didn't bother with a lie.

Piers took to training like a duck to water and, under Bertram's tutelage, developed into the model agent his grandsire knew he would be. As all agents did, he adopted a new name. It functioned, in essence, like a shield, becoming a persona to hide behind to keep his true self safe from the horrors of the work he would be asked to do.

Like Frederich, Connor was polite and affable. He knew how to smile his way through subterfuge and engage convincingly in deceit. Sorin would be heartbroken to know what he had become, but Sorin was gone now, and Bertram was bound by his duty. One day he would find a way to apologize, but until then, he honored Sorin as best he could by training Piers to only depend on Connor when absolutely necessary. It would not be like it had been with Bertram, who'd been pressured to shed his old life and live as Frederich permanently. Piers would get to stay with his brothers during his training and, through his connection to them, keep his childhood.

He would not lose his family.

And if Bertram had any say in it, he would not lose himself, either.

It was not an easy time. Bertram was kept busy with Piers's training, but even at his busiest, there were quiet moments during the day when his mind was prone to wander, and it always went to Sorin. Where he was, and what he was doing. If he was well. If, in his travels, he'd already managed to change some small part of the world, or if now that he was on his own, larger change was coming.

Bertram couldn't say.

When he'd met Sorin, he'd been determined to kill all dragons and set their captive omegas free, but the man Sorin was now didn't match who he'd been then any more than Bertram resembled his past self. He imagined that Sorin would want to stick to the plan they'd come up with, and that he'd found his way from Braemar to the Vanguard, where he could directly help those in need.

But without correspondence, it was hard to tell, and Sorin did not write.

Bertram couldn't blame him.

Ever since the incident with Osbert, Bertram had ceased communications with the Vanguard as well. There was far too great a risk the council was keeping him under surveillance, and if the council discovered his betrayal on top of everything else that had happened, he would surely be put to death.

It pained him to stay silent, but the omegas of the Vanguard were as hardy as they were sharp-witted and determined, and they would be fine in his absence. If Sorin was with them, even better.

He had taught them well.

The Vanguard would be fine.

Still, his thoughts strayed to them often, and when the first group of agents from the other clans arrived to train Piers, Bertram saw his chance. With his son's education now out of his hands and his time now no one's but his own, he kissed the rest of his boys goodbye and instructed them to mind Agnes and Hamish while he was away.

There was someone he needed to see.

Someone who deserved to know the truth.

39

SORIN

The vineyard was awakening, having shed the dreary grays of winter for vibrant, budding greens. It would be a fruitful year, according to the resident omegas. The mild winter and bright, sunny days were favorable conditions for grape growing, and thanks to them, the harvest was sure to be impressive. Some of the most ambitious grapevines had already begun to produce shoots, and while it would be another few months before any fruit appeared, it was a sign of good things to come.

There would be plenty of wine to sell come autumn, Sorin thought to himself as he tended to a broken trellis late that morning, which meant the Vanguard was well on its way to self-sustainability. No more would they be dependent on Bertram's coin.

It was a bittersweet blessing.

The Vanguard deserved independence in all its forms, but...

Sorin's heart gave a painful pang, and he abandoned his work with the trellis to simply sit on his haunches and breathe. In the six months since he'd left Scotland, he hadn't heard from Bertram once.

Was he still alive?

The uncertainty of not knowing woke the voices in Sorin's head, and as they wailed, he carded his fingers through his hair and tugged in a futile attempt to distract himself from the pain.

Would the council have made an attempt on Bertram's life, too?

Could they have succeeded?

It killed him that he didn't know, and that there was no safe way to check.

The children are all alone because of you, whispered the darkness inside him. *One father dead, the other a danger to them. They'd be better off if you handed yourself over to the council. At least then, they wouldn't have to live with the pain of knowing you abandoned them.*

It was too much. Sorin gasped, hunching over, as his head began to throb. The pain was overwhelming, and it was only getting worse. If he didn't find a way to talk himself down, he would never find his way out.

"It wasn't my fault," he said out loud, struggling to get the words out. "I did what I had to do. I didn't abandon them. Their safety had to come first. If I had stayed, they could have died."

You're horrible, the voice rebutted. *You hurt them.*

The voice needn't have wasted its breath.

He knew it.

But for the sake of his well-being, he needed to forgive himself. The screaming only ever seemed to settle when he cleared his mind and let go of his guilt... and with Bertram gone, he had to be strong. The Vanguard needed him. He was their sole leader now, and he had to keep it together—if not for himself, then for his team, and every suffering omega awaiting salvation.

"I'm okay," he told himself even as his dark thoughts tried to tell him otherwise. Slowly, he sat up straight and let his head fall back, neck stretched as far as it would go, so his face was soaked in sunshine. "I'm okay," he repeated as the sun warmed him. The darkness behind his closed eyelids turned red, the light chasing the shadows away. "I did the best I could, and I will keep doing my best. I will. No matter what happens, I will keep trying. I won't stop. Everything I do, I do for good."

It took time, but slowly, the edge came off. The dark thoughts receded, and the screaming went with it, quieting until it was barely a murmur—there, but tolerable. Once it was controlled, Sorin took a deep, grounding breath and picked his head back up.

He opened his eyes.

Everything was as he'd left it, the trellis right there in front of him with its broken picket, tools scattered around him and a replacement piece at the ready. Nothing had changed. Nothing but him. But he was strong, and he was learning, and maybe someday, he'd find the right tool to fix himself, too.

Sorin resumed his work after that, prying the broken picket from the trellis and tossing it aside. He fitted the new picket in place and, after double-checking it was correctly sized, was reaching for his hammer when a terror-filled shriek split the air— this one not in his head.

"Amélie," he said with a gasp, jumping to his feet. He sprinted down the vineyard row and around the side of the winery toward where he thought he'd heard the scream and found Amélie near the winery door, a dropped jug of water spilling out by her feet.

She was not alone.

A stranger was with her. He was wrapped in a traveler's cape, its hood up and obscuring his face, and sat atop a great brute of a horse, seventeen hands tall and black as midnight. Upon spotting Sorin, the horse's nostrils flared, prompting the stranger to set a hand on its neck and whisper something against the back of its ear. The horse flicked its ears and snorted but did not take its dark eyes off Sorin—which was fine, as Sorin couldn't look away, either.

He recognized that horse.

But Amélie did not.

"Dragon!" she sputtered, accidentally kicking the jug in her mad scramble to get away. Water sloshed across the stonework and pooled beneath Sorin's feet, but still, he stood there.

Motionless.

In shock as he took in the horse and its rider.

He remained there until Amélie, the sweet thing that she was, realized he wasn't running away with her and rushed out in front of him, arms out, blocking him from the stranger's view.

"Run!" she urged Sorin. "Alert the others. I'll hold him off as long as I can from here."

"There's no need." Sorin capped her shoulder and squeezed. "But thank you for your bravery. Would you please go collect the others and bring them inside until I give the all clear?"

Amélie gave him an uncertain look, but she did not argue and, after one last glance at the stranger, scurried away. Once she was gone, Sorin stepped out of the puddle and crossed his arms loosely over his chest, trying his best to look foreboding, but coming across as moody at best.

"You're risking your life to be here," he said in English, speaking to the stranger. "And for what? You know I can't come home."

The traveler gave the impression of a laugh—an exhale of breath through his nose—and pulled off his hood to reveal what Sorin already knew.

"I'm aware," Bertram said, and smiled that easy smile of his, love softening his eyes. "But there are important matters we must discuss that merit the risk. Is there somewhere we can speak privately?"

"We can speak here."

Bertram arched an eyebrow and glanced over Sorin's shoulder, where several of the resident omegas had gathered in the doorway of the winery to eavesdrop. When they noticed they were spotted, they all gasped and darted back inside, but Sorin was no fool—he knew they'd gone to hide by the windows, or just beyond the doorframe out of sight and out of mind.

If they spoke here, they would surely be overheard.

Sorin mulled it over, then nodded in the direction of the vineyard.

"Stable your horse and come walk with me through the rows," he said. "Out there, we'll be alone."

SORIN

Bertram, darkly handsome in his traveler's garb, strolled unhurriedly through the vineyard with his chin slightly upturned and his eyes on the sky. He kept his hands tucked on the small of his back and maintained a respectful distance between himself and Sorin, but every now and then, he glanced longingly at Sorin from the corner of his eye as though he badly wanted to be next to him, touching him, their hands clasped and their fingers interwoven, like it had been before Sorin had been forced to flee.

Truthfully, Sorin wanted it, too, but as much as his heart begged him, he knew he couldn't.

It was far too much of a risk.

"I thought, perhaps, you had been killed," Sorin admitted quietly as they found a place two-thirds of the way down the row where their only company was the trellises and their budding grapevines. He folded his arms over his chest and tucked his hands away to make sure he kept them to himself. "I left in such a hurry, I didn't even consider the council might have been trying to eliminate you at the same time they tried to eliminate me. Did they hurt you?" He glanced worriedly down Bertram's body, imagining the scars he might be hiding behind his heavy cloak.

"Not knowing has been agony. You shouldn't have come, but... I'm glad to know you're alive."

"I am uninjured." Bertram paused, looking down Sorin's body with the same quiet concern Sorin had just shown him. His love-stricken expression turned somber. "But I know the same can't be said for you. It seems you have recovered. Are you well?"

"My injuries are healed."

"But are you *well?*"

Sorin pursed his lips to keep his bottom lip from trembling. "I think you already know the answer to that."

A heartbroken expression crossed Bertram's face. Without thinking, he reached out for Sorin as though wanting to pull him into his arms, but remembered himself and dropped his arms back to his side. "I'm sorry."

"It's not your doing." Sorin looked away, tucking his arms tighter around himself. "You couldn't have prevented it. We knew what we were doing could lead to something like this."

"It doesn't mean I can't be sorry. The pain everything has caused you—"

"*Please—*" Sorin took a shuddering breath. "Let's not talk about it. It is what it is, and I am learning to live with it. Picking it to pieces won't help. I just..." He glanced at Bertram's heartbroken face and had to look away again. "Please tell me the boys are well. I just want them to be okay."

"They are doing well," Bertram promised. "They miss you, but they are thriving, and growing bigger and smarter every day. You needn't worry."

"And Agnes and Hamish?"

"Still as healthy as they are stubborn."

"And you?"

This gave Bertram pause.

"I give my all for our children," he said, neatly dodging the question, "but the state of my well-being was not what brought me to seek you out. There are some things that have happened you must be made aware of, and since I cannot write for fear my letters may be intercepted, I have come to deliver the news in person."

Sorin's stomach sank. "What news?"

"I don't know where to begin," Bertram admitted. "So, I suppose I will get the worst of it out of the way first. After the death of the Amethyst agent who was sent to dispose of you, my father has elected a new agent to take his place... and he has chosen Piers."

Sorin's blood turned to ice. "You can't be serious."

"I wish I could tell you I'm not." Bertram folded his arms over his chest and dropped his gaze. "But I have been tasked with training him, and I have been doing everything in my power to make sure he doesn't lose himself along the way. He will get to stay with his brothers, and he will know the love of his family. His duty will not overshadow his individual worth. I cannot keep him from the work he will be asked to do, but I have done everything I can to protect the young man he is growing into. He will not turn out like me."

The noise in Sorin's head stirred, and his dark thoughts came back.

This never would have happened if you hadn't been so self-involved. Who do you think you are, anyway, trying to change the world? You can't even keep your own family out of harm's way. Who would want your help when you can't even help yourself?

"Sorin?" Bertram asked, alarmed.

Sorin snapped back into the moment and realized his hands were in his hair and his shoulders were pinched to his neck. His whole body had gone tight.

"I'm fine," he murmured, dropping his hands. "At least... at least you are there to look after him. I trust you. I know you won't let him wander down any dark paths."

"I won't," Bertram promised. "And while I would never have put him in this position had I my druthers, perhaps it won't be all that bad—with two of the three Amethyst agents on our side, it's far more likely my connection to the Vanguard will never be discovered and disclosed to the council. It's a small silver lining at best, but at least it's something."

"Is that the good news?" Sorin asked.

"No." Bertram looked Sorin over, and a flicker of love warmed his eyes. "The good news is you're my mate."

Everything stopped all at once—the noise in his head, and the beating of his heart.

"Your mate?" he asked in a small and unsteady voice. "Bertram, that's not possible. How do you know? How could it be?"

"When you were attacked, I felt your pain." Bertram chuckled. "I nearly blacked out in the tavern, surrounded by my fellow agents. Surely they thought I was losing my mind, and for a moment, I might have believed it myself, but then I realized it wasn't me—it was you. I left right away and flew through the night hoping I could save you, but by the time I arrived, you were already gone."

Sorin knew he should say something, but in light of this revelation, a part of him that had been dormant for a great many years began to wake, dragging him back to when he'd lived in his cloister, before he'd been sold by his matron and taken away. Freshly finished with a lesson on how best to plea-sure a dragon, he'd found himself in the ruins of the Byzantine garden outside, having been coerced into skipping his next lesson by two of his rowdier classmates. The three of them sat beneath the shade of the garden's old, gnarled acacia, and while they chatted, Sorin contemplated the mangled remains of a nearby bronze statue. He thought it somewhat resembled a lamb.

"Can you imagine going through all the trouble of laying a clutch only to find out you've mated with your dragon?" one of his friends, Zehra, said with a snort. "I think I would rather die."

"Why?" asked Sorin. He traced the dents in the statue with his eyes, imagining the kind of force it would take to crumple metal in the way the statue had been crumpled.

"Why?" Eren, the third member of their group, chuckled. "Have you not been listening to our matron, Sorin? If you are able to lay a clutch, you are sent away to live in luxury, never to have to bed a dragon again."

"But if you mate a dragon," Zehra said, a note of warning in her voice, "that dragon will own you for the rest of your life, and will claim you over and over again. No, thank you. If I am to be forced into the bed of some haggard creature I care nothing about, I want to be paid handsomely for my services, and I only want to have to do it once."

There were four gouges in the bronze.

Four deep indentations, almost as if something large, clawed, and unfairly powerful had smashed its foot down on top of it, causing the metal to cave.

"I wouldn't worry yourself, Zehra," said Eren, with mischief in his voice. "No dragon in his right mind would ever try for a clutch with you."

Zehra had cried out in indignation and scrambled to her feet to smack Eren over the head with her slipper, and, laughing, the three of them had moved on from the conversation and never come back to it again.

None of them had known the truth.

None of them could have known.

But in those dark days after he'd been taken, forced to bear clutch upon clutch to dragons who meant nothing to him, sometimes Sorin's only consolation was knowing that he was not mated to these monsters. That his pain wouldn't last forever—it would only be for now.

Had he known then that, against all odds, he would end up mated, he would have ended his suffering then and there.

But Sorin wasn't that person anymore.

He would never forgive dragons for what they'd done to him,

but somehow, impossibly, he was *happy*. Happy to know that this particular monster was his for all of time.

But his happiness was temporary.

The bond had formed too late.

Now that Sorin knew about his magic, he couldn't be with Bertram.

Couldn't go back to Braemar.

Couldn't see their children for fear the evil inside him would kill them, too.

The truth of what he was feeling must have shown on his face, for Bertram frowned. "I must admit—I wasn't expecting you to react to the news we are bonded like this. Did your cloister not teach you what it means to be mates with a dragon? You will be mine forever, and I will be forever yours."

"You speak as though we have a future," Sorin murmured.

"We do."

"No, we don't." It broke Sorin's heart to say it, but it was the truth. "The mate bond changes nothing. I told you in my letter and I will tell you again now—as long as this evil magic lives unchecked inside of me, I cannot risk being with you. I've killed two dragons already and I can't promise I won't kill again. You must keep your distance. Think of us as a couple no more."

"You're missing the point." Bertram stepped forward, closing some of the space between them. "Do you not see? You're looking at the world through the eyes of a man, but you are no common man anymore. You need to see things from my perspective. Now that we've bonded, we have time we didn't have before. Time to find you someone who can help. Time to tame your magic. We may not be able to be together for now, but that may not always be the case, for a dragon's mate lives as long as his dragon... and sometimes, even longer than that."

A chill ran down Sorin's spine.

His heart, already battered by the spectrum of emotions he'd put it through, pounded like he was running for his life.

Dragons lived for thousands of years. In the past decade alone, he'd liberated two cloisters and helped organize successful rescue missions for over a dozen other entrapped omegas.

What more could he do with a hundred years?

Five hundred? A thousand?

Not only would he have the time he needed to truly make a difference, he would have time to find a way to be with the dragon he loved.

"Do you see now?" Bertram said, and only then did Sorin notice he'd come closer another few steps and closed the distance between them. Gently, Bertram lifted his chin with a curled finger until they were looking into each other's eyes. "We may have to live apart for now," he whispered, smiling. "But I vow on my life it won't always be that way. I will figure out how to bring us together. I promise. I will do anything for you, Sorin. No matter how impossible, I will fight for us, and I will win. The council will not hold me back, and your magic will not stop me. I am a dragon, and I always find a way to get what I want—I will not stop until I bring home what's mine."

"Yours," Sorin whispered numbly. Dumbly. The screaming in his mind—those ghostly echoes from the past—hadn't gone away, but in light of everything, they had faded into the background. Or maybe it was that the screaming had been dampened—it felt as though his mind had turned to fluff, like a dandelion gone to seed.

Whatever the true cause, the relief was intoxicating, and Sorin gave in to it readily. He closed his eyes and parted his lips, inviting Bertram's kiss, and when Bertram took him up on his offer, Sorin wrapped his arms around him and claimed his lips over and over again.

There was a tree not far from the end of the vineyard row—a mature cork oak that had likely been ferried there by a squirrel when it was only a seed. Hands planted on Sorin's ass, Bertram backed Sorin against it and deepened the kiss, tasting his mouth, demanding his tongue, making Sorin want so much more.

He knew deep down that he should stop—that his body was as much a weapon as any sword or mace—but despite everything, he was still human.

Human, and in love, and in want of his lover.

His one perfect mate.

"We shouldn't," Sorin gasped into Bertram's mouth, but in the same breath, he reached down and grabbed Bertram through his codpiece.

Bertram was already hard.

"I could be the death of you," he added breathlessly, groping, squeezing, wanting more than anything to feel Bertram inside of him. To know his touch, and to be with him again.

"You always told me I would die by your hand," Bertram said with a little smirk. He nipped Sorin's lip, making him moan, then flexed his hips forward to press himself into Sorin's hand. "Frankly, it's a little embarrassing you haven't managed to kill me yet... so what do you say I give you one last chance? End me, Sorin. Finish what you started all those years ago. I forfeit my life to you."

Sorin shuddered, then pushed his hands through Bertram's hair and gripped it, tugging his head forward. Their lips crashed together, and the resulting kiss was incendiary, burning down the last of Sorin's resistance and leaving him vulnerable to the demands of his own heart.

In the six months they'd been apart, there hadn't been a day when he hadn't wanted this. Wanted Bertram. Wanted to see him crest the horizon on horseback or by wing, if only to know he was alive. He'd dreamed of the impossible—of waking up in bed to realize it was all a bad dream, or somehow finding a cure for his magic. Of suddenly being saved. And while he wasn't quite there yet, he had half of what he wanted.

Bertram was living, breathing, there for him... and the familiarity in his touch reminded Sorin of who—at his very core—he was meant to be.

He was not an evil witch, cursed to spend eternity without his family.

He wasn't the leader of the Vanguard, an impartial voice of justice and reason who valued the well-being and safety of others even if it came at a detriment to himself.

He was Sorin.

Only Sorin.

Lover. Father. Mate.

And in that moment, even though it was irresponsible, Bertram was his.

All his.

And nothing could change that.

Their souls were bonded now, and they were destined to find their way back to each other over and over again.

That sudden understanding spread through Sorin, sitting warm and heavy in his veins. The situation was far from perfect, but it was tolerable, and it would get better. It had to get better. One day, they would find a way to vanquish his magic, and he would take his place at Bertram's side as his forever mate.

Greedily, unable to help himself, he plunged his hand between their bodies and into Bertram's codpiece, taking his cock in hand. Bertram moaned meekly into his mouth, and his hips gave an involuntary thrust that made Sorin shiver.

God, he wanted it.

The heat of it.

The stretch of his knot, and the raw pleasure it made him feel.

"Fuck me," he gasped against Bertram's lips, and with a growl that rumbled in his throat, Bertram pushed Sorin against the old cork oak and did exactly that.

Pants shucked and cock primed with precum, he hoisted Sorin up and into position, barely giving Sorin time to wrap his legs around Bertram's waist before he pushed inside. Bertram thrust up into him wildly, not giving him a second to catch his breath, and Sorin clung to him for dear life, crying out as Bertram pushed pleasure into him.

His toes curled.

He'd missed this. God, he'd missed this.

What he wouldn't give to come home.

"Breed me," he pleaded into Bertram's ear, clutching him tight as Bertram drove into him over and over again. "Put your knot in me. I need your cum."

Bertram growled again—louder this time—and punched up into Sorin with his hips, bumping into a place inside of him that knocked the breath from Sorin's lungs. Pleasure sparked uncontrollably in his stomach, and crying out, he came, clinging to Bertram as Bertram pounded into that spot without end.

Bertram didn't last long after that. Shuddering, he pushed deep into Sorin's tight hole and came hard, cock twitching as he filled Sorin with his hot cum. His knot swelled, locking them together, and Sorin grinded down on it wantonly. He wanted it as deep inside of him as it would go while Bertram filled him with cum.

"Fuck," Bertram mouthed, barely even loud enough for the word to take shape. He thrust up into Sorin slowly, lazily, chasing out a few last pumps of cum. "*Sorin...*"

Quivering from pleasure, Sorin rode him just as lazily, kissing the words out of his mouth, wishing against reason that he could stay.

"I feel better when I'm with you," Sorin admitted in the comfortable silence that followed. "I wish we didn't have to be apart."

"I know." Bertram nuzzled tenderly into the dip of his shoulder. "I wish it, too."

"Do you really think there is a way to save me?"

Bertram paused for a measured beat. "I believe few things in life are truly impossible."

"But do you include me amongst them?"

"I don't know." Bertram gave a light laugh, but there was no humor in it. "I don't think there is a way to know. Not until I try. But I promise, I won't give up on you. Not even if it takes a thousand years."

Even for a dragon, a thousand years was a long time.

It would mean hundreds of thousands of days spent apart from each other, and hundreds of thousands of nights alone.

"Will you be able to tolerate a millennium on your own?" Sorin asked, suddenly melancholy.

"No," Bertram said simply. Teasingly, he traced his fingers along Sorin's hip, his touch so gentle, Sorin couldn't help but shiver. "But I won't need to."

"What do you mean?"

Bertram nosed into Sorin's hair and pressed a kiss at the base of his ear, letting Sorin feel his smile. "For hundreds of years," he said, "I have followed orders and obeyed every law in the book, but Sorin… I am the villain now. By choosing you, I have betrayed my kind and cast aside the lawful part of myself they shaped from me. I will serve the council to keep up appearances, but outside of what is mandatory, I will no longer do what I am told." His smile grew, and with a touch of playfulness, he took Sorin's earlobe between his teeth in a claiming bite. "Case in point, you told me to stay away," he whispered, his breath hot on Sorin's skin, "yet here I am, and even knowing the risks, I intend to do it again. I will steal every moment I can to be with you. I may not be able to promise when I will see you next, but as long as my heart still beats in my chest, I will see you. I will find a way. And one day, once I've found a way to tame your magic, I will bring you home with me, and we will live in love again."

"I love you." Sorin spoke the words into his skin, melting into Bertram as the true depths of Bertram's love crashed into him— almost more than he could take. "No matter what happens, I will always love you."

"And I will love you until the end of time," Bertram replied, kissing the ridge of his ear, "because my heart is yours for good."

BERTRAM

Bertram left the vineyard before nightfall, and while his body made it back to Braemar, his heart stayed behind. It had done him good to see Sorin safe and well, having adjusted to life with the Vanguard, but secretly—selfishly—it stung.

Sorin's place was meant to be with him.

But between the council and Sorin's magic, there was nothing to be done. Before he could think about sneaking Sorin back into his life, he'd need to do what he'd promised and find a way to tame his wild magic.

But how?

Bertram mulled it over as he spent time with his boys. Everard would be no help. He knew plenty about magic as it pertained to dragons, but he was far too practical to have stuck his nose into something as nonsensical as magic created by man. None of his other brothers were particularly gifted with the craft, and while there were a few agents who had outstanding magical ability, they, too, would likely have no clue as to the ins and outs of mortal magic.

And frankly, Bertram didn't like the idea of asking them.

Agents were naturally curious, and if he were to bring the

topic up, they'd make it their mission to discover why he wanted to know.

Logically, then, the solution was to find a human who had some understanding of magic. The issue was that Bertram knew no such person. He did not associate with any human who was not a dragon's servant, and he knew for a fact that if any of the men or women who served dragonkind displayed magical powers, he would know—they would have long ago been brought before the council.

But he did know one dragon who was familiar with the human world in a rather roundabout sort of way, and so he sent him a friendly letter.

A few weeks later, he received a reply.

Alistair was thrilled to hear from him, and especially delighted to be asked about his precious books. He hadn't known that Bertram was interested in mortal literature! If he had, he would have brought it up ages ago. There were just so many books to talk about. A fact Bertram didn't doubt, as it seemed as though, in his excitement, Alistair had drained two inkpots going into detail about his favorite literary works.

Had Bertram heard of Chaucer, he asked before going on at length about him.

And what of Sir Thomas Malory? He was allegedly quite the scoundrel, but had written such a fascinating Arthurian legend that his sins were to be forgiven.

On and on he went, for pages and pages, book after book and author after author, but of them all, Bertram took interest in one —Le Morte d'Arthur, by that scoundrel Sir Thomas Malory. In it, a wizard by the name of Merlin possessed powers no mortal man should, and while it was fiction, Bertram knew that in every good lie, there was a kernel of truth. Digging deeper into the origin of this character could lead him to answers that might help Sorin.

And so, with Alistair's guidance, Bertram set forth and began to read.

Weeks turned into months. Piers returned from his formative outing with the other agents, and his training at home began anew. Bertram had less time to read than he had before, but he never gave it up, even if it meant sneaking in a few more pages by candlelight after the boys had gone to sleep.

The problem was, there were too many Arthurian legends to comb through, and not all of them were consistent. Many of the authors were anonymous, which he found suspicious, but as he took notes in case he might uncover clues as to their identity, or at least the setting in which their stories took place, he lost hope. The details were vague and inconsistent. Worse, the standard of mortal magic varied from book to book. But he kept reading, hopeful that one of the authors might know more than he should.

These were the only accounts he had of humans who could use magic, and if they couldn't be trusted, what could? Others like Sorin had to be out there. Other humans who were just a bit extraordinary. If he had to read every one of Alistair's recommendations in order to hunt down the truth, he'd do it. He would not stop until he had what he needed to bring Sorin home.

So he read, even when it felt like it was pointless.

He read, and he took notes, and when he was finished with Alistair's recommendations, he wrote to him to ask for more. Alistair was always happy to oblige, and seemed glad to have someone to talk to, but then one day, a few years into their correspondence, his letters stopped. It was strange, as he'd always replied in a timely fashion, almost to the point of predictability.

Had he grown frustrated with Bertram's requests?

It was troubling not only because he was Bertram's only source of information about the mortal world, but because they'd become close thanks to their frequent letters to one another. Bertram had never had a chance to form deep relationships with any of his brothers when he'd been a whelp, and it stung to think the one brother he had somewhat bonded with was pulling away.

Still, he didn't let his feelings get to him.

He was an agent of the council, and he'd played the role of Frederich too long to let emotion addle his brain.

While he waited for Alistair to reply, he compiled a stack of books he'd found the most illuminating and began the painstaking process of picking them apart.

It was on one such night, deep into an Arthurian legend by one of the suspiciously anonymous authors, that Bertram's study door creaked open and a certain someone crept in.

"Piers," Bertram remarked without looking up. He plunged a bauble-headed pin through the map in front of him, marking a spot he thought his current read might be referencing. "I'll blame your lackluster performance on the advanced hour—it's not like you to make so much noise when sneaking into places you shouldn't be. What are you doing up?"

Bertram marked his place in the book, then glanced up from his desk to look upon his son. Piers was beginning to look like a young man now, a little less round in the face and tall enough that the maids sometimes mistook him for Bertram from behind. The last few years of training had put some muscle on him—enough to differentiate him from his brothers, but nothing overly remarkable. Like all agents of the council, his top priority was blending in, so Sebastian he would never be. But that was fine. He was a handsome young man just as he was, and capable. Far stronger than he looked. His skills with handheld blades were only second to his claw, and he was even more agile than Bertram had been at his age—skills he'd likely keep with him for life.

"Father," Piers said charmingly, flashing Bertram Connor's easygoing smile. He came up to Bertram's desk and slid his hand beneath his mantle, producing a letter from within. "Do you wish to explain?"

Bertram arched an eyebrow. "That's a letter, Piers. Surely you know what they're for."

"Don't play games." Piers tossed the letter onto Bertram's desk. The wax seal on the flap had been lifted, and bounced upon impact. "Grandfather asked me to keep an eye on your mail and report any strangeness to him, but so far I have held my tongue. I thought maybe, if I kept observing, I would understand, but it's been several years and I can't make heads nor tails of what you are up to. Why, all of a sudden, are you writing to Uncle Alistair—and about silly books, of all things! You have never been much of a reader. There's something else going on."

Ah, so that was who Grimbold had entrusted with the task. All things considered, it was a fine mission for an agent in training—something with low stakes, but that required a certain amount of finesse. Truthfully, Piers had been doing a fantastic job. Bertram had never noticed any tampering, although he was aware there was a possibility it was happening.

It was why he continued not to write to Sorin or the Vanguard, and why they continued not to write to him.

Still, it was disheartening.

It seemed unfair to pit father against son.

But such was life, he supposed. It was just as Grimbold had said. They were not only fathers—they were leaders, and protectors of the people. Difficult choices sometimes had to be made.

It was just a shame it had come to this.

With a weary sigh, he crossed his arms on his desk and leaned forward to give Piers a long look. He already knew the boy would not relent. He was curious by nature, and his training had only reinforced that curiosity. If Bertram withheld the truth from him now, Piers would sniff it out on his own, and who was to say what conclusions he would come to?

It was better to be honest.

Piers already knew that something strange had happened that had forced Sorin to flee—he was more than old enough now to know the truth.

"You're right," Bertram said once the silence between them had thickened. "There is something more going on, and you have every right to be suspicious. Were I the one in your place, I would be suspicious of me, too. But I'm afraid curiosity sometimes comes with a price."

The neutrality in Piers's expression disappeared. He took a quick, fearful step back, and after a pause, asked, "Father?"

"I shan't harm you, child," Bertram said with a tired laugh. He rose stiffly—not from age, but from the onset of bone-deep exhaustion. "I only apologize for my inability to keep my secret. You were never meant to have discovered it. The truth I have been hiding isn't an easy one, and my failure to keep it from you means you will now be burdened with it, too."

Piers said nothing, and though he did not approach, he did not look away, either. A fierce, stubborn determination burned within him—one Bertram recognized all too well.

He wanted to know.

And although it could mean the end of everything, Bertram had faith in his son.

So he acquiesced, and told him.

Piers listened without interrupting, even after learning that Bertram had not sired his clutch. He took note of Bertram's expression, his posture, and the tension in his body, and when it became obvious that Bertram was telling the truth, he let his guard drop and sat in the empty armchair across from his father, tucking his knees to his chin as he listened to a story that only Sorin and Bertram knew.

It was easy, sometimes, to forget that he was still a child. He wore his maturity too well. But in that moment, Bertram saw him —the boy he'd once carried on his shoulders and cuddled to his chest. The one with mischief in his eyes. Piers did his best to pretend that part of himself had never existed, but he was still there, and it was he who watched his father with round, innocent eyes as he admitted to treason.

"On the day your father went away," Bertram said as he drew near to the conclusion of the story, "he uncovered a terrible secret —inside of him was a dangerous magic. It had slain Unwin all those years ago, and on that day, it claimed the life of another dragon: your predecessor, Osbert. Without an understanding of how his magic works, he fled out of love for our family, for if he were to harm any of us with it, his heart would never recover. I tracked him down after you left to continue your training, and while I was there with him, I swore I would find a way to tame his magic and make things right. Which is why I've been reading so many books. Where else should I look for examples of human magic? Your Uncle Alistair has a great wealth of knowledge on the topic, and has been recommending titles to me, unaware of any of this. Unlike us, he is not the inquisitive type—after his initial confusion at my newfound passion, he never questioned it again."

Piers sat for a long time in silence.

He did not look at Bertram; he kept his gaze lowered, and his arms wrapped around his knees.

"I should report you," Piers finally whispered. "Agents aren't allowed to act outside of direct command."

"Aye," Bertram agreed. "You should."

Silence settled between them. Piers fidgeted in his seat, shifting his weight from one side to the other, more like a child facing down a difficult decision than the agent he purported to be. After too long a time, well past the point where Bertram's heart had twisted itself into breaking, Piers looked him uncertainly in the eyes and said in a small voice, "I can help you."

For a moment, Bertram was too stunned to speak, and when he did regain his wits, the best he could manage was, "What?"

"I can help you," Piers said more confidently. "You and Papa. I can help you both."

"Absolutely not."

"Why?" Piers challenged, sitting up straighter in his chair. "You won't get far on your own. The other agents are just as perceptive as we are. It won't be long before they notice your behavior has changed. You need someone to smooth things over. An ally. Someone you can trust to hide your tracks, especially if you plan on going to see Papa again." He clenched his fists in determination. "What you need is me."

"What I need," Bertram said sharply, "is for you to stay safe, and that means keeping your nose out of this. All I need is for you to keep my secret. I'll be fine on my own."

"Really?" There was fire in Piers's eyes. Excitement. "You were sniffed out by a trainee. What hope do you have of keeping your secret from experienced agents without a co-conspirator?"

"*Piers.*"

"You need me." Piers crossed his arms and sat back in the armchair. The vulnerable child in him was gone. The clever, strong-willed young man he was becoming had taken his place. "There isn't another agent you can trust, Father. No one else would understand."

"It's too risky," Bertram argued. "If I'm caught—"

"You won't be." Piers cut him off before he could get the rest out. "And neither will I. You've trained me too well. I won't fail you, and I know you won't fail me, either."

Bertram's chest ached at the thought of it, but Piers was right. Partnering himself with an ally would be safer, but it also meant that if they were discovered, he wouldn't be the only one tried before the council… nor would he be the only one to suffer from the consequences. "Piers…"

"I'm ready," Piers said. "I want to do this. For you and Papa. For our family. For good."

"You understand that if we're caught—"

"I know," Piers said in a rush. "I understand there will be consequences, and that they will be severe. But how can I do nothing? I love Grandfather, and I love our clan, but if they won't hear us—if they will silence us—then the best way I can help Papa is by swearing loyalty to you."

Bertram looked at Piers. Really looked. Hundreds of years from now, would he agree with the choices he made today? Would he look back at Bertram's story as a grown man with the same sympathetic gaze? There was no way to know for sure—time changed everything in unpredictable ways, and dragons were not exempt—but the stubbornness in the way Piers clenched his jaw and the fierce determination in his eyes made Bertram think he knew the answer.

He rose from his desk, came to stand in front of Piers, and offered him his hand.

Piers looked at Bertram's open palm, at his spread fingers, then lifted his gaze and looked his father in the eyes. He clapped their hands together, and Bertram pulled him to his feet.

"For good," Bertram said solemnly.

"For good," Piers promised, squeezing Bertram's hand.

It was but a single utterance, yet in the undercurrent of those words, unspoken but internalized, they shared another vow: *For Sorin.*

———

Years passed. Piers's training progressed uneventfully, and shortly before his eighteenth birthday, he was inducted into the ranks as an agent of the council in service to the Amethyst clan. Meanwhile, Sorin stayed with the Vanguard and did everything within his power to strengthen the organization from the inside. He wrote to Bertram often to report upon his progress now that it was safe to do so, and Bertram wrote back just as frequently to offer suggestions and relay news of the council.

But not all of their letters were innocent.

He wrote to Sorin not only as a co-conspirator, but as a lover, and on the days when his life seemed at its darkest and most empty, Sorin's correspondence saw him through.

"I'm glad I am no longer obligated to read your missives,

Father," Piers remarked one day not long after Bertram's return from a trip out to the vineyard. He had a letter pinched between his thumb and index finger—just the very tip of its corner—like he knew exactly what kind of filth was inside. "Would you care to remind me how old you are?" he asked, extending the letter toward Bertram as though it were a venomous thing. "You and Papa act as though you're whelps who do not know better. It is most unbecoming."

Bertram cheerfully tucked the letter into his breast pocket. "One day, you'll understand."

Piers made a face. "I think not."

Bertram didn't bother to correct him. At Piers's age, with Frederich already so deeply ingrained in his psyche, he'd also thought himself impervious to love. How glad he was now to have been wrong.

But there was no point in arguing. All children knew best until, suddenly, they didn't. Piers would come around one day, but until then, Bertram would let him be.

Later that evening, when Bertram sat down to read Sorin's letter in the privacy of his own room, he discovered its wax seal had been tampered with, and had himself a good chuckle. That would teach Piers for being nosy.

After that evening, none of Sorin's letters were ever tampered with again.

But the years were not always so carefree. The boys grew up too quickly and left Braemar to lead lives of their own, and Bertram, now an active agent of the council once more, was deployed abroad and sent away. He returned to Scotland, heading into the remote north to care for Hamish in the comfort of his own cottage when his health began to decline after his forced retirement, and after his death, he was there for Agnes as she too faded away. They weren't the first servants Bertram had buried, but their deaths hit him the hardest, and for a while, crushed under the weight of his own grief, it felt like life would never get better. Despite his best efforts, he still hadn't found anything that would help Sorin tame his magic, and now that the boys were men, he couldn't distract himself from his failures with trips out to the loch for flying practice.

He had to sit with his inadequacies, and he had to learn to live with them.

Bertram, who was not used to being incapable, didn't like it one bit, and was glad when he was quickly deployed by the council after Agnes's passing. He had skill out in the field. He could be *useful.* Whether through stealth, or subterfuge, or combat, he could get the job done, and while it didn't get him any closer to bringing Sorin home, it gave him the confidence he needed to keep going despite it all.

The only thing that helped more were the stolen moments he spent in person with Sorin, in the rare times when their paths crossed and Bertram was able to slip away.

He found Sorin in Frisia.

In Persia.

In Spain.

In Prague, they met in secret in Vladislav Hall, where they consecrated one of the darkened knight's stairways.

In Paris, they stole away beneath a bridge spanning the Seine, where Sorin rode Bertram frantically, desperately, grinding his hips and pulling Bertram's hair, neither of them stopping for breath until they were done.

It was reckless—Sorin's magic could activate at any time, killing Bertram the same way it had killed the others—but Sorin was his mate, and Bertram could not stay away. Letters could never replace the way Sorin felt in his arms, the heat of his skin, the honeysuckle smell of his hair...

The risk was worth it.

Bertram *needed* him.

But as time went on, to his dismay, he began to realize that Sorin needed him, too.

Sorin's madness, once dormant, returned with a vengeance. It came in waves, worsening the longer they spent apart. Bertram learned to spot the onset of it in Sorin's letters, and knew that the shakier his handwriting became and the more abrupt his grammar, the worse it was starting to get.

He saw it, too, when they met in person. After long stretches of time apart, he'd find Sorin visibly jittery, paranoid, and seemingly in pain—when he was in the thick of it, it wasn't uncommon to see him wince and tug on his hair. The only thing that seemed to help was when they were able to spend time alone together.

"I wish it would stop," Sorin said in a whisper one day in Guangzhou. They were nude, Bertram on his back with his arms tucked behind his head and Sorin beside him, using his bicep like a pillow. A breeze drifted in through the window of their private room, carrying with it the scent of spices and the distant but lively babble of conversation. The streets outside were bustling. Men and women came and went, trading coin for goods at the local stalls, haggling, arguing, laughing, and blissfully unaware that in their midst, a small group of courageous men and women were helping two recently liberated Pedigree omegas disappear.

"Perhaps one day it will," Bertram said, gazing adoringly at Sorin from the corner of his eye. "If we can find a way to control your magic, there might be a way we can use it to help you escape your pain."

Sorin frowned. "*If* we find a way to control it."

"We will."

"It's been eighty years, Bertram," Sorin chided. "If there was anyone else like me, you would have discovered them by now. Either others like me don't exist, or they're no more skilled at controlling their magic than I am, and have decided to keep their powers a terrible secret for all of time."

"Humans like to gossip," Bertram countered. "No one would be able to keep such a large secret forever, especially if they lacked control over when their magic activates. Someone out there has to know something."

"Do you, of all people, really think that?" Sorin arched a disbelieving eyebrow and poked Bertram in the chest. "How many large and terrible secrets are *you* keeping, Frederich?" There was a hint of flirtation in his voice when he called Bertram by his handle, and though they'd had sex less than an hour ago, heat churned deep inside Bertram, and he started to stiffen again. "Do I need to remind you," Sorin said, nimbly climbing on top of him, "that *I* am a very large secret you've been keeping for a good fourscore years?"

"Dragons are not human," Bertram argued, but without any desire to prove his point. He was distracted by something much more appealing—the gorgeous omega now straddling his hips, who'd positioned himself strategically to grind on Bertram's hardening cock. "With the exception of Everard," Bertram said, "we aren't nosy, and we do not gossip."

"Is that so?" Sorin planted his hands on Bertram's shoulders and leaned down over him until their noses nearly brushed. "Strange. I've unfortunately known quite a few dragons, and all of them have loved to gossip as much as any man."

"How odd." Bertram took Sorin by the hips, pushing him more firmly onto his lap. "I must be quite the exception." He grinned. "How lucky you are to have mated with a dragon who has such mastery over his tongue."

"Beast," Sorin breathed, putting on the air of a man scandalized, but he matched Bertram's grin all the same. "Why don't you show me what that tongue can do?"

Bertram was happy to oblige.

In one smooth movement, he flipped Sorin onto his back and spread his legs while his mate laughed, then went to work with his tongue. With Sorin's legs wrapped around his head, he lapped and stroked and probed until Sorin's thighs were trembling, only to redouble his efforts until, gasping for breath, Sorin came.

Memories of that day—of Sorin pink-cheeked and panting, hazy-eyed from lust—kept Bertram going until the next time they were able to see each other, and the memories they made then kept him going until the next. One encounter at a time, decades turned into centuries, and while Bertram never gave up hope he'd find the answers he needed in order to bring Sorin home, each new lead brought him to a new dead end.

The more he searched, the more it seemed like mortal magic was a myth, but surely that couldn't be. Sorin was proof it existed. He simply had to work harder.

Unfortunately, that proved difficult once the New World was discovered, and Bertram was sent away.

With a vast ocean between himself and the land he knew, Alistair's letters became fewer and farther between until they dried up entirely. Bertram was sad to see them end, but he had next to no way to source books, and on top of that had little time for reading. As humans swept in to colonize the newfound land, Grimbold saw his chance, and the Amethyst clan expanded through Acadia and along the St. Lawrence River with them, vying for territory with the Ruby clan, who had braved the journey first.

Through those harsh, freezing winters and blistering summers, Bertram worried about many things—about Sorin and his madness, about the Vanguard, about the children, and especially about Piers, who had remained in Europe and was acting as a mole for the Vanguard on Bertram's behalf, but worry was all he could do. Europe was too far, and he had his duty to uphold.

Isolated and without hope, they were some of the darkest years of his life.

But eventually, things did get better.

The Amethyst clan settled, technology advanced, and long-distance travel became common. Bertram's brothers made the trip across the pond and came to settle in North America, and not long after, his sons did, too.

The only ones left to worry about were Sorin and Piers, who

stayed in Europe—Sorin with the Vanguard, and Piers on business with the council—and though Bertram couldn't be there to help them, he did what he could by funneling money into the Vanguard's coffers and making trips when it was possible. Between his money and Sorin's leadership, they established new safe houses globally and began to change the world.

Problematic cloisters fell.

Abused omegas were saved.

Sorin even got his wish—with Bertram's blessing and insight into the council's movements from both himself and Piers, the Vanguard slayed a few truly despicable dragons.

Everything was as good as it could be, considering the circumstances, but no good thing could last forever—not even for a dragon. The end came so abruptly, Bertram didn't know to expect it, and it all started with a rumor: Alistair had sired an unsanctioned clutch.

STAY IN TOUCH

Can't get enough omegaverse?
Join Piper Scott's mailing list and get your FREE copy of the oh,
so sexy Yes, Professor
https://www.subscribepage.com/pipersnewletter

Or join Piper's Patreon to read what she's working on as she
writes it!
https://www.patreon.com/piperandemma

Need more men with filthy, snarky mouths?
Subscribe to Lynn Van Dorn's mailing list and stay up to date on
the most addicting new releases you'll ever read
https://lynnvandorncom.wordpress.com/newsletter/

Find Piper Scott on Facebook:
https://www.facebook.com/groups/PiperScott

Find Virginia Kelly, writing as Lynn Van Dorn, on Facebook:
https://www.facebook.com/groups/LynnVanDorn

ALSO BY PIPER SCOTT

Rutledge Brothers Series

His Command Series

Single Dad Support Group Series

Waking the Dragon Series
(with Susi Hawke)

Rent-a-Dom Series
(with Susi Hawke)

Redneck Unicorns Series
(with Susi Hawke)

Forbidden Desires (and Spin-Off) Series
(with Lynn Van Dorn writing as Virginia Kelly)

He's Out of This World Series
(with Renee Fox)

WRITING AS EMMA ALCOTT

Small Town Hearts Series

Masters of Romance Series

ALSO BY VIRGINIA KELLY

Valleywood
In the Pink

Forbidden Desires (with Piper Scott):
Clutch
Bond
Mate

Forbidden Desires Spin-Off (with Piper Scott):
Swallow
Magpie
Finch
Peregrine
Raven: Part One
Raven: Part Two

As Lynn Van Dorn:

North Shore Stories:
Be My Mistake

Damage Control
Daddy Issues
Out of Control

The Oleander Chronicles:
Reunion
Rebound

Stand Alone Stories:
Rule Forty-Seven
Now You See Me
Wild By Nature
Royally Screwed
Misconduct
Straight to the Heart